A WOMAN TORN

She had never found such delirious joy in another man's arms. Jonathan stunned her senses so easily, her response brushed the borders of madness.

It crossed her mind that on even the most romantic of evenings, Fletcher Monroe was not nearly so passionate as Jonathan. That jarring comparison struck Eliza Kate with the chilling force of a cold bath on a winter morn, and mortified, she drew back.

"There's something I should have told you," she confessed in a breathless rush.

Jonathan felt absolutely no need for conversation. "What?" he demanded.

Eliza Kate clamped her hand over his mouth. "Hush!" she scolded. When he gave a grudging nod, she dropped her hand but remained perched on his knee.

"Fletcher has proposed to me. I didn't accept because I feared Mother wasn't well enough to plan a wedding, but I didn't refuse him either."

Jonathan reached up to catch a handful of the curls she had styled atop her head and again claimed her mouth for a wild, possessive kiss which he did not end until she again lay pliant in his arms. "If Fletcher kissed you like that, you'd not be here with me now," he swore darkly.

Phoebe Conn

Wild Desire

LEISURE BOOKS   NEW YORK CITY

To my own dear mother,
Ruby Stanton Conn, my first and most enthusiastic fan.

A LEISURE BOOK®

December 2003

Published by

Dorchester Publishing Co., Inc.
200 Madison Avenue
New York, NY 10016

ISBN 0-8439-5300-4

The name "Leisure Books" and the stylized "L" with design are trademarks of Dorchester Publishing Co., Inc.

Printed in the United States of America.

Visit us on the web at www.dorchesterpub.com.

Wild Desire

O lyric love, half angel and half bird,
And all a wonder and a wild desire!

—*Robert Browning*

Part One

Chapter One

Forth Worth, Texas, Spring 1870

Jonathan Blair hadn't had a peaceful night's sleep since he'd buried his beloved wife and dear little son, but that agony hadn't inspired his latest nightmares. He'd swung south from the Oklahoma Territory intending to pay a visit on Lawrence Bendalin, the best friend he could ever hope to have, but reliving the worst years of his life, as he had in last night's terrors, was an exceedingly high price to pay.

As he cleared away all trace of his camp, he was sorely tempted to ride right on through the Bendalin ranch without stopping by the house. Still, he couldn't shake the eerie sensation that Lawrence needed him now as badly as he had on the awful afternoon his own brother had left him to bleed to death on the battlefield. Disgusted by the memory of Lamar Bendalin's cowardice, Jonathan hunkered down by the Trinity River, scooped up a mouthful of cold, clear water and then blew it out angrily.

Already saddled and anxious to travel, Jonathan's sorrel stallion nickered a soft warning, and the weary man turned to find a primly dressed young woman riding their way. As usual, his horse was on the lookout for a pretty mare, but the last thing Jonathan wanted was company of any kind, especially female. That Red Warrior had noticed this woman's approach before he had distressed him all the more, and as he rose with a lazy stretch, his expression held not a glimmer of welcome.

Eliza Kate Bendalin had begun her dawn rides down to the Trinity River soon after her father and Uncle Lawrence had left home to fight for the Confederacy. Now a habit of nearly ten years, the tranquil interlude was precious to her. She wasn't at all pleased to find a stranger had invaded the mesquite-shaded riverbank she had long regarded as her own private sanctuary.

Then the man looked up, and Eliza Kate felt the searing heat of his narrowed gaze far more intensely than that of the rising sun. Clearly he was as much annoyed to have her interrupt his solitude as she was to have him intrude upon hers, but because she belonged there, while he did not, she raised her chin proudly.

As she greeted the stranger, her voice held a courtesan's seductive low pitch, but rang with unmistakable authority. "This is the Bendalin's Trinity Star Ranch," she announced proudly. "You're welcome to water from the river and a meal if you need one, but don't plan on making it a lengthy stay."

Her broad-brimmed straw hat shaded her eyes, but Jonathan still recognized her in an instant. He cursed softly under his breath, but removed his hat as a gentleman would and slapped it against his thigh to dislodge a thin layer of dust. With his silver spurs providing a faint musical accompaniment, he then moved over the rocky riverbank toward Eliza Kate.

He was dressed all in black, and the thick, straight hair that brushed his collar was so dark the sun lent it the same vivid blue highlights reflected off the Colt Navy revolver worn low on his hip. When he was within six feet of Eliza, he stopped to regard her with smoke-gray eyes.

The James gang had eaten supper with the Bendalins, and Eliza had met nearly a dozen other less celebrated outlaws; but she had never encountered another individual who conveyed the deadly threat of a coiled rattler without so much as a raised brow. The inky blackness of his hair and the bronze cast to his deep tan gave proof of his mixed blood, but Texas was peopled with all manner of humanity, and he would not stand out among them.

Eliza imagined that he had been a handsome youth, and he possessed a young man's tough leanness still, but his expression reflected an ancient sorrow. She had met too many war-weary veterans not to recognize the horror of the Civil War in the fine lines etched at the corners of his strange light eyes and the permanent harsh set to his mouth.

A lesser woman would have hightailed it for home, but she'd run her family's ranch as a child, and now nineteen, felt completely at ease regardless of what manner of man she found trespassing. She expected this stranger to produce a reply as harshly grating as his looks, but when he finally spoke, his deep voice caressed her ears with a courtly southern flavor.

"Good morning, Miss Bendalin." Jonathan forced himself to be pleasant, but he was disappointed that her untimely arrival would compel him to visit Lawrence whether he chose to do so or not.

"I appreciate your kind offer of food and water," he assured her, "but I expect a great deal more in the way of hospitality from the Bendalins."

Jonathan's glance wandered over Eliza's gentle curves as though he had every right to study her so closely. "Lamar used to talk about his little girl, but I guess she's not so little anymore."

Eliza Kate's hair was hidden beneath a silk scarf and wide hat. Her starched white shirt was tucked neatly into a gray split skirt that dipped over the tops of black boots.

Her hands were encased in her favorite pair of leather riding gloves, but despite being fully clothed, she was becoming increasingly uncomfortable under the man's lazy perusal.

That he knew her father's name didn't surprise her, but she was still wary. "Yes, I'm Eliza Kate. Do you know my uncle William as well?" she asked, hoping to catch him in a lie.

"As far as I know, you don't have an Uncle William, but I'm well acquainted with your uncle Lawrence," Jonathan answered with a soft chuckle.

At the mention of his old friend, Jonathan's features had softened into a smile of such genuine pleasure that Eliza quickly revised her initial impression: He was a handsome man still. Somehow that discovery was far more unsettling than his dark frown had been, for it offered a teasing glimpse of the true man, and a most appealing one at that. Unfortunately, his sudden smile faded all too soon, leaving Eliza with an inexplicable sorrow that she'd not been the one to inspire it.

She tightened her hold on her reins, more to control the shockingly inappropriate direction of her thoughts than to subdue her lively mare. "Forgive me for testing you in such a clumsy fashion," she offered in a breathless rush. "Let's go on up to the house, Mr.—"

"Jonathan Blair," he replied with a mock bow.

Eliza knew the name well but stared at Jonathan a moment too long; he was not at all what she had imagined him to be. When he turned in a slow circle to allow her a better view, the heat of a bright blush flooded her cheeks. An inch or so above six feet in height, Jonathan was an impressive sight from any angle, but she had not meant to gawk rudely.

"I'm so sorry. I didn't mean to stare," she apologized, all the while knowing she had not seen nearly enough. Her uncle had raised her on wild tales of his adventures with Jonathan Blair, and it was difficult to believe the storied hero had finally appeared in the flesh. Lawrence had marveled at Jonathan's courage and daring, but not once described his looks. She had mistakenly believed his appearance would be quite ordinary, and it most definitely was not.

"My uncle speaks of you often," she continued after an uncomfortable pause. "Had I known who you were, I would have been more cordial. It was merely . . . well . . ." Too late, Eliza realized she could not possibly justify her initial cool reaction without insulting him anew.

Jonathan shrugged off her apology. "Most folks don't take to me right off, so I don't blame you." He stepped closer and hooked his thumbs in her mare's bridle. The pretty little brown-and-white pinto eyed him only briefly, then turned her glance back to his handsome stallion.

"Tell me about Lawrence," Jonathan urged. He was now standing close enough to see past the deep shadow thrown by her hat. Her features were delicate, and he had to admit quite pretty if he discounted the fact that she'd inherited her father's vivid blue eyes. Unfortunately, her pose held as much starch as her crisply ironed shirt, and he doubted she ever gave her gentlemen callers more than a coolly turned cheek.

Eliza loved her uncle dearly, and thinking how best to describe his situation, she missed the closeness of Jonathan's scrutiny. After sighing softly in frustration, she shrugged unhappily. "Thanks to your courage, Mr. Blair, my uncle survived the war. That's all that truly matters."

She'd unwittingly confirmed Jonathan's worst fears, and believing Lawrence's need might truly be desperate, he drew in a deep breath and released it slowly. "I'd still appreciate your telling me just what to expect."

Jonathan stepped back and placed his hat on the back of his head. When he looked up at Eliza, his glance shimmered with steel, and she took his softly voiced request as an order. Even with the reassurance that he was a friend, her apprehension grew, and she found it easier to concentrate on the dancing river than to return Jonathan's disconcerting gaze.

The tumbling current sent a fine spray into the air that caught and reflected the morning light in a thousand tiny rainbows. Fearing her thoughts would be equally scattered, Eliza chose her words with care. "If you're wondering whether it was worth risking your life to save his, the answer's yes. Lawrence isn't strong, and he walks with a slight limp, but he keeps our books and does his share of the work for the family."

Immediately taking exception to her words, Jonathan's posture stiffened as though he'd been slapped. He made no effort to hide his disgust as he spit out his response. "Lawrence is the finest man I've ever known, and I didn't waste a second considering the threat to my own life before I saved his. You must have had some pretty sorry specimens ride through here for that thought to even cross your mind." Including your own rat of a father, he thoughtfully did not add.

Now noticing that Jonathan was watching her far too intently, Eliza became desperately eager to return to the safety of home. "I can't argue with that," she admitted flippantly. "I truly am sorry if I've insulted you, Mr. Blair. Let's go, or Father might soon be tempted to send a search party out after me."

"Do you always go riding alone?" he asked.

The disapproving note had remained in his voice, but Eliza refused to defend her habits. "Sometimes," she replied, rather than reveal how much she cherished her freedom.

Jonathan had a bedroll tied behind his saddle and saddlebags, but they weren't bulging with provisions. Eliza hoped a renewed offer of food would entice him away from the river.

"I'm getting awfully hungry," she coaxed. "Wouldn't you enjoy some breakfast too?"

After a lengthy pause, during which Jonathan appeared to be carefully weighing the matter, he finally gave a grudging nod. "Breakfast would be real nice, Miss Bendalin. Just lead the way."

As he turned toward his mount, Eliza called to him. "Just a minute. My mother may not recall hearing your name even though my uncle frequently speaks of you. Our family physician believes Mother may have suffered a slight stroke. For whatever reason, her memory just isn't what it should be."

"I understand," Jonathan assured her.

He gave Eliza a lazy salute before he walked back to his horse, but she wasn't certain the gesture hadn't held more insolence than respect. Not wanting his unnerving gaze focused on her shoulder blades, she waited for him to mount his stallion and ride up beside her. Then as they got under way, she urged her little pinto to quicken her pace to keep up with the big red horse.

"There's nothing wrong with my memory, but I don't recall Lawrence mentioning that you were coming for a visit," Eliza Kate mused aloud. "Is he expecting you?"

Jonathan wasn't surprised to find such a straitlaced young woman to be a stickler on etiquette, but he refused to apologize for showing up without notice. "No, I can't say that he is," he replied.

Until Eliza Kate had asked him to be considerate of her mother, Jonathan hadn't thought much of her. Except for the blue of her eyes, she didn't resemble Lamar, but her haughty manner could have come from no one else. He sure hoped she didn't expect him to make polite conversation the whole way home.

"I like traveling alone," he said, "and making my plans as I go."

Jonathan hadn't told Eliza anything she couldn't see at a glance. Clearly he was a loner through and through, and taking what surely hadn't been a subtle hint, she refrained from making any further attempt to draw him out. Still, she stole an occasional glimpse of him through her thick lashes.

Jonathan cast several sidelong glances of his own, but his thoughts were running in an entirely different direction. In the years since the war, he had heard a lot of talk about forgiveness, but he would hate Lamar Bendalin until the day the bastard died. Then he might hate him awhile longer just for spite.

Until the nightmares had begun, he had been looking forward to spending a few days with Lawrence giving Lamar as little thought as possible; but now that he'd met Eliza Kate, the old resentment was flooding him with a near-choking dread.

He would never understand how a family could have produced two such different sons. Lawrence was intelligent, compassionate and kind, while Lamar was an arrogant coward who'd gone screaming from the battlefield rather than help carry his own brother to safety. Lawrence had been too badly wounded to realize how quickly Lamar had abandoned him; but Jonathan had seen it all, and Lamar knew it too.

Lamar's stomach would surely cramp with terror when Jonathan came moseying in and joined him at the breakfast table. Jonathan doubted he would have much appetite himself, but damn, it might just be worth the ordeal to make Lamar sweat in his own home. Surprisingly amused by the thought, Jonathan couldn't stifle a chuckle.

Believing her companion had spoken, Eliza Kate turned toward him, but Jonathan was looking away, not making any effort to speak with her after all. Disappointed, and yet relieved she'd been spared the effort of supplying a witty reply, Eliza glanced up at the clear blue sky. It would be another lovely spring day, but she had lost what little time she would have had to savor its beauty, thanks to Jonathan's unanticipated arrival.

As the trail curved toward home, Eliza tried to concentrate on how glad her uncle would be to see his old friend, but there was a darkness to Jonathan Blair that extended well beyond his coloring and clothes. She wished she knew more about him than Lawrence's tales had revealed. At the same time, she was equally convinced she'd probably be wise to avoid him altogether.

Eliza shot Jonathan another furtive glance, and tried to

reconcile Lawrence's light-hearted description of his old
friend with the solemn individual who rode beside her.
When he glanced her way, as though she had actually
voiced her confusion, a chill skittered down her spine.
Jonathan's piercing glance demanded a response, and unable to think of anything else to say, she immediately directed his attention toward their home on the next rise.

"My father and Uncle Lawrence built our house before
the war. The stone's from the riverbed and the wood is
native pine, oak and cedar. Admittedly it's an eclectic
blend of Victorian elements, and perhaps completely out
of place on the Texas plain, but I've always loved it."

Jonathan couldn't speak for Lawrence's tastes, but he
wasn't surprised Lamar hadn't been satisfied with a simple
ranch house when he had had the means to construct a
three-story mansion. The place was ridiculously elegant,
but the lush profusion of spring flowers spilling over the
low wall of the surrounding garden softened the ambitious dwelling's sharp angles.

"Nice flowers," Jonathan murmured, grateful a sincere
compliment had finally come to mind.

"Thank you. My mother lives for her garden." The
strained morning had left Eliza restless and eager for the
reassuring comfort of her family. She hurried their pace,
and once home, guided Jonathan toward the barn where
they left their mounts with one of the hands.

Eliza again led the way as they crossed the dusty yard
to the house. They climbed the front steps where a wide
porch offered shelter from the elements but as Eliza
pressed toward the ornately carved front door, Jonathan
paused to admire the garden.

"I've known women to plant a flower or two by the front
door," he murmured appreciatively, "but you've got your
own private park here."

Striving to be a polite hostess, Eliza hesitated. She expected Jonathan's appraisal of her mother's garden to be
brief, but he took it all in with an almost palpable hunger.
She was surprised such a hard man would be drawn to

something as fragile as her mother's luscious blooms.

Reluctantly she crossed the porch, but took care not to stand too close to him. From the front of the house, they had a splendid view of the winding garden paths and each of the well-tended flower beds. An exotic blend of fragrances only teased their senses now, but could prove nearly overwhelming in the heat of midday.

"The roses are my mother's favorites," Eliza confided softly, "but I rather like the honeysuckle vines. We have jasmine that blooms late in the summer, and it's always so—"

Jonathan turned toward her, but rather than displaying the interest in the garden she had assumed he'd show, his gaze was as vacant as a dead man's. Eliza took a sudden backward step toward the door.

"Wait," Jonathan urged. "It's what?"

Eliza could not even recall what they had been discussing, and fearing she must appear as forgetful as her mother, she removed her hat and scarf to free her long, golden curls. She shook her head and let the tumbling ringlets spill down over her shoulders. Although it had been a foolish feminine ploy deliberately calculated to distract him, when she glanced up through her lashes, she was shocked by just how successful she had been.

A bright flash of desire lit Jonathan's silvery gaze for no more than an instant, but Eliza recognized the bold male response for what it had been and was thoroughly ashamed of herself for provoking it. She had mistakenly believed inspiring amusement—or even revulsion—would be an improvement over Jonathan's terrifyingly blank stare, but she had not meant to awaken his passions. She trusted her instincts where men were concerned and knew better than to trifle with this man's affections.

She blamed such a serious lapse in judgment on the fact she had had not even a second to collect her thoughts at the river. She finally recalled that Jonathan had been admiring the garden. She then used her hat in so broad a gesture, she nearly flung it over the porch rail. Forced to grab for it by the trailing ribbons, she pressed it to her bosom and wondered if the day could possibly get any worse.

She knew some women were so badly flustered by a man's attentions that their every move turned clumsy, but she had never suffered from such a painful degree of self-consciousness with another man. She couldn't abide the thought that Jonathan Blair might have such an effect on her. After all, she had raised two younger brothers and perhaps knew more about men than any gently bred young woman ought to.

Clinging to the belief she was simply tense for a multitude of reasons that had absolutely nothing to do with Jonathan, she drew in a calming breath and strove to be gracious. "If you have time later," she invited warmly, "I know my mother would love to show you her flowers. We've put identifying tags on them all, so remembering their names won't be a problem for her."

Even more startled by his primal reaction to Eliza than she had been, Jonathan knelt and nearly ripped the spurs from his boots. Lamar Bendalin's daughter was the very last woman he'd ever want, but in the one glorious moment when he'd seen just how beautiful she truly was, he'd longed to lace his fingers in her tawny curls, kiss her until sundown, and then make love to her until dawn. Such lunacy absolutely appalled him.

"It's a shame most problems can't be solved that easily," he muttered. It had just been all that golden hair, he told himself. After the night he'd had, Eliza had distracted him so thoroughly that his imagination had gotten the better of him. Still, he knew damn well that what she'd grabbed hadn't been his imagination.

When he straightened, his expression was again an unreadable mask. Eliza held the front door open for him, but he left his hat, spurs and gun belt on the bench beside the door. Again sorry he'd had no choice about coming, he followed her inside.

After the bright outdoors, the entry hall of the spacious

home appeared dim. Wanting both a clear head and clear vision, Eliza Kate paused after hanging her hat and scarf on the hall tree. The parlor was off to the right, and she waited until Jonathan had had a glimpse of the well-appointed room before leading him into the dining room on the left. A bay window on the west gave the whole room a golden glow and provided another excellent view of the lush garden.

The six places at the dining table were set with fine English bone china and Mexican silver. A delectable aroma of fried bacon and freshly baked bread wafted in from the adjacent kitchen. Before Eliza Kate could summon the servants to add a setting to the table, her eleven-year-old brother, Robby, came bounding down the stairs and with a triumphant rebel yell entered the room.

Robby was a handsome lad. His blond hair wasn't as curly as Eliza Kate's, but his eyes were just as bright a blue. He greeted Jonathan with an impetuous grin and pulled another chair up to the table.

"Set yourself down right here beside me, mister. I figure you must be somebody important, 'cause Eliza Kate sends most strangers away with a cold biscuit."

Jonathan thought he'd had a pretty good sample of the way Eliza usually banished travelers, but he felt instantly drawn to Robby. "Is that a fact?" he asked, and he shot Eliza an unexpectedly amused glance. "Well, then, I feel doubly honored."

Eliza took hold of the extra chair and moved it over slightly to provide Jonathan with more room. "Robby, please. This is Uncle Lawrence's good friend, Jonathan Blair, and we don't want him to believe that we treat strangers unkindly."

Before Robby could reply, Lamar came to the doorway with his wife, Delia, on his arm. He did not instantly recognize their guest, but when Jonathan turned toward him, all color drained from his face. He drew Delia closer to his side and with his free hand made a quick grab for the solid security of the doorjamb.

"Jonathan," he uttered in strained disbelief.

Eliza had always known her father to be a supremely confident individual, but with the wind sucked out of him by his startled gasp, he wore the first crestfallen expression she had ever seen. Her dear mother, bless her, slipped from his grasp and moved forward unsteadily with her arms outstretched.

"Jonathan, my dear," Delia exclaimed. "How wonderful it is to see you again."

Eliza Kate sent Jonathan a frantic glance, silently imploring him not to correct her mother's misconception, for in truth, the pair had never met. After a barely perceptible nod, Jonathan took a quick step forward to catch Delia's hand before she lost her balance. He slipped his arm around her narrow waist to escort her the last few steps to the table, then eased her down into the chair at the end.

"Yes, ma'am," he replied. "It's awfully good to see you again too." Then he glanced over her head to where Lamar still stood transfixed. "I'm sure you know how I feel about seeing you, Lamar," he added coldly.

Eliza Kate was enormously relieved that Jonathan had greeted her mother so warmly. Despite her warning, she knew her mother must appear far more frail than he could have anticipated. Delia was in her early forties, but her fair hair shimmered with silvery highlights, and her translucent skin seemed stretched over bones too fragile to bear even her slight weight.

Her pale lavender gown was as lovely as her tenderly cultivated flowers, but Eliza Kate did not know how much longer her mother would be able to summon the strength to do more than merely gaze at them from her bedroom window. Her thoughts growing increasingly troubled, she welcomed the sound of her uncle Lawrence's slow, uneven step.

The Bendalin brothers each stood nearly six feet tall and shared the same fair coloring, but their resemblance ended there. At forty-three, Lamar was in robust good health. His build was sturdy and muscular while at thirty-four, Lawrence was painfully thin and strands of gray were already woven into his light brown hair. Puzzled to find his elder brother blocking the doorway, he slid past him with a clumsy stretch, then saw Jonathan, and with an ecstatic cry lurched on into the dining room.

Lawrence rushed forward to draw Jonathan into an exuberant hug, which his old friend tolerated with a patience Eliza regarded as truly admirable. Jonathan apparently didn't know what to do with his hands, but after a slight hesitation, he slowly raised them to lightly pat Lawrence on the back. Lawrence's bony shoulder blades poked through his soft woolen coat; Eliza supposed he must have lost at least forty pounds since the day Jonathan had carried him to safety.

Overwhelmed by the emotional greeting, Jonathan stepped back and gave Lawrence's wiry biceps a hearty squeeze. "It's so good to see you again. We must talk, later," he stressed.

Eliza's glance swept her uncle's finely drawn features, then lingered over Jonathan Blair's starkly chiseled face. Though complete opposites in appearance, clearly the men were still good friends, but Lawrence no longer possessed the virile strength that marked Jonathan's every gesture. She wondered if they would find anything more than old times to discuss and was flustered by the stab of envy that came with the realization of how quickly she would be excluded.

Then her father's frozen stance caught her eye, and she was again mystified by his peculiar reaction to Jonathan's arrival. She sent him a questioning glance, and he quickly composed himself, responded with a nervous smile, and without coming forward to shake Jonathan's hand, moved on toward his place at the head of the long table.

Eliza was appalled by her father's rudeness, but when the front door slammed shut with a jarring thud, her brother Ricky caught her full attention. "Ricky, please," she called. "You must try harder to close the door quietly."

Ricky was seventeen, not quite as tall as his father, but well-built and strong. As he strode in, he quickly scanned the room for an unfamiliar face, then went toward Jonathan and stuck out his hand. Like Eliza Kate, he favored their mother and with a dimpled chin and ready grin, made friends easily.

"That must be your red stallion out by the barn, and a horse that size has to be fast. How about a race later?" he asked.

"You'll have to make it worth my while," Jonathan replied as soon as Lawrence had introduced them.

"I sure will." Ricky slapped Jonathan on the shoulder and walked around the table to take the extra chair between Robby and Eliza Kate's. "Come on, everyone. Let's sit down and eat before one of us faints from hunger."

Lawrence gestured for Jonathan to take the chair between his and Delia's. Eliza Kate went to the door leading to the butler's pantry to inform the help there would be a guest and as soon as she had taken her seat, the men took theirs. Delia rang a sterling silver bell with a graceful flourish, and two young Mexican girls entered, first bringing a plate and utensils for Jonathan, then carrying trays laden with bacon, fried eggs, hot biscuits, and bowls of grits and gravy.

They took great care as they placed the heaping platters along the length of the table, but sent lingering glances Jonathan's way before withdrawing to fetch pitchers of milk and freshly brewed coffee. Eliza Kate was embarrassed by the girls' obvious interest in their handsome guest, and surprised when he seemed not to notice.

"Just grab whatever you want," Robby offered as he reached for a piece of bacon.

Delia clutched her napkin to her breast in horror. "My gracious, son. I hope you'll forgive us for being so informal this morning, Mr. Blair. We'll surely display far better manners tonight at supper."

"Please pass the platter of bacon, Robby," Eliza Kate

ordered under her breath, and her younger brother grabbed two more pieces before passing it along to his mother.

The heavy serving dish wobbled precariously in Delia's trembling hands, and Jonathan quickly took a firm hold on it. "I appreciate the invitation, ma'am, but I just stopped by to say hello, and I'll be moving on before sundown."

"Absolutely not," Lawrence insisted emphatically. "You'll have to spend at least one night with us. As you can see, we have plenty of room, and I'll not hear of your leaving us so soon."

Eliza doubted it was ever wise to argue with Jonathan Blair, but she was amused by how easily her uncle countered his friend's every objection. Then Ricky joined in with another plea for a race, and her mother remarked wistfully upon how much she wanted to show him through her garden. Robby was anxious to learn if Jonathan had seen any sign of the Kiowa or Comanche, who had been raiding in the next county. What with passing the platters and trying to respond to all the comments and questions sent his way, Jonathan swallowed only one mouthful.

"Let's give Mr. Blair a chance to enjoy his breakfast," Eliza suggested firmly, "or he'll not have the strength to answer any more questions."

"Thank you," Jonathan replied, and he raised his coffee cup in a silent toast.

Eliza Kate held his cool gray gaze for only a second and then had to look away. Her brothers continued the animated conversation, but their words were blurred by the pounding of her heart. Jonathan Blair was easily the most coldly distant man she had ever met, but for some inexplicable reason, she felt drawn to him.

It was such a frighteningly irrational response that Eliza prayed he would spend no more than a single night under their roof and then race his big red stallion right out of their lives first thing in the morning.

Chapter Two

After breakfast, Lawrence ushered Jonathan into the book-lined study off the parlor. He eased himself down into his chair behind the massive desk, leaned back and nodded thoughtfully. "I swear you look the same as the day Lee surrendered, but now if I fling out my arms, I'll be mistaken for a scarecrow."

Lawrence had hoped to make Jonathan laugh, and having failed, he leaned forward slightly. "Tell me about the pretty little Cherokee maiden you'd hoped to marry. Was she waiting for you?"

Feeling trapped, Jonathan pushed out of his chair and crossed to the window. On that side of the house, Delia's flower garden gave way to vegetables, and the two girls who had served breakfast were moving along the rows of green beans. They were giggling rather than carefully perusing the crop, and Jonathan wondered how long it usually took them to fill their baskets. When at the end of a row they linked elbows to dance, he turned his back toward them and leaned against the windowsill.

Although the news was no longer fresh, the agony of relating it was no less intense. "Yes, she was," Jonathan responded softly, "but I lost her and our son to a fever two winters ago."

The heartbreak of that tragedy brought tears to Lawrence's eyes, and he hurriedly reached for his handkerchief. "Oh, Jonathan, I'm so sorry. I've thought of you often and always hoped that you were happy."

Lawrence's sorrow over his friend's loss while he, himself, was barely alive embarrassed Jonathan even more deeply than the joyous welcoming hug. "We were," he answered gruffly, "but the Indian Territory is empty for me without them, and I'm on my way to California."

Lawrence nodded and sensing his friend was uncomfortable with sympathy, he blew his nose and stuffed his handkerchief back in his pocket. "You're too late for the gold," he admonished.

A slow smile tickled the corner of Jonathan's mouth. "So I've heard. Maybe I'll plant orange trees."

Leaning back again, Lawrence sent a roving glance from the scuffed tips of Jonathan's boots up to his thick, black hair. There had been a time when he could have wrestled him to the ground, but clearly that day was long past. "You're no farmer," he swore convincingly. "Stay here with us."

Jonathan found it easier to note the clutter piled on his friend's desk than look him in the eye. "If it were only you, I'd be tempted, but you've got more people living here than reside in most hotels."

"There's not that many of us," Lawrence argued, "and we could sure use your help. Lamar spends most of his time in town while Ricky's always out looking for trouble. Don't let him talk you into a race, by the way, unless your mount is swift or he'll take whatever stake you might have."

Amused by that unlikely prospect, Jonathan couldn't help chuckling. "I doubt it." Unable to hide his curiosity, he forced himself to sound only mildly interested. "What's Lamar find so fascinating in town? Does he gamble?"

"He does enjoy an occasional game of cards, but mainly he just tends to business. He and a man named Fletcher Monroe have been supplying whiskey to the saloons in Fort Worth and Dallas. I've no part of that enterprise, but Lamar and I have bought some property in Fort Worth and built a few little shops. It's nothing too ambitious, but Lamar's anxious to construct some more. You know him. He likes to surround himself with people and would probably run for mayor if Delia's health weren't such a concern."

Lamar had always had a thirst for liquor, and Jonathan wasn't surprised to learn that he now sold it. While that surely made him popular in some quarters, it was no guarantee he'd be an exemplary public official. As for the delicate Delia, Jonathan just felt terribly sorry for her.

"It's difficult for me to picture your brother as a devoted husband," Jonathan replied.

Lawrence frowned slightly. "Well, you've got to remember that you met Lamar during the war when none of us were strangers to the ladies, if they could even be called that."

Jonathan wouldn't dignify the painted women who had entertained the troops with such a respectful title and shook his head sadly. "No, they sure couldn't, but you and I weren't married then, and Lamar was."

Lawrence's blue eyes filled with a perceptive light. "I may walk more slowly now, but that doesn't mean I've grown stupid. You never did like Lamar much, did you?"

Jonathan did not even know words vile enough to express what he truly thought of Lamar Bendalin, but when Lawrence chose not to see his brother's faults, there was no point in his listing them. After all, he would soon be gone, and Lawrence had to live with the bastard.

"Come on," Jonathan hedged. "You know I wouldn't win any popularity contests either."

"Damn it all, Jon. Why is it always impossible to get a straight answer from you?"

Jonathan had forgotten how easy it was to tease Lawrence and how much he had enjoyed it. "Maybe you just ask real peculiar questions."

Amused that Jonathan had confounded him again, Lawrence laughed to himself, then couldn't remember the last time he had so much as chuckled. "How about this one? What do you think of Eliza Kate? Isn't she about the prettiest girl you've ever seen?"

At the mention of her name, the scene out on the porch flashed through Jonathan's mind with astonishing clarity, and he had to turn back toward the window to hide his dismay. Eliza Kate was most definitely a beauty, but she had looked as priggish as a schoolteacher until she'd whipped off her hat and shaken out a wild mane of blond curls.

Jonathan couldn't remember the last time he had been with a woman, but he was still appalled by how powerfully he'd been attracted to Eliza Kate.

God almighty, he swore under his breath. How had a weasel like Lamar Bendalin produced such a striking daughter? Of course, she did favor her mother, but it was still Lamar's blood that flowed in her veins. He would have to make a point of remembering that fact, but it was going to be a real challenge.

The Mexican girls had gone inside, and Jonathan watched a crow dip low over the garden. "I still miss my wife," he breathed out truthfully. "Please don't ask me to comment on other women."

Lawrence was deeply ashamed he had failed to consider his friend's tragic loss. He cleared his throat with a nervous gulp and quickly changed the subject. "Forgive me for being so thoughtless. What I really need is your opinion of Fletcher Monroe. He's been courting Eliza Kate. In addition to being Lamar's partner, he owns a ranch as fine as ours. That makes him an excellent prospect, I know, but I just can't abide the man.

"He quotes Shakespeare as though he knew him and brags incessantly about his horses. If that stallion of yours beats Ricky's, I'd be much obliged if you'd stick around long enough to race one of Fletcher's prize horses."

Still shaking off the seductive memory of Eliza Kate's beauty, Jonathan wasn't even tempted to hang around. In fact, he was becoming almost desperately eager to leave. "No, thanks. I'd rather be on my way to California."

A light tap on the door signaled the arrival of a dark-eyed young woman. Petite and pretty, her lustrous sable hair was knotted atop her head, and she was dressed in a crisp white blouse and brown skirt. She sent Jonathan a glancing smile, then spoke to Lawrence.

"Mrs. Bendalin thought you two might want some lemonade, but perhaps you'd prefer something stronger?"

Lawrence's slow smile grew a touch too wide, and Jonathan saw more than a mere discussion of refreshments pass between them. "Nothing for me, thanks," he said.

"Nor me either, Carmen," Lawrence added. "Please tell Delia we'll join her in the garden in a few minutes."

"As you wish."

As soon as the door closed behind her, Jonathan began to laugh. "And who, pray tell, was she?"

Lawrence dipped his head and began to contemplate his neatly trimmed nails. "I can see what you're thinking, but Carmen is Delia's maid, and she's much too young for me." He drew in a deep breath and released it in a poignant sigh. "Not that any woman would have me when I couldn't waltz her around the room without collapsing."

Jonathan had suffered too much grief of his own to accept another man's self-pity. He immediately circled the desk, grabbed Lawrence by the arms and hauled him up out of his chair. "Then you'll have to find yourself a lady who doesn't like dancing. Now let's go and admire Delia's flowers."

"Damn you, Jonathan," Lawrence swore angrily. He didn't appreciate being handled like an oversized rag doll but he couldn't stay mad at his friend and soon gave in to laughter. "I've really missed you. Now promise me you'll spend the night with us."

It had been a long while since anyone had cared what Jonathan did, and again touched by the frankness of Lawrence's affection, he gave a grudging nod. "I guess I owe you that much," he admitted reluctantly.

Lawrence opened his mouth to argue that Jonathan didn't owe him a thing, but he quickly realized that for once he had gotten his way with his stubborn friend and kept quiet. Now all that remained was to enlist his help in proving to Eliza Kate that Fletcher Monroe was too great a jackass to marry.

"Now about that race," Lawrence murmured, and he ushered Jonathan on out the door.

* * *

Eliza Kate and her mother were seated on a wooden bench beside the lily pond. Shaded by a leafy pepper tree, they were planning menus for the coming week. Leaving nothing to chance, Eliza kept careful notes in a small leather-bound journal to make certain her mother's wishes were followed to the letter before the dear woman forgot them.

The soft scrape of the men's boots on the brick path alerted Eliza to their approach and she set the book aside along with her pen and ink. The morning had remained pleasantly warm, and the air was crisp and clear, but Eliza was all too aware of Jonathan's presence to enjoy the beauty of the day.

She turned toward him slowly and was relieved to find Lawrence was providing such a lengthy commentary, it would be several minutes before they reached the bench. Jonathan bent to sample the fragrance of a rose, and Eliza was struck by the tenderness with which he cupped the delicate blossom. She had never before envied a flower, nor noted such stunning grace in a man.

Delia leaned over to dip her fingertips into the pond. "You ought not to stare quite so boldly, my dear," she whispered softly.

Caught in the act, Eliza Kate made no attempt to deny how closely she had been regarding Jonathan Blair. "I'm sorry, Mama, but he's, well, just so—"

"Handsome?" Delia offered.

The bright sparkle in her mother's eyes gave proof of her opinion of their guest, but Eliza Kate had no such facile answer to describe his deeply unsettling effect on her. "He's nothing like us," she blurted out instead.

Delia straightened and adjusted the drape of her shawl, which had slipped down to her elbows. Woven of feather-soft wool, it was a pearl gray that blended perfectly with her pastel gown. She eyed the men, who were perhaps a dozen steps away and had again paused to compare the fragrances of her red and white roses.

"We could do with some new blood," Delia murmured

pointedly, and her glance lingered over Jonathan.

Eliza Kate did not want to consider where that surprising opinion might lead, but as she stole another quick peek at Jonathan, she found him studying her rather than the magnificent flowers. His gaze was as openly appreciative as she feared hers must be, and she quickly turned back toward her mother.

"Fletcher's coming to dinner tonight, and though I'm glad Lawrence finally has the opportunity to entertain his friend, I certainly don't want Jonathan to feel awkward if he has no fine clothes."

Delia smiled knowingly and inclined her head. "I doubt the man's clothing will be the problem."

Lamar had left for town and taken Robby to school on his way before Eliza Kate had had a chance to speak with him, but he had been so uncharacteristically mute at breakfast that she was convinced he was not nearly as fond of Jonathan as her uncle and mother.

"Perhaps not," Eliza agreed, "but I don't believe Father likes him."

Delia's gently arched brows knit in confusion. "Really? Did he say something I missed, or have I merely forgotten?"

Eliza hadn't meant to trouble her mother and leaned close to rest her hand lightly on Delia's arm. "Forgive me. It was merely a fleeting impression. I've no idea what he really thinks of the man."

Greatly relieved, Delia smiled warmly and called out to the men. "Do come and join us." She gestured toward the bench opposite the one she and her daughter occupied and Lawrence came and took a seat, but Jonathan circled the lily pond, leaned back against the pepper tree, and folded his arms over his chest.

"This is a splendid garden, Mrs. Bendalin," Jonathan offered, his praise coupled with a sincere smile. "You've every right to be proud."

"Thank you so much," Delia replied. "I would love to continue the tour, but I'm feeling rather tired this morning. I wonder if you'd show Jonathan the rest, Eliza Kate, while Lawrence and I make the last plans for tonight's dinner."

"Would you please, Eliza?" Lawrence echoed. "My leg's bothering me something awful today, and I could sure use a moment to rest here in the shade."

Eliza would have preferred to cozy up to one of the lizards skittering through the cactus garden than provide Jonathan with an attentive escort, but with neither her mother nor uncle in good health, she could scarcely refuse their requests. Fearing she had already hesitated too long, she rose so quickly, she knocked the bottle of ink off the bench. It broke, splattering the contents over the brick walkway.

"Oh dear," she exclaimed. "Wait just a minute, please. I need to clean up this mess."

"I'll get it," Jonathan offered and he scooped up a handful of soil from beneath the pepper tree, bent down, and sifted it through his fingers to cover the spill. "There. The dirt will blot up the ink, and we can sweep up the glass later."

"Thank you," Eliza murmured, amazed by how promptly he had come forward to ease her distress and ashamed that she had not been more gracious in the first place. As Jonathan stood and brushed the last trace of dust from his hands, she turned to precede him up the walk. A sudden chill coursed down her spine, but she was uncertain whether it was one of anticipation or dread.

Unused to such conflicting thoughts, she did her best to concentrate on the garden and called over her shoulder. "Mother planted the roses, then wanted the lily pond. It's only a few inches deep and Robby used to wade in it when he was small. Over the years, Mother has kept expanding the garden, and it's carefully planted so the colors harmonize and provide flowers all year."

She paused at a small toolshed where a lush profusion of sweet peas grew on a twine trellis strung up the side. She plucked a pink blossom and twirled it gently between her fingers. "We collect the seeds and replant these pretty flowers every autumn."

The sweet peas' delicate fragrance scented the air, but Eliza watched in awed silence as Jonathan stepped close, placed his hand over hers, and inclined his head to inhale deeply of the single bloom she held. His fingers were long and slim and felt warm against the back of her hand, but when he slid his thumb over her palm, a rippling tingle flashed up her arm and coiled around her chest. Her breath caught in her throat. Startled, she yanked her hand from Jonathan's, and the sweet pea floated to the ground.

Eliza raised her hand to push her curls off her brow but the hurried gesture failed to erase the pleasure of Jonathan's touch. "I'm dropping everything it seems," she apologized. "I don't know what's happened to me today."

Jonathan knew exactly what he'd done, but the need to touch her had overwhelmed his usual reserve, and having succumbed to temptation, he'd not apologize. He picked up the fragile blossom but rather than hand it back to Eliza, he threaded it into a curl at her temple. He wasn't his usual steady self that day either, but doubted she felt the tremble in his fingers.

"Really? I think you do," he countered with an easy grin.

That earlier Eliza had wished to inspire such a handsome smile was forgotten now. And it had been his touch rather than his teasing expression that had affected her so deeply. Now understanding precisely how greatly the rose must have enjoyed his caress, she clasped her hands together tightly and vowed not to pick another bloom and invite her own undoing.

"You're right," she admitted with forced charm. "I missed the time I usually spend by myself at the river, and whenever it's lost, I never seem to catch up."

She moved on down the path before Jonathan could distract her again. They soon reached a grassy lawn enclosed by neatly clipped hedges, and she led him across it with a brisk step. "We come out here for picnics sometimes. Every summer, the orchard at the back of the garden produces more fruit than we can eat and so much jam and jelly that we usually have to give most of it away."

Eliza angled off on another path that led to the blackberry vines and grape arbor, then decided she ought not to go that far away from the others. Meaning to retrace her steps, she stopped and turned so suddenly, Jonathan would have run right into her had his reflexes not been so quick.

He reached out to grab her shoulders to prevent a collision, then quickly dropped his hands to his sides. "I didn't mean to make you so nervous," he confided. "Let's go back and sit with your mother and Lawrence. It doesn't sound as though he has many friends, and I don't want to neglect him while I'm here."

"That's very kind of you," Eliza answered in a voice she scarcely recognized as her own.

She had felt the heat of his hands through her blouse, but could not understand why Jonathan's touch was so stirring. That he was continually so thoughtful made her feel even worse. When she had first sighted him that morning, his menacing glance had frightened her, but like so many things in life, he was not what he seemed.

She wanted to step back again to put more space between them, but fearing she would trip over her own feet, she forced herself to remain where she stood. She then reminded herself that her own discomfort ought not to interfere with what could be an immensely rewarding visit for her dear uncle.

"You're right about Lawrence," she explained. "He keeps to himself more than he should. I've introduced him to half a dozen young women I thought he might genuinely enjoy knowing, but he's failed to pursue any of them. I'm simply at a loss for what to do now."

Jonathan nodded to encourage her to continue along the path. "I imagine Lawrence will find his own woman when he's ready."

"Not if he doesn't look," Eliza Kate argued.

The brick walkways were wide enough for two in many places, but Eliza preferred to walk in single file until she realized Jonathan might find the sway of her hips immensely entertaining. Struck by a sudden inspiration, and hoping to avoid another abrupt halt, she detoured around the cactus garden.

"This is our latest addition. Cacti require so little care and come in so many entertaining varieties, we've encouraged everyone we know to bring us one whenever they come across them in their travels."

She gave Jonathan a few seconds to survey the sandy soil studded with the spiny plants, white flowering yucca, and an artfully arranged collection of river-tumbled stones. Although her uncle could not possibly overhear, she took the precaution of lowering her voice to a hushed whisper.

"I hope this won't sound terribly presumptuous of me, and I realize it would require a change in plans for you, but for Lawrence's sake, would you please consider spending more than a single day with us?"

Jonathan didn't know which was more distracting, the gentle softening of her pose, or the imploring gleam in her pretty blue eyes. Silently cursing his own weakness for the appealing young woman, he knew he'd have to disappoint her. "You're right. That is presumptuous."

He knelt to examine a small cactus with what appeared to be a wild mop of white hair. "This one looks like a little old man," he observed in surprise.

"Yes, it does." Eliza Kate knelt beside him, then realized her mistake when he turned toward her. They were mere inches apart, and it was very difficult to recall it was Lawrence they were discussing. She had noticed the unusual color of Jonathan's eyes when they'd met, but his dark lashes were as long and thick as her own and enhanced the soft light of his gaze.

A small scar crossed the left corner of his upper lip, but melted away as he began to smile. She licked her lips nervously and fought not to wonder how his kisses would taste, but it was all she could do not to lean against his shoulder to savor his warmth. Her mind was wandering terribly she knew, but her senses had never been more acute.

A guilty flush crept up her cheeks as she began to sincerely doubt it had merely been concern for her uncle that had prompted her request. She was accustomed to young men pursuing her, not the other way around, but whatever would she do if she were to actually succeed with Jonathan? This ranch was her whole world, and he was merely passing though. At that sobering thought she become determined to concentrate solely on her uncle's needs.

"Speaking of old men," she continued with renewed purpose, "Lawrence is going to be a very lonely old man if he doesn't find the courage to seek a wife. I don't want that for him. Do you?"

Jonathan shrugged slightly. "Of course not, but if you can't find a woman who interests him from among your friends, where do you imagine that I'll find one?"

Eliza feared her thinking wasn't nearly clear enough to stay ahead of Jonathan's. "I'm sorry. I didn't mean to confuse you. I don't expect you to find the woman but merely to inspire him to search."

Jonathan ran the tip of his index finger over the cacti's white hair and found it as coarse as wood shavings rather than soft as it appeared. "I'm sorry, too, but you've got the wrong man." He rose then, and offered her his hand.

Eliza Kate had not forgotten the magic of his touch and allowed her fingers to trail across his palm before taking a firm grip on his hand. When he grabbed hold and yanked her to her feet, she was stunned by his reaction. That she obviously affected him as strongly as he affected her should not have come as a surprise after the way he had looked at her out on the front porch, but she'd failed to anticipate his current anger.

"I was married myself once," Jonathan blurted. "My wife died the day after our son, and I buried him in her arms.

I wouldn't wish that pain on anyone, least of all Lawrence."

He was crushing Eliza's hand in a brutal grip, but she was certain he was unwittingly transmitting his own anguish rather than intentionally causing her pain, and she refused to cry out. "I had no idea you'd suffered such a terrible loss. You have my deepest sympathy. But even the frailest of women will undoubtedly outlive Lawrence. She'll be the one left to go on alone, but that ought to be her choice, not his. Now I'm so fair I bruise easily, so you must let go of my hand."

Shocked to find he had not already done so, Jonathan released her instantly, but the outline of his fingers remained clearly imprinted on her creamy smooth skin. "Forgive me. I shouldn't have come here."

"On the contrary, I think you should have paid us a visit much sooner." Eliza Kate had never been involved in such an intense exchange, but believing she had been given a valuable insight into her own character as well as his, she led the way back to the lily pond with a confident stride.

They passed beneath an arched trellis covered with honeysuckle and on by the jasmine, but she did not tarry to admire either one. She could feel Jonathan walking a few paces behind her, his step slow and steady, but her wildly beating heart drowned out the sound. She feared her mother would note her flushed cheeks but what excuse could she possibly give other than that being with Jonathan was both madly perplexing and deliciously exhilarating?

By the time they reached the lily pond, Carmen had swept up the broken ink bottle and brought out a pitcher of lemonade. Eliza Kate was grateful the maid had already begun to fill the accompanying glasses because her right hand ached so much she would surely have dropped the pitcher and broken it too. She reached out to take her lemonade with her left hand, then again chose the place beside her mother while this time Jonathan sat down opposite her next to Lawrence.

Jonathan thanked Carmen for the refreshing drink, but his gaze did not follow her progress as she returned to the house. Appreciating the ample room to stretch out his legs, he made himself comfortable. "Your garden is as charming as you and your daughter, Mrs. Bendalin. Eliza Kate is a most informative guide."

Eliza recognized the sarcasm in that compliment, but Delia beamed with pride. "Thank you. Now I'd love to hear something about your home, Jonathan. Please forgive me if you've already told me all about your family. Regrettably, my memory is no better than a sieve nowadays."

Immediately coming to his friend's aid, Lawrence straightened out his slumped pose. "I'm sure there are other topics Jonathan would rather discuss."

Jonathan took a long drink of lemonade, then looked straight at Eliza Kate. His gaze darkened as he gathered his thoughts. "I don't mind talking about myself. It's just difficult to know where to begin. I guess I should start back in Georgia where the family tree had two main branches.

"My grandfather was a Cherokee who owned a prosperous farm and took a white wife. My father was their only child. He also married a white woman."

Delia responded with a polite nod while Eliza Kate anticipated what was coming with growing dread. Lawrence shot her an anxious glance, for he was also well aware the Cherokee had been forcibly removed from their lands. To compound the tragedy, their men had fought for the Confederacy and again been punished by the loss of a portion of their new tribal lands in the Indian territory.

Jonathan continued the sad tale in a weary monotone. "When the government of the United States ceased honoring treaties and began evicting all the Indians living east of the Mississippi, my mother's family threatened to disown her if she would not divorce my father. She refused and went right along with him. It's a long way from Georgia to Oklahoma, and while thousands died on the journey, I was born along the way.

"I suppose a few of my mother's relations might still be scattered around Georgia, but my grandparents and parents are dead. I had a family of my own for a while, but they're gone now, too, so I'm all that's left."

"You were born on the Trail of Tears?" Eliza Kate asked. It had taken place in the fall of 1838, which meant Jonathan would turn thirty-two that autumn. He was such a serious individual, she could not even imagine him ever being as fun-loving a boy as either of her brothers. Just the same, she wished there were a way to glimpse more of his past than what he'd revealed.

Jonathan took another sip of lemonade, but appeared far from refreshed. "Yes, I sure was. It's a sad legacy, isn't it?"

He was daring Eliza to show him sympathy he would stubbornly refuse, but she recognized the trap for what it was and remained silent. Jonathan Blair was a difficult man to get to know, but she sensed he would be well worth the effort. If only he stayed with them long enough for that miracle to occur.

"You've no brothers or sisters?" Delia inquired.

Jonathan shook his head. "My mother died when I was small, and my father never remarried. Now that's enough of that pitiful tale. If you're feeling better, Lawrence, let's go find Ricky, and I'll race him to win whatever he wants to wager."

"You're awfully confident," Eliza interjected. "Ricky might surprise you."

Jonathan finished his lemonade, then rose and set the glass on the tray Carmen had left resting at the edge of the lily pond. "You've seen my horse. I call him Red Warrior, and he's never been beaten."

"I doubt anyone gets the better of you either, Jonathan," Delia mused aloud. "I hope you'll excuse me. I need to rest now, but I'll look forward to hearing about the race this evening."

Eliza Kate took her mother's arm to walk her to the house, but she looked back over her shoulder and called to the men. "Please wait for me. I might want to place a wager too."

"I won't take your money," Jonathan replied.

His gaze swept over Eliza in a taunting challenge, but she merely nodded and made a silent vow not to risk anything of value where he was concerned.

Chapter Three

As they entered Delia's bedroom, Eliza Kate's mother gave her hand a fond squeeze. "Will you please help me select a gown for this evening?" she asked. "I do so want everything to be perfect when we have guests."

Eliza Kate's heart fell, and not because her mother's request would make her late for the race, but because Delia had obviously forgotten there was going to be one. Not wanting to rush her mother, Eliza set aside her own need for haste and slowly sorted through Delia's extensive wardrobe. It was a task she usually enjoyed, and she provided thoughtful suggestions until one finally appealed to Delia.

Eliza then left her mother in Carmen's equally attentive care, raced down the stairs, donned her scarf and hat, and hurried out front where she was elated to find her uncle still waiting for her in the buckboard. She surveyed the yard with a hasty glance before climbing up beside him on the high seat.

"There's simply no way to hurry Mother when she needs me, but I'm sorry to have kept you waiting so long. Where are Ricky and Jonathan?"

"They knew better than to gallop past the house and coat your mother's beautiful furnishings with dust, so they've ridden out a ways. Don't worry, they promised to wait for us." Lawrence clucked to the mules, and as the team moved forward, the buckboard gave one shuddering lurch then rolled steadily down the trail Eliza Kate followed each morning to the river.

"What did you think of Red Warrior?" Eliza asked to distract herself from thoughts of his handsome owner.

"He's a beauty, but Ricky's pinto has wings for feet so it should be an exciting contest."

Lawrence paused to reflect a moment, then regarded Eliza Kate with an apologetic smile. "I've an enormous favor to ask. I'm really worried about Jonathan. I'm afraid he's adrift on a sea of grief and riding out to California might be the worst mistake he could ever make. Will you please do whatever you can to convince him to remain with us awhile?"

Caught off guard, Eliza couldn't possibly admit she'd already begged Jonathan to extend his stay, but she felt horribly uncomfortable being on the opposite side of a similar plea. Lawrence was only fifteen years her senior, and they were as close as brother and sister, so keeping secrets from him hurt her conscience badly.

"I'm doing my very best to be gracious, Uncle," Eliza assured him, struggling to hide her frustration. "What more do you suggest?"

Lawrence pursed his lips thoughtfully. "I haven't had much time to consider the matter but because love makes the best of anchors, perhaps you could introduce him to one of those charming young women you'd hoped would be perfect for me. Then it will be up to her to make Jonathan lose interest in leaving Texas."

"That's a tall order when he's only agreed to spend one night," Eliza pointed out, but she had never received a more painful request.

A complete stranger to the anguish of jealousy, it took her a moment to recognize the shameful emotion for what it was. After knowing Jonathan only a few hours, how could she possibly be jealous? she wondered. It made no sense at all to her, and yet such level-headed reasoning failed to dissolve the disquieting ache in the pit of her stomach.

The friends she had chosen for Lawrence had all been bright, beautiful, and sweet. She was glad that he remembered them fondly, but when Jonathan fascinated her so, she could not bring herself to consider which were still available. Of course, she wasn't truly free herself because Fletcher had proposed several months ago. Rather than accept, however, she had beseeched him to be patient.

At the time, she had been torn by a terrible dilemma for it would be too great a strain on her mother to help plan the type of wedding the Bendalins would surely insist upon hosting for their only daughter, and yet how could Eliza postpone her wedding when her mother might not live to see another spring?

That dismal prospect inspired a rush of tears, and Eliza Kate bit down on her lip to stem them, then coughed to clear her throat. "Did you have someone in particular in mind?" she asked hoarsely.

Lawrence had been mulling over the choices and offered what he considered a fine option. "Carol Ann has an impish sparkle. She might be precisely what Jonathan needs to brighten his mood."

Carol Ann Ferguson was an adorable redhead with translucent skin and golden-brown eyes but Eliza Kate could not abide the thought of Jonathan even holding her hand, let alone becoming seriously involved with her. That Lawrence had once provided the perfect reason to reject Carol Ann brought Eliza an enormous sense of relief.

Now suppressing a smile, she spoke with studied nonchalance. "Didn't you describe her giggle as shrill and annoying?"

Lawrence swore under his breath. "Is Carol Ann the one who giggles constantly?"

"Incessantly," Eliza Kate stressed. "You have an admirable forbearance, but I fear Jonathan might soon strangle her."

Lawrence laughed at that dire prediction and thought again how wonderful it was to have Jonathan near. "I'd almost forgotten how to laugh," he confessed shyly. "Please help me keep Jonathan here. Think of someone less exuberant."

Eliza Kate could not even force her mind around that request and instead, pointed excitedly. "Look. They're waiting by the Hanging Tree."

As a child, Ricky had given the oak that grotesque name, and the whole family had soon adopted it. As far as anyone knew though, no one had actually been hanged from its gnarled old branches.

In another minute they were close enough for Eliza Kate to see that Jonathan had discarded his shirt and exchanged his boots for moccasins. He had also stripped Red Warrior of his saddle and was riding bareback. When he reached up to hang his hat from an overhanging branch, his jet-black hair caught the sun, and he looked thoroughly Indian.

Recalling her mother's warning, Eliza tried not to stare but Jonathan's hard-muscled body drew a long, admiring glance. She had never seen Fletcher without a shirt, but he wasn't in the least athletic and could not possibly be anywhere near as appealing physically.

Ashamed for having such disloyal thoughts, Eliza Kate struggled to focus on the race and grasped Lawrence's sleeve. "I hope you didn't allow Ricky to wager much."

"No, of course not. I took him aside and told him I doubted Jonathan could afford to lose more than a few dollars. Ricky's a good kid; he understood the need for restraint."

Ricky waved to her, and Eliza cupped her hands around her mouth to shout, "Have you already set the course?"

Before Ricky could answer, Jonathan rode up to the buckboard. "I told him Red Warrior would leave him in the dust whether he chose fifty yards or a mile. Perhaps we should ask you to set the distance."

Lawrence pulled the mules to a halt beneath the oak

where they'd have a shaded view of the race without having to leave the buckboard. Eliza doubted her knees would hold her and seized the excuse to remain seated. She had never fainted, but feared it was a distinct possibility that day when her thoughts and feelings were twisted in such hopeless knots.

"What do you say?" she asked Lawrence. "Should we make it a sprint, or insist upon distance?"

"Distance," Lawrence chose immediately. "I'm eager to see Red Warrior run."

Jonathan's grin stretched wide. "We'll be lost over the horizon before you can count to ten."

Annoyed by that arrogant boast, Eliza Kate sent a dismissive glance over Jonathan's broad chest, but her resolve faltered as her gaze grazed his tautly sculpted belly. It was then as difficult to ignore his well-muscled thighs as it was his proud pose. Her roving glance traveled clear to the toes of his moccasins before again rising to his face, and the amusement dancing in his light eyes made it plain he reveled in her attention.

Flustered, Eliza hurriedly scanned the surrounding terrain. "With a dinner party tonight, I haven't all day to sit out here in the sun. That outcropping of rock must be half a mile away. Why don't you race there and back?"

Ricky stood in his stirrups to judge the distance. "That's fine with me," he called and a gentle tap of his heels sent his black-and-white pinto forward with light dancing steps. Harlequin was as high-spirited a horse as Red Warrior and eager to run.

"Come on, Jonathan," Ricky urged. "Let's see if that stallion runs as fast as you talk."

Jonathan turned his mount in a tight circle. "Better take a quick look because during the race all you're going to see is his tail."

The lively banter reminded Lawrence of the many happy times he and Jonathan had shared despite the war, and he could barely contain his laughter as Jonathan and Ricky moved into place. Lawrence then grabbed Eliza

Kate's hand. "Let's all count to three," he said.

Eliza Kate couldn't find the breath to force the words over her lips and merely mouthed them, but the instant the men reached three, both stallions leaped forward, leaving a dusty haze in their wake. Harlequin had tremendous speed, and for the first twenty yards kept pace with Red Warrior, but with what appeared to be near effortless ease, Jonathan's stallion gradually began to draw away.

Ricky used the trailing ends of his reins as a whip against Harlequin's rump, but failed to cut the lead Red Warrior increased with every stride. Crouched low, Jonathan controlled his mount with such a light hand he seemed almost to float above him as a bronze-and-black blur. Jonathan and Red Warrior reached the rocks first, circled them in a tight spin and came streaking back toward the Hanging Tree.

The magnificent sorrel's snowy mane was whipped by the wind, and his luxuriant tail flowed out in a billowing stream like steam trailing a locomotive. Nearly flying, the red stallion's hooves struck the prairie with the challenging rhythm of war drums, and he crossed the finish line at the ancient oak half a dozen lengths ahead of Harlequin.

"My God!" Lawrence screamed, for he had never seen another horse with Red Warrior's lightning speed. He grabbed Eliza Kate in a jubilant embrace, knocking her hat askew, but she simply stared numbly as Jonathan turned his stallion in a wide arc and then trotted back to the buckboard.

Ricky, astonished to have finished such a poor second, slid out of his saddle, and led Harlequin over to his uncle and sister. The pinto was breathing hard, but Red Warrior had not even come close to the limit of his endurance.

"Thank God no one else saw this race," Ricky exclaimed excitedly, "because we're going to win ourselves a fortune on the next one."

Jonathan drew in a deep breath and squared his shoulders proudly. "There's not going to be another race. Now just hand over the hundred dollars you owe me."

Ricky removed his hat and fanned himself with brisk strokes. "Tell him I'm good for it, Eliza Kate."

"I'll do no such thing," Eliza announced. She paused to adjust her hat, then shook her finger at her brother. "You'll pay up right now, or—"

"Or what?" Jonathan asked in a lazy drawl.

Eliza Kate was shocked by the insinuation in his tone. Fortunately, both Ricky and Lawrence were paying closer attention to Red Warrior's splendid conformation than Jonathan's expression and missed his veiled meaning entirely.

"Or I'll have Father make you drive one of his freight wagons until you've earned the money you ought not to have wagered unless it was in your hand," Eliza finished with forced calm.

Ricky plunked his hat back on his head. "Calm down, Sis. I'll pay him just as soon as we get back to the house." He swung himself back up on Harlequin, and still in high spirits, began to coax Jonathan into having another race where they would invite the public.

Lawrence misread Eliza Kate's anxious frown, and believing she was in a rush to get back home, slapped the reins against the mules' haunches and left Jonathan to argue with Ricky. He didn't care how the dispute ended, but he fully intended to convince his old friend to challenge Fletcher Monroe. In his mind's eye, he replayed the race he had just witnessed and ended with an admiring whistle.

"I've never seen the equal of Red Warrior, have you?" he asked.

"No, indeed," Eliza agreed, but the fleet stallion was merely a horse, while to her mind, Jonathan Blair was infinitely more remarkable.

The Bendalins employed a staff that truly endeavored to please them, and appreciating their loyalty, Eliza Kate provided firm, but light supervision. Though she and Delia did the initial planning for the household together, it was Eliza who ordered the food not grown on the ranch and oversaw its preparation. The house was immaculately kept because of her insistence and with whatever spare time she might have, she also provided the decorative touches that gave the attractive house its charm.

Although Fletcher Monroe was a frequent dinner guest, Delia always insisted upon making the occasion as festive as a formal party. That meant additional work for Eliza, for the food had to be not merely delicious, but superb. The table linens had to be sparkling white and pressed to crisp perfection. The silver had to be polished to a near blinding gleam, and fresh flowers had to be artfully arranged not only for the centerpiece in the dining room, but for the entryway and parlor as well.

Ricky could be expected to come to dinner in a suit, but Robby always required Eliza's attention. Knowing it was their mother's touch he missed, she usually found the necessary patience, but that night it was all she could do not to scold her younger brother mercilessly. Knowing how little he liked wearing his good clothes, she bit her tongue, but when she checked on him a third time and he still was not ready, she nearly lost her tenuous hold on her temper.

"Robby, please," she cajoled. "Stand still or I'll never get your tie straight."

"Why do I have to go to so much trouble to look good for Fletcher?" Robby complained. "He's just here to see you, and he doesn't even notice me."

"It's not for Fletcher," Eliza insisted. "It's for Mama." She slicked back his hair as best she could without taking the time to trim his curls.

"There now," she encouraged, "that will have to do." She opened Robby's door to shoo him on downstairs and found Jonathan passing by in the hall.

Lawrence had loaned Jonathan a suit, and Eliza Kate could scarcely believe how completely it had transformed his appearance. Except for the white shirt, he was again clothed in black, but the change wasn't merely one of attire. The elegant cut of his frock coat, waistcoat, and trousers showed off his handsome build to every advantage, but freshly shaven and with his hair neatly combed, there was no trace of the Indian brave who had ridden Red Warrior to such a stunning victory.

There was also no hint of the rogue Eliza had first glimpsed at the river. She could not help wondering in what guise Jonathan might next appear, but it wasn't until he reached out to chuck her chin that she realized how rudely she had been gaping.

"Forgive me," she begged. "I didn't realize Lawrence's clothes would fit you so well."

Jonathan's glance swept over the ruffles and pleats adorning Eliza's fashionable taffeta gown. A rich sapphire color, the lustrous fabric matched her eyes perfectly and the square neckline provided an exquisite frame for her bosom's soft swell. Her curls were twisted atop her head in a graceful swirl, but she had left several tendrils free to tickle her neck and invite the kisses he dared not give.

"Would it be improper for me to comment on just how well your gown fits you?" Jonathan teased.

From the intensity of his gaze, Eliza Kate assumed his thoughts were as improper as his comment, but her little brother spoke up before she could offer that opinion.

"She's got more than a dozen gowns," Robby interjected. "Ricky told me your horse barely nosed by his to win the race. Is that how you saw it?"

Jonathan laughed at that outrageous lie. "No, it sure isn't, but I'll bet you know exactly how far your brother usually stretches the truth when the facts don't suit him."

Eliza Kate heard Fletcher's voice and realized it was inexcusable that she had not been downstairs to greet him. She raised her hem to reveal pale blue stockings and kid slippers dyed a deeper shade of blue to match her gown. "Please excuse me," she requested politely.

Jonathan responded by moving into her path rather than to the side, confounding her escape. Had Robby not

been there, she would have shoved Jonathan aside; but
she dared not behave so rudely when her brother would
provide a talkative witness. All she could do was scold Jonathan with her eyes, but he just smiled as though she had
not made her intentions plain.

"Let's all go downstairs," Eliza suggested more forcefully
and this time took Robby's hand. With Robby leading the
way, she slipped past Jonathan before he could again
block the move, and she was inordinately pleased to have
outsmarted him. She loved her little brother dearly, but
until that night she had never realized just how useful his
presence could be.

As they reached the stairs, she took hold of the banister;
she could still make out the pale imprint of Jonathan's
fingers on the back of her hand, but she was confident
no one else would notice. Still, it was a taunting reminder
of a day, and a man, she'd not soon forget.

Beaming happily, Fletcher stood at the bottom of the
stairs. As Eliza Kate and Robby began their descent, he
greeted her with a mock bow. "You're radiant as always,
my dear."

Eliza waited for him to comment on how nice Robby
looked, too, but just as the boy had complained, Fletcher
failed to notice him. Of medium height with a slender
build, Fletcher had wavy brown hair and hazel eyes. He
took great pride in his appearance; though he usually
wore tweeds during the day, he preferred more formal
attire when he dined with them and was dressed in black.

Robby pulled his hand free of his sister's and bounded
ahead of her without so much as a murmur of welcome
for Fletcher. Understanding why Robby's feelings were
hurt, Eliza Kate did not call him back to remind him of
his manners. It was also difficult for her to consider
Fletcher rude when she was so flattered by his devotion.
As he continued to regard her with an adoring gaze, she
wondered how he could overlook Jonathan Blair, who was
only a single step behind her.

Then Jonathan slid his fingertips lightly across the small

of Eliza's back and a shivering thrill shot clear through her. Even without that shockingly inappropriate reminder, she certainly hadn't forgotten him. A challenging light lit her eyes as she paused on the bottom step and turned to look up at him.

Jonathan dropped his hand to his side, but his smile was tinged with regret as though he knew he deserved a good scolding. Eliza could not imagine why he would attempt to create a scene in front of Fletcher, but she intended to disappoint him and with a forced smile, provided polite introductions.

In a smoothly proprietary gesture, Fletcher drew Eliza Kate down the last step to his side. He waited for Jonathan to also reach the bottom of the stairs and then shook his hand enthusiastically. "I've heard Lawrence speak of you, and I'm proud to meet a genuine hero. Perhaps if our side had had more men with your courage, the war might have ended differently."

Rather than being honored by Fletcher's effusive praise, Jonathan took immediate exception to it. "There was no shortage of brave men serving with the Confederacy, Mr. Monroe, and it's a cause of great sorrow that more did not survive."

Startled by Jonathan's vehement tone, Fletcher stared at his back as Jonathan promptly left them to enter the parlor. Recovering quickly, he leaned over to kiss Eliza's cheek. "Is Blair merely an extremely modest individual, or was what I said truly offensive?"

Also shocked by how quickly Jonathan had dismissed Fletcher, Eliza Kate refused to make excuses for him. "I really don't know him well enough to judge, but perhaps like Father, he simply prefers not to discuss the war. Shall we join the others?"

Fletcher slid his arm around Eliza's waist. His touch was pleasant, but for the first time she began to wonder if she shouldn't feel something more for the man she intended to marry. She felt safe with Fletcher, for he cherished her with the same adoration her father showed her mother, but as they joined the others in the parlor, it was Jonathan's presence she sought, not more of Fletcher's flattering praise.

Jonathan was standing near the windows conferring with Lawrence, and reminded of her uncle's plea for help, Eliza hoped something clever would occur to her. After all, she would have to appear to be seeking a suitable feminine companion for Jonathan while at the same time carefully avoiding even a brush with success. It was a formidable challenge, but the only choice her heart allowed.

"Beloved?" Fletcher whispered insistently. "It is my imagination, or are you completely ignoring me this evening?"

Appalled that she had not heard a word he had said, Eliza Kate promptly apologized. "I want our dinner party to be perfect, and I'm afraid I was preoccupied with the menu."

"Your cook is far too accomplished to make such worries necessary, my dearest. Come. Let's chat a bit with your mother. She looks quite well this evening, don't you agree?"

Delia's satin gown was a rich burgundy shade that imparted a rosy glow to her pale complexion. The patterned overshirt was drawn back to form a stylish bustle and Eliza Kate felt sure it was the lovely gown that had enhanced her mother's natural beauty rather than any real improvement in her health. She did not want to argue with Fletcher, however, and nodded to encourage the compliments she was positive he would bestow.

Her mother had always been charmed by Fletcher's engaging personality, and for the most part, so was Eliza Kate. Still, no matter how hard she tried to be attentive to him, her gaze kept drifting toward Jonathan Blair. She moved closer to Fletcher, even gripped his arm tightly, but while she heard her mother's lilting laughter, her thoughts continued to wander in the same maddening direction. She feared it was going to be a very long and trying evening.

When dinner was announced, Delia and Lamar led everyone into the dining room where Eliza Kate had carefully arranged the places to seat Jonathan at Delia's right, then Lawrence, and Ricky on that side of the table. Fletcher's place card was at Lamar's right. Eliza took the seat beside his, and as usual, Robby was on his mother's left.

Grateful not to be opposite Jonathan, Eliza nonetheless remained exquisitely aware of his presence and barely tasted the delicate cream of chicken soup. The main course was a sumptuous leg of lamb surrounded by fresh vegetables, but she did not take a bite until Jonathan added his compliments to those voiced by Fletcher and the rest of her family. Her father appeared to be in no better spirits that night than he had been in the morning, but she had discarded her earlier plan to question him about Jonathan for fear she'd reveal an unsuitable curiosity that he might swiftly convey to Fletcher.

The very last thing she wished was to make Fletcher jealous, but even as she smiled to encourage his conversation, she heard little of what he said. Fortunately, her mother found his description of Fort Worth's latest arrivals highly entertaining; on the opposite side of the table, Lawrence and Jonathan were quietly conversing on the same topic.

"There's a marvelous new bookstore that carries quality literature rather than dime novels. I found a beautiful volume of Shakespeare's sonnets there," Fletcher confided as the meal drew to a close. "I wasn't certain whether or not you owned one, Delia, but if not, I'll make you a present of it on my next visit."

Unable to recall just what filled the shelves of their family library, Delia frowned slightly, and Eliza Kate spoke to spare her mother more than a few seconds confusion. "No. We don't have a copy, and it would be so thoughtful of you to bring us one. It would make for lovely reading in the garden."

"Thank you, Fletcher," Delia added graciously. "I shall look forward to receiving it."

Ricky waited until lemon sherbet and sugar cookies had been served for dessert, then diminishing his loss considerably, he gave a brief account of the morning's race. "You ought to see Red Warrior, Mr. Monroe. Although I sincerely doubt you own a mount that could come any closer to beating him than Harlequin did."

"Surely you jest," Fletcher replied with an amused chuckle.

Eliza Kate dared a glance toward Jonathan and found him regarding Fletcher with a sly smile. After his caustic reply to Fletcher's greeting, she certainly hoped he was not about to begin a similar hostile exchange at the table.

"I'm positive Jonathan told us he wasn't interested in another race, Rick," Eliza reminded him. "Didn't you believe him?"

Ricky leaned out to look around Lawrence so as to better judge Jonathan's reaction. "Sure. I believe him, but that doesn't mean I won't keep trying to change his mind. Just as soon as Mr. Monroe sees Red Warrior, I'll bet he will too. Couldn't you use a larger stake to set yourself up in California?"

Jonathan shrugged. "If I run out of money, I can always race Red Warrior out there."

Fletcher had begun by scoffing, but as Ricky continued to praise Red Warrior's impressive speed, he swiftly grew intrigued. "I'll tell you what," Fletcher offered. "Let's give your horse a couple of days to rest, and then I'll take Coal Dust, the best horse in my stable, and race you."

Jonathan's resolve didn't waver. "Sorry, but I'm in a hurry to leave. It's a long way to California, and I want to cross the Arizona desert before it gets too hot."

Jonathan then forced a reluctant turn in the conversation to travel, but all Eliza Kate heard in his voice was an eagerness to flee her family. She gave her uncle a wistful smile, and he nodded, but she could see Lawrence was as disappointed as she. Fletcher reached over to take her hand, and hidden by the tablecloth she gave his fingers a light squeeze, but there was no magic in his touch, and she was beginning to fear there might never be.

Long after the house had grown silent, Eliza Kate was unable to sleep. Uncomfortable in every pose, she lay upon her tangled sheets until remaining in bed struck her as absurd. Too restless to merely pace her room, she left to explore the garden, but although the pale moonlight softened the shadows, peace continued to elude her on the curving paths.

She sat for a while by the lily pond, but the memories of Jonathan's sad revelations were too strong there. "A sad legacy, indeed," she murmured. She readily understood why he wished to move clear across the country, but in escaping his sorrow, he would also miss any hope for them ever to know each other well.

A tear spilled over her lashes, and she wiped it on the ruffled hem of her nightgown. She was so fair her eyes remained puffy for hours whenever she cried. Not wanting to explain why she'd been crying the following morning, she dared weep no more.

She pushed herself to her feet and reluctantly returned to the house. Filled with an aching sense of loss for something she had never really known, she was halfway up the stairs before she noticed Jonathan standing above her on the landing. Clad only in a pair of black trousers, he again reminded her of an Indian brave, but no savage, he waited calmly for her to climb the stairs.

Eliza Kate paused several steps below the landing and kept a firm grip on the bannister. Her parents' and uncle's bedrooms were in the rear of the house, and her brothers slept too soundly to overhear what might transpire on the stairs, but she doubted Jonathan had been looking for conversation. He came down a step and then another, but Eliza was unable to express her heart's desperate yearning and waited for him to speak.

Jonathan had been given a spacious guest room on the

third floor, but having fine accommodations had not
helped him sleep. He knew he should walk right on by
Eliza Kate without so much as a polite nod, but framed
by the gentle moonlight filtered through the windows
above, her slender figure held an angel's grace and her
fair curls a heavenly glow.

Hungry for a touch of that sweetness, he reached out,
meaning only to wrap a single curl around his finger and
then let go; but trembling with desire his hand brushed
her cheek. He then stood frozen on the edge of a longing
so strong it sucked every bit of wind from his lungs. Seemingly unaware of his fierce battle for control, Eliza dipped
her head to place a tender kiss in his palm.

Overwhelmed, Jonathan smothered an anguished cry
against her temple, then pulled her down beside him on
the stairs. He held her locked in his arms, and at the same
time, prayed she'd struggle to break free. Instead, Eliza
relaxed into his fervent embrace and rested her cheek
upon his bare shoulder.

He smelled of spicy soap rather than imported cologne
but Eliza felt far more comfortable in Jonathan's arms
than she had ever been in Fletcher's. She rubbed her
hand over his chest to savor his warmth, then pressed her
fingertips against his heart. She felt it beating as wildly as
her own, then slid her hand up to his shoulder where of
their own accord, her fingers wound themselves in his
hair.

She raised her mouth to his, and as their lips met, he
pulled back but his resistance lasted no more than an
instant. Then he nearly crushed her in his arms. Eliza
opened her mouth to swallow his anguished moan and
turn it into a deep, hungry kiss.

Watching him race Red Warrior had been a delicious
thrill, but nothing Eliza had ever experienced had prepared her for the exquisite excitement coursing through
her now. Breathless and eager, she returned Jonathan's
devouring kisses, sucking his tongue in a wild craving for
an even deeper intimacy. Pressing for it, she molded her

supple body to his until their reckless ardor threatened to send them tumbling headlong down the stairs.

Sliding down a step, Jonathan gasped for air and grasped Eliza Kate's arms to steady them both. She pushed her tangled curls out of her eyes, and wished she could see his face clearly but in the dim light, it was enough to know he was smiling. She wanted the choice to be solely his and stilled an ardent plea, but she longed for him to stay with her always.

When Jonathan remained silent, Eliza drew the sad conclusion that even if she invited him to spend the night in her bed, he would still bid her good-bye the next morning. Perhaps there was only room for one woman in his heart, and his late wife still filled it. That idea was easier to accept than the possibility she was no more than a pretty young woman who'd provided a bit of amusement on a sleepless night.

"Let me go," she ordered softly, and it broke her heart when he released her with no more than a softly voiced sigh.

Chapter Four

Early the next morning, Eliza Kate left the house not knowing whether Jonathan Blair might still be there. She had no sense of his presence, only a lingering anguish over the regrettable way they had met and the shocking passion with which they'd parted.

She rode her mare in a slumped pose and was grateful the gentle horse would make her way to the river on her own. In the past, Eliza had almost floated on the blissful calm of the early morning, but that day, she simply felt incredibly sad and alone.

When she reached the Hanging Tree, she glanced up at the branch where Jonathan had hung his hat and pulled her pinto to a halt. While growing up, she had not shared in Ricky's raucous games, but he had often climbed the old oak tree, and now Robby loved to play there.

As she studied the branches' beckoning curves she finally saw how easy it would be to use the lowest as a convenient step to the next. Instantly abandoning her usual routine, she dismounted, left her horse to graze on the lush spring grass, and began to climb the tree.

Ricky had often gone clear to the top to pretend he was a pirate high in the rigging of a ship bound for the azure waters of the Caribbean. Robby preferred to pretend he was a monkey in the jungle and swing through the branches. Eliza's mood was anything but playful, and she was content to sit and rest just ten feet above the ground.

She was surprised by how comfortable a perch a gently angled limb made and let her feet dangle while she marveled at how different the familiar countryside appeared when viewed from this new perspective. A soft cooing drew her attention upward, and she wondered how many baby doves had been hatched in nests cradled in the old oak's branches and if they would return the following spring to build their own nests there.

She envied the sweetly voiced birds their freedom to soar above the treetops and view the world from afar. Her own world was so very beautiful, but as fragile as her mother's health. She held tightly to the tree trunk, as though even this small separation from home were too great to bear.

"Eliza Kate?"

The sound of Jonathan's deep voice filled Eliza with such a dizzying thrill she had to consciously summon a merely curious expression before looking down. She had not expected ever to see him again, and quickly reached up to adjust the angle of her hat to hide the growing width of her smile.

"Good morning," she replied with a friendliness she wished she'd displayed at their first meeting.

"I meant to go riding with you," Jonathan explained. "I didn't realize you'd leave so early, and I sure didn't expect to find you sitting up in that tree."

He laughed in spite of himself. "Not that you don't look real pretty, because you most certainly do. It's just that, well, I doubt many young ladies of your breeding would care to do such a crazy thing."

"Crazy?" Eliza repeated numbly. Last night she might have taken leave of her senses when she had kissed him with such desperate abandon, but now she was merely contemplating her surroundings from an elevated perch, which wasn't crazy at all.

She didn't understand how she could have failed to hear Jonathan approach. She watched him swing down from Red Warrior's back, and suddenly afraid he might also climb the tree, she felt compelled to defend herself.

"I love climbing trees," she proclaimed loudly, "and do so often. But like riding, I prefer to enjoy the pastime alone."

She had slept poorly and ridden away from home blaming herself for touching Jonathan's passions rather than his heart. Now his cocky grin almost made her sorry she had cared. *Almost.* "I thought you'd be on your way to California by now."

Jonathan dropped his reins to allow Red Warrior to graze alongside her mare. He leaned back against the oak's thick trunk, and folded his arms across his chest before glancing up at her. "I didn't get much sleep last night and thought it a poor day for travel."

Eliza knew precisely how out of sorts he must feel, but was far too self-conscious to describe her own distress. "I can't imagine why you didn't enjoy a peaceful night," she said instead. "Our other guests haven't complained. Didn't you find your bed comfortable?"

Jonathan discounted her flippant comment with a knowing shrug. "The problem was the sharp angles of my thoughts rather than annoying lumps in the feather mattress."

Eliza Kate didn't dare hope that she had inspired those troublesome thoughts. She licked her lips nervously. Instantly reminded of Jonathan's luscious kiss, she silently cursed her own folly. She had never had any difficulty conversing with other young men, but nothing was as it should be with Jonathan Blair.

He obviously favored black in his clothing, but yesterday's guarded expression had left his eyes. Without the suspicious gleam, they were a warm, smoky gray. Eliza supposed his light eyes came from his mother's side of the family, but the confident way he carried himself and the easy grace of his motions were pure Cherokee.

"Yes, thoughts can be deeply disturbing," she finally agreed.

"Yes, ma'am. I kept thinking of what you'd said about Lawrence ending up a lonely old man. That's such a pathetic vision that I just can't allow it to happen. So I'll stay on here awhile and do whatever I can to help him find the love of his life. But as I said yesterday, I've no idea where to begin, so I'll rely on your help to succeed."

Eliza Kate clung to the oak with a frantic grasp. She had left home believing all hope of knowing Jonathan was lost, but by some miracle, he was willing to extend his visit. While she prayed it was not solely because of Lawrence, she knew she'd have to adopt a more effective strategy than she'd used in the past to make their efforts on her uncle's behalf worthwhile.

"I really appreciate this," she replied with sincere gratitude. Whatever Jonathan's reason for remaining on the Trinity Star, she expected Lawrence to reap the benefit. "Our family has a few acquaintances in Dallas. Perhaps we'll have more success if we widen our search for an appealing young woman."

"Dallas?" Jonathan considered the city a moment and then nodded. "Sure. It's just down the road. Maybe I could ride over, stand on the corner of the main street, and hand a flyer to every pretty woman who walks by."

"Jonathan Blair, you'll do no such thing!"

Jonathan stepped away from the tree to look up at her. "I'm teasing you, Eliza Kate. I know we have to be discreet. If Lawrence were to discover what we were up to, he'd be furious with us both, and I don't want to risk that. After all, I could just head out for California, but you'd be left here to deal with his anger."

Eliza swept him with a leisurely glance. She had to continually remind herself not to stare, but he was awfully nice to look at, and it was difficult not to observe him too closely. "Why are you so set on going to California?" she inquired softly.

Jonathan tipped his hat back. "Let's just say I need a complete change of scene. I've seen the Atlantic Ocean, and the Gulf, but I'd like to see the Pacific Ocean too. I understand the scenery's real pretty in California."

Even on that cool spring morning, he could have melted chocolate with the bright warmth of his gaze, and Eliza Kate understood he considered his present view extremely enjoyable too. Last night she had longed for him to remain with her, but in the clear light of day, she feared she had absolutely no idea what to do with him now that he'd agreed to stay. That she knew precisely what she wanted to do sent a tingling blush rushing up from the tips of her toes.

"It would help if we knew what type of woman Lawrence craves," Eliza offered in a hurried attempt to shift her concentration to her uncle. "I never succeeded in getting his views on the subject. Do you think he might confide his preferences in you?"

"He might, and if we knew then, it would make our job a lot easier."

Believing Jonathan's wife must have been Cherokee, Eliza Kate felt certain she would have been a dark-eyed beauty with long ebony hair. It saddened her to consider how different she must be, but because she could not possibly remind him of his late wife, she hoped her fair coloring might work to her advantage. She had never been interested in a widower, so Jonathan presented a challenge she was unprepared to face.

"Yes. It would narrow our search if we knew he was partial to petite redheads or preferred willowy blondes," Eliza replied.

"Don't tell him I said this," Jonathan confided, "but he's worried about not being able to dance. So it would be a real shame to find him precisely the type of woman he wants, if she loved to waltz."

Because Jonathan possessed a natural grace, Eliza knew he would be a marvelous dancer, and she could easily imagine herself in his arms. Yet she dared not ask him if he enjoyed moving to music and risk having him show her right there.

"You're right, of course," she admitted. "Perhaps I should have been more concerned with finding him a woman who shared his interests, rather than merely introducing him to attractive young women I thought he'd like. I fear I've gone about this all wrong, and I really do appreciate your help."

"It'll be my pleasure. Is there anything else you'll need while I'm here?"

Jonathan's smile was teasing, and Eliza wondered if he truly expected her to request more of the delicious affection he had lavished on her last night. She did, indeed, long for more, but she could not bear to suffer the humiliation of having to ask.

"Well, yes, there is something you could do," she responded brightly. "Catch me if I fall."

Eliza hoped climbing down the tree would be as easy as going up. Because she had boasted she climbed trees often, she attempted to look as though she knew precisely what she was doing. Almost before she knew it, her feet touched the ground. She was elated by the accomplishment until she realized she had foolishly missed an opportunity to fall straight into Jonathan's arms.

Eliza pushed away from the tree's gnarled trunk and

brushed off her gloved hands. "Well, now. I need to get back home."

Jonathan had stepped away from the tree to give her sufficient room to climb down, but was deliberately blocking the path to her mare. "Wait a minute. We need to get our stories straight."

Fearing he was referring to the escapade on the stairs, Eliza Kate gasped sharply. "You mean someone saw us together last night?"

Jonathan laughed at her horror-stricken expression. "No, thank God. But at dinner I was real insistent about leaving this morning, and I don't want Lawrence to suspect that I'm sticking around because I feel sorry for him."

Not appreciating his laughter, Eliza Kate simply stared up at him. It was heartbreaking to be so close and not reach out to touch him, but she didn't want him to use an attraction to her as an excuse if that was all she would be. When he kept his hands firmly tucked in his hip pockets rather than drawing her into his arms for a kiss, she was sadly disappointed.

"You could say you've changed your mind about racing Fletcher," she offered smoothly.

Jonathan nodded thoughtfully. "Perfect. Now why didn't I think of that?"

He was teasing her again, and Eliza chose to go along with it. "I'm sure the idea would have occurred to you before we reached the house." That said, she circled him and grabbed for her mare's reins. "I'd challenge you to a race myself, but Patches here wouldn't stand a chance against Red Warrior."

"I could give you a big head start," Jonathan offered graciously.

"Then it would look as though you were chasing me, and one of the hands might shoot you. I'll not risk that calamity."

"Thank you. I'd rather not take that risk either." Jonathan waited for Eliza to mount her mare, then swung himself up into his saddle. "Robby asked me about Indians yesterday. If they're raiding as close as the next county, I don't think it's wise for you to ride this far from the house alone. Wait for me in the morning."

Yesterday Eliza had been annoyed by his concern for her safety, but today she simply laughed. "Why? You're an Indian yourself and probably pose a greater threat to me than the Kiowa."

Amused rather than insulted, Jonathan urged Red Warrior forward. "The Cherokee are one of the so-called civilized tribes, ma'am, and I'm not even tempted to scalp you. I doubt a Kiowa brave would be either, but that doesn't mean he'd provide you with a safe escort home."

Eliza doubted she was truly safe with Jonathan either, but for the time being, the morning had regained its glorious promise, and in his charming company, hope soon erased her earlier despair.

At breakfast, Jonathan announced he had reconsidered and would remain at the Trinity Star Ranch to race Fletcher Monroe. With the exception of Lamar, who promptly choked on a bite of biscuit, the Bendalin family welcomed his decision. Jonathan sat back and listened as Ricky and Lawrence recounted several exciting races, but as soon as they were all finished eating, he cornered Lamar.

"I know Robby has to get to school," Jonathan began in an urgent whisper, "but I need to speak with you a minute, in private."

Jonathan's softly voiced request touched Lamar's ears as a grating command. A glow of pure terror filled his eyes, but he led the way into the study and carefully closed the door.

Jonathan intentionally kept his voice low to prevent their conversation from carrying into the parlor. "It's plain you don't want me here, Lamar, and I don't blame you. If this weren't where Lawrence lives, I sure as hell wouldn't have come within ten miles of your spread. When I was growing up, I had a pet snake with more character than you possess, but no one chooses his relatives, and Lawrence is cursed with you."

Lamar hadn't slept well either the previous night, and faint circles marred the skin beneath his eyes. "Jonathan, I don't think—"

Jonathan's grasp on his temper was sorely strained and he swore a filthy oath. He took a step forward, and Lamar shrank back against the door. "No, you're always thinking, but only of yourself. The fighting outside Richmond was fierce, and Lawrence was too badly wounded to question why I was the one to carry him to safety rather than you. I've no hope that if he ever begins to wonder about that awful day, you'll finally admit to having left him for dead."

The memory filled Jonathan with disgust, and he dropped his voice to an even more threatening tone. "But's it's not something I'll ever forget, or forgive."

Lamar's hands began to shake and he shoved them into his coat pockets to hide the incriminating tremor. "What do you want from me, Jonathan? If it's money—"

Jonathan would have spit had they been outdoors. Instead, he merely swore another bitter curse. "There's not enough money in the entire world to buy my silence, but I'll continue to keep your wretched secret for Lawrence's sake. For him, and also for the rest of your family, who don't deserve to suffer the shame of your cowardice."

Jonathan took another step toward Lamar and broke into a wicked grin when in his eagerness to get away, Lamar bumped into the door with a jarring thud. "You're still a coward," Jonathan murmured.

"It makes me sick to look at you, but I'm staying because I don't like what's happened to Lawrence. You've let him hide here behind your ledgers rather than encouraging him to enjoy life, marry, and raise a family of his own. I plan on remedying that sorry situation, and you're going to welcome every last one of my suggestions. Is that understood, Lamar?"

Beads of perspiration had sprung on Lamar's forehead,

and he grabbed for his handkerchief to mop his brow. "Yes. Indeed it is."

"Good. Now let's make everyone believe we were just having ourselves a friendly chat about the race you'll set up with Fletcher, and you take Robby to school with a smile on your face."

"I'll be glad to handle the race. I don't want any trouble with you," Lamar insisted.

"Then you should have been the one to brave the rifle and cannon fire to rescue your brother." Jonathan shouldered Lamar out of his way, yanked open the door, and stepped through it before the sight of Lamar's quivering lips made him puke on one of Delia's fine carpets.

Eliza Kate wore another stunning gown to dinner that evening. Fashioned of blue-gray taffeta, the flounced skirt was adorned with an overskirt in a dainty floral print gathered to form an elegant bustle. The high neckline brushed her chin with a delicate ruffle while the tight-fitting bodice hugged the soft swell of her bosom and narrowed her already slender waist. It was a far more modest gown than the one she had worn the previous evening and yet even more provocative for what it concealed.

Eliza took note of Jonathan's admiring glance and fought to keep a heady glow of pleasure from showing in her expression. He was Lawrence's guest, after all, rather than her beau, and she would not flirt with him in front of her family. She stayed by her mother's side as they entered the dining room, and then took her time making her way around the table to her place.

She had added a few white roses to the centerpiece and airy sprays of fern to screen the opposite side of the table so she would not be tempted to stare at Jonathan. To her shame, she now found herself adjusting the placement of her chair to improve her view of him. He appeared to be genuinely interested in how the others had spent the day but at the same time responded to questions about his own with no more than evasive shrugs and good-natured smiles.

The meal began with a hearty vegetable soup and as soon as everyone had been served a flavorful bowl, Lamar cleared his throat loudly. "Fletcher would like to schedule the race between Coal Dust and Red Warrior for this coming Saturday. Will that fit into your plans, Jonathan?"

Lamar seemed to be fascinated by the ornate handle of his soup spoon, and Jonathan was highly amused by his host's discomfort. However, if the man could still swallow, then he was not nearly as uneasy as Jonathan wished him to be. "I'm afraid I've completely lost track of the days. Is this Tuesday or Wednesday?"

"Tuesday," the entire table murmured in a soft chorus.

"All right, then," Jonathan mused aloud. "Saturday will be fine. Just let me know where and when, and Red Warrior and I will be there."

"You should make Fletcher come here," Ricky leaned forward to suggest. "There's no sense in giving him the advantage of racing at his own ranch."

"He'll have no advantage regardless of where he sets the course," Jonathan replied, "but I like the way you think, Ricky. Tell Monroe I want to race down by the river, Lamar. The ground's level, and Ricky and I found the landmarks easy to read."

"You know where he means, Father," Ricky exclaimed. "It's near the Hanging Tree."

Lamar considered the location a moment and then nodded. "It's as good a place as any, I suppose. How does noon suit you?"

The spring weather had been mild, and Jonathan had no objection to that hour. "That's fine with me. Will you come and watch, Delia?"

Delia raised her napkin to blot her mouth lightly. "Is it far?"

Jonathan was surprised she wasn't familiar with the location, then realized she must simply have forgotten. Embarrassed for her, he glanced toward Eliza Kate.

Touched by his unspoken plea, Eliza hastened to reassure her mother. "It's a short ride from the house and will be a pleasant outing, Mother. I do hope you'll feel up to joining us."

Until recently, Delia had known the ranch as intimately as the rest of the family. That she could no longer recall where the Hanging Tree stood pained Eliza greatly. It was such a small matter and of no real consequence, but provided further painful evidence of how the vibrant woman Delia had once been was slowly slipping away. Eliza longed to leave her place and hug her mother tightly, but restrained the impulse, which would have alarmed Delia and everyone else.

"All right, then," Delia responded. "I'll look forward to joining you all on Saturday."

"Fletcher intends to hold a victory celebration afterward," Lamar announced, "although I warned him those preparations were decidedly premature."

"He can still host the victory party," Jonathan offered with a lazy chuckle. "If he isn't heartbroken when Red Warrior and I win."

Robby leaned close to poke his sister. "You believe Red Warrior will win, don't you?"

Eliza Kate certainly hoped so, but knowing she ought to favor Fletcher's stallion, she could only smile knowingly. "We'll just have to wait and see."

She caught Lawrence's eye and included him in her smile. Despite their talented cook's varied menus, her uncle often displayed little appetite in the evenings, and Eliza was pleased to see he had already finished his soup. Apparently Jonathan's company was more beneficial than any of Dr. Burnett's tonics, and she seized the hope Lawrence might swiftly become interested in women again on his own. He was such a dear man, and she regretted giving up her matchmaking efforts simply because she hadn't met with immediate success.

After supper, Eliza Kate took Robby upstairs to his room to review his homework. He was a bright child, but had made several careless errors in his arithmetic. She insisted he redo the problems before they read from Jules Verne's *20,000 Leagues Under the Sea*.

Robby had a keen imagination and got so caught up in the exciting tale he did not consider having to read a chore as he did the rest of his homework. Eliza Kate had been enjoying the book, too, but that night she was far too distracted to pay close attention to the magical plot. She had to keep glancing at the clock on the desk to prevent Robby from staying up too late. He was old enough to put himself to bed and had grown increasingly bashful about being kissed good night.

Eliza kissed him anyway and shut his door quietly. Now able to join the others, she dared not appear overly eager for Jonathan's company. She descended the stairs with a slow, measured step and then paused unobserved, at the entrance of the parlor. Her glance wandered over her family before lingering on their attractive guest.

Her father and Ricky were seated in front of the unlit fireplace continuing the current game in a lengthy chess tournament. Her mother was curled up on the sofa perusing an issue of *Lippincott's Magazine*. Lawrence and Jonathan were seated near the windows where with unusually animated gestures, Lawrence was recounting an incident Jonathan had apparently forgotten but now found highly amusing.

They were all content without her, and filled with secret longings she was unable to express, Eliza was far too restless to read with her mother. Not wanting to interrupt the chess match nor intrude upon her uncle and Jonathan's conversation, she continued down the hall, past the study, and out into the garden.

Lanterns were lit along the pathways each evening at dusk, and she frequently came outside for a stroll. She drank in the sweetly scented air but had not moved past the rose garden before she heard someone approaching. That she could recognize the sound of Jonathan's step after such a brief acquaintance was ample proof of how closely she had been observing him. She turned slowly, as though his presence weren't exceedingly welcome.

Jonathan had again dressed for dinner in the dark suit Lawrence had loaned him, but while he may have blended into the shadows, Eliza Kate was exquisitely aware of him. When he reached her side, he took her arm and quickly propelled her along toward the lily pond.

"The race is on Saturday," Eliza reminded him pointedly.

"Sorry, I didn't mean to rush you. When your father mentioned a party after the race, it occurred to me we ought not to waste such a fine opportunity to surround Lawrence with beautiful young women. Are there any you'd like to invite to the race from either Fort Worth or Dallas?"

Jonathan released his hold on Eliza Kate once they reached the pond, and she chose the solid security of a bench rather than remain standing. She had not expected him to pursue her and in a futile attempt to quell her growing apprehension, she fussed with the drape of her skirt before looking up.

"Fletcher loves to entertain, so he's sure to invite everyone I know. I'll give it some thought though, and if there's anyone, even a chance acquaintance who ought to be included, I'll make certain she's there."

Jonathan propped his boot on the edge of the pond and peered down at the slick black surface of the water. "I don't actually believe Fletcher will feel much like hosting a party on Saturday. Will your friends come here after the race to celebrate with me?"

"It would be most unsportsmanlike of them not to, and Lord knows, Father can certainly supply plenty of liquor."

"Wouldn't your guests expect something to eat as well?"

A frown crossed Eliza's brow. "Yes, I suppose they would." She had not fully considered what would be required in shifting the location of the party from Fletcher's ranch to theirs. As she did, her spirits fell.

"I'm sorry," she murmured. "I simply wasn't thinking.

Unless Mother took to her bed, an impromptu party would completely overwhelm her. You can't be expected to host a party in town either; regardless of how much money you win, it would be prohibitively expensive."

Jonathan sat down beside Eliza Kate. "I don't give a damn about the cost. I just want Lawrence to have a chance to meet a nice woman."

He was now studying the soft circle of light cast by the lantern rather than glancing her way, and Eliza longed to ask if he weren't lonely too. Afraid he would regard the question as a pathetic plea on her own behalf, she held her tongue but it was all she could do not to slip her hand into his and caress his palm.

"Lawrence is fortunate to have such a good friend," she confided in a hushed whisper.

Jonathan straightened, and believing their conversation over, Eliza Kate started to rise, but with an easy stretch, Jonathan slid his arm around her waist and pulled her back down into his embrace. She rested her palms on his chest but felt no more steady.

"Jonathan," she cautioned against his lips, but her faint protest went unheeded, and he kissed her with the same delicious urgency she had tasted at midnight.

She had a fleeting thought that this was why he had led her away from the house, but whatever his original purpose for choosing the seclusion of the pond, she'd not complain. Instead, she relaxed in his embrace and slid her hand inside his coat to savor his warmth. She had enjoyed the feel of his bare skin too greatly last night to accept him fully clothed now, and with trembling fingertips began to unbutton his waistcoat.

In response, Jonathan pulled Eliza across his lap and deepened the kiss. He tasted of the peach cobbler they had had for dessert. Lost in him, Eliza Kate fought to free the buttons on his shirt. In another moment, she had a couple undone and slipped her hand inside the cotton garment to caress his bare chest.

She felt his breath quicken, and growing dizzy herself,

she had to make a conscious effort to breathe. When they
had been with her family, she had successfully kept her
desire hidden but there was no pretense in her gestures
now. She craved a thousand of Jonathan's deep, eager
kisses; filled with their sweetness, she clung to him, encouraging a thousand more.

She had never found such delirious joy in another
man's arms. Jonathan stunned her senses so easily, her
response brushed the borders of madness. She leaned
into him as he shifted his position slightly, but then
leaned away to encourage the slow, teasing circles he had
begun to trace over her breasts. Even fully clothed it was
exquisite torture, and her nipples peaked in eager response.

It crossed her mind that on even the most romantic of
evenings, Fletcher Monroe was not nearly so passionate a
man as Jonathan. That jarring comparison struck Eliza
Kate with the chilling force of a cold bath on a winter
morn and mortified, she drew back.

"There's something I should have told you," she confessed in a breathless rush.

Jonathan felt absolutely no need for conversation.
"What?" he demanded.

Eliza Kate clamped her hand over his mouth. "Hush!"
she scolded. When he gave a grudging nod, she dropped
her hand but remained perched on his knee.

"Fletcher has proposed to me. I didn't accept because
I feared Mother wasn't well enough to plan a wedding,
but I didn't refuse him either."

Jonathan reached up to catch a handful of the curls she
had styled atop her head and again claimed her mouth
for a wild, possessive kiss which he did not end until she
again lay pliant in his arms. "If Fletcher kissed you like
that, you'd not be here with me now," he swore darkly.

Fletcher's kisses were chaste and sweet, and unlike Jonathan's, they had never quickened Eliza's heartbeat. Even
with her thoughts too full of Jonathan to reason clearly,

she was positive that in every respect the men could not have been more dissimilar.

Fletcher offered a great deal, however—intelligence, culture, and an abiding sense of steadfast security. What did Jonathan offer, she agonized, other than a heated passion that seared her heart and left her shamelessly yearning for more?

Even surrounded by the lush sweetness of her mother's garden, Eliza felt her world spiraling out of control. She rested her forehead against Jonathan's in a valiant attempt to dispel the fog that blurred her hopes for a serene future whenever he was near. Her only comfort was the crickets' familiar chirped cadence.

A long moment passed before Eliza recalled his comment. Feeling compelled to answer, she sat up straight to face him. His light eyes caught the lanterns' gleam with a mirror's silvery brightness but held no trace of her torment.

"You're right," she admitted freely. "His kisses aren't nearly as marvelous as yours, but that scarcely justifies how badly I've betrayed him."

Jonathan replied with a rueful laugh. "Fletcher Monroe has more polish than substance, and you should never have wasted your time on him in the first place."

That he would dismiss her anguish over Fletcher as merely misplaced loyalty distressed Eliza. But then came the dawning realization that when Jonathan had chosen to rely on the fervor of his kisses rather than demand that she end her relationship with Fletcher, he had revealed all she truly needed to know.

Before Jonathan could stop her, she slid off his lap. She hurriedly combed her curls back into place with her fingers, then shook out her skirt as she started back up the walk toward the house. Her back ramrod straight, there was no mistaking the fury of her mood even in the moonlight.

"Eliza Kate!" Jonathan spoke her name in a harsh whisper.

He followed so closely that she did not have to stop to be heard. "Regardless of how little you think of Fletcher, his happiness means a great deal to me. It's Lawrence's happiness that concerns you though, remember? Obviously, not mine," she added under her breath. She raised her hem, quickened her step, and was relieved when Jonathan fell back to allow her to enter the house alone.

As for Jonathan, he was simply stunned by the abrupt change in Eliza Kate's mood. He had told Lawrence he needed not only fresh air, but some time alone. Now that Eliza had rather forcefully granted his wish, he felt drained and retraced their steps to the lily pond.

He sank on the bench they had just shared and stared into the water. He knew he should count himself lucky that Eliza Kate hadn't shoved him right into the shallow pool, but he didn't understand why she had suddenly gotten so angry with him.

"Oh, hell," he said, sighing. He was the one who ought to be angry. How could Eliza honestly believe he would be flattered to have her mention Fletcher Monroe when he was so lost in her he couldn't think at all? Her kisses were luscious, and his hands still tingled from the feel of her silken skin and softly rounded bosom.

And she was worried about Fletcher's feelings? What about his? he moaned. He leaned forward and rested his head in his hands. God help him, he had been numb for so long he had forgotten how it felt to want to please a woman. He was confident he had always delighted Mary Claire. She had been such a dear young woman, and he could not recall their ever having the slightest misunderstanding, let alone a heated argument.

Mary Claire hadn't lacked spirit either. She had been so full of life and love, their brief marriage had overflowed with joy. Thrilled by the birth of their son, they had expected David to be the first of many beautiful children. There had been so much they'd wanted to teach the bright little boy, but David had died knowing only how dearly his parents loved him.

A still unbearable grief stung Jonathan's eyes, but he refused to give in to tears. If only he had been able to keep David alive, he knew he would not have lost Mary Claire; but when her darling babe died, she had simply surrendered to the fever and let it take her as well. That the precious mother and son were together in the next world was the only comfort Jonathan had, but he wished they had not left him so alone in this one.

Ashamed not to be stronger, he sat up and took a deep breath. He had buried too many loved ones, and the awful suspicion that somehow he was to blame for their deaths weighed heavily on his heart. He could barely remember his mother, but his father had never forgotten her. Without her love their home had been a cold and lonely place. His grandparents had soon followed his mother to the grave, and his father had spent years chasing death before it finally took him.

Jonathan was sick of treading on graves, but he was a child of the Trail of Tears, and death was his birthright. He had fought in a terrible war where the dead and wounded had been heaped all around him, and yet he'd not received so much as a nick from a ricocheting bullet. Whether it had been due to luck, or destiny, he had survived, but he envied the dead who did not have to live on with their blood-soaked memories.

He had returned home from the war a haunted shell of a man, and Mary Claire had loved him still. She had given him not only abundant love, but the hope for a future untouched by senseless loss. She had had such a beautiful smile, she had made even the rainy days bright, and it had shattered his soul to bury her and David in the icy cradle of the ground.

Struggling against the wretched tide of his memories, Jonathan pushed himself to his feet. Unmindful of the beauty all around him, he strode through the garden and went on out to the corral near the barn where Red Warrior stood. The stallion nickered softly as Jonathan approached, and the lonely man greeted the horse, his only source of pride, with a low whistle.

Red Warrior was the perfect companion for his tormented master. He demanded nothing and yet gave of a silent compassion that had no end. He lived only to run, and with Jonathan on his back, to race the wind.

"What am I going to do?" Jonathan asked, as though the handsome horse were a wise friend who'd offer sage advice. "I've found a woman who makes me feel alive again. More than alive," he admitted with a painful catch in his voice, "but all my love ever brings is death. I can't let that curse touch Eliza Kate, Red, but I don't know where I'll find the courage to walk away."

To have lost his wife and son was a tragedy Jonathan would mourn forever, but even as his chest ached with the pain of their loss, he grew ever more certain that to allow himself no more than a brief flirtation with Eliza Kate Bendalin would be equally tragic. If only the choice were truly his, he agonized, but he'd been punished too severely to have any faith in love.

Chapter Five

Grateful for the cover of darkness, Eliza Kate waited a long moment before slipping in the back door. Her composure still tenuous, she moved down the hall at a ladylike pace, but as she passed the study, Lawrence called her name. A rush of guilt halted her step with a nervous jump far removed from her usual grace.

Coming to the open doorway, Lawrence sent a hasty glance down the hall. "Is Jonathan still wandering the garden?"

Eliza Kate feared the tremor in her voice would give her away and coughed as though her throat were merely dry. "Why yes, I believe he is. It's a lovely night."

"Good." Lawrence took his niece's hand in a fond clasp, drew her into the study, and closed the door. "I was hoping we'd have a moment to talk."

Certain she would never be able to sit still, Eliza Kate moved to the desk and leaned back against it. "Is there some problem, Uncle?"

"No. I didn't mean to alarm you. It's just that I wanted to make certain you'd invite all your friends to the race on Saturday so Jonathan will have an opportunity to meet them. He's sure to win, and even if he weren't handsome, that fact alone will make him popular with the ladies. I just don't want to leave anything to chance. Perhaps if you were to suggest to Carol Ann that Jonathan prefers more serious women, she'd take care not to make him dizzy with her childish giggles."

Eliza Kate's hands were hidden behind her, but she kept a firm grip on the edge of the desk as Lawrence named several more of her friends whom he hoped Jonathan might find appealing. It was so easy to want Lawrence to find a special woman, but painfully awkward to listen to her uncle's hopes for Jonathan.

Feigning interest, she was enormously relieved her uncle had not guessed she and Jonathan might have been enjoying more than a leisurely stroll and strove not to arouse his curiosity with a careless remark. Her deep disappointment in Jonathan was extremely difficult to hide, however.

"Let's consider this more carefully," Eliza began after another forced cough to free the tension from her voice. "After all, Jonathan is one of your best friends, but you've really no idea what sort of husband he made."

Puzzled, Lawrence crossed to the chair opposite the desk and eased himself down into it before responding. "He's kind, considerate. Why wouldn't he have made a good husband, Eliza Kate? Have you noticed something about him that I've missed?"

Eliza was positive she had seen a side of Jonathan Blair that Lawrence would never have an opportunity to glimpse. Still embarrassed by her shocking weakness for him, she dipped her head and raised her hand to coax an errant curl back into place.

"I'm sure you understand these things far better than I ever will, Uncle Lawrence, but there are men who simply use women rather than cherish them. A woman can sacrifice all she holds dear for such a man, but he'll simply abandon her in disgrace once he's sated his passions."

Lawrence was amazed by the peculiar direction of Eliza's thoughts and shrugged helplessly. "Indeed there are such scoundrels, and far too many I'm ashamed to say, but Jonathan isn't among them. He treats ladies with respect. Hasn't his behavior toward you and your mother been above reproach?"

In Eliza Kate's view, all Jonathan had proven was how quickly he took whatever he wanted without any regard for those who might be hurt. The garden was dark and inviting. How far would he have gone had her conscience not provided a tardy reminder that she owed Fletcher more consideration than she was showing?

Even more troubling was that she had been so thrilled by Jonathan's ardent kisses and tender touch that the arrival of dawn and the men who tended the garden might have been all that would have pried her from his arms. She had not even suspected she possessed such a wanton nature, and the discovery terrified her.

"Eliza Kate?" Lawrence prompted. "Has Jonathan insulted you somehow?"

"No, of course not," Eliza responded softly. Jonathan touched her emotions and tormented her soul, but there was no way she could confide that agony to her uncle without destroying his respect for her in the process. That would only serve to intensify her shame rather than ease it.

"He's been a perfect gentleman," she emphasized. "I was merely thinking out loud, but I trust your judgment of your friend." *If not my own*, she worried.

Afraid she was merely confusing Lawrence, Eliza

straightened. "Fletcher will invite all my friends to the race, and between us, we can make certain Jonathan meets every one. Is there anything else that concerns you?"

Lawrence was perplexed their conversation hadn't gone nearly as smoothly as he'd expected, then suddenly realized why and shoved himself out of his chair. "I'm sorry if I've put you in an awkward position. Surely you must want Fletcher to win the race."

Eliza smiled sweetly as though that were precisely her concern and moved toward the door. "I'll be content to see the swiftest horse win."

Lawrence chuckled softly. "What a diplomatic response, but that's what you're sure to see come Saturday."

Eliza brushed his cheek with a light kiss. "It's so good to see you smiling. Good night." She left him before he noticed just how close she was to tears.

Eliza Kate's bedroom was decorated in a delicate rose tint and each morning the first rays of the rising sun pierced the lace curtains and bathed the spacious room in a golden light. Snuggled beneath the quilts in her gleaming brass bed, Eliza usually welcomed the bright glow of dawn as a sign of a promising new day, but after another restless night, any such optimistic hopes seemed absurd.

She didn't really feel up to riding, but convinced she needed the exercise and solitude, she pushed herself to make the effort. Dressed and sitting on the side of her bed, she struggled to compose a suitably indifferent greeting in case Jonathan was waiting for her downstairs.

Unfortunately, she was too tired to be witty, and she absolutely refused to be trite. She finally decided to allow him to greet her, and thus have the advantage of being able to play off his words rather than having to come up with an original comment on her own.

Feigning a confidence she certainly didn't feel, she left her room with a purposeful stride and went downstairs. When Jonathan wasn't in the entryway, she expected to find him outside lounging against the porch rail enjoying the garden, but he wasn't there either. As she approached the barn, she was surprised to see an unsaddled Red Warrior still in the adjacent corral.

That she was again ready to ride before Jonathan was up and about gave her a fiery burst of satisfaction that kept her smiling while she saddled Patches. If she could not avoid the irritating man, she could at least force him to come looking for her, and she rode toward the river at an easy canter.

Buoyed by the brisk morning air, Eliza Kate's spirits rose with each yard she traveled from home. When she reached the Hanging Tree, she circled it twice but rode on rather than risk feeling as helpless as a treed opossum should Jonathan find her aloft in the branches a second time.

That his presence had made her so giddy yesterday now struck her as lunacy. She now possessed an insight into his character that had been absent then, and she intended to use her newfound wisdom as an impenetrable barrier against the powerful attraction that had nearly consumed her last night.

She rode on by the stand of mesquite and then farther along the riverbank than was her custom. When she at last stopped to dismount, she stretched out on a grassy knoll where she had a splendid view down river and would be certain to see Jonathan coming long before he saw her. She was not intentionally posed, but merely relaxed, as she had been each morning before he'd arrived at the Trinity Star.

It was a lovely tranquil spot, and normally Eliza Kate would have been able to clear her mind and restore her soul, but she feared her next conversation with Jonathan would go as badly as their last and grew increasingly anxious for him to appear. She fidgeted for half an hour before accepting the obvious: He had not followed her after all. The resulting sense of relief lasted only an instant, and then was swiftly replaced with the insult of being abandoned, and she lost her temper all over again.

Apparently his interest in her safety had merely been a convenient pretense he no longer found useful. That alone was infuriating, but she still believed he owed her an apology for ridiculing her attachment to Fletcher Monroe. She could not believe he wished to offer it at the breakfast table in front of her whole family.

Then again, she fumed, he might have planned to do just that. He was clever enough to speak in sufficiently vague terms not to alarm her parents and brothers. Though the taunt would be clear in his strange light eyes, she'd not dare throw his comment right back in his face and arouse her family's suspicions.

"Bastard," she muttered under her breath. She ripped off her gloves as she got to her feet. She marched down to the water with an angry sway, but as she bent to scoop up a drink, she noticed a dancing pattern of hoof prints scattered across the mud. She'd not felt the eerie sensation of being watched, but quickly cast a furtive glance over her shoulder to make certain the riders were no longer nearby.

The tracks had been made by unshod ponies, which meant it hadn't been any of their *vaqueros* who had watered their mounts there. It might only have been a small band of renegades rather than a painted war party of Kiowa or Comanche, but clearly Indians had boldly ventured across Bendalin land.

She would have to issue an immediate warning, while at the same time not frighten her mother out of her wits. Eliza was suddenly grateful that Jonathan hadn't come looking for her, for he would surely have distracted her so completely she would never have seen the telltale tracks. The Bendalins employed too many well-armed hands for the Trinity Star to be overrun by hostile Indians, but they had a great many fine horses and enough cattle to make a raid on the outlying acres of the ranch well worth the risk.

Shaken by her discovery, Eliza Kate rode Patches home

at a gallop. She cursed the fact that Jonathan Blair had been right, and she ought not to have strayed so far from home, but she would be damned if she'd ever thank him for his advice. When she rode into the yard, she found Ricky standing outside the barn currying Harlequin's spotted coat. As she slid off Patches, the hand cleaning out the stalls came out of the barn to meet her, and she handed him the mare's reins.

"What are you doing?" Ricky called to her. "Training pretty little Patches to race?"

Eliza Kate reached his side in three long strides. "Don't start yelling," she warned, and in a low, urgent whisper described what she'd seen.

"Tell the foreman to have the men keep a sharp lookout for Indians," she continued. "They might have only stopped by the river to water their horses and quickly moved on, or they might still be close enough to help themselves to our stock. I don't want to cause Mama any worry though."

Ricky nodded but kept right on brushing Harlequin's glossy hide. "I understand, but I didn't think there had been any Indian raids within fifty miles of here."

"Neither did I, but now fifty miles doesn't sound all that far away. Don't you go out looking for renegades on your own, Rick. They'd shoot you just to steal Harlequin, and it would kill Mama if something awful happened to you." Eliza reached out to grasp his arm. "The rest of us would be devastated as well."

Eliza appeared sincerely pained by that morbid thought, and Ricky was quick to reassure her. "I've no intention of being one of the last casualties of the Indian wars. Now if you don't want Mama to worry, you'd better find a smile before we go in for breakfast. Don't you worry none either. I'll warn the men to keep a close eye on themselves as well as the stock, but let's wait until Mama's not around to tell Father about what you found."

"Do you think he might cancel the race?" The possibility flooded Eliza with a sinking fear, because without the race, Jonathan would have no excuse to extend his stay. That she could still care filled her with a renewed burst of shame.

"No, of course not," Ricky replied. "Besides, there's sure to be too big a crowd for a few Indians to stage an attack. Now you go on inside. I'll be there in a minute."

Eliza Kate envied Ricky his boundless confidence, but as she started across the yard she was still his big sister. "Please don't be late and don't slam the front door again either."

Ricky just laughed at her warning, but Eliza was serious. Their father had left a veritable army of tough Mexican *vaqueros* to protect them while he and Lawrence were away fighting in the war, but Eliza had never truly felt safe. Preoccupied as she entered the house, she failed to notice Jonathan leaning against the entrance to the parlor.

"Did you have a nice ride?" he inquired in a lazy drawl.

Eliza Kate whipped off her hat and scarf as she wheeled to face him. "Could you shoot a Kiowa brave if you had to?" she asked in a challenging whisper.

Jonathan yanked himself upright and came toward her. "My God. Did you actually see one?"

"Just answer me," Eliza insisted darkly.

Jonathan read the fright in her gaze and silently cursed the fact that danger had apparently found her even without his being there to serve as death's lightning rod. He could not have borne it had she been hurt simply because he'd been too damn proud to accompany her on her morning ride. He had to glance away momentarily as a cold shiver shot down his spine, but he had a ready reply.

"If someone took a shot at you or me, I wouldn't stop to consider who, or what, he might be. I killed too many fine young men in the war to have any qualms about killing one, or a dozen, more."

His eyes had taken on the same icy gleam Eliza Kate had previously found so alarming, and she believed him. She had recognized him as dangerous on sight, but with his jaw clenched, he looked ready to take on a whole war party on his own. She had no doubt that should such a battle occur, he would be the only man left standing. Rather than being reassured by the force of his resolve, however, she was sickened by how easily he had promised death to anyone who might harm her.

"Well, did you see a Kiowa brave, or not?" Jonathan demanded.

Lamar reached the landing in time to hear Jonathan's question and rushed down the stairs before Eliza Kate could reply. "Please," he begged. "Delia needed a moment longer to dress or she'd have been with me. If Indians have been sighted on our land, I don't want it discussed within her hearing."

Strengthened by her father's arrival, Eliza Kate moved close and looped her arm through his. "I'm sorry. I came upon some suspicious tracks. I told Ricky about them, and he and the foreman will investigate."

Quickly dismissing the threat her information implied, Lamar gave her a hug. "That's my girl."

Delia's skirt made a soft swishing sound as she approached the second-floor landing, and Lamar slid away from Eliza's grasp to go back up the stairs and provide his wife with an escort.

Jonathan leaned close to Eliza Kate's ear and inquired in an anxious whisper, "Are tracks all you found?"

"That's all," Eliza Kate responded truthfully, then turned away from him to greet her mother. "Good morning. How are you feeling?"

Delia held on to the banister as well as her husband's arm as she descended the stairs with carefully placed steps. "Quite well, thank you, but unfortunately, it didn't help me dress any faster."

"You're beautiful as always, my dear," Lamar insisted, and he moved aside to allow Robby to squeeze by them.

Ricky came through the front door just as his parents and little brother reached the bottom of the stairs. He tousled his brother's hair, brushed his mother's cheek with a kiss, then winked at Eliza Kate. "This is going to be one fine day," he said. "You want to race me again, Jonathan? Harlequin just might beat you today."

Jonathan shook off the challenge with an easy laugh, but he considered Ricky foolhardy in the extreme for being excited rather than wary after what Eliza Kate had reported.

Lawrence had already been at work in his study and hearing his family's voices, came down the hall to join them for breakfast. "I have to go into Fort Worth this morning," he told Jonathan. "Why don't you come with me? It will give you a chance to see something of the town."

Jonathan waited for Robby to scoot by him to take his seat at the crowded table. Though he would rather have gone with Ricky to search for renegades, he didn't want Lawrence out riding alone, so he promptly accepted his invitation. "Sure. I'd like that," he replied with as relaxed a smile as he could manage.

That morning they were served pancakes as light as sugar wafers, but Jonathan kept imagining Eliza Kate being carried off by garishly painted warriors, and it was all he could do to swallow without choking on every bite.

Lawrence rode a bay gelding that until that day had never seemed small, but with Jonathan astride Red Warrior, he had to look up when he spoke to him. "I don't get into town often, so I'm afraid I've allowed a lot of rather tedious errands to pile up."

Lamar and Robby had apparently passed that way safely in the buggy, but Jonathan still scanned the outcropping of boulders up ahead and didn't draw an easy breath until they were close enough to be certain there were no Kiowa nor Comanche braves lurking among the rocks.

"Take your time," he said encouragingly. "Don't forget I'm used to keeping myself entertained. I'll just wander around on my own and be fine."

Although well aware Jonathan wasn't given to idle chatter, his mood that morning still struck Lawrence as subdued and he could imagine only one reason why. "Are you worried about the race?" he asked.

"No, not at all," Jonathan replied. He couldn't name a single thing that was going right, but not wanting to burden Lawrence with his troubles, he urged his friend to describe the shops he owned with Lamar and the others they might build. When they parted company in Fort Worth, Jonathan left Red Warrior at the livery stable where Lamar kept his buggy and struck out on foot.

It was a fine day for a walk, and Jonathan paused frequently to peer into shop windows and read the extravagant claims for the fine new products being sold inside. He was impressed with the town's wide streets and stately brick buildings, but he had never liked crowds and soon tired of threading his way through the people out on the walkways.

He had agreed to meet Lawrence in front of Lamar's office on Commerce Street, but he didn't want to arrive early and be forced to chat with Fletcher and Lamar until Lawrence arrived. Choosing to make better use of his time, he entered a barbershop located closeby and requested a trim.

Just as he had expected, the barber was a talkative soul, who with every comb and snip provided a tidbit of knowledge about the good citizens of Fort Worth. Jonathan murmured appreciatively and with an occasional offhand remark cleverly steered the conversation to Lamar Bendalin.

"Lamar is one of our most enterprising businessmen," the barber exclaimed. He was a stocky man named Earl, whose white apron was stretched tightly across his broad stomach. He wore his graying hair slicked straight back, which served to emphasize the fullness of his florid cheeks.

"Not much goes on in this town that Lamar doesn't have a say in, or earn a dollar on, if you know what I mean," Earl confided.

"I heard he sold liquor," Jonathan replied.

"Oh yes, that's true, but he also owns several popular shops," the barber lowered his voice and bent down, "and the Rosedale Hotel, which isn't actually a hotel, if you catch my meaning. He's got the prettiest girls in Texas working there. His mistress, Flossie Mae Kemble, is the madam. She won't tolerate rude cowboys, or lazy girls for that matter, so it's a real nice place to visit if you're seeking that type of entertainment."

Jonathan wasn't shocked to learn Lamar kept a whore for a mistress, but he sure hoped Delia didn't know about her. "What does Lamar's wife think of the Rosedale?" he asked.

Earl sucked in such a sharp breath his mouth formed a tight circle. "Lamar would never tell her about it and no one else would either. No, sir. Delia's a mighty fine woman, although she's never been real strong. I can't even recall the last time I saw her here in town.

"Their daughter's a real beauty, and she brings her little brother to me sometimes for haircuts. As for Ricky—he's Lamar's elder son—I think one of girls at the Rosedale trims his curls."

Earl chuckled at the impropriety of that. "He's a lucky young man. I sure wish my daddy had owned a whorehouse."

Jonathan wasn't nearly as amused as the barber by that prospect and pulled the towel off his shoulders. "I think that's short enough."

"Well, sure. If you say so. You're blessed with hair as thick as an Indian's, not that I've ever cut a brave's hair, mind you. Now that I think of it, they don't bother with haircuts, do they?"

Jonathan climbed out of the barber chair and handed Earl his money plus a tip. "Only when a loved one dies," he informed him, and he had to laugh when the barber's eyes filled with a dawning light of recognition. Jonathan never gave much thought to his appearance, but he knew if anyone bothered to look close enough, the truth of his Cherokee roots was apparent.

He didn't ask for directions to the Rosedale on his way out, because that was the last place he cared to visit; but he thought it a good bet Ricky had worn a path from the ranch to the brothel. Eliza Kate might even know about its existence. With the exception of Robby, it seemed likely the whole Bendalin clan was sitting on a nest of secrets. Sickened to be in on the very worst of them, Jonathan was looking down as he approached Lamar's office. He was startled when Lawrence reached out to tap him on the shoulder.

"Are you ready to go home?" Lawrence asked. "Or we could get something to eat first if you're hungry."

Jonathan's appetite had fled when Eliza had first mentioned the Kiowa, and it wasn't likely to return anytime soon. Still, he knew it wouldn't hurt to be gracious. "The cook at the ranch is supplying me with such wonderful meals, I'd just as soon go on home," he replied.

Lawrence nodded. "That's fine with me." He had ridden his horse around town, and again mounted him while Jonathan went around the corner to fetch Red Warrior.

"I invited everyone I saw this morning to come to the race. There's sure to be a big crowd," Lawrence said enthusiastically.

"I'll do my best to win," Jonathan promised. "But please don't expect me to entertain anyone afterward."

Lawrence tipped his hat to two young women passing by on the walk. "Those were Eliza Kate's friends," he mentioned pointedly. "She has so many pretty acquaintances, but I have a hard time keeping their names straight."

"Just call them all sweetheart," Jonathan suggested, and in spite of himself, he began to chuckle at the thought of Lawrence being surrounded by adoring females.

"Will that actually work?" Lawrence asked. "Won't they soon become suspicious?"

"Well, now, I suppose if you called on the same woman for months without remembering or discovering her name, she might begin to wonder if you knew it. But I wouldn't worry. Eliza will be there on Saturday to help you with names."

Lawrence had been so busy worrying about involving Jonathan in a romance, he'd not given any thought to himself and immediately began to fret. "That's true, but I always feel so awkward when she introduces me to her friends that nothing ever comes of it. I doubt if any of them will even notice me on Saturday."

Not wanting to appear too eager to encourage him, Jonathan nodded thoughtfully, but it was difficult to listen while his friend was being so pessimistic. "Just stand beside Eliza Kate, that way when her friends stop to chat, you'll be impossible to ignore."

"Yeah, I suppose I could do that without looking too silly."

"No one would ever accuse you of looking silly," Jonathan argued. "You're smart, part owner of a fine ranch, and even if you are thin, you're still a good-looking man."

"I wish I believed that."

"Well, just pretend to believe it this Saturday afternoon." Jonathan turned to make certain they weren't being followed, but they were the only ones on the road. Not reassured, he continued to keep a close watch on the surrounding terrain.

"Call all the women sweetheart and pretend to be handsome? What if I succeed?" Lawrence agonized.

"What's the worst that could happen?" Jonathan teased. "You might find yourself with an adoring bride in no time at all."

Overwhelmed by that possibility, Lawrence was quiet several minutes. Finally he spoke in a voice barely loud enough to hear above the soft thud of the horses' hooves. "You've been married. Would you recommend it?"

After working to build Lawrence's confidence, Jonathan didn't want to discourage his friend. "For you, yes, but I'll not marry again."

"But why not? You said you were happy with your wife."

Jonathan felt a familiar painful tightening in his chest

but answered honestly. "Yes, I was, but tragedy strikes me so regularly, I'm better off alone. The same doesn't go for you though, so just keep a smile on your face Saturday, and I'll bet you'll do just fine with the ladies."

Lawrence fell silent, and Jonathan hoped his friend's mind was filled with charming possibilities. Johathan's thoughts were a whirl of Eliza Kate. After Mary Claire's death, he'd not expected another woman to ever touch his emotions, but now that Eliza Kate most definitely had, he'd have to force himself to pretend otherwise.

Who was he to criticize the Bendalins? he wondered, when he had no choice about keeping secrets himself. Unlike Lamar, however, his reason was honorable, but that made it no easier to silence the bittersweet yearning overflowing his broken heart.

Chapter Six

Lawrence had bookkeeping that required his attention that afternoon, and Jonathan rode down to the Trinity River on his own to examine the tracks Eliza Kate had reported. Ricky had assured him they were a couple of days old, but he needed to see them for himself. With Ricky's directions, he found the suspicious hoofprints easily enough, but then he walked along the riverbank, searching for something more the men from the ranch might have missed.

He did not particularly care that he had arrived at the Trinity Star within hours, if not minutes, of happening upon a band of renegades watering their mounts. But he was deeply concerned about Eliza Kate's safety. Her little mare couldn't outrun a burro, let alone a fierce Kiowa brave astride a fleet pony.

Though he felt certain any man would judge Eliza far too pretty to kill, he didn't even want to imagine how she'd suffer as a hostage. He was sickened that she ignored such an awful risk to ride wherever she pleased. He gazed out over the prairie and fought to convince himself that however she chose to live her life ought to be her own business rather than an abiding concern of his.

The distant scenery was a soothing blend of sandy beige with an occasional splash of gray-green, but Jonathan found no comfort in the serenity of the view. He wondered if he had simply been alone too long, or perhaps not nearly long enough, to dull the need Eliza had aroused. He hurled a stone into the river with a loud curse, for he was not torn by mere physical craving, but by an intense yearning that was far more precious and rare. He dared not care deeply for Eliza Kate, but God help him, he already did, and he needed no reminder that his affection was a deadly desire.

Reluctantly giving up his search for further evidence of an Indian presence nearby, Jonathan walked back to Red Warrior and caught hold of his trailing reins. The stallion sent him a slanted glance that held more than a hint of annoyance at being forced to leave so much of the tender spring grass uneaten.

"What?" Jonathan responded. "Do you think I've nothing better to do than to watch you grow fat?"

Red Warrior tossed his head and blew out a disgusted snort.

Jonathan knew his question had been ridiculous but refused to apologize to the high-spirited horse. "You don't appreciate just how lucky you are," he said.

The handsome horse had been a wedding present from Mary Claire's father, but it was Jonathan's gentle hand that tamed the ungainly colt. He had always felt the powerful stallion merely tolerated his weight on his back, while his heart remained wild and free.

Admiring the beautiful horse, Jonathan glanced back toward the rushing river and wished he could say the same for his own.

* * *

Lawrence tried to concentrate on transcribing neat rows
of figures in his ledger, but he was too frequently distracted by visions of beautiful young women to get much
accomplished. His imagination painted such delightful
creatures, then abandoned him with the lingering dread
that he might have already foolishly squandered whatever
slim hope there had been to impress one of Eliza Kate's
friends. No longer able to work, he threw down his pen
and left the study.

He knew Jonathan's encouragement had been sincere,
but he longed for a woman's opinion. Delia was such a
dear person, but she would be napping now. When he
didn't find Eliza Kate in the parlor, he went outside to
the garden, but he had to go a long way before he found
her reading John Keats's poetry in the shade of the grape
arbor.

"What are you doing way out here?" he called to her.
"I expected to find you by the lily pond."

The pond was one of Eliza's favorite places, but she'd
been seeking inner peace that day more than the privacy
to read. She would never hide from Lawrence, however,
and greeted him with a smile. "What is it, Uncle? You look
ready to burst so it must be good news."

Lawrence feared his hopes were running away with him,
but they were impossible to contain. He grabbed hold of
an end post supporting the arbor and leaned against it.
"Jonathan's a good friend, so his opinion of me is probably as biased as yours, but he's been encouraging me to
make more of an effort to impress your friends. They'll
all be at the party after the race on Saturday, but I wonder
if they'll even remember me."

The faint twinkle of hope in his eyes tore at Eliza Kate's
heart, and she marked her place and set John Keats aside.
"Of course, they will," she assured him. "It should be a
lovely day. Everyone will be in a festive mood, and if you'll
just share some of the charm you shower on Mother and
me, all my friends will be delighted to see more of you."

Elated by that prediction, Lawrence wanted to shout for

joy, but he was far too shy now to express his happiness that openly. "I'm afraid I'll make a fool of myself by getting everyone's name confused."

"I'll stay close and supply whatever names you need. Or you could always call everyone sweetheart," she teased.

"That's exactly what Jonathan suggested," Lawrence replied. "Oh, now that I think of it, he told me he has no plans ever to remarry, so I guess there's no point in your introducing him to all your pretty friends after the race."

The shock of Lawrence's softly voiced announcement left a jagged tear in Eliza Kate's heart, but she was far too proud to allow him even a glimpse of her pain. Instead, she reached for her book of poetry and absently shifted through the pages. "He's a very young man to make such a final decision. What exactly did he say?"

Lawrence hated to admit he had been so absorbed in tantalizing thoughts of her friends that he'd not been paying all that close attention. "Well, I don't recall his exact words, but there was something about tragedy stalking him. Whatever it was, he was quite emphatic about it."

Eliza could well imagine. "Yes, I understand. Jonathan is the emphatic type, isn't he? Well, if he refuses to consider a second marriage, then it would be a waste of my friends' time to meet him because they all long for a husband and family."

"Yes, of course they do," Lawrence agreed. His own expectations soaring in that regard, he took his time and wandered through the garden before returning to the work that awaited him inside.

Once alone, Eliza Kate retreated into the narrow paths separating the blackberry vines, but she left the ripening fruit untouched. Jonathan's dark vow to remain alone had confirmed her worst suspicions. She had been no more than an amusing diversion, after all, and it sickened her to recall just how willingly she'd played her part. No, she corrected herself sharply, she'd been desperately eager. Hot tears of shame filled her eyes, and she bit down on her lip to force them away.

She'd not weep over Jonathan, nor over her own girlish dreams of love. Her mother had once told her men were very different from women and adept at separating their bodies from their hearts as women never could. The demure Delia had left Eliza to wonder about prostitutes, for surely they sold their bodies without ever allowing their hearts to enter into the transaction.

Eliza did not understand how such unfortunate women could bear to undress in front of a stranger, let alone tolerate his touch. But now she longed for a similar cool detachment to enable her to hide the depth of her disappointment from Jonathan.

A wayward blackberry branch caught her skirt, and she bent down to yank the fabric free of the thorns. "I'll have to do the same with my heart," she murmured softly, but the thought would prove far easier than the deed.

By the time Eliza Kate dressed for supper that evening, she had suffered through a wildly whirling kaleidoscope of emotions. Her initial shame had given way to furious anger for the way Jonathan had offered such a generous sample of love, and then told Lawrence rather than her that he intended to live out his life alone.

All too soon the driving beat of her anger had throbbed into a painful headache. She had lain down to rest, but her mind had continued to spin painful images of Jonathan Blair. She'd felt the agony of his loss when he'd described the deaths of his loved ones. But it was his wife and child who had died, not he. So why should he choose a solitary life?

Recalling Jonathan's sorrow, compassion briefly warmed Eliza's mood, but then the lingering suspicion that he had merely used her to assuage his grief rekindled her temper. She was a woman with a heart, not a pretty plaything to be toyed with on a moonlit evening and then casually tossed aside.

And he had enjoyed her affection! She was sure of it. His pleasure had flavored his every kiss, but he still intended to go on to California as alone as he had arrived. She hated him for not wanting more, for settling for what was easy rather than choosing the more challenging path. Most of all, she hated him for not wanting her as badly as she wanted him.

She slammed her door as she started downstairs, then had to stop and strangle her fury, as she would have liked to strangle Jonathan Blair, before her family discovered just how stupidly she had behaved. She had chosen a prim gray gown she had never particularly liked, but the muted satin was still far brighter than her mood.

Rather than enter the parlor, she went straight to the dining room and turned the centerpiece to expose everyone to a new view of the attractive arrangement and make it appear as though she had just created a new one. When the others arrived, she sat down without glancing toward Jonathan and did not look his way a single time during the meal.

Eliza took only a few bites of her food and failed to taste even that. She just wanted supper over so she could retreat to Robby's room and concentrate on his homework. That was at least a useful endeavor, and she inquired as to whether he had much to do that evening.

"Too much," Robby complained. "There's gonna be nothing left to study next year."

As taciturn as his daughter of late, Lamar was grateful for a subject he could pursue. "Lawrence, do you recall the schoolmaster you absolutely despised? He was a short little fellow who was as big around as he was tall. What was his name?"

"Whitley," Lawrence replied with a shudder. "Chester Whitley. It wasn't that he gave us too much homework, Robby. It was that he loved to talk, and he wouldn't just present a history lesson, he would also illustrate it with wild diagrams all over the blackboard. He was so short he often had to leap to add the final detail. Of course, we'd all laugh, because it truly was a ridiculous spectacle. Then he'd wheel around and like some squat little cannon take aim for his favorite target, which for some unfortunate reason, was me."

Robby appeared confused. "But why? You're awfully quiet, and the quiet ones are always the teacher's favorites."

Although Robby wasn't old enough to recall, Eliza Kate remembered how gregarious Lawrence had been before the war. In sore need of a laugh, she had been charmed by his tale. "Uncle Lawrence was a lively boy, just like you, Robby. I'll bet you made your own share of mischief, Father."

Lamar shook his head. "No, indeed. I was a very studious lad."

Jonathan had been surprised to find Eliza Kate waiting in the dining room rather than the parlor. She had yet to glance his way, so apparently she was still aggravated with him. She had spoken to him that morning, but now she was ignoring him as though he weren't there.

"What about you, Eliza Kate?" Jonathan asked pointedly. "Were you the darling little girl with beribboned curls all the teachers loved?"

A tray of freshly baked rolls sat to Eliza's right, and it was all she could do not to hurl one at him. "I was too busy keeping an eye on Ricky to care what they thought of me," she answered crossly, and with that encouragement Ricky began an involved tale of how he and his friends had stolen one schoolmaster's long underwear and tied them to the flagpole where the whole town saw them flying as people rode to church that Sunday morning.

"The prank occurred after I'd graduated," Eliza added quickly as the others laughed, but it embarrassed her still, and she absolutely refused to look at Jonathan.

"I don't believe we ought to be making fun of schoolmasters," Delia interjected sweetly. "Their job is a difficult one at best, and they receive so little pay and even less appreciation."

"You're absolutely right, my darling," Lamar concurred,

and thinking the evening a success, he continued eating with gusto.

After dinner, as the Bendalins left the table and moved toward the parlor, Jonathan dropped back to allow Delia to precede him and quickly stepped into Eliza Kate's path. "Meet me later in the garden," he whispered.

Forced to confront him, Eliza Kate narrowed her eyes to a threatening glare. She had not noticed until then that he had trimmed his hair; though she had liked it long, the slight change was immensely flattering. It made him appear to be a gentleman, which she knew was merely a convenient pose.

"I plan to retire early," she told him.

"I'll need only a moment," Jonathan stressed.

Eliza Kate knew precisely what he would do with whatever time she gave him. He would say what he wished, and then draw her into his arms. He would kiss her until the garden, the starry night, and indeed the whole universe, dissolved into him. To her everlasting shame, she was tempted, but she refused to overlook what she had learned that afternoon.

"I'm sorry, but that's impossible," she said without conveying a shred of regret. She moved by him and followed Robby up the stairs. She wanted to pause on the landing to look down at Jonathan and savor the hurt in his eyes at her rebuff, but knowing it would bring no real sense of triumph, she hurried to catch up with her little brother.

Despite what she had told Jonathan, Eliza Kate had no real intention of retiring early. After encouraging Robby to complete his homework, she read with him awhile longer than usual. When she left him to prepare for bed, she went on to her mother's room and rapped lightly at the door. Believing Carmen would have already helped Delia into her nightgown, she expected to find her mother alone.

When it was her father who invited her to come inside, she fought to conceal her dismay. Her parents had been seated on the side of the bed reviewing the treasured letters her father had sent home during the war. It was something her mother loved to do and with her memory fading, the missives were always fresh. Eliza was touched by the patience with which her father indulged his cherished wife.

"I'm so sorry, I merely had a question about menus. I didn't mean to intrude," Eliza hastened to explain.

Wrapped in ruffled white silk, Delia was as pretty as her white roses. She gestured with a faded letter. "You're never a bother, sweetheart. Please do come in."

Eliza had simply wished to spend a few minutes with her mother, and perhaps seek her advice without ever admitting how much Jonathan Blair's presence tormented her. She could scarcely admit to any romantic dilemmas in front of her father, however, when he believed she and Fletcher were a perfect match. Until Eliza had met Jonathan, she had agreed.

Eliza Kate came forward to kiss her parents good night. "The menus can wait, but I do want to let you know how well Robby's doing. He has a good grasp of arithmetic and reads quite well."

"Thank you so much for looking after him," Delia murmured. "I don't know how we'd all survive here without you."

Eliza would once have treasured that compliment, but tonight her many responsibilities weighed too heavily on her shoulders. After kissing her parents good night, she left them to reread the faded letters and enjoy the time they had left to share.

As Eliza closed her mother's door behind her, she couldn't help wondering if she would ever receive any love letters of her own. Fletcher hadn't traveled since he had begun calling on her so there had been no need for him to write. As for Jonathan, Eliza was positive after he was gone, she would never enter his thoughts, let alone inspire any anguished declarations of love he'd commit to paper.

Eliza tore the pins from her hair as she entered her bedroom, but she had not reached her dressing table before she was interrupted by a gentle knock at her door. Thinking it must be Carmen or one of the servants with a question about tomorrow's routine, she hurried to respond.

With her golden curls falling about her shoulders in wild disarray, Eliza Kate was so very beautiful that Jonathan could barely find his breath to speak. For a long moment he simply stared, then remembering how rudely she had snubbed him earlier, he delivered his message before she could again get the better of him.

"Everyone will have gone to bed in an hour. Meet me downstairs in the parlor then."

Eliza opened her mouth to refuse, but Jonathan placed a fingertip on her lips to silence the objection before she could voice it.

"Just be there," he ordered firmly, then pulled her door closed and was gone.

Eliza Kate reached for the doorknob, but caught herself before following Jonathan out into the hallway where the angry confrontation that would surely ensue would be overheard by one and all. She would meet him later, all right and waste no time in telling him exactly what she thought of him in words he could not possibly misunderstand.

Ricky waited until the house was quiet and then went next door to his brother's room. "You've got to be quiet about this," he warned, "and I'm not just talking about sneaking out of the house."

Robby broke into a mischievous grin. "I understand, but Father's gonna know what we did when next year's colts all look like Red Warrior."

"So what? There won't be a damn thing he can do about it then." He cracked open the door and glanced up and down the hallway before gesturing for Robby to follow him down the back stairs. None of the servants lived in

the house, but the boys tiptoed out the rear door as
though they had had to elude the whole staff.

"What about Patches?" Robby asked as soon as they
started across the yard.

Ricky slapped his hand over his little brother's mouth.
"Hush!" he hissed, and he didn't let go until he was certain Robby would keep still. He then shoved him toward
the barn. When they reached it, Ricky yanked him inside
and shook him.

"Voices carry on the night air, and I won't let you come
with me again if you can't keep that mouth of yours shut."

"I promise," Robby whispered grudgingly, but clearly he
didn't relish taking orders from Ricky. "Now what about
Patches?"

"Patches is as pretty as can be, but she's too small to
make much of a brood mare. I want another stallion as
swift as Red Warrior, and we'll have the best chance of
creating one using our best mares."

"Suppose Red Warrior don't like 'em?"

Ricky began to laugh, then remembered the necessity
for silence and swallowed his chuckles. "Stallions aren't
choosy, Robby. The timing has to be right for the mares,
but believe me, horses aren't nearly as particular as people. I figure we can't put more than a couple of mares in
with Red Warrior per night, or he's liable to make such
a racket servicing them we'll get caught for sure. I'll get
the first of the mares; you go on over by the corral and
get ready to open the gate."

Robby peeked out the doorway and finding none of the
hands about, he tiptoed over to the corral with exaggerated care. Red Warrior came over to him, and he was sorry
he hadn't thought to bring him a treat, but decided with
a mare or two for company, the stallion wasn't likely to
complain.

As Eliza Kate descended the stairs, her mouth was set in
a grim line. She had removed her kid slippers to ensure
her steps would be silent, but was otherwise still dressed.

As she entered the parlor, her long curls bounced with each angry stride.

Jonathan had lit a lamp but turned it down low, and it took her a moment to locate him in the dimly lit room. He was in his shirtsleeves, which she considered much too informal for what she had to say. Regrettably, Jonathan came forward and spoke before Eliza could begin her carefully rehearsed speech.

"Has Lawrence told you he's actually becoming interested in your friends?"

Eliza was so surprised, her long lashes nearly swept her brows. "You insisted we meet here to discuss Lawrence?"

"Of course. What did you suppose?"

Eliza just shook her head, and her golden curls caught the sunny warmth of the lamp's soft glow. Here she was ready to have it out with Jonathan Blair, and as usual, his thoughts were on anything but her. In her present dark mood, she found that revelation deeply insulting.

"That doesn't really matter now, does it?" she confided in a hushed whisper. "Yes, Lawrence spoke to me. He was simply anxious before, but now he seems almost desperately eager to please."

Jonathan studied Eliza's troubled expression and answered in a wary whisper. "I just hope he doesn't set his sights on some fickle young woman who'll break his heart."

Eliza Kate took a step closer to him. "For some reason, it's difficult for me to believe that you'd care."

"I don't want to see anyone get hurt," Jonathan assured her.

Eliza Kate's voice was low, but the viciousness of her tone still stung the air. "That, you miserable coward, is a damn lie!"

Before Jonathan could reply to her astonishing accusation, they heard the hinges whine on the back door. He looked over his shoulder, then shot Eliza Kate an anxious glance, but she shrugged and shook her head as though she'd also believed they were the only ones up and about.

Eliza quickly extinguished the lamp and with a nudge from Jonathan, moved behind him as he turned toward the noise. The Bendalins didn't lock their doors at night, but she thought it more likely the cook or Carmen had entered the house than some malicious intruder.

She regarded Jonathan's quick action to shield her from possible danger as pure instinct and doubted it was necessary. Then she paused to consider just how difficult it would be to explain what they were doing together in the darkened room. She almost hoped it was a thief, for then explanations would be unnecessary.

Jonathan was unarmed, but he stood poised to attack whomever was slowly creeping up the hall. Realizing the servants would have no reason for such stealth, Eliza Kate began to share his obvious apprehension. Not wanting him to have to confront the unseen enemy alone, she remained close. She prayed the house wasn't rapidly filling with bloodthirsty renegades out for scalps and strained to hear the sound of footsteps to track the villains' approach.

Jonathan stood perfectly still, but it was all Eliza could do not to shriek and run from the room. A sudden thump out in the hallway jolted her, but it was followed by a scolding whisper. Recognizing Ricky's voice, she grabbed Jonathan's arm to tug him back toward the wall just as her brothers reached the dark opening of the doorway.

"I'm sure I saw a light," Robby whispered.

"Well, it's out now. Let's hurry on up to bed," Ricky answered.

Eliza ran her hand down Jonathan's arm, and he caught her fingers in a firm grasp. It would have been awkward to have had Carmen walk in on them, but the maid would not have teased them mercilessly as Ricky was sure to do should he find them together. Nor would Carmen have told everyone she knew.

God help them, if Ricky found out, Fletcher would be sure to hear about it before noon. By one o'clock, he would come calling, and what could she possibly tell him that would make any sense?

Unable to draw a breath, she pressed against Jonathan's back as they waited for Ricky to follow Robby up the back stairs, but instead, he entered the study and could be heard rummaging through Lawrence's desk.

"What's he doing?" Jonathan inquired softly.

Eliza Kate rose on her tiptoes to whisper in his ear. "He's probably looking for the key to the liquor cabinet." It would not be the first time either. Ricky would find it in an instant, and she and Jonathan were standing not two feet away from the ornate chest. She pulled on his hand and drew him toward the front entrance to the parlor. With any luck, they could duck out of the room as Ricky entered and climb the stairs unseen.

Unfortunately, they were only halfway across the room when they heard Ricky slam a drawer shut. "Oh damn," Eliza cried. They were going to be caught for sure. Trembling, she feared being caught with Jonathan might have far worse consequences than being attacked by Indians.

Chapter Seven

Remaining cool under the threat of discovery, Jonathan gracefully tucked Eliza Kate in his arms. He then moved with a silent step to guide her behind the velvet sofa, where with a gentle tug, he pulled her down beside him in the deep shadows. They had no time to separate or arrange themselves in a comfortable pose before Ricky entered the parlor, but at least they were hidden from view.

Eliza Kate was pressed close to Jonathan's chest and feared he had just worsened their situation rather than improved it. When he began to massage her shoulder with a lazy caress, she assumed he meant only to keep her calm; but his touch affected her so strongly she found it nearly impossible to breathe.

Distracting herself from Jonathan's heady allure, Eliza strained to listen as Ricky crossed the parlor. She heard him fumble with the lock on the liquor cabinet, and for a brief instant hoped that he'd give up and leave. But he simply swore an inventive oath and swiftly succeeded in opening the chest.

In addition to alcohol, it contained cut-glass tumblers in several sizes. Believing he was alone, Ricky conducted a noisy search for the one he preferred. He then filled it with their father's best bourbon, and to Eliza Kate's absolute horror, sat down not six feet away in their father's favorite chair to enjoy his drink.

Apparently resigned to a lengthy wait, Jonathan adjusted his position slightly, but Eliza was too frightened to move. It was so unlike her to be caught in a compromising position that she had no previous success at eluding discovery to provide hope. She simply felt trapped and was so awkwardly posed in Jonathan's arms it was all she could do not to scream.

Occasionally Ricky set his glass on the rosewood table beside his chair, and each time Eliza expected him to be on his way, but then her brother would take up the glass again, and her wait would begin anew. She thought eventually Ricky might fall asleep where he sat, and then they'd be able to flee, but the delay had already proved uncomfortably long.

Growing stiff in a heap of angles, Eliza turned slightly and was forced to rest her palm lightly on Jonathan's chest. She felt the slow, steady beat of his heart and marveled at the ease with which he avoided panic. With a concerted effort, she matched her breathing to the slow, steady rhythm of his.

It helped her some, but again focused her thoughts squarely on him. His arms were looped around her in a softly protective embrace, and she couldn't recall the last time she'd been cradled in such a fond clasp. Perhaps it hadn't been since she was a small child. Her family all came to her for comfort now, and seldom, if ever, offered her their own.

Jonathan, however, was unlike anyone she had ever met. It was difficult to remember they had only known each other three days. Three strained days in which he'd both frightened and fascinated her. Again all too aware of him, Eliza slid her hand up the placket on his shirt to the open collar. She laid her fingertips against the pulse at the base of his throat and silently counted the slow cadence.

Jonathan had survived a terrible war. Surely having to hide from her brother was no more than a minor prank to him, and the incident would probably not linger in his memory any longer than she did. How could she have harbored the absurd hope that Jonathan would set aside his heavy burden of grief to pursue her? she wondered.

It had been a preposterous desire, but at least she had kept it to herself until she'd foolishly called him a coward. Embarrassed by such selfish behavior, she struggled to form a coherent apology, but the words wouldn't come, and all she truly wanted to do was flee without having to acknowledge her stupidity.

Apparently in no need of an apology, Jonathan raised his hand to her neck and rubbed small, soothing circles that gradually drifted up into her scalp. He combed her hair with his fingers, untangled the tousled curls, then traced the line of her jaw before inclining her face toward his.

When his mouth covered hers for a slow, deep kiss that seemed to have no end, Eliza gloried in it, even as she feared he'd lost his mind. Or perhaps with Ricky so near, he was merely paying her back for insulting him. *Who's the coward now?* she thought, and nearly limp with shame, she knew which one of them deserved the name.

When Ricky chose that very moment to leave the deeply cushioned chair, Eliza was so startled by the sound of his footsteps, she would have cried out had Jonathan not

smothered her voice with his lips. She dug her fingers into
his shoulders and shoved, but he refused to release her
until they'd heard Ricky return the key to the desk drawer
in the study and start up the back stairs.

"Oh no," Jonathan whispered against Eliza's cheek.
"You're not going anywhere until we finish our little chat."

Now imprisoned in his arms, Eliza began to apologize
in a breathless rush. "I was unforgivably rude. I had no
reason to call you names and—"

"Eliza," Jonathan cautioned as gently as a prayer. He
then stood and drew her up beside him.

"I couldn't be more sorry." Eliza swayed against him.
After being confined in such a cramped pose, her legs felt
numb, and she was forced to cling to him even though
she was desperately eager to get away.

"You're forgiven. By the way, your perfume is absolutely
luscious. Now good night. Go on up to bed."

For one awful moment, Eliza Kate wasn't sure what he'd
said about her perfume, but then grateful to be dismissed,
she turned, and with a stumbling gait, ran from the room.

On Thursday morning, Eliza longed to escape her cares
at the river, but that morning she was positive Jonathan
would be waiting for her, and she simply couldn't face
him. Instead, she remained seated on the side of her bed
with her hands clasped tightly in her lap until it was time
for breakfast. As she entered the dining room, Jonathan
slanted her a darkly curious glance, but she responded
with only part of the truth.

"I slept poorly and didn't feel up to riding today. I hope
I didn't keep you waiting."

When Eliza hurried to her seat as though just looking
at him hurt, Jonathan wondered if she were ashamed of
herself or of being with him. The latter possibility stung
until he realized that whatever her reason, at least she'd
avoided the risk of being captured by renegades this
morning.

"No," he replied with the same disregard for the truth.

"I'm usually up early, and I'd just as soon give Red Warrior a couple days' rest."

"Of course, that makes sense." Eliza was greatly relieved when her family immediately began discussing the coming race. Jonathan smiled at some comments and laughed out loud at others, but she simply found it torture to be in the same room with him now and avoided him for the remainder of the day.

After dinner, she reviewed Robby's homework, and then went straight to her own room where she intended to stay. Unable to read or even think, she paced with an anxious stride. On other such restless nights, she'd gone to the garden, but now its seductive shadows were far too dangerous. When there was again a light knock at her door, she could barely bring herself to answer.

Jonathan was surprised Eliza hadn't been brushing her hair and preparing for bed, but her curls were still wound atop her head as though she'd been expecting him to come calling; the idea was damn disconcerting. He'd yet to have a good night's sleep in the Bendalins' house, but after a day when his thoughts and feelings had been such an uncomfortable fit, he knew his demons would chase him all night if he didn't make things right with her.

"I'm not sure where to begin," he said.

Just looking at him made Eliza feel sick with longing for something she couldn't even name. The awful yearning was the very last thing she'd ever admit to him, however. "Perhaps you should just bid me good night."

Jonathan took a quick step forward to prevent her from closing the door. "No, there's something important I need to say." Looking away, he fought to corral his thoughts, but it wasn't all that easy.

"Sometimes a man and woman meet, and the attraction between them is so strong they pursue it without any regard for the consequences. I'm afraid that's what I've been doing, and I owe you an apology, Miss Bendalin. I've been too forward, and I'm sorry for insulting you the other night. I shouldn't have criticized your beau, and I'll do my best not to make him look bad come Saturday."

His reference to her as Miss Bendalin, which was not merely polite, but coldly distant, broke Eliza's heart. She was far too proud to throw herself at his feet and sob, but she had to dig her nails into her palms to keep from weeping openly.

"Fletcher really is a good man," she replied, "but I understand there's a natural rivalry between horsemen."

"Well, now, I suppose that's one way of looking at it." Jonathan couldn't believe she didn't understand that she was at the heart of whatever rivalry existed between Fletcher and him. "I do hope we can remain friends though, especially for Lawrence's sake."

"Yes, of course. I'll just have to give more serious thought to planning Lawrence's wedding as well as Fletcher's and mine to avoid any undue stress for my mother."

Jonathan's stomach lurched at the thought of Eliza becoming Mrs. Fletcher Monroe. He leaned against the doorjamb and crossed his arms over his chest to hold in the pain. "I imagine Fletcher will be real helpful in that regard."

"Yes, he's always wonderfully considerate," Eliza explained without any sense of joy or pride. "He's offered to come here to live rather than have us reside at his ranch. It's the best choice for me while Mother's ill, but not many men would be so accommodating."

Jonathan searched her face for a sparkle of excitement or a trace of tenderness when she spoke Fletcher's name, but there wasn't a hint of affection in her expression. He saw only the same sorrow mirrored in his own reflection, and he couldn't help feeling he might be partly to blame.

"It sounds as though Fletcher intends to fit himself neatly into your life," he summarized. "That's very generous of him, but wouldn't the two of you rather create a life of your own?"

Eliza fought to hold back her tears. "Please, I can't bear

to think what life will bring when my mother's gone. It causes too much pain to contemplate."

Jonathan had meant to sever whatever tenuous tie might exist between them, but in spite of his best intentions, his anger got the better of him. He pulled himself up to his full height and handed her a totally honest opinion.

"Sweetheart, you don't even know the meaning of the word *pain*. Just wait until you wake to the awful realization that you've pledged your whole life to the wrong man."

Realizing what he'd done, he broke into a rueful smile. "Damn. I came here to apologize, and here I've gone and insulted Fletcher all over again. Guess it's time to say good night."

Unable to draw the breath to speak, Eliza closed her door and leaned back against it. She didn't understand why he'd come to her room simply to torment her. In the last few days, she'd developed grave doubts about Fletcher on her own, but who was Jonathan Blair to give her advice? All he'd offered were a few stolen kisses and a resulting loneliness she feared might linger a lifetime.

Early Friday morning, Fletcher arrived to beg for Eliza Kate's help with the final plans for Saturday's party, and she was delighted for any excuse to be away from home for the day. After she secured his consent to host the party regardless of who won the race, she scarcely listened for the remainder of the buggy ride to his ranch. However, she did catch enough to understand just how greatly he was looking forward to winning the race and hosting the spring's most spectacular celebration.

Fletcher's single-story adobe ranch house was built around a central patio, and as they strolled through it, Eliza smiled and nodded, and tried her best to appear interested in his plans, but her heart simply wasn't in it. She didn't care a bit about where the decorations were placed or what food he served. She loved to dance, but not even the promise of talented musicians made her look forward to the coming day.

"It would be a fine time to announce our engagement," Fletcher suggested on their return trip to her home.

With the introduction of that subject, Fletcher at last captured Eliza's full attention. She nearly choked, forcing down a suffocating dread, then rested her hand on his sleeve. "I need a while longer, Fletcher. You've been so wonderfully understanding, and I hate to take advantage of your patience, but I'm just not ready yet."

"The spring is the best time for a wedding, my dearest. I've already spoken with your father, and he's—"

"You two have discussed the wedding?" she said, gasping. Her father thought so highly of his partner, he'd certainly not object to her marrying him, but she didn't want to be handed over as though she were an extravagant bonus Fletcher had somehow earned.

Fletcher shot her an incredulous glance. "Well, yes, of course, I have. As I'm sure you know, it's customary for a man to seek the father's permission before he proposes to the woman he loves."

Eliza swallowed hard. She'd played with the food on her plate at noon rather than eaten a bite but still felt sick to her stomach. "I thought the man was supposed to propose to the woman first, and then ask for her father's permission to marry."

"Good Lord, Eliza Kate. Let's not quibble. We've already decided to marry. You were simply hesitant to set the date because of your mother's poor health. I think she's doing much better now, and your father agrees."

Eliza stopped listening right there. She had meant what she'd said about postponing their marriage when she'd suggested it months ago, but at the time she'd expected so little of the institution, she'd not fully realized what a dreadful match they would make. "Please, let's wait a little longer," she begged.

"Even if Mother goes to the race, she has no plans to attend tomorrow's party, and I'll not announce my engagement without her present. That would be very cruel, don't you see?"

All Fletcher saw were the huge tears welling up in Eliza Kate's beautiful blue eyes, and fearing he'd offended her, he immediately agreed. "Whatever you wish, my dearest. I didn't mean to upset you so much."

"Thank you." Eliza found a lacy handkerchief in her pocket and quickly dried her eyes. "Let's just concentrate on tomorrow's race and party. That's more than enough for now."

Fletcher reluctantly concurred, but Eliza Kate cared little about either event and was too confused to know what she thought about anything else.

Saturday morning, Lawrence found Jonathan out by the barn grooming Red Warrior with long, easy brush strokes. "He looks awfully good," he greeted him.

"That he does. I intend to ride bareback. Will Monroe object?"

"How can he? You're the larger man, so riding without your saddle will help to even out the weight. If he complains, just refuse to race. He's made such a fuss about it with his party plans and all, he won't dare let you back out."

"Don't worry. There's no danger of my backing out." Jonathan stepped back to admire his stallion and found a rough spot on his shoulder he'd missed. He added one last swipe to erase the mark and set the brush aside on the tree stump some used to mount their horses.

"I thought I'd go on out to the Hanging Tree to beat the crowd. Want to come along?" Jonathan asked.

"Yeah, sure." Lawrence looked back toward the house to make certain they were alone, but still took the precaution of lowering his voice. "I should have thought of this sooner, but if Red Warrior were to lose this race by a nose, Fletcher would boast all the louder. He'd brag about Coal Dust to anyone who'd listen, and he'd also look all the more ridiculous when his horse loses the rematch by several lengths."

Although flabbergasted, Jonathan calmly adjusted the angle of his hat, then rested his hands on his narrow hips. "Now let me get this straight. Are you asking me to deliberately lose today's race?"

"I know it's crazy, but you didn't see Fletcher strutting around here yesterday when he brought Eliza Kate home. To hear him tell it, this won't be much of a contest, but the party afterward will make up for it." Lawrence took a step closer and his tone became all the more urgent.

"Forgive me if this seems desperate, but there's something new to dislike about Fletcher every time I see him, and Eliza Kate simply deserves better. I'll have to place a bet on Red Warrior in today's race, but I won't mind losing a few dollars if it will set Fletcher up for an enormous humiliation when Coal Dust is badly beaten in the rematch.

"I'm hoping the way he gloats today and the tantrum he'll surely throw when he loses next time will enable Eliza Kate to see his true colors. With any luck, she'll not want anything more to do with him. What do you say?"

Jonathan nodded thoughtfully. "Truthfully? I'm disappointed. I thought you were one of the few honest men on Earth."

Lawrence swung his arms in such a broad gesture he lost his balance, but a quick hand from Jonathan saved him from falling. "I've always thought of myself as an honest man, too, but damn it all, I'm desperate. Though I've tried to pretend otherwise, I'd give anything to have a loving wife, and Eliza Kate's done her best to find me one. I can't stand idly by and allow her to choose a husband who's going to make her miserable by always thinking more of himself than he ever does of her."

"Eliza Kate strikes me as a real sensible young woman. Why don't you give her your opinion of Fletcher straight out?" Jonathan suggested.

"Don't think I haven't considered it, but she's too sweet

a girl to believe ill of anyone, and criticism would only prompt her to defend him."

Jonathan had already heard Eliza defend Fletcher in a spirited fashion, and readily sympathized with Lawrence. "That's probably true. But even if I agreed to your plan, I doubt Red Warrior here would go along. He loves to run, and the possibility of losing to Coal Dust won't enter his mind."

Utterly defeated by that thought, Lawrence shrugged helplessly. "You're right, of course. It was a stupid idea, and I shouldn't have bothered you with it."

Jonathan reached out to grab hold of Lawrence's shoulders in a brief encouraging clutch. "No, it's a damn good idea. But even though I agreed to stay on here to race Fletcher, I'm still anxious to leave for California. Having to hang around for a second race would force me to postpone my plans all over again.

"Now let's forget the race for a moment, and concentrate on the party. You must have some favorites among Eliza's friends, to say nothing of the other pretty girls in town. Who's caught your eye?"

Lawrence's face flooded with color, and flustered, he ran a finger around the inside of his collar. "They all have. Oh no, that makes me sound desperate, doesn't it?"

Jonathan couldn't help laughing. "No, not at all. You're a good-looking man with every right to have a fondness for the ladies. Now saddle your horse, and let's get going before Fletcher and all his friends crowd up the trail."

As Lawrence entered the barn, Jonathan swore under his breath and turned to Red Warrior. "Don't look at me like that. This wouldn't be the first race that was fixed, but if Eliza Kate can't already see what kind of man Fletcher Monroe is, then there's not much we can do to open her eyes."

Red Warrior raised his nose to sniff the wind, then tossed his freshly brushed mane as though he shared his master's conclusion.

* * *

Eliza Kate rode out to the race in the buggy with her parents while Ricky and Robby rode their horses. She wore a flattering new pink gown and carried a matching parasol her mother had insisted she bring along, but she was far too anxious to twirl it slowly and flirt as so many other young women were doing. Instead, she let it rest lightly upon her shoulder as she wandered through the noisy crowd.

Jonathan was easy enough to find with that big red horse of his, but she'd always considered Coal Dust a fine stallion too. He was as dark as midnight and danced in place with a high prancing step as Fletcher laughed and joked with his friends. Eliza knew she was expected to approach her beau and cheer for him wildly, but she'd seen Red Warrior run and thought he'd be the more likely winner.

That expected outcome kept her circling away from Fletcher, and when she saw Lawrence standing off by himself, she hastened to join him. "I fear Fletcher will lose," she whispered softly as she reached him.

"Probably," Lawrence responded, "but he shouldn't take it too badly." He had great difficulty keeping his face straight as he made that comment when he was praying for Fletcher to make a complete fool of himself in front of half the town. He moved quickly to distract Eliza by pointing out a willowy brunette standing half a dozen paces to their left.

"That's Miss Wilson, isn't it? I didn't remember her being so attractive, and I wouldn't mind renewing my acquaintance with her. Is her first name Marsha?" he asked.

"No, it's Martha, and she isn't Miss Wilson anymore. She married Arliss Anderson a couple of months ago. He's the young pharmacist who began working at the apothecary shop last year. Perhaps you've met him in town."

"No, I don't believe so," Lawrence replied. "I hope they're very happy together," he added rather wistfully.

"Why, yes, I believe they are." Hoping to cheer him,

Eliza directed his attention toward a young woman with exquisite pale skin and thick auburn hair. "That's Sandra Sloan. She was quite fond of you, as I recall, and she's still available."

Lawrence turned his back toward the woman in question. "I remember Sandra all too well. She's not simply shy and difficult to converse with; she's absolutely silent. I could probably have a more diverting conversation with that feathered hat she's wearing than with her."

Eliza linked her arm with her uncle's and gave him an encouraging squeeze. "Let's wait until the party to strike up any conversations. Then we won't be interrupted."

"If that giggling Carol Ann appears, I'll be grateful for the interruption!"

"Uncle, please," Eliza cautioned, but he had her smiling for the first time that day.

Eliza had paid no attention to him, but Jonathan had noted her arrival and watched her progress through the crowd. He was puzzled that she appeared to be in no hurry to speak with Fletcher and offer a good-luck kiss. She looked so pretty in her pale pink gown, but not at all like the confident young woman who'd urged him not to tarry on the Bendalin's Trinity Star Ranch.

Today she was all sweet femininity and lace, but she was a long way from Fletcher's side where a woman as devoted as she pretended to be ought to stand. He shrugged off another woman's cool touch and began to unbutton his shirt. It was coming up on noon, and he wanted the race run on time.

"Let's go," he called to Fletcher. "Anyone who hasn't got a bet down is just too late."

Fletcher's glance swung from Jonathan's bronze chest to his moccasins, and he shook his head in dismay. "You really intend on riding bareback like an Indian?"

"I sure do," Jonathan shouted back at him.

"You fall off in the dust, don't expect me to give you a rematch," Fletcher warned with a hearty chuckle.

"You just worry about yourself, Mr. Monroe," Jonathan cautioned.

The course had been marked with bright pennants, and as Jonathan brought Red Warrior into place, he turned for a last glimpse of Eliza Kate. She was watching him now, and he responded with a wink and a lazy salute.

Noting the direction of Jonathan's gaze, Fletcher nearly snarled. "That's my girl, and don't you forget it."

Jonathan took a firmer grip on his reins before he coolly dismissed Fletcher's complaint. "Looks to me as though Eliza Kate's the one who can't remember."

The race began with a pistol shot before Fletcher could think of a suitably cutting reply, and his coarsely worded curse was drowned out by the swelling noise of the crowd. Coal Dust got off to a flying start, and then it took all of Fletcher's concentration to steer him through his best race, but he was all too aware of Red Warrior's place at his side to feel anything but scared.

As always, Jonathan meant to win. Coal Dust was surprisingly strong and swift but no match for Red Warrior. Jonathan kept a tight hold on his horse's reins, however. He held Red Warrior back, intending to let the stallion fly as soon as they made the turn and headed back toward the Hanging Tree. They'd cross the finish line, and maybe not even stop to collect their winnings before setting out for California.

But as Jonathan rounded the turn, he could think only of Eliza Kate. She was no more than a small pink blur at the finish line, but he could feel her presence as though she were cradled in his arms. Dust swirled around him, but the taunting fragrance of her perfume filled his senses.

The options were clear. He could give Red Warrior his head, win the race, and leave for California, or pull him wide to allow Coal Dust to streak by them. In a heartbeat, he made his choice.

Coal Dust crossed the finish line first, and Eliza Kate could not believe her eyes. She turned to Lawrence, who appeared to be equally stunned. "What happened?" she shouted above the cheering crowd. "I never expected Red Warrior to lose."

Lawrence shrugged as though dumbfounded. Although Jonathan hadn't agreed to throw the race when he'd proposed it, that was exactly what he'd done. For whatever reason, he'd set the plan to discredit Fletcher Monroe in motion, and Lawrence struggled to look suitably disappointed by Red Warrior's defeat.

"We'll demand a rematch right now," he vowed forcefully.

Eliza continued to hold her uncle's arm as they approached Fletcher, who'd already dismounted to accept hearty congratulations from his friends, but her glance followed Jonathan as he rode away alone, as she feared he'd always be.

Chapter Eight

Robby's brows knit in a mask of confusion. "Shucks. You said this would be an easy win for Red Warrior."

The brothers were seated astride their horses at the edge of the crowd where they'd had an excellent view of the race. When Ricky didn't answer, Robby glanced over in time to see all the color drain from his big brother's face. "What's the matter? You gonna be sick?"

There were too many people standing nearby for Ricky to lean over and vomit on the ground, but he had bet far more than he should have and had just lost it all. Even worse, he feared Red Warrior hadn't run his best race because of him.

"Yeah, I'm gonna be real sick," he answered, struggling to overcome the sudden attack of nausea. "I think we ought to catch Uncle Lawrence before he leaves for the party."

"What's Uncle Lawrence gonna do?" Robby wondered aloud, but he followed Ricky's lead and skirted the spectators returning to their buggies and horses and took up a position at the side of the trail.

When Ricky finally spotted their uncle, he stood in his stirrups to wave. Then he searched for a way to explain what they'd done without looking like the idiots they surely were.

"I'm afraid I've some bad news," he began.

"Can't be any worse than seeing Red Warrior lose," Lawrence replied, but having no prior experience with deceit, he had a hard time keeping his smile from growing too wide. Ricky caught his attention immediately, however, with his confession and then Lawrence gaped in sincere astonishment.

"You've been putting mares in the corral with Red Warrior?" he said, groaning. He knew Jonathan must have lost the race on purpose, but now Ricky had provided a logical excuse, which made him wonder if fate hadn't played a major hand in their success. "My God," he fumed dramatically. "Didn't it occur to you that Red Warrior might get just a wee bit tired?"

Robby now understood just how much trouble they were in and quickly tried to get himself clear. "It was Ricky's idea. You know it couldn't have been mine."

Ignoring Robby, Lawrence did his best to produce another burst of righteous indignation. "Plans are already under way for a second race, so we'll have to pray we can set things right then. For the time being, you two just get on home and stay there."

"Please don't tell Mr. Blair," Ricky begged.

"Of course I'm going to tell him. What you did wasn't merely thoughtless, it was wrong, and I'll leave it up to him to decide your punishment. Wouldn't surprise me if he didn't demand that you pay him stud fees though, and I'll bet you two haven't got a nickel between you."

"I've got six bucks saved," Robby offered hopefully.

"Somehow I don't believe that's going to be nearly enough," Lawrence replied coolly.

Robby's eyes grew wide with fright. "I sure don't want Mr. Blair mad at us."

"I don't either," Ricky swore. "Can't you talk with him for us, Uncle Lawrence? You two are best friends and all. He'll take it a lot better coming from you than from us."

Lawrence stared at his nephews a long moment. He and Lamar had been an entirely different set of boys, but upon occasion they'd also gotten themselves in some deep trouble. Besides, Ricky and Robby weren't as guilty as they believed, and he was inclined to be lenient with them.

"I'll consider it," he offered, "but right now, you two better get on home."

"We're on our way," Ricky promised, and he and his little brother swung around the buggies on the trail and rode away.

Lawrence couldn't believe his good luck. Not only was everything progressing according to plan, but Ricky had even provided a damn good reason for Red Warrior's loss, and once the information was circulated, nobody would suspect the first race wasn't as honest as the second was sure to be. He laughed to himself and hoped he'd have similar luck with the ladies that afternoon.

Eliza Kate had gone to check on her mother's comfort while Lawrence and Fletcher held their preliminary discussion of a rematch. Just as Eliza had expected, Delia had enjoyed the race, but found the swirling crowd overwhelming and was eager to leave for home. Eliza was about to rejoin her parents in the buggy when Fletcher caught up to them.

"Wasn't that the best race you've ever seen?" he asked, his grin wide.

"Your horse was magnificent," Delia assured him.

"I certainly enjoyed the race," Lamar added, and he patted the fattened billfold in his breast pocket.

When the attention shifted to Eliza, she quickly pro-

duced a noncommittal compliment. "It was very exciting,"
she said, but her spirits had plummeted when Jonathan
had lost and showed no sign of rising.

Fletcher extended his hand. "Come with me, Eliza Kate.
I had one of my hands bring my buggy. He'll see that
Coal Dust gets home so we can ride to my place together.
Thank you so much for coming out here today, Delia. I'll
understand if you find the party too taxing."

"Thank you, but Lamar will be there. Won't you, dear?"

"Maybe later," Lamar replied, and he dipped beneath
her straw hat to kiss her cheek. "I want to make certain
you're settled at home first."

Eliza noted how easily her parents exchanged affectionate gestures and envied them the depth of emotion behind every glance and touch. She felt Fletcher's hand at
her elbow leading her away, but he could have been anyone escorting her to a buggy, and she drew no comfort
from his touch.

Someone called her name, and she turned to find Bess
Perry waving from her family's buggy. Bess was small and
slender with silky blond hair. Eliza made a mental note
to make certain Lawrence had a chance to speak with her
at the party.

"I should have placed a larger bet," Fletcher confided
softly as he helped Eliza up into his buggy. "Now I know
better, and I'll win a small fortune on the next race."

Eliza provided Fletcher with an appropriately optimistic
murmur, but she was worried Jonathan might have wagered and lost a great deal. Fletcher continued to wave
and shout to his friends as they made their way to his
ranch in a joyous parade, but she felt every bit as detached
as she had on Friday. Everyone else was in such a buoyant
mood, but the crowd's gaiety didn't touch her.

When they entered Fletcher's home, he led his guests
out to the patio and opened the first bottle of champagne,
then excused himself to freshen up and change his
clothes before the rest of his guests arrived.

Eliza Kate was left to play hostess for the moment, and

with Lawrence's happiness a major concern, it was a role she assumed gladly. She handed him a glass of sparkling wine and encouraged him to drink up while she took only a sip of her own.

"Here comes Bess Perry," Eliza whispered. "I saw her at the race and hoped you two would have a chance to talk."

Grateful Eliza had supplied the attractive blonde's name, Lawrence greeted her cheerfully. "Miss Perry, I know it's been months, but it's so nice to see you today."

"Lawrence, Eliza Kate," Betty responded sweetly, then searched the crowd with an impatient gaze. "Where's your friend? I thought maybe he'd need a bit of consoling, and I'd be real happy to provide it."

"My friend? Oh, you mean Jonathan Blair," Lawrence replied, his initial delight that she'd sought him out rapidly fading. "He told me this morning that he'd not be here. He's a widower, you see, and not given to frivolous entertainments."

"A widower?" Greatly intrigued, Bess licked her pale pink lips. "How tragic. How long ago did he lose his wife?"

"A couple of years, I believe," Lawrence stated politely. He then glanced over her head to seek out more agreeable company from those gathering on the patio.

Eliza Kate didn't blame her uncle for losing interest when clearly Bess wanted to meet Jonathan rather than spend any time with him. She absolutely refused to consider whether Jonathan might have liked Bess. Instead, she urged Lawrence toward another group, which included Deborah and Rachel Webster, attractive sisters a couple of years older than she.

"Where's your friend?" they asked in unison.

"Jonathan doesn't care much for parties," Lawrence hastened to explain, but he sent Eliza an exasperated glance. "I'll give him your regards."

"Oh, please do," Deborah replied.

"I fear it's been too long since we paid a call on you and your mother, Eliza," Rachel added. "Would Monday be a convenient day for a visit?"

When it was obvious it was their handsome house guest rather than her dear mother the sisters wished to see, Eliza promised to contact them when a good time presented itself and promptly steered Lawrence away. "Oh no," she said, sighing, "here comes Carol Ann."

Thinking he could stand a few giggles if Carol Ann could discuss something other than Jonathan Blair, Lawrence greeted her warmly. "How pretty you look, Miss Ferguson. I do believe yellow is your color."

Carol Ann dipped her head and looked up at him through her lashes, then burst into a lilting giggle. "Thank you so much, Mr. Bendalin. It's always good to see you out and about. Where's your friend?"

"He may be on his way to California for all I know," Lawrence shot right back at her.

Carol Ann jumped back a step. "My goodness. Was he so disappointed about losing the race that he would leave the state?"

"You must excuse me, Miss Ferguson, I fear I may have gotten too much sun. I need to move into the shade."

"I'll chat with you later, Carol Ann," Eliza promised, and she held tightly to her uncle's arm as he moved toward a shady corner. "Isn't there going to be a second race?" she inquired, cautiously, focusing her question on the race rather than Jonathan.

"Yes, and probably a third if Fletcher demands it." Lawrence removed his handkerchief and wiped his brow. "Was I unforgivably rude, Eliza Kate?"

"You were a mite abrupt, but you already knew you weren't interested in Carol Ann."

"Still, I shouldn't have been so curt with her. I just didn't expect all the women here to be pining for Jonathan."

"He's a dashing figure. It's only natural women—and probably most of the men here as well—would be curious about him. That doesn't mean they aren't pleased to see you though."

Lawrence just rolled his eyes, jammed his handkerchief

back into his pocket, and sank down upon a narrow
wooden bench. "You go on and enjoy the party. I really
do need to rest."

Eliza watched his shoulders sag, and equally sad,
couldn't leave him. "No. I could use a chance to catch my
breath too." She sat beside him and smoothed the soft
folds of her skirt. If she hadn't known how negative his
reaction would be, she would have asked him about Jonathan, too, and that made her feel very guilty.

"There's Diana Ballard," she whispered, and then waved
to the petite, doll-like young woman. "Here she comes."

Lawrence hauled himself to his feet, and then straightened his shoulders as though just standing weren't such
an effort. "Miss Ballard. I believe I saw you in town this
week."

"Indeed you did, Mr. Bendalin." Diana raised a fluttering hand to her thick, black curls, and opened her brown
eyes wide. "I was with Paulette O'Toole, and you were with
your friend. I believe his name is Jonathan Blair. Has he
arrived yet?"

Still primping, Diane surveyed the crowded patio. She
even stretched up on her toes for a moment to get a better look at a gentleman who'd joined the Webster sisters.
Quickly discounting him, she smiled at Lawrence, then
tipped her head slightly to prompt his response.

"Jonathan is unlikely to arrive, Miss Ballard. He's far
more fond of his horse than he is of women."

"You don't say," Diana cried, obviously shocked. "Well,
I declare. It's good to see you too, Eliza Kate. I hope you'll
excuse me. I promised my mother I'd ask after one of her
friends, and I see her standing near the champagne."

Lawrence sat back down on the bench. "Perhaps I
should ask Fletcher for a piece of paper. I'll just print in
block letters that Jonathan won't be here, and pin it on
my coat. Then people won't have to keep bothering me
about him."

Eliza took his hand in a fond clasp. "You've not been
to a party in so long. Please be a little more patient and

give everyone the chance to appreciate the fact you're here."

"The women my age are all married," Lawrence muttered glumly. "And your friends are so young they're not interested in me. I know you mean well, but there's no reason to pretend otherwise."

Eliza Kate opened her mouth to argue, but Fletcher arrived to refill their glasses, and she'd not share her uncle's poor opinion of himself with her beau. She'd not considered the fact that Fletcher wasn't the type in whom she could confide until that very moment. He provided charming company, and that had always been enough until Jonathan had invaded not only her favorite place at the river, but also the lonely places in her heart.

She would have cried at that thought but her mother hadn't raised her to create embarrassing scenes at parties, and so she withdrew into herself and ignored Fletcher's continued praise for Coal Dust and how handily they'd won the race.

Equally bored with the subject, Lawrence wasn't listening either. Instead, he drank his champagne and studied the latest arrivals. Striving to be pleasant, even if he wasn't enjoying himself, he smiled whenever anyone looked his way and prayed at least one woman would smile in return.

Fletcher's cook was nearly as talented as the Bendalins'. When the food was ready, Eliza urged her uncle to eat but herself sampled no more than a tiny bite of the barbecued beef, glazed carrots, savory rice, and hot biscuits. There were fruit pies for dessert with delicate crusts, but again she swallowed no more than a single mouthful.

While the guests dined, the musicians provided a lovely serenade with their fiddles and guitars, but once the dishes were cleared away, the music became far more lively and the dancing began. Eliza had plenty of charming partners, all of whom laughed, claimed Fletcher had won the race easily, and expected her to be of a like mind.

She smiled until her cheeks ached and didn't admit to anyone how deeply disappointed she truly felt. Instead, she relied on gracious manners and commented on the beauty of the afternoon or the joy of good friends. Everyone else was enjoying the party, but she swiftly began to suspect that should she wed Fletcher Monroe, she would spend the rest of her life talking about nothing of any importance and pretending a happiness she didn't feel.

He wanted children, and a family was also her fondest hope, but it was becoming increasingly doubtful that they'd have those dear little babies together. When her father arrived at the party, she danced with him, too, but she was no longer his darling little girl who had once felt so grown up in his arms.

"When did you fall in love with Mother?" she asked as the musicians paused for a break.

Lamar raised his brows in surprise. "What a strange question."

Eliza Kate saw Fletcher approaching and urged him to answer. "No, please, I'm serious."

Lamar's expression softened with the memory. "I fell in love with Delia when we were children. I don't recall if the first time I saw her was at church or in school, but she was so awfully pretty all the little boys fell in love with her. I was just the lucky one she loved back."

"How wonderful to have loved each other your whole lives," Eliza mused aloud, and when her father quickly glanced away, she knew he feared her mother's life wouldn't be nearly as long as his own.

"Come dance with me again," Fletcher invited as he reached her side.

"There's no music for the moment," Eliza pointed out.

"A minor problem," Fletcher teased, and he kept hold of her hand.

Eliza had stayed close to her uncle whenever possible that afternoon, but having lost sight of him while dancing with her father, she looked past Fletcher, hoping to locate him. "Have you seen Lawrence?" she asked. "I do so want him to have a good time but he tends to stray off into the corners and keep to himself."

"He left for home a few minutes ago," Fletcher replied.
"He said his leg was bothering him too badly to stay."

Eliza glanced up at her father. "Well, I did my best to
encourage Lawrence to circulate among the guests while
he was here."

Lamar sighed wearily. "Don't worry about your uncle.
I'll think of something to cheer him up if he needs it."

"What he most definitely needs is *someone*," Eliza emphasized.

Lamar rocked back on his heels. "Someone. Yes, I understand."

Jonathan Blair's criticism that he had not done more
for his brother rankled anew, but he nodded thoughtfully
as though his daughter's idea was most welcome.

The musicians returned, and Fletcher swept Eliza Kate
into his arms for as graceful a waltz as they could manage
across the slightly uneven surface of his patio. "You've appeared preoccupied all afternoon, my dearest," he whispered. "I'd no idea you were so concerned about your
uncle's happiness."

Eliza's smile faltered, but she managed a quick nod.
Then another of Fletcher's friends slapped him on the
shoulder and congratulated him on the race, and she was
spared the ordeal of saying more.

As the shadows lengthened across the patio, the tem-
perature dipped, and growing chilled, some of Fletcher's
guests began moving indoors to continue their conversations while others departed for home. When Lamar announced he was ready to leave, Eliza Kate hurriedly bid
Fletcher good night.

"But I wanted to take you home," Fletcher complained.

"Your guests are still having such a good time. You
should stay here with them. It was a lovely party. I'll see
you again soon." She brushed his cheek with a hasty kiss,
and then forgot him entirely as she rode home in her
father's buggy.

When they entered the house, Lamar went upstairs to
Delia's room, while Eliza Kate was disappointed not to

find Jonathan in the parlor. Her brothers were there playing checkers, and restless, she joined them to play the
winner, but quickly lost the match.

"Checkers never was my game," she uttered in a frustrated sigh. "I'm going on up to bed. It's been a long day."

"You can say that again," Ricky mumbled.

Eliza paused at the doorway and briefly considered
warning him to stay away from the liquor cabinet if he
wished for better days. Then recalling how she had come
to know that he helped himself to their father's bourbon,
she pushed herself straight on up the stairs.

She was exhausted, but so anxious her skin felt as
though it were a size too small. She quickly peeled off her
clothes, but it was too late to heat water and soak in a
soothing bath as she would have liked. The only alternative was to use the cool water in the pitcher on her washstand to scrub herself clean before slipping on a white
linen nightgown whose ruffles and lace were nearly as
fancy as her day gowns. She had no real hope of going to
sleep though and paced as she brushed out her hair with
long, savage strokes.

Now she was sorry she'd not quizzed Ricky and Robby
about Jonathan's mood, but she doubted he would have
confided in the boys regardless of how upset he might
have been. Perhaps when Lawrence had returned home
from the party, he and Jonathan had talked over the race,
but she'd not disturb her uncle when his day had been
so far from good.

As for Jonathan, if she went upstairs to his room, he'd
simply be annoyed if she woke him. If he were still awake,
he'd probably call her Miss Bendalin again and bid her a
terse good night. Neither option held any appeal, but
long after she'd heard her brothers close the doors of
their rooms, she was still wide awake.

Jonathan filled her thoughts, as indeed he had all day.
He was so proud of Red Warrior, and she feared he had
been heartbroken to lose a race to a man he heartily dis-
liked. She felt sick with disappointment herself, so how

much worse must he feel? she agonized. In the end, it was concern for him that inspired her to grab a shawl, and before she lost her courage, climb the stairs to the third floor, and knock lightly at his door. She waited in the hall's gloomy darkness, her heart firmly lodged in her throat.

Just when she'd begun to suspect Jonathan wasn't in his room and might even have left for California, he swung the door open wide. The single lamp burning atop the dresser gave his face and bare chest a burnished glow while his dark trousers melted into the shadows.

Perhaps it was the obvious strength of his muscular body or the sheer masculine beauty of all that bronze flesh. It might have been the way his hair dipped boyishly over his forehead or the wicked light in his eyes. For whatever reason, Eliza continued to stare, memorizing every detail of his appearance, exactly as she had whenever they were together.

"Something you wanted to say?" Jonathan prompted before the silence grew uncomfortably long.

"I was afraid you'd be despondent," Eliza blurted out.

"Really? So you waited, what has it been, ten hours or more since the race, to check up on me?" He couldn't help laughing. "Obviously you were deeply concerned."

Insulted by how easily he'd made her look foolish, Eliza drew her shawl more tightly around her shoulders. Perhaps her tardiness was inexcusable, but not when she considered Lawrence was supposed to be the only link between them. "You're obviously in much better spirits than I feared. I don't know what happened to Red Warrior today, but he's sure to beat Coal Dust the next time you race."

Jonathan had laughed so hard he'd nearly cried when Lawrence had revealed what her brothers had been up to, and he was surprised Eliza appeared to be unaware of Ricky's scheme. With her standing so close though, he didn't have much interest in talking about horses.

It was the light dusting of freckles across the bridge of

her nose that caught his attention, and unable to subdue the impulse, he reached out to touch her flushed cheek. "It looks as though you forgot to use that pretty parasol of yours. If you're not more careful, you'll get as freckled as some sharecropper's daughter."

"That's highly unlikely." Eliza was amazed he'd noticed she was carrying a parasol, but nevertheless batted his hand away. "It's a shame you didn't attend Fletcher's party. All the women were asking after you, but I suppose Lawrence already told you that."

"Can't say that he did. He didn't look too happy though. How'd he get along?"

Eliza didn't notice that he'd taken a step closer and now nearly filled the doorway, but she'd caught a glimpse of his bed, and the spread was still smoothed neatly across it. Apparently he'd known he wouldn't get much sleep that night either.

"Not too well, I'm afraid," she replied sadly. "He's so shy, and when all the women inquired about you, he was pretty discouraged."

Distressed by that news, Jonathan breathed out an impatient sigh. "Is Fort Worth overrun with stupid women? I'll be gone soon, but Lawrence has a fine family and nice home here. Maybe I should have gone to the party and insulted everyone who spoke to me. Maybe then the women would have appreciated that Lawrence is the much better catch."

When the conversation had shifted to Lawrence, Eliza had drawn a deep breath, but now that Jonathan was talking about himself, he was again regarding her much too closely—as closely as she always studied him—and she couldn't breathe at all.

"I should go," she murmured hesitantly.

"Yes, you should," Jonathan agreed, but as she took a step away, he reached out to catch her arm, drew her into his room, and closed the door behind her. He released her only to capture her between his outstretched arms.

He'd moved so quickly Eliza hadn't had time to utter a

sound, and now backed up against the solid oak door, she could only stare up at him, her eyes wide. He'd trapped her so easily, but for the first time, she felt truly free. "I can't marry Fletcher," she announced suddenly.

She was full of surprises that night, but Jonathan didn't even try to stifle his chuckles. Instead, he leaned close and rested his forehead against hers for a moment before straightening. "That's probably the most sensible thing you've said since we met. What did you tell him?"

"I haven't told him yet," Eliza admitted softly, and for a dreadful instant, she feared Jonathan was going to open his door and shove her right back through it. She saw the thought flash across his gaze as clear as lightning, but then it was gone, and a teasing smile tugged at the corner of his mouth.

"I will tell him though and soon," she promised.

Jonathan barely heard her above the rapid pounding of his heart. Her eyes caught the lamp's golden light, and with her curls tumbling past her shoulders, she again resembled the angel he'd met one night on the stairs. He didn't know how he'd let her go then, but it was impossible now.

He dropped his arms to encircle her waist and inclined his head to feather a trail of kisses across her gently arched brow, over the pretty blush on her cheek, and down her slender throat. "Just touching you always feels so damn good," he swore softly.

The shawl slid from Eliza Kate's shoulders as she stepped into his arms. She wrapped her arms around his waist, and her fingertips skipped down his spine. Content for the first time all day, she rested her cheek on his bare shoulder and leaned into him. His skin was so smooth and warm, his breath against her temple as gentle as his caress.

He'd warned of consequences to pursuing the attraction between them, but she cared little about whatever repercussions there might be. He'd been with her all day, clouding her thoughts, heightening her senses, but she held him now with an aching need that was far from assuaged. It burned through her, yet she could not pull away from the flame.

Jonathan rubbed his cheek against her curls. Her hair always smelled as delicious as her garden, and just when he thought he recognized the scent of one flower, it melted into the fragrance of another. It was an amazingly complex perfume, and yet as innocently beautiful as she was.

It made him long to taste her, but he was in no rush to make her his woman. He stood quietly as she explored the broad plains of his back, the rippling flatness of his stomach, before he caught her hands and brought them to his lips. He kissed her palms, and then with a gentle tug, drew her across the room to the bed.

He cupped her face in his hands as he began to kiss her, and in a matter of seconds he was so lost in desire, he didn't realize she was the one to pull him down onto the feather mattress. He just knew they were a lot more comfortable than they'd been been hidden behind the sofa in the parlor. Now freely given, her kisses were so sweet he knew they'd be together until dawn.

He ran his hand over the soft swells of her lithe body and gloried in the tenderness of her touch. When he could stand no more of the lazy circles she'd traced on his skin, he caught her hand and rubbed it against his rigid shaft. He wanted her to feel how badly he needed her, but when she unbuttoned his waistband and slid her hand inside his trousers, he thought he'd die.

He managed one last deep kiss, then rolled over the side of the bed to strip off what little clothing he wore. He hadn't meant to frighten her though, and reached out to turn down the lamp.

"Leave it alone," Eliza begged in a sultry whisper. "I want to see you."

"I was afraid you might not want to see so much," Jonathan replied.

Eliza knew how men were made, and though she'd never seen another fully aroused, she thought Jonathan

even more handsome than she had before. Immediately
inspired to remove her nightgown, she sat up to peel it
off and flung it over the end of the high, iron bed. She
had never imagined she could give herself to a man with
such shocking abandon, but then she hadn't expected to
fall in love with Jonathan Blair.

She savored the thought as she held out her hand, and
he rejoined her on the bed. She had never felt so vulnerable as she did nestled in his arms, and at the same time,
so safe and protected. When Jonathan's fevered kisses
strayed to the fullness of her breasts to playfully bite, tease,
and suck, she wrapped her arms around his head to encourage more of his lavish attentions.

He shifted position to slide his tongue into her navel,
and she laughed with sheer joy, but when his tender kisses
traveled lower, she was too shocked to cry out. Then she
was lost in such an exquisite sensation she could only lace
her fingers in his hair and sob his name. Inspired by her
response, he continued to taunt her with his fingertips
and lips until a shuddering climax rocked her very soul.

The pleasure was so intense it was nearly pain and as it
uncoiled through her core and swept down her legs, Jonathan moved over her to claim her for his own. He slid
on her own slippery wetness and entered her slowly, with
shallow teasing thrusts. With every dip and withdrawal he
created within her a deep, throbbing ache for still more.

Lost in him, Eliza clutched his shoulders as he made a
final, deep plunge that tore through the last barrier between them, and with a blinding ecstasy, overwhelmed the
pain that threatened to slice her in two. Much later she
was only dimly aware that she had felt his bliss as deeply
as her own. Too content to move, she fell asleep in his
arms.

The pearl-gray light of dawn had barely begun to fill the
room when a tear slipped from Jonathan's eyes and
splashed on Eliza's bare breast. Startled awake, she raised
herself slightly, but found her lover still sound asleep. She

adored him and thought him heartbreakingly handsome, even with a slight growth of beard shadowing his cheeks.

She lay silently observing another tear trickle slowly down his face and came to the sad realization that no matter what they might have shared, in his dreams he still wept for the family he'd lost. He was her first love, but she would never hold the same sacred place in his heart.

Suddenly feeling very sad and alone, she kissed his damp cheek and tasted the salty tears. She carefully eased herself out of his bed so as not to wake him, then hurriedly slipped her nightgown over her head and grabbed her shawl from the floor as she ran from his room downstairs to the silent sanctuary of her own.

Part Two

Chapter Nine

Lamar pulled back the lace curtains and looked down on the dusty street three stories below where a fistfight was quickly drawing a rowdy crowd. He owned the building located southwest of Fort Worth in a colorful collection of saloons and brothels known as Hell's Half Acre. Everyone still referred to the place as the Rosedale Hotel, but it had been a bordello for years and next to whiskey, was Lamar's most profitable enterprise.

Flossie Mae Kemble was seated at the vanity brushing out her light brown hair. She used a liberal application of lemon juice to create a frame of golden highlights around her face but she still envied Lamar his fair curls and wished her hair weren't as straight as her corset laces.

She was the madam of this proud establishment and slept only with Lamar. She didn't usually see him this early on a Monday, but she knew him too well to miss the fatigue shadowing his eyes, and concluded he'd had a lousy weekend.

"Something's wrong," she observed. "Is Delia having a

difficult time, or is there a problem with business?"

"Neither," Lamar replied absently. The fight had been won by the stockier of the pair brawling below, and after satisfying himself that the crowd was moving on without interfering with the men visiting the hotel, he adjusted the curtains and stepped back from the window.

In his shirtsleeves, he began to pace the rose-patterned carpet with a long, even stride. "One of Lawrence's friends from the war is paying us an extended visit."

Flossie set her brush aside and turned from her mirror. She was wearing only a sheer chemise whose neckline dipped so low over her ample breasts a hint of dark nipple showed clearly above the lace trim. "And you're not pleased?"

Lamar snorted derisively. "I despise the bastard."

"Lawrence must not feel the same way." She had never met Lamar's younger brother, but he spoke of Lawrence so often she felt as though they were well acquainted. In fact, Lamar had related so many intimate details of his home and family that she could clearly envision the whole clan seated around the dinner table each night. She expected to join them herself after Delia died.

Lamar turned on his heel and continued his restless pacing. "Unfortunately, Lawrence is completely taken with him; but he's common, Flossie Mae. He's just some mixed-blood Cherokee who should have had the sense to stay put in the Indian territory."

"My goodness." Flossie endeavored to affect a refined manner, but hated to hear Lamar describe anyone as common when the term could so easily be applied to her as well. "You really don't like him much, do you?"

Lamar snarled, "It sickens me to have him in the house."

"Then send him here. I'll have the girls entertain him so thoroughly that he'll forget Lawrence even exists, let alone recall where your ranch is."

Lamar swore under his breath. "A half-dozen girls

would probably run off with him, and then where would we be?"

"Is he that remarkably good-looking?" Flossie asked, her curiosity piqued.

Lamar fixed Flossie with an evil stare. "Is the devil himself handsome?"

Flossie laughed and again picked up the silver-handled hairbrush Lamar had given her for her twenty-seventh birthday. "Satan must be as beautiful as a god, or so many of us wouldn't have been lured from the righteous path. I hate to see you so distressed though. Is this troublesome visitor staying long?"

"He lost a race to Fletcher on Saturday, so he's hanging around for a rematch. That's bad enough, but he has some absurd notion that Lawrence suffers from neglect. I've always looked out for my kid brother's best interests, and I don't appreciate Jonathan's meddling one bit."

Flossie Mae studied Lamar's troubled expression more closely. He was a man of few layers, and while he usually presented a charming façade, his true thoughts were often devious at best. Today she caught a glimpse of a deeper dilemma than he was apparently prepared to admit. It was unlike him not to fling his troubles at her feet and demand her reassurance that he would prevail. The uncharacteristic change in his behavior troubled her.

"This Jonathan knows something, doesn't he?" she asked perceptively.

Lamar halted in mid-stride. "What could he know?"

Flossie had once been an innocent young widow who'd trusted every man to be as kind as her late husband. Quickly betrayed, she'd learned how to survive with her wits as well as her voluptuous body, which was why she was the madam at the Rosedale rather than one of the whores. Lamar might not be lying, but he was definitely withholding an important piece of information, and it was most likely a secret that showed him in an unflattering light.

She hadn't meant to alarm him with her insight. She

smiled seductively and lowered her voice to an enticing purr. "I've no idea, but I've never seen you so agitated, my love. Why don't you come back to bed and tell me about it later?"

Stubbornly ignoring her invitation, Lamar clamped his jaws shut. "There's nothing more to tell. The man's a bad influence on Lawrence, and I can't wait for him to be gone."

"Then perhaps you ought to send Lawrence here, and we'll keep him entertained until his guest leaves."

"Now there's an idea." Lamar laughed in spite of the darkness of his mood, and his whole expression brightened. "There was a time when Lawrence could have had any woman he wanted, but now, well, as I've said, he's little better than an invalid."

Flossie leaned forward slightly, and her chemise slipped off her shoulders, wantonly exposing her generous curves. "If he's still breathing, he can be pleased."

Lamar's hungry glance slid over her, and swiftly falling prey to her allure, he reached her in a single stride. He dropped to his knees between her legs, licked her exposed breasts, and moaned way back in his throat. "I'll never have enough of you. Each day may be Delia's last, and then I'll have you in my bed every night."

He began to suckle so hard Flossie's nipple became tender, but she stroked his hair lightly as though she loved his mock nursing. "After a suitable period of mourning, I assume?"

Lamar switched his adoring attentions to her other breast. "Hmm. I do so want you to appear respectable." He slid his hand under her chemise to stroke her pale white thighs, and then hurriedly sought her moist cleft. "My goddess," he murmured, and dipped his fingers into her.

Flossie Mae leaned back to rest her elbows on the vanity. She tilted her hips upward and spread her thighs obligingly. "Oh, Lamar," she said, sighing appreciatively. "That feels heavenly."

She had him convinced he was the best lover she'd ever had. While she was genuinely fond of him, in truth, she was completely indifferent to his touch. A man of his immense pride was easy to fool, and after she offered a few throaty moans, he rose to carry her over to the brass bed and sated his desires as quickly as he had less than an hour earlier.

When he rolled away from her this time, Flossie Mae remained in bed and watched him dress with an admiring gaze. His well-tailored suits cloaked him in respectability, and she longed for the day when she would share his family's prestige as his wife. Savoring the thought, she raised her arms above her head for a lazy stretch.

"Although I can't solve your current problem," she murmured in a satisfied whisper. "I do hope I've eased its pain."

Lamar laughed with her as he gave his coat sleeves a tug to improve the fit. "Indeed you have." He leaned over to kiss her, and as he straightened, his expression grew thoughtful.

"Perhaps I was too hasty to dismiss your suggestion. If Lawrence were suddenly presented with a delicious distraction, he'd have far less time to spend with Jonathan."

Pleased that he'd liked her idea, Flossie Mae sat up and plumped a pillow to serve as a backrest. "Which of the girls did you have in mind?"

"We boast that the Rosedale has the most beautiful women in Fort Worth, or the whole state of Texas for that matter, but you're the only one I'd trust with Lawrence."

Stunned by his totally unexpected choice, Flossie Mae leaned forward to hug her bent knees. "Oh no. You can't possibly be serious."

"Of course, I am," Lamar assured her. "After all, you're the only one I can count on to do precisely what I ask rather than take advantage of my brother. You'll sleep with him a few times, convince him he can satisfy any woman he meets, and then encourage him to court the daughter of one of Fort Worth's other fine families." Obviously pleased with the proposition, Lamar slid his hands into his trouser pockets and rocked back on his heels.

Flossie Mae was furious and opened her mouth to point out the glaring flaw in his plan, but then with a sickening chill she recognized his promise of marriage for the clever lie it had been. If he had ever had any intention of marrying her, then he would never ask her to sleep with Lawrence when the three of them would eventually share the same house.

She wanted to scream the ugly names that would make it clear what she thought of him and hurt him as badly as he had just hurt her. Had she had a knife handy, she would have sprung from her bed to lunge for his throat, but she kept no weapons of any kind in her room. Wanting him gone, she relied upon fierce self-control to keep the bitterness of her reaction to herself and pulled the sheet up over her now-swollen breasts.

"When should I expect Lawrence to arrive?" she asked with a calculated calm.

"I can't send him here," Lamar countered sarcastically. He frowned slightly as he considered his options. "There's a millinery shop in one of our buildings downtown. I'll ask Lawrence to collect the rent due this week. Only instead of Madame Leroux, he'll find you. I trust you'll know how to take it from there."

Flossie had prided herself on being adept at hiding her emotions, but Lamar had just handed her such a cruel disappointment she could barely conceal her dismay. "I'm to be Madame Leroux?" she asked numbly.

"Yes. She's a sweet little widow, perhaps fifty years old, who will surely be delighted to cooperate when I offer to reduce her next month's rent in exchange for the use of her shop for a few afternoons."

Lamar was elated by his cleverness and grinning widely, but Flossie Mae had seldom felt worse. Rather than being openly belligerent, she became deliberately obtuse. "I'm afraid I simply don't follow your plan."

Lamar began to pace again, but this time his step was

light rather than plodding. "It will be a simple ruse, my dearest. Be charming. Invite Lawrence into your living quarters in the rear of the shop for tea. He'll accept, and as I said, I trust you to protect his feelings while at the same time renewing his faith in himself as a man. Then you can claim undying love for your late husband and suggest he court some fresh ingenue. You might even shed a few tears as you bid him *adieu*. He's such a trusting soul, he'll never question your motives."

Flossie Mae waited for Lamar to explain just how he planned to introduce her later as his future bride, but he simply smiled as though he had already covered all the pertinent details. She sighed softly as she accepted the dreary fact that to his mind, he had.

"Whatever you wish, Lamar," she promised as she had so often in the past simply to get rid of him. "Just make certain I know when I'm to play the part of Madame Leroux so Lawrence will be certain to find me at her shop."

Relieved to have the matter settled, Lamar brushed her cheek with a fleeting kiss. "I'll send a note as soon as it's arranged." He headed for the door, then paused before leaving. "Better keep a closer eye on Agnes. I think she's giving out free samples to that long-legged boyfriend of hers, and I don't want her doing it during business hours."

"Consider it done," Flossie replied.

Lamar closed the door behind him, and she got up quickly to lock it, then returned to bed. She wondered how long it would take him to realize just how much his pathetic plan had revealed. Perhaps everything he had ever told her was a lie, and Delia was in the best of health rather than frail.

"Lying bastard," she hissed. If her husband hadn't been such a fine man, she would swear all men were swine, but Jason Kemble had been truly good. She released a weary sigh and glanced around the room. The walls were as deep a crimson as her shame, and as her pride overcame her studied indifference, she wept bitter tears for the beautiful dream that would never come true.

She would have made such a good wife for Lamar, and he would have provided a lovely home for her. She had expected to give him more children and had names picked out for the dear little babes who had now lost the chance to be born. Devastated, she cried herself to sleep, and when she awakened, it was nearly noon. She shoved her hair out of her eyes, and refusing to lie in bed all day like some poor little girl who'd lost her first boyfriend, got up.

She always kept her room neat, and as she hurriedly made up her bed, she supposed she should thank Lamar for providing a vivid reminder of how little a woman could trust a man; but she was far too resentful to be grateful for such an unwanted lesson.

"Unless—" she murmured to herself as the spark of an idea glowed ever more brightly in her mind. Unwittingly, Lamar had just taught her that she'd been a fool to trust him, but she could turn the same trick right back on him. Lawrence might have been badly injured in the war, but as Lamar's younger brother, he couldn't possibly be totally unappealing.

Lamar had asked her to seduce him, then send him into the arms of another woman, but why shouldn't she keep Lawrence for herself? They could marry before Lamar even knew he had been double-crossed, and he'd never dare reveal that his original plan had been to denounce her.

Inspired, Flossie Mae flung open the doors to her wardrobe and began to sort through the garish gowns her profession required, searching for the one black garment she'd worn when newly widowed. It was shoved to the back, and she removed it quickly, and carried it to the window to have better light.

The dress was adorably quaint, and knowing Lawrence well from Lamar's description, she was positive if she affected the proper combination of ladylike poise and touching vulnerability, he'd never question her sincerity when she invited him into Madame Leroux's bed. Holding the somber gown in front of her, she waltzed in a slow circle before pausing in front of her vanity mirror.

She had longed to become Mrs. Bendalin, and she practiced Lawrence's name in a tender sigh. She vowed to pull off Lamar's ruse better than he had ever dreamed, and rejoice when she became Lamar's devoted sister-in-law rather than his second wife. Maybe she'd even become Delia's best friend when they all lived together on the Trinity Star Ranch.

Somehow she doubted Lamar would approve of her marriage, but he wouldn't be able to do a damn thing about it without breaking both his wife's and brother's hearts. All that remained of her own heart were fragmented bits the size of confetti, and they'd been tossed in the air so often, they'd probably disappear in the next breeze.

Monday found Jonathan as restless as he'd been on Sunday when after such an incredible night, he'd not expected to wake up alone. He'd gotten up and hurriedly rinsed the evidence of Eliza's lost innocence from the bedclothes. He'd then shaved, dressed, and gone tearing down the stairs only to find Eliza Kate had already gone into town to attend church with her father and brothers. Unable to bear the thought of facing a Sunday dinner where he'd have to make polite conversation for Delia's benefit without once winking at Eliza Kate, he'd made his excuses to Lawrence and had gone out searching for Kiowa.

Now he'd been gone a day and hadn't found any sign of the band who'd stopped at the river. Maybe they'd split up and gone their separate ways, but there didn't appear to be any looming threat of trouble from renegades.

That left him free to contemplate what trouble he might be in with Eliza Kate. Perhaps she'd left his bed because she feared he'd not be discreet, but he knew how to protect a lady's reputation as well as her feelings. Hell, he'd meet her wherever she wanted, down by the river or out in the barn. He didn't care what place she chose, but he was a long way from finished with her, and he sure hoped she didn't think she was through with him because it would cost him a lot of valuable time to prove her wrong.

When he finally returned to the house, he left Red Warrior in the corral, where he was now positive the stallion wouldn't be entertaining company. He carried his gear upstairs and then leaned out the window to get the best view he could of the garden. He was hoping to locate Eliza Kate out there somewhere, and when he spotted a touch of gray, he hoped it was her riding skirt. He'd dress for dinner later, but for now, he just washed up, put on a clean shirt, and went on outside.

Eliza was curled up on the bench near the grape arbor, the book of Shakespeare's sonnets Fletcher had given her mother unopened in her lap. Too distracted to read or even think clearly, she was struggling mightily to focus on the single cloud in the sky. When someone approached whistling a happy tune, she expected Ricky and was amazed to find Jonathan coming down the path. Elated, and at the same time embarrassed to care so deeply, she swung her feet off the bench to make room for him.

He looked tired, but when he tipped his hat and eased himself down beside her, she thought he'd never been more handsome. She had difficulty catching her breath and managed only a few hushed words. "I was hoping you'd come back," she greeted him softly.

Jonathan shot her an incredulous glance. "Thank you, ma'am, but was there any real doubt in your mind?"

Terror was the correct word, a gnawing terror that had left her feeling flayed, but still alive. Eliza was loath to admit that, however. "Some," she dismissed with a slight shrug.

"I needed to get away," Jonathan explained truthfully, but the resulting hurt in her eyes made him instantly sorry. "I'm not blaming you for leaving my bed without waking me, but I'm a real light sleeper, so it was obvious you left my room as quietly as you could. You needn't have worried. I'll not tell anyone we were together."

"It never occurred to me that you would," Eliza Kate assured him. "It's not the type of thing a gentleman announces."

Jonathan thought better of mentioning he'd not have had to announce anything if the girls who cleaned the house had seen his bed. He'd not embarrass her by mentioning it, however. "Are you stretching the word *gentleman* to cover me?"

Eliza had to look away. A crow sat atop a nearby trellis, his head tilted as though he were straining to follow their conversation. "I don't believe there are any words to describe you," she responded with a slight catch in her voice. She'd relived every second of Saturday night a thousand times in her mind. It always left her breathless; but his tears on Sunday morning would haunt her forever.

Her tone had been too wistfully complimentary for Jonathan to take offense, but he could tell something was very wrong. He wished she'd come running to him and thrown herself in his arms, but clearly she wasn't ready for any spontaneous displays of affection. As long as she was loving when they were alone together, he'd not complain.

There was no one around, but he still took the precaution of lowering his voice. "I know I hurt you, and I'm sorry. I promise it will be better for you the next time."

Eliza Kate was stunned by that vow, for if making love with him got any better, she'd simply die and float right up to heaven—if she'd still be eligible for heaven after what they'd done. She'd always been so responsible, such a sensible person. Ricky was the one who caused all the trouble, while her behavior had always been above reproach. At least it had been until Saturday night, but strangely, she didn't feel a bit of shame. Her only worry was losing him.

"I don't need any promises," she replied after a long delay.

"Sure you do," Jonathan advised.

Eliza just shook her head, sending her thick curls flying. She'd strayed so far from the comfortable path her life had always taken, and she still felt as though she were falling from an incredible height. It was the same eerie sensation that had made her feet tingle when she'd sat in the Hanging Tree. She wanted to grab Jonathan and hold on tight, but that would only be pathetic, so she gripped the book of sonnets and let her heart glide toward the unforgiving ground.

"If people see us out here together too often," she cautioned, "they're going to get suspicious. One of us ought to go inside."

Jonathan had been whistling happily a few minutes ago, but there wasn't a trace of good humor in his face now. "I didn't have to come back, Eliza Kate."

"Yes, I know." From her place across the table, she had studied every nuance of his expression as he talked with her family, but somehow whenever he looked her way, everything changed. She didn't want him ever to leave her again, but she couldn't share that heartfelt desire when he'd vowed not to remarry.

Eliza was so withdrawn, Jonathan scarcely recognized her, and he came to the most obvious conclusion. "Does my Indian blood bother you?"

"No, not at all," Eliza promptly assured him. "I wish you'd grow that glossy black hair of yours clear to your waist and lace it with eagle feathers."

She'd spoken the astonishing request so fervently, Jonathan didn't doubt her sincerity, and he slid his hand over hers. "That's quite an image, but I told you the Cherokee are one of the civilized tribes, and our men don't generally sport manes longer than our horses'."

"Of course, if that's what you want, I'll give it my best effort, but I want to be with you again long before my hair grows out. Just tell me what you want me to do, and I'll gladly do it. I'll come to your room tonight, or you can come to mine again if you'd rather."

Eliza considered the options, and certain her own bed

would become unbearably lonely if he were ever to share it, she quickly made her choice, and then rose on unsteady legs. "I'll come to you," she promised softly, and she left him to enjoy the beauty of the garden all alone.

Chapter Ten

Eliza Kate moved through the rest of the afternoon in a dreamlike fog. Before Jonathan Blair had sent her life careening wildly out of control, she'd spent her days efficiently checking off chores and then confidently pushing on to the next. Now she could scarcely place one foot in front of the other without forgetting where she was bound.

She had spent years maintaining order. Although she may have done it splendidly, why had it never occurred to her that making time for love was infinitely more important? she wondered. Why had she not even suspected what treasures love might bring? The answer to the second question was obvious even in her befuddled state: she'd not known Jonathan Blair.

Now she sat impatiently waiting for her beautifully managed home to fill with a contented silence so that she might dash up the stairs to Jonathan's room. Of course, she couldn't actually run up to the third floor with such unladylike haste. She would have to glide slowly through the shadows and arrive at his door with an admirable display of calm. As though she had every right to be there, as though she belonged with him wherever he might be.

She cherished their romance with all her heart, but still recognized it for the ephemeral dream it was. "I'll not forget you, Jonathan," she promised in an anguished sigh, "for it would be forgetting my very soul."

She shut away the eventual pain as quietly as she closed her bedroom door. Then with a deep breath, she went up the stairs. When she reached the third-floor landing, she saw Jonathan had left his door slightly ajar, perhaps to light her way with his lamp, or perhaps, she dared hope, because he was as anxious to see her as she was to see him. Nearly floating on that joyous prospect, she rapped lightly at his door and peered inside.

The guest room had become a cage to Jonathan, and he turned away from his window where he'd feared the sun would arrive before Eliza Kate. He wanted to scold her for making him wait, and an enraged cry was already traveling up his throat, but she was regarding him with a tender gaze rather than petulant defiance, and his anger dissolved instantly.

Whenever they were apart, he carried her memory like a talisman, but each time they were reunited, he was shocked by how much he had missed her. Filled with an instinctive need to protect her, he quickly crossed the distance between them, dropped his arm around her shoulders and pulled her into a fond embrace as he closed and locked the door.

Longing to hold her, he rested his chin atop her flowing curls and drank in her perfume. "You smell like gardenias tonight."

Eliza Kate nuzzled against his bare chest. He smelled of their soap, which Delia scented with cloves, but it was the solid, muscular feel of him that thrilled her so deeply. Like the tendrils of a tenacious vine, the bond between them was coiling itself ever more tightly around her heart. It was a strange sensation and more than a little frightening.

"Eliza Kate?" He felt her whole body tremble, swung her up into his arms, and carried her not to the bed, but to the comfortable wing chair near the window.

He cuddled her in his lap and wished he had a gift for the pretty speeches he knew women loved. Tragically, he'd learned just how impossible it was to keep loving promises when he'd failed to protect his family from harm. He drew in a ragged breath to suppress those awful memories before their sorrow touched Eliza Kate.

He hadn't forgotten who she was or the life she'd been raised to lead, but for him, there was the hope of another night with her, and he was far too grateful to complain or curse the future they'd never share. Then she raised her hand to his face, and her gentle caress erased all his cares.

He had just wanted to touch her, but with that first tentative gesture, the curl wrapped around his finger on a starry night, he'd been lost in desire. He dipped his head to meet her kiss and prayed the night would never end.

Tuesday morning, Lawrence agreed to collect the rent from Madame Leroux, but because Lamar was in town every day, and he rather seldom, he hadn't been particularly gracious about it. Preoccupied, he walked right by the millinery shop without realizing it. Disgusted his inattention had cost him several extra steps, he turned back before he had strayed too far.

At the entrance, half a dozen brass bells sewn to a green velvet ribbon created a musical trill to announce his arrival, and startled, he took care to close the door without initiating another jangling chorus. He succeeded in that, but then the sweetly scented air of the elegant shop teased his senses with half-forgotten memories of exotic perfumes. Surrounded by bolts of silk, lace, and bright ribbons, he felt as out of place as he would have in an elegant lady's boudoir.

He caught a glimpse of himself in the full-length mirror standing in the corner, and not pleased by the reflection of his pale, thin face, he quickly turned away. He then noticed a pretty young woman observing him from behind a counter stacked with wide-brimmed straw hats. Eager to conclude his errand, he removed his hat and greeted her with a nervous smile.

"Good morning. Will you please summon Madame Leroux? Tell her Mr. Bendalin is here. I believe she has something for me."

Flossie Mae Kemble's appraising glance lingered over Lawrence a moment longer than was politely permissible. Very pleased with what she saw, she smiled brightly as she came forward to welcome him. "I'm Mrs. Leroux," she confided in a soft, ladylike tone.

"I chose to refer to myself as Madame when I opened this shop. It's a foolish affectation, I know, but because French designers are more highly regarded than our own, it's proved good for business. I'd rather you called me Mae."

Because Lamar had described Madame Leroux as a widow, Lawrence had assumed she would be a much older woman. This stunning creature was clothed in black, however, and he was embarrassed not to have recognized her from her manner of dress, but he was by no means disappointed to find her so youthful and attractive.

"We needn't be so informal simply because I'm the landlord, and you're the tenant," he argued.

Lawrence was actually blushing, and Flossie Mae was delighted he was such a shy young man; it would make endearing herself to him ever so much easier. She approached him with a gentle sway. "Please forgive me if I've insulted you, Mr. Bendalin, but I'm so thankful to be doing business in such a beautiful shop that I like to consider the Bendalin brothers my partners."

A slight smile played across Lawrence's lips. "Really? Well, now, Madame—Mrs. Leroux, that is—I'm sure we're both pleased that you feel at home here."

Flossie Mae moved closer still. "Oh, indeed, I do." She slipped her arm through his and although she felt him flinch slightly, she held on. "Won't you come to my desk with me? I have your check ready."

Lawrence braced himself. He could not even recall when he had last been this close to a woman other than Delia or Eliza Kate. Pressed against his side, Mae Leroux felt very soft and curvaceous, and her perfume was so utterly delicious it was making him dizzy. Entranced by her, he needed a moment to recall just what she had suggested.

"You'll have to lead the way," he insisted, "or I'll just trip over your skirt, and I would hate to cause us both a painful fall."

Flossie Mae gave his arm a slight squeeze before stepping away. "Why, Mr. Bendalin, I doubt you are ever clumsy."

Thinking she must not have observed him walk in, Lawrence hated to disillusion her. He struggled to find words that would merely inform rather than invoke pity. "I was injured in the war and limp rather badly."

Playing her part to perfection, Flossie Mae raised her brows in a show of concern. "I had no idea. Now I must insist that you come and sit down for a moment before you go on your way." Confident he would follow, she turned and walked toward the green velvet curtain that separated the front of the shop from the workroom.

Lawrence took a deep breath and forcing himself to move slowly, walked as smoothly as he possibly could. He stepped through the curtain and nodded toward the two seamstresses who were busy fashioning elaborate satin bonnets. He looked around, expecting to find Mrs. Leroux's desk nearby, but she gestured for him to follow her through the door into her living quarters.

Lawrence hesitated slightly, but after recalling that he and Lamar owned the building and that he had every right to be there, he again pursued the fetching Mae Leroux. The widow's modest furnishings had been arranged to create a sitting room in front and a bedroom at the rear of the apartment's single room, but he still felt as though he were intruding upon her privacy. Wanting to be proper, he left the door to the workroom ajar.

"It looks as though your business is thriving," he blurted, then silently cursed his own lack of originality.

"Which is good for us both, isn't it?" Flossie Mae replied with a charming laugh. She again reached for his arm.

"Now come and sit down here at my desk. May I offer you a cup of tea?"

Lawrence doubted he could swallow a drop without spilling the rest down the front of his suit. He took the straight-backed chair she indicated, but nothing more. "Thank you. I haven't the time today."

Flossie Mae made herself comfortable at the desk and continued to regard Lawrence with a fond gaze. His eyes were as clear a blue as Lamar's, and she rather liked the silvery cast to his hair. Even if he were not in robust good health, Lawrence Bendalin was a handsome young man. Best of all, while his suit was expertly tailored, he displayed none of his elder brother's proud swagger.

She raised her hand to her hair and toyed with a strand that had escaped her chignon. "Do you come into town often?" she asked.

Lawrence didn't know what to do with his hat. He didn't want to lay it on her desk, nor did he want to balance it on his knee. Finally he bent and leaned it against his chair leg. "No. I work at home rather than at Lamar's office. I do all our bookkeeping, and quiet surroundings make the necessary concentration much easier."

Flossie Mae licked her lips with a provocative swirl. "Perhaps concentration is what I lack, because I have the most dreadful time balancing my books. The shop truly is doing well, but the more money I make, the more sales there are to record and the more sums there are to calculate. I do my best to tally the receipts at the end of each day, but sometimes I'm simply too tired and fall behind."

She ran her hand over the ledger lying open on her desk. "I love designing hats, and an occasional gown, but it's such a chore to keep my figures in straight columns."

She had very beautiful hands, Lawrence noted. Her fingers were long and slim, and her nails were filed to gentle ovals. Her only jewelry was a thin gold wedding band. Her gestures were filled with grace, and he longed to have her touch him again. That he was so lonely he would daydream about a woman he had just met struck him as deplorable. He straightened his shoulders in an attempt to shake off that additional embarrassment.

"Perhaps I could be of some service in that regard," he offered graciously, hoping he did not sound so dreadfully eager that she would merely be amused.

"Oh, could you?" Flossie replied, her hazel eyes aglow. "I would be ever so grateful. You needn't worry that you'll be wasting your time, because I'll endeavor to implement every procedure you suggest."

It had been a long while since a young woman had regarded him with such open admiration, and Lawrence drank it in for as long as he dared. "Please, you mustn't consider it such a large favor because it is obviously in my best interests to have your shop do well."

Flossie Mae reached out to caress his sleeve. "Of course, it is, Mr. Bendalin. We're partners, remember?"

Lawrence found it nearly impossible to remember anything when her smile was so inviting. "Have you been a widow long?" he asked, and instantly regretted it. "I'm so sorry. I shouldn't have pried into your private life. That was very tactless of me."

Flossie Mae found his embarrassment charming and curled her fingers over his arm. Lamar had been good to her, but his every action was calculated for effect, and Lawrence was almost painfully sincere. She had been prepared to make him like her with whatever means necessary, but she had never expected to find him so appealing.

She could feel his bones beneath the soft wool of his sleeve and wished she had some choice delicacy to feed him. Lacking refreshments, she gave his arm a gentle squeeze before sitting back in her chair.

"I lost my dear husband in 1862 at the Battle of Shiloh."

Eight years ago! Lawrence rejoiced silently, but he struggled to appear sympathetic. "That was tragic, I know. That dreadful war left far too many widows."

"Yes, the women on both sides suffered terribly," Flossie Mae agreed, then quickly lightened the subject. "I hope to make a whole new life here, and this shop has provided a wonderful beginning."

"Indeed it has." Even clothed in an austere gown, she was lovely, Lawrence thought. He assumed the blond highlights at her temples came from the sun, and that the subtle rose tint of her lips was quite natural. Her eyes were filled with such delicate shades of gold, brown, and green that he could have stared into them for hours.

Had he not heard the bells on the front door chime, he might have sat there all morning, but fearing he had already stayed too long, he picked up his hat, grabbed hold of the edge of the desk and hauled himself to his feet. "You've a customer to see, and I should be on my way."

Flossie Mae noted his reluctance to depart and considered their first meeting a tremendous success. She plucked the check the real owner of the shop had written from one of the cubbyholes in the desk and handed it to him as she rose. "You don't want to forget this."

Lawrence slipped the check into his breast pocket. "Thank you, Mrs. Leroux." She'd provided the perfect excuse to return before the next month's rent was due, and he quickly followed up on it. "Now about your bookkeeping," he remarked in an offhand manner. "I could come back into town day after tomorrow. Would that be convenient for you?"

"It would be perfect," Flossie Mae exclaimed. "Most of my customers shop in the morning, so could we make it in the afternoon?"

Lawrence would have agreed to meet her any time she named, but counted to five before he responded to make it appear as though he were thoughtfully considering her request. "Yes. Shall we say around three?"

"Thank you. I'll look forward to it." Flossie Mae led the way out of the private apartment. When she reached the velvet curtain, she drew it back and held it so that Lawrence would precede her out front. Just as he had claimed, he did have a pronounced limp, but she did not find it troubling.

One of the seamstresses was showing the woman who had just entered a bolt of lace, and Flossie Mae hurriedly guided Lawrence by them and bid him good-bye at the door. She then quickly retraced her steps and left the shop by the back door before the customer had caught more than a brief glimpse of her.

As Flossie Mae climbed into the waiting buggy, she was relieved Lamar's ruse had gone so smoothly, but the prospect of seeing Lawrence again in just two days lit her whole face with genuine pleasure.

Jonathan had again accompanied him into town, and Lawrence found him outside a jewelry store admiring the window display. "Think you might buy that gold watch with your winnings from the next race?" he asked. "It's a beauty."

Jonathan had been debating whether to purchase a delicate gold locket for Eliza Kate. He assumed she already owned such beautiful jewelry she might think the pretty heart an insignificant addition to her collection. Then again, she might treasure it always. He was uncertain which was correct, but he'd not share his dilemma with Lawrence.

"That's a thought," he said instead. "Are you ready to head for home?" He was ashamed at how anxious he was to get back to Eliza Kate and glanced down the street as though he were in no rush.

"Yes, I've already been by the bank." Though it nearly killed him, Lawrence waited until they had ridden a ways out of town before he described just how well one of his errands had gone.

"Madame Leroux wasn't what I'd expected," he then revealed. "She's as pretty as her fanciful hats. I sure hope this isn't just wishful thinking, but I believe she liked me too."

"I'm sure she did," Jonathan assured him. "How often can you drop by to collect the rent?"

"Not nearly often enough, I'm afraid, but she mentioned needing help with her bookkeeping, and I told her I'd be delighted to provide it."

Lawrence looked so pleased with himself, Jonathan hoped Madame Leroux wasn't simply trying to get a break on her rent. "It might be a good idea to begin with real basic lessons so you can draw them out over a couple of months."

Lawrence nodded thoughtfully. "I'd not considered doing that, but it's an excellent suggestion. Thank you. I'm dreadfully out of practice when it comes to impressing women, but Mrs. Leroux was so charming that I almost forgot how unattractive I've become."

"As usual, you're being too critical of yourself, Lawrence. None of us looks as good as we did ten years ago, but I sure hope we're a hell of a lot smarter."

"I'll grant you I've learned a thing or two, but I can't carry a glass of water more than two steps without spilling it. Do you suppose Mae loves to dance?"

"Oh, so now it's Mae, is it?" Jonathan couldn't help chuckling. "That's a pretty name, but let's hope she'd prefer to just listen to music. Has she been a widow long?"

"Eight years! Isn't that wonderful? Oh, I don't mean it's wonderful that Mr. Leroux died so young, but that's got to be enough time for her to have gotten over him, don't you think?"

"For your sake, I certainly hope so."

"Yes, so do I, but I'll tell you something, Jonathan. When she spoke to me, she reached out to touch me. She did it more than once too. Perhaps she really misses having a man around."

Jonathan raised his hand. "Stop right there. It never pays to try to analyze a woman's actions. You'll only end up more confused than you were to begin with. Just believe that if she touched you, it was because she liked you. Don't try to make things more complicated than that.

Now tell me something more about Mae Leroux. What does she look like?"

Lawrence hummed a few bars of a favorite tune. "Maybe if I took it real slow, I could learn to dance again." He did not want his hopes soaring too high, however, and quickly roped them in. "Mae's petite, probably not more than five feet one or two, and she's as delicate as an angel."

Jonathan moaned. "Please, no more. I can't stand it."

"I sound really stupid, don't I?"

Jonathan thought of how he'd describe Eliza Kate, and knowing he'd sound just as daft, shook his head. "No. You don't sound stupid at all. *Smitten* is the word, and I'm real happy for you."

Lawrence's smile spread wide. "It's been so long since I felt anything for a woman, I didn't actually believe I even could. God, I hope her bookkeeping is absolutely awful!"

Jonathan laughed with his friend, but he dared not confess how recently he'd made a similar discovery about himself.

Delia had brought a pillowcase to embroider out to the garden, but rather than concentrate on her stitches, she found herself studying her daughter. Eliza Kate had a marvelously expressive face, and it was so easy to see she was troubled. Delia couldn't help wondering why.

"You look rather sad, my darling. Has Fletcher been neglecting you?" she asked.

"Fletcher?" Eliza Kate shrugged, for truly she'd not thought of him in days. "No, not at all. We were together last Friday and Saturday, and I expect I'll see him again soon."

When Eliza Kate quickly looked away, Delia understood how little interest her daughter had in her suitor. "My memory may have become hazy lately, but that doesn't mean I can't still think." She ran her needle through the fine linen to anchor it and set the pillowcase aside.

"You're becoming increasingly distracted, and there's

only one charming distraction here at the ranch," Delia suggested softly. "I've noticed Jonathan glances your way rather often when we're all together for meals. Have you been able to spend any time alone with him?"

Eliza Kate blushed all the way to the roots of her hair. She didn't want to lie to her mother, but she couldn't bring herself to confide how wanton her behavior had become either. "I suppose on a few occasions we may have been here in the garden together," she admitted hesitantly.

"Is he attentive then, or merely interested in talking about himself?" Delia inquired.

Attentive wasn't nearly strong enough a word to describe Jonathan's behavior, but Eliza refused to share how generous he was with his affection. Instead, she murmured what bothered her most. "He'll be gone soon."

Eliza Kate appeared to be on the verge of tears, and Delia had the answer she'd been seeking. "I thought you might care for him, and I see that you do. Perhaps he'd stay forever if you asked him to."

"I shouldn't have to ask," Eliza Kate replied. "Besides, you may not recall that he's a widower, but he told Lawrence he'd not remarry. I'd rather have him gone than here if we could never be husband and wife."

There were days when Delia felt as though she were merely floating on the edge of her family, but today, the situation was almost painfully clear. Her stomach tightened with a familiar ache she knew her daughter must also feel.

"Men do change their minds," she advised thoughtfully. "You're a resourceful young woman, and if Jonathan is the man you want, then I'm sure you'll find a way to convince him that you're his heart's desire."

Eliza tried to smile, but she had no real hope such a miracle would ever occur. There were also Fletcher's feelings to consider. The next time they were together, she'd have to tell him she'd changed her mind about becoming his wife. It made her sick to think of how devastated he'd be, but it would be worse to allow him to believe she still planned to marry him.

"The spring weather has been lovely," she remarked absently.

"Hasn't it though?" Delia agreed, but she was deeply concerned for her daughter, and rather than review old love letters that night, she confided in her husband.

Lamar had been brushing Delia's hair, but when she mentioned Eliza Kate and Jonathan Blair in the same sentence, the brush flew right out of his hand. He leaned over as much to hide his dismay as to retrieve it. "Perhaps she finds him an amusing guest, but she and Fletcher are as good as engaged," he argued.

"That may be Fletcher's belief, but Eliza Kate seems to have changed her mind. Jonathan's such a handsome man. They'd make very beautiful children together, don't you think?"

Lamar never swore in front of his wife, but he had never been so sorely tempted either. He gathered her long silken hair in a firm grip and brushed the ends over his fist. "His looks aren't really the issue, my dearest. Eliza Kate deserves a husband who can provide the finer things in life, the things I've worked so hard to give you. Please don't encourage our daughter to consider such an unsuitable match.

"As far as we know, Jonathan still intends to make his home in California. Don't you want your grandchildren born here where we can love them?" he asked.

Delia took the brush from her husband and laid it on the vanity. "I'd not thought about the grandbabies," she admitted, "but you're right, of course. I don't want Eliza Kate to go away."

Lamar forced a smile, helped her into bed, and kissed her good night before turning down the lamp. "You leave everything to me, Delia, dear. I'll see you in the morning."

Lamar held his temper only long enough to close Delia's door, and then he went straight to Eliza Kate's room rather than his own. He didn't knock lightly either; he beat on her door as though the house were in flames.

Eliza Kate yanked open her door and nearly tripped over her nightgown when her father shoved her aside to storm into the room. She quickly closed the door behind him, and fearing the worst, spoke in a hoarse whisper. "What's happened? Mother seemed fine half an hour ago."

Lamar's glance darted around Eliza Kate's room, seeking damning evidence that Delia was right about their daughter's feelings for Jonathan. Nothing was amiss, however. The spacious room held only his daughter's belongings, and the only scent was her perfume. He'd not really expected to find a pair of Jonathan's pants hanging over the back of a chair, but still, he was worried.

He turned back toward Eliza Kate, his eyes narrowed and cold. "Your mother is resting quietly, thank God, but I sincerely doubt I will. I want you to understand I'll always be grateful to Jonathan for saving my brother's life, but I'll be damned if I'll accept him as a son-in-law. Is that clear, Eliza Kate?"

"Has he asked for my hand?" she asked, gasping.

A look of pure joy spread over her face as she took a step toward him, but filled with revulsion, Lamar just as quickly moved back. He could not even imagine a worse happenstance, but clearly she was thrilled by a prospect that sickened him through and through.

"No, he has not, and if he were ever to make such an outrageous request, I'd refuse him. This is Lawrence's home as well as mine, or Blair would not even be here. Obviously it was a mistake to schedule a second race, as we'd all be better off if he'd left for California last Saturday."

Her hopes dashed to brittle bits, Eliza Kate fought to hide what she feared she'd already revealed. "It's been plain you don't like him since the day he arrived. What happened between you two?"

Lamar glared at her. "Nothing that isn't better left forgotten, but that doesn't change the simple fact that he'd be no fit husband for you. Now I'll lock you in your room if I must, but you'll not so much as smile at the man ever again. Is that understood?"

"Yes," Eliza replied meekly, but she had absolutely no intention of obeying.

"Good. I'll not mention this sorry episode to Fletcher, and I'll trust you to know where your affections should lie."

Eliza Kate bowed her head. "Yes, Father."

Believing the matter settled, Lamar left her bedroom without wishing her a good night, but Eliza Kate was so relieved he hadn't guessed how far her friendship with Jonathan had actually progressed that she wasn't insulted by the oversight. She simply vowed not to drop her guard and allow her feelings to show, no matter what the future provocation.

She might not be nearly as resourceful as her mother believed when it came to changing Jonathan's plans for the future, but she could at least protect them both from her father's wrath better than she had that day. As a precaution, she waited even longer that night before rumpling her bed and sneaking upstairs to Jonathan's room, but she didn't reveal her father's suspicions. It would only sound as though she were begging for the proposal he had no wish to make. Wrapped in Jonathan's loving embrace, it was merely another secret, and like her deepening love for him, one she dared not share.

Her passion that night was filled with an almost palpable fear, but his response was just as desperately hungry. For a few brief hours they created a world from a single room where their contented sighs echoed until the threat of dawn.

Eliza brushed Jonathan's lips with a last frantic kiss before donning her nightgown. "Ride with me to the river?" she asked.

"You know I don't want you going anywhere alone," Jonathan responded.

Eliza nodded and took the back stairs down to the first

floor. She then walked down the hall to the main staircase
and went up. She saw no one, but she could have offered
half a dozen excuses for being downstairs and none for
being on the floor Jonathan occupied. She feared it must
surely be madness to want him as she did, but to avoid
him as her father had insisted would have been intolera-
ble.

She crawled into bed, and already missing Jonathan,
refused to cry. These days she spent with him would surely
be the best of her life, and she clung to her joy as though
that truth were all that mattered. When a few minutes
later her father opened her door and peeked in, she pretended to be asleep, but she was shocked by how narrowly
she'd escaped disaster.

Chapter Eleven

Jonathan and Eliza Kate left Red Warrior and Patches to
graze near the river while they sought the shade of the
mesquite thicket. Jonathan sat behind Eliza Kate, removed
her hat and scarf, and pulled her back against his chest,
where she fit very comfortably between his outstretched
legs. He could have sat there all day enjoying the feel of
her supple young body pressed close to his while he allowed her to innocently believe he was merely admiring
the river. She wasn't nearly so relaxed, however, and as
difficult to hold as a sack of puppies.

"You're as jumpy as the night we were trapped behind
the sofa," he observed with a chuckle. "Are you worried
Ricky might show up here?"

"No. He's usually not up this early." Eliza looped her
arms around Jonathan's thighs. There were so many paths
of conversation she wished to explore, and yet each one
led straight into the same disheartening labyrinth. The
past belonged to his wife and son, and there was no point

speculating on a future they'd not share. She ran a numbing variety of questions through her mind, but there was no way she could demand answers without revealing the depths of her hopeless longing, and she was much too proud for that.

"Eliza Kate?" Jonathan leaned forward to nuzzle her ear. "Talk to me."

Having given up all hope of discussing anything of any importance, she replied with a softly voiced complaint, "Words just get in our way."

Dumbfounded by that comment, Jonathan waited a long moment for her to elaborate, but when she chose not to, he didn't press her. He wouldn't risk provoking an argument on an otherwise perfect morning. Knowing how deeply she cared for Lawrence, he hoped to inspire a conversation about him.

"Lawrence didn't mention meeting Madame Leroux at supper last night. Did he say anything about her to you in private?"

"No. Who is Madame Leroux?" Eliza turned to look up at Jonathan. He responded with a teasing grin that was so handsome it took her breath away. She could only stare at him then and recall how wrong she'd been ever to consider him either cold or distant when there was a warmth to him as dazzling as the noonday sun.

"She owns a millinery shop located in one of the Bendalin buildings," Jonathan explained. "Lawrence is quite taken with her. I was hoping you might have met her and could say she's as nice as Lawrence believes."

Eliza Kate frowned thoughtfully. "I've not heard of her, but then I've not gone into town to shop in quite a while. Perhaps I could pay Madame Leroux's establishment a visit, and then I'd be better able to offer an opinion."

"That's sweet of you, but she'd surely mention meeting you to Lawrence, and I don't want him to believe that we're spying on her. Let's just leave well enough alone. At any rate, I'm relieved he seems to have found his own woman."

"Just as you predicted," Eliza mused aloud.

"Yeah, but I didn't have any real hope of that happening when I said it."

Eliza again adjusted her position to face him squarely. "Really? But you sounded so convincing."

"You caught me, ma'am, 'cause when the occasion demands it, I'm real good at that." Jonathan winked at her, then hugged her close for a near-endless kiss. When he finally drew away, he sighed sadly. "It's getting late. We ought to be heading back for breakfast."

Eliza saw the river's dancing reflection in his openly adoring gaze and realized no matter how it might sound, she had to warn him about her father's suspicions. She ran her hand down his arm and laced her fingers in his. Thinking it best just to get it over with, she rushed along quickly.

"My mother's noticed there's something between us. Apparently she said as much to my father, and he denounced you rather angrily last night. He claims he's grateful you saved Lawrence's life, but that you're no friend of his nor suitable companion for me."

Caught off guard, Jonathan silently cursed the narrowness of his own vision, which had been focused almost exclusively on the beautiful young woman in his arms. Now understanding the cause of her earlier silence, he hurriedly released her, rose to his feet, and then extended his hand to help her up.

"I'm sorry you were subjected to that misery, but no matter how mad Lamar was, it couldn't have had much effect, or you'd not have spent last night in my bed."

Reveling in his bed was how Eliza would have described it, and turning shy, she looked away as she brushed the dust from her riding skirt before donning her scarf and hat. "There appears to be a great deal more going on here than either of you is willing to admit." Of course, there was an enormous amount she wasn't eager to confide either, which made her doubly ashamed.

"Leave it alone, Eliza Kate," Jonathan scolded softly, and he left her to fetch their horses.

Eliza would have told him how early her father had come to her room that morning, but thinking the most likely result would be Jonathan's swift departure, she kept still as he'd ordered and followed him down to the river. They rode back to the house in as uncomfortable a silence as on their first such journey together. Then as they entered the yard, Eliza Kate noticed Fletcher's buggy parked in front of the house.

In that terrible instant, she was positive that despite her father's promise, he'd sent for his partner. "Fletcher's here," she breathed out in an anguished whisper, "I think I'm going to be sick."

"Can't say I blame you when he's always had that same effect on me. I'm going to pass on breakfast this morning. Don't bother giving your caller my regards." He slid down off Red Warrior, and taking the reins in a loose grasp, angled off toward the barn.

Eliza Kate watched him cross the dusty yard with a long, easy stride. The pride in his bearing was unmistakable, and she wished she had even a fraction of his unfailing confidence. At least he hadn't prodded her to break the unfortunate engagement she'd drifted into without a conscious thought. She'd certainly had the opportunity to consider it fully now though, and squaring her shoulders, vowed to seize this unexpected opportunity to make a clean break with Fletcher.

She left Patches tethered by the gate and hastily gathered her thoughts as she climbed the steps, but just as she reached the porch, Fletcher came barreling out the front door. As he came forward, he reached out as though he meant to embrace her, but instead caught her in a rough grasp and held her at arm's length.

"Where's Blair?" he nearly shouted. His face was flushed, his mood obviously agitated.

Knowing it was her own fault she'd not been honest with him long before this, Eliza Kate gave up any hope of

inviting him into the coolness of the garden for an intimate chat. Instead, she took a deep breath and attempted
to say what she had to in as kind a manner as possible.

"Please, Fletcher, let's leave Jonathan out of this," she
reasoned with forced calm. "All that need concern us is
what's best for both you and me."

Fletcher's hostile frown merely deepened. "What the
devil are you talking about?" he responded rudely. "We've
got major problems in Galveston with a captain who refuses to unload a shipment of Irish whiskey that's right-
fully ours. I can't worry about a horse race while I'm
dealing with that mess. Now have you seen Blair this
morning or not?"

Out of the corner of her eye, Eliza Kate caught sight of
her father inching toward the doorway. She wondered
how long he'd been standing in the shadows and if he'd
considered her comment as odd as Fletcher had. Feeling
faint from a curious mixture of dread and relief, she
pulled away from Fletcher to lean against the porch rail.

"I might have seen him enter the barn when I returned
from my ride. Why don't you look for him there?"

Without another word, Fletcher bounded down the
steps and across the yard with his coattails flapping. Eliza
watched him go and couldn't help comparing his brisk
dust-kicking step with Jonathan's far smoother gait. She'd
forgotten all about the second race, and when she cast an
anxious glance toward the empty doorway, she wondered
if she'd actually seen her father there, or if a guilty conscience had simply played her a nasty trick.

Near the barn, Jonathan's stance was deceptively relaxed as he pretended to listen to Fletcher Monroe's sputtering tirade on the boundless greed of a certain
thoroughly unprincipled sea captain. His real interest,
however, lay just over Fletcher's left shoulder where Eliza
Kate could be seen pacing the porch and fanning herself
with her straw hat.

As always, her restless motions made it plain she was
upset. While he was grateful he never had any trouble

reading her emotions, he wished to God she were more forthcoming with her thoughts; he seldom had any idea what she was thinking.

Mary Claire had never been so reticent about expressing herself. No indeed, she had had a way of gracefully sweeping back her coal-black hair before looking up at him that had been a clear warning she was about to poke him in the chest and ask, "Do you know what I think?" She'd then explain her ideas in great detail.

Jonathan caught himself comparing the two women just as Ricky came through the front door and leaned close to speak with his sister. Eliza Kate sent one last fleeting glance toward Fletcher and him, and then followed her brother into the house. With a weary sigh, Jonathan swung his attention to Fletcher, who at last got to the point.

"Well, Blair, will you agree to postpone a week or not?" he asked.

Jonathan tried to imagine Eliza Kate ever being even mildly amused by Fletcher, but he knew she must have encouraged his attentions or the couple would not have become engaged. Still, it was difficult to believe the Eliza he knew had ever been satisfied with such a superficial sort. But then, perhaps Fletcher reminded her of her father.

"Damn it, man," Fletcher fumed. "What's it to be?"

Jonathan shrugged, for really Eliza Kate was what was important to him rather than winning any race. "I'll probably regret the delay when I reach the Arizona Territory, but I'm sure to beat you this time so I won't cancel."

Fletcher responded with an amused chuckle, and after slapping Jonathan soundly on the upper arm, turned toward his buggy. Jonathan was sorely tempted to kick the arrogant swine in the seat while he was still within range, but knowing the coming race would probably permanently erase his smirk, he forced himself to be patient.

He had very little patience where Eliza Kate was concerned, but he knew she'd come to him again that night and offer the same sweet surrender he'd never been able to refuse. Perhaps she was right in believing words merely got in their way; when what they did share was so incredibly sweet, he'd not waste a moment in senseless debate.

He was puzzled when Fletcher drove away in his buggy without stopping to say good-bye to Eliza Kate. Maybe he wouldn't miss her. Jonathan couldn't help hoping the jackass fell off a pier in Galveston and drowned.

Thursday noon, Lamar stopped by the Rosedale Hotel. Flossie Mae was clad for the afternoon trade in a deep purple gown that allowed an alluring glimpse of her full bosom before nipping in her tiny waist. An ebony ostrich plume adorned the curls wound atop her head, and she tapped a black lace fan against his chest as she greeted him with a flirtatious flourish.

"My first visit with Lawrence went extremely well, and I'm looking forward to seeing him again this afternoon. He's every bit as shy as you claimed, but I do believe he'll warm to me soon."

Lamar placed a quick kiss on her forehead and then began to pace her small office. "You needn't cultivate his friendship with the care you'd show flowering shrubs, Flossie. Don't waste a minute on chitchat. Just get him out of his clothes and keep him in the good milliner's bed until sundown."

As usual, Lamar had been easily misled, but Flossie Mae found it impossible to look him in the eye while she imagined such an abandoned scene with his younger brother. She had not thought she could still blush, but the warmth filling her cheeks was real. She made a coy turn away from her paramour and adopted a more ladylike tone.

"I don't want to rush things, Lamar, and this afternoon would be much too soon for someone as reserved as Lawrence and Madame Leroux to become lovers."

Something about the way Flossie's voice had softened when she murmured his brother's name set Lamar on edge. He reached out to catch her arm and yanked her back toward him. "Tie him to the bed with red ribbons if you must, but begin the affair today," he ordered sternly.

Flossie Mae looked up slowly, and then batted her eye-lashes, which usually worked well to distract him, but the force of his bruising grip didn't slacken. His narrowed glance frightened her, but she again spoke sweetly. "You needn't shout or squeeze me so hard. This has to be done with the appropriate finesse. I can't just yank up my skirt and invite Lawrence to fuck me."

That crass comment brought a burst of hearty laughter that erased Lamar's tense frown. After a quick peck on her cheek, he released her. "Why not? It certainly worked well with me."

Flossie Mae ran her fingertips up his lapels. "That's not the way I remember it, but you and your brother are very different men. It's been a long while since Lawrence has slept with a woman, and I don't want him to be so apprehensive, if not downright terrified, that he won't enjoy it. He'd never come back to me then, and your whole plan would be ruined."

Lamar nodded to acknowledge her point and then rested his hands on her shoulders. "Just remember this isn't a formal courtship that can drag on for months, Flossie. I want Lawrence so thoroughly intoxicated by your charms that he won't be able to think of anything else. You may have been my first choice for the job, but if you fail me, I won't hesitate to bring in someone else."

The threat smoldered in his eyes, and convinced he meant it, Flossie Mae was quick to argue. "Have you forgotten that you said I was the only woman you'd trust not to take advantage of Lawrence? If I'm to build his confidence in himself, and then inspire him to pursue another woman, my actions have to hold a subtle yet enticing reluctance. I can't possibly be as bold as you suggest. It would defeat the whole purpose. Besides, how could you even consider replacing me? What explanation could you possibly give for my sudden disappearance?"

Not about to accept the logic of her argument, Lamar dug his fingers into her shoulders. "Lawrence will believe

whatever fanciful lie I tell him. Now give me your word
that you'll begin the affair this very day, or I'll put another
girl in the shop who will."

When Lamar was in such an intractable mood, Flossie
knew better than to push him. She glanced down as
though she felt utterly defeated and slumped her posture
slightly. "I suppose I could cry. He'll surely rush to console
me, and with a bed in the room, I can coax him into it
before he even knows what's happened."

His eyes lighting with triumph, Lamar lowered his head
for a demanding kiss and then released her. "That's precisely what I had in mind. Lure him into your bed with
tears, and then in a week or two when you swear you were
lost in memories of your late husband, he'll be sure to
believe you."

Flossie Mae returned Lamar's parting kiss, but she still
felt shaken long after he'd departed the Rosedale. According to him, Lawrence seldom left the ranch, and if
he fell for her as he was supposed to, as she sincerely
hoped he would, he was bound to tell Lamar. Perhaps in
a plea to protect her reputation, she could swear him to
secrecy.

She would definitely have to think of something to silence him, because she could not bear to have him confide the details of their affair to his elder brother. Any
show of true emotion would surely bring Lamar that
much closer to demanding she end their romance.

Her thoughts awhirl, she paced her garishly decorated
office in an erratic circle. There was absolutely no margin
for error in her plan. Lawrence had to fall in love with
her, propose, and elope with her before Lamar had the
slightest doubt that she wasn't following his orders to the
letter. Unfortunately, she feared she must have already
aroused his suspicions, or he'd not have turned so vicious
that day.

She rubbed her arms and paused to peer in the gilt-
framed mirror near the door. She was going to have to
be much more careful when next they discussed

Lawrence. She would have to provide Lamar with a detailed report that was both colorful and crude, but that did not mean she'd actually confess to anything truthful.

She was far too smart to lie to herself, however, and knew a fine man like Lawrence would merely be revolted by the painted woman she saw reflected in the mirror. There was far more to her than the feathers and rouge though, and portraying the chaste Madame Leroux had given her an opportunity to reclaim the virtuous young woman she had once been. Lawrence had been drawn to her, she knew that he had, and she could not help being touched by the shy young man.

She would not allow him to be hurt in this scheme either. After they were wed, she would be a devoted wife, and Lamar would not be able to say a single word against her. A satisfied smile gave her lips a provocative curve, and she left her office intent upon running the Rosedale for the next couple of hours with the wit and flair that had made her uniquely popular in a city with many flamboyant madams.

Lawrence was nearly beside himself with anxiety by the time three o'clock arrived. He did so want to be helpful, but at the same time, he feared he would be so distracted by the lovely Mae Leroux that nothing he said would make any sense. Her ledger would then end up an impossible mess, and whatever respect she might have had for him would promptly evaporate.

When he reached the millinery shop and found a closed sign on the door he nearly wept with relief, then was embarrassed to recall that Mae had promised to close early so that they wouldn't be disturbed while they worked. "I never should have offered my help," he muttered under his breath, but he bravely raised his hand and knocked lightly at the door.

A nasty dispute between one of the girls and a businessman from Dallas had taken longer to settle than Flossie Mae had anticipated, and she was still buttoning up her black dress as she rushed to admit Lawrence. Half expecting to still find an ostrich feather in her hair, she ran a quick hand over her curls as he entered.

"Mr. Bendalin," she greeted him warmly. "It's so good of you to take your valuable time to help me. I'm ever so grateful."

Lawrence inhaled the shop's wonderfully exotic perfumes and longed for the days when he'd been at ease with a beautiful woman. "Your gratitude is definitely premature, Mrs. Leroux, but I'll do my very best for you."

He was blushing again, and flattered he found her appealing, Mae took his arm for a brief moment before leading the way to her apartment. "It's Mae. I hope you won't mind, but I thought we might have a cup of tea before we examine my books. The confectioner's at the corner has such delicious tarts, I couldn't resist buying a few. I do hope you'll share them with me."

Mae had placed a small table near the desk, and a china teapot and the tarts she'd described were waiting for them. The pastries were heart and diamond shaped, heaped with berries, and dusted with confectioner's sugar. Lawrence had been too nervous to taste the noon meal, but now found himself ravenously hungry.

"You've made this a party rather than work, and I don't know when I've seen anything that looked so good," he blurted out, then feared he'd sounded as eager as a small child presented with a surprise treat.

Mae indicated the chair he'd used on his previous visit and poured him a cup of tea to go with the pastries. She took only a small bite of hers, but successfully urged Lawrence to have two, and then three. By his last bite, his coat was lightly dusted with the powdered sugar, but he seemed not to notice. Unwilling to call his attention to it, Mae merely leaned over and brushed away the sugar with her own napkin.

"Forgive me, but it's been so long since I've had a man to fuss over, I did that without thinking," she apologized quickly, and the memory of far more innocent days quickly filled her eyes with the tears she'd hoped to affect.

Lawrence immediately set his plate and cup aside on the small table. Drawn to touch her, he reached out to catch a tear on his fingertip, but he'd not noticed a drop of berry clinging to his hand, and it smeared across her cheek. "Oh dear, look what I've done," he worried aloud, and grabbing his napkin, he rushed to blot away the errant fruit.

That was all the opening Mae required, and she slid her hand over his. They were now so close, she could have easily brushed her lips across his mouth, but instead, she placed a shy kiss in his palm. She felt his hand tremble, and looked up at him through her tear-spiked lashes.

Lawrence knew he ought to say something witty, or do something gallant, but what he saw in Mae Leroux's golden gaze was the very same hunger a thousand berry tarts couldn't assuage. Since Tuesday, he'd reined in his initial hopes, not daring to count on more than a pleasant hour while he struggled to concentrate on her ledger rather than her, but now, anything seemed possible.

Mae waited, silently willing him to lean closer rather than draw away, and in the next instant Lawrence kissed her. It was a somewhat clumsy kiss, and yet so incredibly dear that she raised her free hand to encircle his neck to encourage another, and yet another. He tasted sweet, and as his kisses grew increasingly bold, her softly encouraging sighs were completely sincere. It had been so long since she had felt the desire flooding through her now that she could think only of Lawrence and how much she truly wished to please him.

Equally lost in her, Lawrence swiftly grew dizzy from lack of air. He'd been with women, lots of them, in his youth, but none had ever touched his heart as Mae Leroux did so easily. Passion was almost enough to make him forget how unattractive he'd become, but as he paused to draw in a deep breath, he remembered.

"I'm so sorry," he nearly moaned. "I didn't mean to, well, to take advantage."

Mae was used to loud, swaggering men who rudely demanded what they wanted from a woman, and she found
Lawrence's hesitant apology so delightfully quaint, it was
easy to smile. "You're a gentleman as always, but you've
not taken advantage of me, Lawrence. On the contrary,
that was wonderful."

Lawrence appeared slightly startled. "Really? I'm afraid
I'm dreadfully out of practice."

Mae laughed and gave her lips a suggestive lick. "Not
at all. Your kisses are absolutely delicious, although if you
really feel that you require further practice, I'll be glad to
oblige."

When she leaned toward him, Lawrence didn't make
her beg for another kiss. Instead, he reached out to catch
her around the waist and lifted her onto his lap where
they snuggled together as their kisses grew increasingly
passionate. It took him a long while to find the courage
to slide his hand over her bosom, but Mae responded by
unbuttoning her bodice, and her bare skin was so smooth
and soft he began to dream of still more.

Mae was so comfortable in his embrace, she also longed
for more. She ran her hand down his shirt placket and
slipped the buttons out of their holes with one hand. She
then slid her hand inside his shirt to caress his bare skin.
He was warm, his chest lightly furred, and she drew enticing circles around his nipples as she returned his fevered
kisses.

Unable to stand any more of her enticing gestures,
Lawrence caught Mae's hand and held it as he pressed
her close. "You must think me unforgivably forward," he
whispered against her ear.

Mae sat back slightly and regarded him with a curious
gaze. "When I fit so perfectly in your arms, nothing you
could possibly do would strike me as being too forward."

Her expression was one of such angelic sweetness,
Lawrence wondered if she really meant what she'd said.
Certain that she could not possibly be inviting further in-
timacy, he glanced toward the ledger that lay forgotten

on her desk. "I was supposed to help you with your books," he offered with a shy smile.

"Will you be dreadfully disappointed if we don't have time for them today?" Mae asked.

"I'm afraid I've completely lost track of the time," Lawrence replied.

"Good," Mae encouraged, and she gave his lower lip a teasing nibble.

Lawrence had never been with such a delightfully uninhibited woman, but reminding himself that Mae was the only widow he'd known, he thought perhaps she and her husband had been an unusually affectionate couple. For whatever reason, she seemed to actually want him, and he didn't want to disappoint her.

Again drawing back, Lawrence fought to make sense without making a fool of himself. "I told you I was injured in the war," he began.

Mae was sprawled across his lap, and she could feel his arousal without having to slide her hand up his leg. Discounting impotence, she rushed to reassure him. "Scars don't bother me. But if you'd rather make love in the dark, I'll put out the lamp."

Now that she'd actually issued the invitation, Lawrence searched her face for any hint of revulsion, but only the light of an enticing possibility shone in her pretty eyes. "That's awfully tempting," he confessed, "but then I'd not be able to see you."

Touched, Mae rested her forehead against his. She knew he'd consider her lush figure lovely, but she was deeply grateful he'd not be able to see past her pale skin to the years when a shapely body had been her only means to survive. For a split second she longed to tell him the truth, and how everything she'd done in the last eight years had been a dreadful mistake she knew he could never forgive.

The impulse was fleeting, however, and as she sat up she knew each and every one of those mistakes had brought her that much closer to meeting him. "I never expected this," she murmured.

Lawrence knew exactly what she meant, but he'd fallen in love with her the first time she'd smiled and reached out to touch him. Now all he wanted was to share the joy she'd given in such abundance, and his hands shook as he helped her off his lap and out of her clothes.

Mae held her breath, praying he'd not change his mind, but Lawrence swiftly joined her in the bed, and his motions weren't in the least bit awkward as he made love to her with the same tenderness that filled his kiss. She had felt nothing with all the other men, and had sincerely believed her heart had been buried with her husband. But now, her body was so sensitive that every caress, every slow, adoring kiss was ecstasy, and when Lawrence at last slid inside her, his passion burned clear to her soul.

When her climax burst forth with his, a delicious warmth spread to her fingertips and toes and lingered as a soft blanket of love. As she fell asleep still locked in Lawrence's embrace, she thanked God for her foresight in giving the real Madame Leroux the money to spend the night in a hotel. It wasn't until the next morning when she heard Lawrence swearing that she realized how truly lucky she had really been.

"I'm so sorry," Lawrence repeated over and over. "You're so fair, and last night I didn't realize how badly I'd bruised you."

Mae had been in too great a rush when she'd gotten dressed before leaving the Rosedale to notice Lamar had left deep purple bruises on her shoulders and arms. Now Lawrence believed he'd carelessly caused the telltale marks, and she couldn't bring herself to tell him his brother was to blame.

She reached out a hand. "Obviously you're much stronger than you thought, but you didn't hurt me last night, and I know you won't hurt me now."

Lawrence had expected her to be mad at the very least, but Mae just wanted more of him, and he rejoined her on the bed. "I haven't stayed out all night since the war," he confided softly. "But I doubt anyone missed me."

Mae rolled over him, and now wondering why she'd ever thought he would need to be carefully coaxed into her bed, she made love to him with a joy she'd no wish to hide. More than an hour passed before he again left the bed so that she could prepare for the day, but she walked him to the door wrapped in a rumpled sheet.

"I'm going to insist that you come back to help me with my books, Mr. Bendalin," she teased.

"Oh yes, you can be sure of that, Mrs. Leroux. Will tonight be too soon?"

As Mae assured him it wouldn't be, she wondered how she was going to wait that long. Then she thought of how eager Lamar would be for a full report, and regretted the day had ever dawned.

Chapter Twelve

Lawrence was still wearing a decidedly sappy grin when he arrived home. He'd missed breakfast but was too happy to care. Fearing he must look as though he'd slept in his suit, he hurried up to his room to bathe, shave, and dress in clean clothes before going out to the garden to share his good news with Delia and Eliza Kate.

Though Delia had no idea Lawrence had been out all night, Eliza Kate was well aware of it, and a single glimpse of her uncle's ecstatic expression was enough to convince her Madame Leroux must be a very charming companion. Of course, he'd not mentioned the woman to her, and she'd not reveal what Jonathan had confided for fear her dear uncle would begin to wonder how close she and his good friend might have become.

Lawrence sat down opposite his sister-in-law and niece and after politely inquiring as to their health, he blurted out the reason for his uncharacteristic joy. "I've met the most remarkable young woman, and for some inexplicable reason, she likes me too."

"Why wouldn't she?" Delia inquired sweetly. "You're one of Fort Worth's most eligible bachelors."

Lawrence laughed at the compliment he usually brushed aside. "You've assured me of that quite often, but I've never believed it until now. Mae Leroux brings out the best in me so easily. I can't help wishing I'd met her years ago."

"Who are her people, dear? Do we know them?" Delia glanced toward her daughter.

"I don't believe so, Mother. Does she have family here?" Eliza Kate hated playing this silly game.

Lawrence appeared puzzled for a brief moment, and then shook his head. "No, I don't believe so, but I'll inquire after her family when I see her again this evening. Did I mention that she's a widow?"

Eliza Kate nodded politely as Lawrence described Mae Leroux as an enchanting creature and pronounced her millinery shop a superb addition to Fort Worth's growing business community. She couldn't help wondering if Jonathan would describe *her* in such effusive terms. It had not occurred to her until that very moment that keeping quiet about their romance might be as difficult for him as it was for her. After all, he was a man of honor, certainly not one given to telling convenient lies, but she supposed just as she had chosen to do, he simply said nothing at all.

Eliza Kate's attention was wandering woefully, but the longer her uncle praised Mae Leroux's intelligence and wit, the more distracted she became. "I can't wait to meet her," she interjected when he slowed for a breath.

"I wish we'd not had to postpone the race a week, but I'll invite her to join us then," Lawrence replied. "I just hope she won't mind opening her shop a little later than usual, or even closing for the day."

"Perhaps she'd rather join us for Sunday dinner," Eliza suggested. "Then her shop's hours won't pose a conflict."

"What a wonderful idea," Delia agreed. "We all want to meet her, dear. Do invite her to dine with us this Sunday."

Lawrence nodded, then paused as he got to his feet. "You don't think it's too soon for me to present her to the family, do you? I wouldn't want her to feel over-whelmed."

Delia was amused by that thought. "We are a well-mannered family, Lawrence. None of us will embarrass you or do anything in the least bit rude."

"No, of course not," he conceded. "I just don't want to rush things."

He looked so sincerely worried, Eliza Kate couldn't help sympathizing with him. "You do whatever you think is best, Uncle. We're happy you've made the acquaintance of such a lovely woman, and we'll be delighted to enter-tain her whenever you're comfortable doing so."

"Thank you. I believe I'd really rather wait for the race." Lawrence kissed them both on the cheek, and then started off toward the house with frequent stops to smell the roses.

"Oh, dear," Delia whispered. "He's really smitten, isn't he?"

"Yes, and I for one think it's wonderful." Of course, she knew precisely how Lawrence felt and understood why he could barely contain his happiness.

"I don't mean to be indelicate," Delia continued softly, "but it's rather obvious Mae Leroux's been quite generous with her favors. I'd never want to see Lawrence hurt, but I doubt she's the type of woman he ought to marry."

"Simply because she's been 'quite generous with her favors'? Perhaps she's every bit as fond of Lawrence as he is of her." Eliza Kate held her breath, but regardless of how much Mae Leroux might adore Lawrence, she knew her mother would never approve of any woman with less than impeccable virtue.

Delia dipped her head slightly. "I realize she's a widow, and therefore experienced, but still, a woman of quality waits for marriage before displaying the depth of her affection for a man. Surely I taught you that."

"Oh yes, Mother, indeed you did," Eliza Kate declared convincingly, but she would not have traded a moment she'd spent in Jonathan's arms to regain her lost innocence.

In addition to loving her mother, she'd always admired her enormously as a model of feminine perfection. She'd never questioned Delia's views on what constituted acceptable conduct until Jonathan Blair had shown her there was far more to knowing a man than a flirtatious exchange designed to conceal far more than it ever revealed.

As they sat quietly observing a hummingbird dart through the roses, Eliza couldn't help wishing her mother were still the vibrant woman she'd once been. She could have engaged in a spirited debate with that woman and, perhaps, even convinced her that a woman's greatest obligation was to her own heart rather than the sterile rules society imposed.

Jarred by her own unwillingness to proclaim that view aloud, Eliza Kate longed to possess Mae Leroux's courage and silently wished her and Lawrence an abundance of the same heady passion she and Jonathan shared.

That same morning, Flossie Mae had bathed and dressed only in a lavender silk dressing gown, but she was more than ready for Lamar's visit. Before he had taken two steps into her room, she loosened her belt and turned her back toward him. Then with a careless shrug, she let the smooth silk slide low to reveal her shoulders and upper arms.

"Everything went as you'd hoped," she declared confidently. "And Lawrence actually thought he'd put these awful bruises on me. You'll have to be more careful in the future, because he'll not believe that absurd lie a second time."

Lamar scoffed at her warning and swung the door closed. "I'd meant only to make my point, but since the bruises worked to our advantage, I'll not apologize."

Flossie Mae quickly adjusted the drape of her dressing gown and securely knotted the belt before facing him. "I fail to see how your leaving me black and blue helped our cause."

"Guilt is a plus, dearest, because it means Lawrence will try all the harder to impress you the next time he sees you. It's almost a shame he doesn't realize how easy you'd be to impress regardless of what foolish mistakes he might make."

Flossie bit her tongue rather than defend Lawrence as she would have liked, but she tolerated only the briefest of kisses before grabbing up her brush to style her damp hair. "I'm meeting him again tonight."

"Good, and keep him out all night again. The less sleep he gets, the easier he'll be to confuse when you tell him you've had a sudden change of heart."

Flossie Mae sat down at her vanity and caught Lamar's eye in the mirror. "Your brother's feelings don't concern you at all, do they?"

Lamar moved to the window where he could observe the street as they talked. Friday was payday for many in town and always profitable at the Rosedale. From the amount of foot traffic already filling the walks, today would be no exception. "On second thought, send Lawrence home tonight. Then you can tend to business here."

Flossie Mae had sworn not to say anything Lamar could ever repeat to Lawrence, but it was difficult not to refer to the shy young man when he filled her thoughts so completely. "I suppose I could yawn frequently and tell him Saturday is one of my busiest days. As I said, he's very considerate and will undoubtedly believe I need my rest."

Lamar left the window to walk up behind her. He laid his hands lightly on her shoulders, but then gave her a squeeze that made her wince. "Is he a considerate lover as well?" he asked.

Flossie Mae was anxious to escape his grasp, but forced

herself to remain still. With a convincingly wistful smile, she told the truth in a way he completely misunderstood. "There's no comparison between you, if that's your real question."

Lamar released her with a rude laugh. "I already knew that. Unfortunately, with Fletcher out of town, I can't stay long enough to remind you which of us is the better man, but I doubt you'll forget anytime soon."

"No, it's highly unlikely," Flossie claimed sweetly, but she held her breath until he'd closed her door on his way out. After the years they'd been together, she'd not expected to feel such revulsion at his touch, but in the past, their partnership had never included such a heartless scheme.

She hadn't realized her hands were trembling until she laid her brush on the vanity. She'd been too tired to match wits with Lamar, and thank God, he'd displayed only a passing interest in Lawrence's prowess as a lover. She wasn't certain what she would have done had he wanted to assert his own dominance and sleep with her. After having been with Lawrence, she couldn't be intimate with Lamar ever again. She rested her elbows on the vanity and placed her hands over her eyes.

Lawrence had slept so contentedly in her arms, but she'd lain awake most of the night. He'd not been a real person to her when she'd vowed to become his wife, but now he was far too dear to betray. She was so confused she didn't know what course to pursue, but believing it was sleep she needed most, she lay down for a nap, and hoped the coming night would be as good as the last, even if she couldn't remain with Lawrence until dawn.

By that afternoon, Flossie Mae was fully refreshed, but in no mood to wear black again. On her infrequent visits to the bank, she wore a gray suit adorned with swirling black trim on the cuffs and hem. Lamar preferred to make their deposits himself, but in an occasional emergency, she had donned the modest suit to appear presentable and conduct their business without drawing undue notice from the bank's other patrons.

It had been several months since she'd worn the stylish garment, and it was wedged between a purple velvet and a lime green gown. After laying it carefully on the bed, she returned to her wardrobe to survey the bright silks and satins, but there wasn't a single dress she'd care to model for Lawrence. That meant she had no need for any of them, and with a sudden burst of inspiration, she decided to get rid of the whole lot by parceling them out to the girls.

With an exuberant grace, she began tossing the colorful clothes on the floor. An entire rainbow of high-heeled slippers were next to join the heap, then the fancy fans, ostrich plumes, black net stockings, and red lingerie. Everything Lamar had ever bought and insisted she wear to titillate their clientele went cascading to the floor.

Then with a rollicking laugh, Flossie called the girls and made a party of it. "I need a whole new wardrobe," she exclaimed, "and with a tuck here and there, or letting out a seam, my clothes will fit all of you. Take only one dress to begin with and the matching shoes if they'll fit you. If there's anything left, we'll go around again."

While her companions were still staring at the chaos in Flossie's usually immaculate room, Agnes grabbed for the purple velvet gown. "I can't believe you'd part with this pretty thing."

"It'll be even prettier on you," Flossie replied graciously. "What about you, Belle? Isn't yellow your favorite color?"

"You know it is," Belle replied, and she snatched up a gown of yellow brocade that had once been Flossie's pride and joy.

Flossie had to break up an argument or two, but in half an hour, her private apartment was again neat, and her once bulging wardrobe, nearly empty. For a brief moment, Flossie was tempted to pack up what little she had left and convince Lawrence to elope that very night. But with the weekend coming, Lamar would be out at the

ranch, and she'd have another couple of days to inspire
Lawrence to propose on his own.

Praying things continued to go better than she'd had
any right to hope, she donned the modest outfit she'd
chosen and hurried on over to Madame Leroux's. While
she fully intended to follow Lamar's directions and send
Lawrence home early, she thought that just might prove
impossible to do, so again provided the milliner with the
money to spend the night in a hotel. Fortunately, the
Frenchwoman was enjoying the brief escape from her
shop and offered to continue to assist in her landlord's
plans in whatever way she could.

Lawrence was very pleasantly surprised to find Mae
dressed in a lacy white blouse and tailored gray skirt with
elegant black trim. It was nearly as prim and proper an
ensemble as her black gown but the light colors spoke
volumes about her change in attitude. Hoping he was responsible, he brushed her cheek with a kiss as he handed
her an enormous bouquet of red roses.

"Oh, Lawrence. Where did you find such beautiful
roses?" Flossie hugged them to her breast and inhaled
their lush perfume. She couldn't recall the last time a
man had brought her flowers and was so touched she
nearly wept.

"Delia, my sister-in-law, has surrounded our house with
an enormous garden. I was afraid the roses might wilt
before I got here, but they seem to have survived the journey. Do you have a nice vase for them?"

Flossie regarded him with an adoring smile as she frantically wondered where Madame Leroux might keep a
vase if she owned one. "I know I have one here somewhere," she finally replied, "but I've been rearranging my
stock and in the process misplaced nearly everything. I
thought we might have wine with supper, so let's just put
these in the teapot for now."

"The teapot?" Lawrence thought the idea daft, but he
was so distracted by the mention of supper, he followed

Flossie into her private apartment without objecting. "I didn't mean for you to cook for me. I should have mentioned that we'd dine out."

Flossie quickly poured water from the pitcher on her washstand into the teapot. While her hands moved with quick motions to arrange the roses, she sought a reasonable excuse, but there was absolutely no way she and Lawrence could appear in public until they were wed. Even then, she did not look forward to what would surely be openly curious, if not downright hostile, stares.

When she stepped back to admire her surprisingly artful bouquet, her answer flowed easily. "I can boil water on the small coal stove used for heat, but I can't really cook here, my darling. I simply ordered chicken and dumplings from the Lone Star Cafe. Then if we actually do want to work on my books, or even if we don't, we won't have wasted precious time by going out to dine."

Her suggestive smile warmed Lawrence clear through, and he completely lost interest in leaving her apartment. A covered dish wrapped in a blue-and-white dish towel sat on the table with the same small plates they'd used for the tarts. Lawrence eagerly drank in the delicious aroma.

"I wasn't certain you were even real," he murmured softly. "And here you are providing another meal. I'm beginning to suspect you're hoping to fatten me up."

Flossie came forward to loop her arms around his waist. "Suspect whatever you wish," she teased, "but I like you just the way you are."

Lawrence wrapped his arms around her and hugged her tight. He rested his cheek against her curls, and then began to pluck the combs from her hair. It fell past her waist in soft waves, and he wrapped a strand around his hand to draw her closer still.

"I've never brushed a woman's hair," he confessed shyly. "Maybe you wouldn't mind my brushing yours later."

"Not at all, but I'm going to insist that you sample some of this chicken first to keep up your strength." Flossie Mae hadn't eaten all day, but it wasn't hunger that made her feel weak, and it was all she could do to leave his arms to fill their plates.

The chicken tasted as good as it smelled, and Lawrence was on his second plate before he recalled his promise to Delia. "We've not had a chance to talk about ourselves. Except for the war, I've been here all my life. You mentioned coming to Fort Worth, but I've no idea from where."

Flossie took a sip of wine before replying. She wanted to tell him the truth, but it was so awfully unflattering, she was reluctant to do so. "I'm from a little town in Georgia. I'm sure you've never heard of it, but we were close to the Alabama border near Columbus."

"I marched through Georgia. It's a beautiful state, so green compared to Texas. Tell me about your family."

His interest was obviously sincere as well as keen, but Flossie turned shy. "I never talk about my family or reminisce about my childhood. It just seems so terribly long ago."

"It can't be that long," Lawrence chuckled. "You're not thirty surely. I know I'm being dreadfully impertinent, but I like you so much that I really want to know you better. If it's too soon, please forgive me, but I've hardly spoken with a woman outside my family in years, and—"

Flossie reached for his hand, then left her chair to circle the small table. "I want to be certain I don't hurt you when I sit on your lap."

Somewhat startled by her request, Lawrence still had the presence of mind to ease her down on his good leg. "No, not this way, but I'd not complain even if it did."

His face was lit was such innocent delight, Flossie could not help loving him. She gave him a quick hug, then leaned back slightly. "I don't usually tell this story because it's simply too sad. My mother died shortly after I was born. My father handed me to my maternal grandmother to raise, and from the way she told it, he just wandered off and never returned."

"But that's awful," Lawrence responded. "I know he must have been heartbroken, but to just walk away?"

"Yes, it is awful. When I got old enough, I could understand his grief at losing my mother, but I could never fathom why he didn't pay us an occasional visit to see how I'd turned out. Maybe he died in some horrible accident. I'll never know. Now take another bite or I'll stop talking."

"Yes, ma'am." Lawrence thought he might actually regain some weight if she'd perch on his knee every night. Amused by that thought, he chewed a flavorful bite of chicken and savored a somewhat soggy dumpling. "There. So your grandmother raised you by herself?"

Flossie had always considered the tale too pathetic to relate, then had found no one who even cared enough to ask about her background. The men she'd known had been nothing like Lawrence, however. She forced a smile, and he winked at her.

"Yes. Things were never easy for us either. We had just a tiny farm where we scarcely grew enough food to feed ourselves, let alone any extra produce to sell. My grandmother taught me to sew, and I helped with the mending she took in so we could buy the necessities."

"And that's what led you to become a milliner?" Lawrence took another bite before she could insist upon it.

Flossie stared at him a moment before recalling she was actually supposed to be a milliner. "Yes, you could say my early training made millinery a natural choice." She was immediately struck with the absurdity of attempting to relate the truth about her past while veiling the present and swiftly grew as morose as her story.

"I had only one friend. His name was Jason, and he lived on a farm that wasn't all that much bigger than ours, but his parents thought a great deal of themselves and never let him forget I was dirt poor. He didn't care though, and we used to run back and forth between my farm and his. As soon as we were old enough, we married, but his family didn't approve and refused to attend the wedding. I couldn't go to them when Jason was killed, but I've managed to survive on my own."

Lawrence watched her fight back tears and tightened his embrace. He bet she'd worn long braids, and he could imagine her hiking up her skirt to race the freckled boy Jason must have been. He'd had no childhood sweetheart, but now he wished Mae could have been his rather than Jason's.

"I can't run anymore," he whispered against her throat.

Flossie combed her fingers through his hair to tilt his face up to hers. "Now that I've found you, I've no reason to run, so please don't worry about having to chase me."

Lawrence responded with such a handsome grin it was easy to see what a charming man he'd once been, and with a loving wife, could be again. As she wrapped her arms around his neck, she knew a few enticing hints would inspire him to propose. She longed for the tender proposal he'd make on his own though, and she wanted him to surprise her as he had with the armful of gorgeous roses. That way she'd be assured she'd really been his choice, not simply a clever woman who'd tricked him into marriage.

The problem was, Lamar hadn't given her nearly enough time for that. Still, she didn't want to rush things any more than she had to. "I've also lost all interest in balancing my books," she confessed boldly.

"What books?" Lawrence murmured as he caught her mouth in a deep, hungry kiss that left no doubt as to his plans for the rest of the evening. He was so lost in loving her, the night dissolved in an instant, and he didn't remember how much he'd wanted to brush her hair until the morning. Then there wasn't time for such playful attentions before her shop opened.

"I want to see you again tonight," he murmured as he kissed her good-bye. "But I don't want to risk your growing tired of me."

He was teasing her now with such good-natured fun, Flossie could scarcely remember the timid young man who'd first asked to see Madame Leroux. "Then I promise to warn you should it ever become a danger," she replied with equal zest.

After he left, she leaned against the back door, confident she deserved the credit for restoring his belief in himself, but he had had a far more profound effect on her. With him it was so easy to be the joyful girl she'd once been, rather than the cynical whore who'd learned all of life's worst lessons too late. Having decided which woman she now wished to be, she took her time getting back to the Rosedale, never expecting Lamar to be there waiting for her.

He was seated in her office adding up the girls' earnings for Friday night. It had been a surprisingly good evening considering Flossie hadn't been there, but he had no intention of telling her so. He shut the cash box, quickly drew her into the office, and shut the door.

"You were supposed to be here last night." He leaned back against the desk and folded his arms over his chest. "What happened?"

Flossie was still filled with a dreamy warmth, but she strove to project a jaded indifference. "Lawrence felt like talking, and it simply got too late to send him home."

Flossie was staring at the floor and fiddling with her hair, as though her evening had been of little consequence, but Lamar wasn't fooled. "When I tell you to do something, I expect you to do it," he reminded her sternly.

Flossie covered a wide yawn as she glanced up. "I am doing exactly what you expect, Lamar. I've seduced your brother without making him in the least bit suspicious as to my motives. It hasn't been easy either."

"I distinctly recall telling you to send him home early," Lamar repeated, "and you knew what would happen if you disobeyed me."

Flossie shrugged. "Why are you making such an issue of this? I had every intention of sending him home before

ten, but he was in a talkative mood, and I had to listen. I
didn't dare be rude."

Lamar's stance didn't soften. "He talked the whole
night through?" he challenged skeptically.

"No, of course not."

"Let's go upstairs, and you can show me exactly what
you and he did."

Flossie covered another yawn. "Really, Lamar. I do need
to sleep sometime. Just use your imagination."

"That's precisely what you've been doing, isn't it? Well,
your little game is over. I told you what to expect if you
didn't obey me, and unfortunately you've forced me to
tell Lawrence that he's been keeping company with my
favorite whore."

The threat sickened her, but Flossie knew the only
thing Lamar respected was strength, and she had plenty
of that left. "To what purpose, Lamar? You wanted your
brother distracted from his friend, and I must have succeeded in that. Give me the weekend to finish our game,
and on Monday, I'll tell Lawrence I can't see him again."

Lamar shook his head. "I'm the one running this, not
you. Now let's go upstairs."

Flossie Mae knew what it was to be frightened. She'd
grown up with the fear there would be nothing to eat.
Then she'd been afraid Jason would abandon her to
please his parents. Even after she and Jason had wed,
she'd had to live with the unrelenting terror that he'd be
killed in the war. When he'd died, all their hopes and
dreams, and the best part of her, had been buried with
him.

From that moment to this, she didn't recall being truly
afraid, but although fear was now coiling painful knots in
her belly, she knew Lamar was giving her no choice at all.
"I'm not that good an actress," she complained flippantly.
"I can't sleep with both of you and keep my story straight."

"You don't have to," Lamar insisted. "The story's over,
the end. You're my woman, and I want you. Now let's go
on upstairs to your room." He moved toward the door.

Now it was Flossie who crossed her arms over her chest. "No. You're in such an intractable mood, you'll just leave me all battered and bruised. I'd prefer to avoid that misfortune."

Lamar turned away from the door. "Whatever made you think you had a choice?"

Flossie just stared at him. That she had ever expected to marry him and have his children now struck her as one of the stupidest mistakes she made in a life filled with bad choices. "Calm down," she ordered softly. "There's no reason for us to lock horns over this. Let me give Lawrence the best weekend of his life, and I'll send him on his way on Monday. Then on Tuesday, you and I can argue from dawn until sunset if you like. Today, I'm simply too tired to think."

"I'm not asking you to think," Lamar replied harshly. This time he reached for her arm before taking hold of the doorknob. "Come on."

Flossie yanked away from him. "No."

For a brief instant, Lamar appeared to be perplexed, but he quickly recovered and offered a compromise. "What if I promised to allow you to bid Lawrence farewell on Monday? Would you be so grateful that you'd peel off your clothes as you ran up the stairs?"

Flossie could still feel Lawrence, and she wouldn't betray him like that, nor herself either. "You're forgetting how well I know you, Lamar. You'd just sleep with me, and then do as you damned well pleased."

Lamar nodded to concede the point. "As I said, you give me no choice. I'll have to tell Lawrence he's been consorting with a whore."

"Don't do that," Flossie ordered sharply. "You'll only diminish yourself in his eyes as well as break his heart."

"And you don't want his heart broken, do you?" Lamar cooed sarcastically.

"Have you taken leave of your senses?" Flossie took a step toward him, but didn't reach out to him.

"No, not at all," Lamar exclaimed. "I tossed you to Lawrence, and now I'm taking you back."

Grasping a slender hope, Flossie began to smile. "You're jealous. That's ridiculous, Lamar. This was your idea in the first place. Let's play it through."

Lamar reached for his belt buckle. "All right. I'll give you until Monday. Just take care of me here."

Flossie had fought for a way to save Lawrence without having to give in to Lamar, but nothing she'd tried had worked. She didn't trust Lamar to keep his word now, either. With a cold sense of inevitable doom, she shook her head. Even if she couldn't protect Lawrence from the vicious truth Lamar was determined to reveal, she could make this final choice for him, and proudly.

"No," she swore. "I've quit being a whore."

She saw Lamar draw back his hand and tensed for the blow, but he hit her so hard she fell against the desk and struck her head. As she slumped to the floor, all she saw were bright flashes of stars, and when he began to kick her in the ribs, she felt nothing at all.

Chapter Thirteen

Jonathan had just started up the back stairs to wash up for supper when he heard Lamar laugh. Caught by the mirthless, mocking tone coming from the study, he paused on the second step. He was surprised Lawrence was still working on the accounts when he had meant to go into town to visit Mae Leroux again and thought Lamar had chosen a particularly poor time to discuss anything of substance.

Believing Lawrence might appreciate being interrupted if Lamar were giving him a hard time, Jonathan moved off the stairs and toward the study. As he reached for the doorknob, Lamar spoke, and he hesitated to make certain he wasn't butting in where he wasn't needed.

"I know you're taken with her," Lamar remarked dismissively, "and I'm gratified that she's given you such a good time. It's just that she's not what she seems. Her real name isn't Mae Leroux, it's Flossie Mae—"

With stunning clarity, Jonathan recognized the name of Lamar's mistress before he'd reached her surname, and he kicked the door open hard enough to hit Lamar in the shoulder and send him reeling against the desk.

"You rotten son of a bitch," Jonathan spat at him. "What have you done?"

Lamar scrambled to get out of the way, but with Jonathan blocking the only exit, and the desk taking up half the room, there was nowhere to hide. He sent a beseeching glance toward Lawrence, who'd risen from his chair, but his incredulous expression warned Lamar that he was on his own.

"It didn't mean anything!" Lamar shouted in his own defense.

"It meant a great deal to Lawrence," Jonathan countered. His only thought was that if Mae Leroux and Flossie Mae Kemble were one and the same, then Lamar had deliberately played a malicious trick on his younger brother. He was sickened clear through by that shocking lack of loyalty and gave Lamar no chance to beg for mercy before he lit into him with both fists.

"My God!" Lawrence cried, but Jonathan was not only punching Lamar in the face and body, but throwing him against the book-lined walls. It was all Lawrence could do to dodge his friend's furious blows, his brother's flailing arms, and the books sailing through the air. There was no way he could separate the battling pair without making a suicidal dive between them, and he wasn't crazy.

Hearing the commotion, Eliza Kate came running from the parlor, but the scene that greeted her in the study was so completely unexpected that she slid to a clumsy halt at the open doorway and simply gaped. She'd seen tornadoes skidding across the plains, their enormous energy

uprooting trees and shredding wooden structures in a
cloud of whirling debris, but that awful spectacle was mild
compared to this mayhem.

There was only one reason for the two men she loved
most in the world to have come to blows, and she was
consumed with guilt for having caused the fight. Somehow her father must have discovered that she and Jonathan were lovers, and while Jonathan had every right to
defend himself against her father's resulting wrath, it
quickly became apparent that he was the one who was on
the attack.

Her father was the heavier man, but his ineffectual
punches just slid right off Jonathan, who rather than tir-
ing, was actually throwing increasingly vicious blows. Frozen by fear, Eliza watched him methodically beat her
father to his knees.

When Ricky shoved Eliza aside and rushed into the
room, she was sufficiently jarred to take a quick breath.
She was overcome with dread for the heated questions
that would come her way the instant her father was able
to speak. Clearly he thought she had made the worst of
choices, but how could Jonathan have ever believed beating her father into submission was the best way to deal
with the problem?

Jonathan had already stepped back, but Ricky knelt and
wrapped his arms around Lamar's shoulders to shield him
from further harm. "Whatever the hell you're fighting
over, you've won, Blair. Don't kill him, please," Ricky
begged, his voice cracking with emotion.

Grateful for the help in breaking up the fight, Lawrence
quickly grabbed hold of Jonathan's shirt to yank him back
another step. "You needn't tell Ricky what prompted the
fight, but your efforts to protect me were misguided at
best. What possible difference can it make if Mae's name
is Flossie Mae or just plain Mae?"

As shocked as Jonathan had been earlier, Ricky gasped,
but in the crowded study his astonishment went unnoticed. Absolutely dumbfounded, he stared up at his uncle

and then at Jonathan Blair, who still looked ready to kill.

Unable to make sense of that exchange, Eliza clung to the doorjamb as with Ricky's assistance, their father stumbled to his feet. His face was a bloody mask over deathly pale skin. The hatred lighting Jonathan's gaze made it plain he'd relished every punishing blow. Eliza took a shaky step forward to join Ricky and wrapped her hands around their father's upper arm, but he promptly shook them both off.

"Leave me be," Lamar scolded. He fumbled for his handkerchief and dabbed at his bloody mouth with trembling hands. "I can't let your mother see me like this. Tell her I had to go into town, but I'll be in my room."

"Can you make it up the stairs?" Ricky asked anxiously and with a hasty glance toward his uncle and sister, he hurried after his father.

The usually neatly kept room was a shambles, and Eliza Kate wasn't even tempted to navigate the book-strewn carpet to move closer to Jonathan. He'd raked his hair out of his eyes, but his chest was still heaving from exertion. His shirt had been ripped open, and a deep scratch had left a bloody trail across his flat belly where her father must have clawed at him as he'd fallen.

She was horrified by the violence they'd unleashed on each other, but she'd always known Jonathan was dangerous. God help her, from the instant she'd laid eyes on him, she'd recognized the threat inherent in him, but this horror was beyond imagining.

She sent him a questioning glance, and his gaze narrowed in a silent warning to be still; but if this awful fight hadn't been over her, then what could have provoked such senseless rage?

"Uncle," she asked breathlessly, "what happened here?"

Lawrence responded with an incredulous shrug. "Jonathan obviously took violent exception to something Lamar wanted to tell to me about Mae, but I certainly don't need him to censor our conversations. Believe me, I'm every bit as disgusted by this brutal fight as you must be.

"Don't you clean up this mess, Eliza Kate, or I'll never be able to find anything. I'll take care of it tomorrow. Right now I'm going into town to see Mae, and I don't give a damn whether she calls herself Mae or Flossie."

Lawrence's expression hardened as he turned toward his friend. "As for you, Jonathan, try to remember the war's over. I can take real good care of myself now."

Eliza Kate moved aside to allow Lawrence to pass, but then quickly planted her feet to block Jonathan's exit. "Oh, no you don't," she whispered. She knew she was pushing him while his mood must still border on murderous rage, but after he had given her father such a savage beating, the very least he owed her was a lucid explanation as to why.

"If this was about Mae Leroux," she challenged, "is it because you're interested in her too?"

Astonished that she could have reached such a ridiculous conclusion, Jonathan responded with a rude snort. He raised badly bruised hands to rebutton his shirt, but several of the small mother-of-pearl disks were missing, and he was forced to abandon the effort. He was still so disgusted with what Lamar had done, however, that he could barely look at Lamar's lovely daughter.

"Trust me, Eliza Kate. This really doesn't concern you."

Eliza had known there was no love lost between her father and Jonathan, but she refused to allow him to brush her aside as rudely as her father had. She crossed her arms over her bosom and stood her ground. "The hell it doesn't. Now I want the truth, if you're even capable of speaking it."

"I'm not the one telling vicious lies," Jonathan retorted. After that staunch denial, he wrapped his throbbing hands around her narrow waist, and ignoring the pain, plucked her off her feet. His expression grimly determined, he set her out of his way, strode out of the study and right on out of the house.

At that moment, Eliza was so furiously angry with him she didn't care if she ever saw him again. Her lover and her father despised each other, and if being trapped between them didn't concern her, then what did? Her heart was still pounding with fright, and she could barely see the chaos surrounding her through the tears filling her eyes.

"How could Jonathan possibly hold such a preposterous opinion?" she wondered aloud. But perhaps in the ease with which he'd set her aside, he had provided abundant proof of how little he really cared for her. Again growing faint, she sank down amid the scattered books and wept bitter tears for the foolish girl who'd fallen in love with a man she'd always known would break her heart.

As he rode into town, Lawrence kept rehashing the awful fight between Lamar and Jonathan, but he could not for the life of him understand why his old friend had flown into such a furious rage. Perhaps Jonathan had misunderstood Lamar's intentions, but he had already known what his brother was trying to say. After all, one of the first things Mae had confided was that she wasn't really French. Maybe she had also believed Mae to be a more elegant sounding name than Flossie Mae. So what? he asked himself.

He'd not accuse her of trying to be something she wasn't when she had always been so delightfully sincere with him. "What a regrettable incident," Lawrence muttered under his breath, and after a moment's silent debate, he vowed not to tell his darling Mae a word about it.

He left his horse at the livery stable. He was nearly an hour early, but he thought he'd just stop by the millinery shop to let Mae know he'd arrived in town. Then he'd browse the neighboring shops until she was ready to entertain.

He'd grown rather fond of the sound of the brass bells at her shop's door and gave them an extra shake as he entered. There was a gray-haired woman he didn't recognize seated behind the counter, and assuming she must be a new employee, he greeted her warmly.

"Good afternoon. I'd like to speak with Madame Leroux if I may."

"I am Madame Leroux. How may I help you, *monsieur*? If you're seeking a gift for your wife or sweetheart, I have many exceptionally beautiful things to suggest."

Her smile was as lovely as her softly voiced French accent, but Lawrence was far too anxious to see Mae to care why this woman was pretending to be the shop's owner. "I'm Lawrence Bendalin, a friend of Mae's," he assured her. "Perhaps this is an inconvenient time, but please let her know that I'm here."

"Mr. Bendalin and Mae?" Madame Leroux repeated the names with exaggerated care. This was not the Mr. Bendalin from whom she rented her shop, but she could easily discern a family resemblance. That still left her puzzled, but she had been a great beauty in her youth and involved in more than one clandestine affair.

That experience led her to suspect the Miss Kemble who had used her shop in the last week must have been calling herself Mae Leroux. She had agreed only to rent the shop for a few hours and not her own good name along with it. However, she did not want such a profitable and enjoyable interlude to end prematurely.

"You have caught me, *monsieur*," she finally responded, "but regrettably, Madame Leroux is out and not expected to return for another hour or two. Would you care to leave a message?"

Embarrassed by his utterly transparent admiration for Mae Leroux, Lawrence began to back away. "No, thank you. I shouldn't have come so early. I'll see her later." Disappointed, he turned to leave. "I'm sorry to have bothered you."

"A handsome man is never a bother, *monsieur*."

Certain she was merely adept at flattery, Lawrence still chuckled at the compliment. "Good afternoon." As he reached the door, he heard a muted giggle and glanced over his shoulder to find Mae's two seamstresses ducking out of sight. "Obviously they do not agree with you."

"On the contrary," Madame Leroux assured him. "They are laughing because they do."

Lawrence just shook his head as he went out the door, but his spirits were again high. He decided to visit the confectioner's shop, where he purchased half a dozen berry tarts and sat down to wait. After twenty minutes, his euphoria over his coming rendezvous with Mae gave way to a lingering sense of disgust with both Jonathan and Lamar. Then he began to wonder if he weren't partly to blame for the way they coddled him, but he was no longer the depressed semi-invalid he'd once been.

He smiled as he thought of the credit Mae deserved for his transformation. Preoccupied with hopes for the evening, he was startled to see a red-haired young woman dash by in a fancy yellow dress she'd only partly concealed with a long gray shawl. It had been years since he'd been in a brothel, but he recognized her type instantly. He wondered idly where she was bound in such a rush, but before he'd come up with a satisfactory guess, she went sprinting by in the opposite direction.

The confectioner had followed Lawrence's glance and chuckled knowingly. "That's Belle from the Rosedale. I wonder what she's up to in this part of town."

"Not much apparently," Lawrence replied, "because it sure didn't take her long." He knew Lamar owned the Rosedale, but he'd never been there. He'd not had to pay a woman for her favors until the war, and after . . . well, he'd rather be alone than with someone who'd be kind to him merely for the money. He couldn't think of anything sadder than that.

When it came to making love, Mae had definitely been worth the wait, but after watching the activity in the street for nearly an hour, he returned to her shop, only to find the same middle-aged woman behind the counter. "If you don't mind, I'll wait here this time," he announced and moved toward one of the small chairs near the counter.

"*Monsieur*, I am so sorry, but Mae has sent you a note.

I don't believe she'll be able to meet you this evening."

"But why not?" Lawrence made a hasty grab for the proffered note and scanned it quickly. Mae was breaking their date without any explanation. But she did beg his forgiveness.

"Please forgive me?" he murmured aloud. "That's rather dramatic, don't you think?"

Madame Leroux responded with a graceful shrug. "I am sure she is very sorry to disappoint you."

"Well, yes. Let's hope so," Lawrence replied. As he refolded the simple missive, it struck him that the writing more closely resembled a childish scrawl than the elegant script in the shop's ledger. "Wait a minute. I don't believe Mae even wrote this. Who brought it?"

"The young woman is not among our regular clientele, and she was in such a great hurry, there was no time to ask her name."

A young woman in a hurry? Lawrence didn't want to entertain his first thought, but it was too pressing to ignore. "Did she have bright red hair, a yellow dress, and a gray shawl?" he asked.

"Why yes, she was the one. Do you know her?"

"I do now," Lawrence replied tersely. He recalled Mae mentioning that she designed an occasional gown. Perhaps that's why she'd gone to the Rosedale, but even so, she'd need an escort home that night. He shoved the brief note in his pocket and again smiled at the clerk.

"Thank you. You've been very helpful." He couldn't enter a place like the Rosedale carrying a box of berry tarts and handed the box to her instead. "I meant these treats for Mae, but I'd rather you shared them with the other ladies here."

"Thank you, *Monsieur* Bendalin. I know we will enjoy them."

Lawrence nodded politely, but he left the shop frustrated and confused. He would have to fetch his horse to ride over to the Rosedale, and with every step toward the livery stable, his limp grew more pronounced. He could so easily devise perfectly innocent reasons for Mae to be at the Rosedale, but he was haunted by Lamar's taunting laugh.

He had to stop to catch his breath and took a moment to reread Mae's note. The handwriting still puzzled him, but perhaps Mae had been altering a gown and dictated the note to—what had the confectioner called her—Belle?

"Yes. That's probably it," he assured himself. Mae had sent the message, but had been too busy to write it herself. Relieved that explanation made such good sense, he was able to retrieve his horse from the stable and ride to his brother's brothel with a renewed sense of purpose. He trusted his Mae, and if she'd sent a note from the Rosedale, then she was certainly there for a legitimate, rather than scandalous, purpose.

Belle rapped lightly on Flossie Mae's door, then entered the darkened room without waiting for a response. She tiptoed up to the bed where Flossie lay curled up in a tight ball and leaned close. "Flossie Mae? Are you awake?"

She dared not touch the badly battered madam but was encouraged when Flossie turned toward the sound of her voice, and her swollen eyes opened to narrow slits. "Lamar's brother is downstairs," Belle continued in a hushed whisper. "I swear I didn't see him when I delivered your note, so I've no idea how he followed me here. He's asking for Mae Leroux. He seems to think you're here to sew."

Wracked with pain, Flossie could barely comprehend what had happened. She'd not really expected Lawrence to turn up at the millinery shop after Lamar had told him the truth about her, but from what Belle said, he still thought she was Mae Leroux. "That doesn't make any sense," she murmured softly.

"Why not? I imagine a woman who makes fancy hats can sew real well," Belle argued.

Flossie hadn't been referring to talent with a needle but

lacked the energy to correct the misunderstanding. She
pulled her knees closer to her chest and stifled a low
moan. If Lamar hadn't told Lawrence who she was, then
it had to be because he wanted his kid brother to make
the awful discovery himself. That was even more cruel
than what Lamar had done to her, but her thoughts were
too muddled by pain to know what to do.

"Lawrence is here?" she repeated numbly.

"Yes, ma'am. He sure is. He's a nice-looking man too.
Now what shall I tell him?"

Drifting in and out of consciousness, Flossie Mae
longed to simply disappear so she'd not have to see the
sick look on her dear Lawrence's face when he finally
realized what she was. "Despicable," she breathed out
softly.

Belle bent closer. "Mr. Lawrence, ma'am?"

"No, me. Tell him I'm dead."

Belle slanted a hip across the foot of the bed. "You're
not making a lick of sense. We should have called Doc
Burnett first thing this morning like I wanted to. If you
really think you're dying, I'll run get him right now."

The addition of Belle's weight on the mattress sent a
fresh burst of pain rippling through Flossie's badly
bruised body, and she cringed as she shook her head. "No
doctor can help me. Now go on downstairs and tell
Lawrence that Mae Leroux is dead. Do it!" she ordered
forcefully but began to cough and could barely stand the
resulting agony circling her cracked ribs.

Reluctantly, Belle rose and backed away toward the
door. "I doubt he'll believe me." She waited a long moment, but when Flossie remained silent, she shrugged and
went on downstairs.

Belle found Lawrence standing right by the door where
she'd left him. His expression brightened when she approached, but he was glancing past her, expecting Mae to
be following close behind. He looked a little like Lamar,
but she could tell he was a lot nicer.

"Now I realize this won't make a bit of sense," Belle

informed him, "but Mae instructed me to tell you that she's dead."

Belle delivered the message with the stilted perfection of an actress totally lacking in talent, and Lawrence simply shook his head. "That's absurd. If she were actually dead, she couldn't have told you to say that."

Belle nodded. "My thoughts exactly, sir. I think you'd better leave. Unless, of course," she added coyly, "you wouldn't mind spending a little time with me this evening?"

That Belle would flirt with him didn't really surprise Lawrence. After all, she worked in a brothel and was expected to entertain her share of the men who came through the door. "I've no idea what's going on here," he replied as coolly as he could possibly manage under such ridiculous circumstances, "but I'm not going anywhere until I see Mae."

He took a step toward the wide staircase. "Just tell me where she is, and I'll find her myself."

Belle grabbed for Lawrence's arm, unwittingly threw him off balance, and nearly caused him to fall. When he lurched into her, she stumbled into Marlene, who'd been inching close to eavesdrop on their conversation. "I'm so sorry," Belle cried when they'd all three recovered, and an equally apologetic Marlene turned away. "But Mae doesn't want you to come up to her room, not tonight, not ever."

Lamar's cocky grin flashed in Lawrence's mind, and he finally understood what had prompted Jonathan's attack. He was stunned by the same disbelief that had rocked him when he'd been shot. Knowing exactly what was coming, he steeled himself against the excruciating pain.

The scent of Belle's cheap perfume floated on the foggy layer of cigar smoke drifting out of the parlor, where a man was playing a lively tune on the piano to encourage a party mood. The noisy conversation, which had dropped to a hush when he'd nearly fallen, again erupted, and in the cacophony, he was certain he heard his name among the laughter. Still, he stubbornly grasped for hope.

"Mae has her own room here?" he asked skeptically.

Belle raised her hand to fuss with a stray curl. Most men loved her red hair, but Lawrence apparently hadn't noticed anything remarkable about her, which was a real shame.

"Sure," she replied. "But her name isn't really Mae Leroux. It's Flossie Mae Kemble, and she's the madam here."

Lawrence noticed Belle's red hair then, but only because the whole room was now swimming in a sickening blood red. It had all been a bold-faced lie. From that first sweet brush of her hand, Flossie Mae had played him for the pathetic fool he surely was. How she and Lamar must have laughed at him!

Thoroughly humiliated, he relied on what little dignity he had left and went straight out the door without telling Belle that if Mae was the madam of the Rosedale, then he was overjoyed to learn she was dead.

He recognized a white blur as the dapple-gray gelding he'd ridden into town, but once mounted, he didn't know where he could go that people wouldn't snicker at him behind their hands or cluck their tongues in pity.

Part Three

Chapter Fourteen

Jonathan was still standing outside the barn soaking his hands in the watering trough when Robby rode into the yard on a palomino pony. The boy took one look at the disheveled man and leaped to the most exciting conclusion.

"Hey, Jonathan!" he yelled as he slid off the pony's back. "What happened?" Eager to hear all about it, he rushed to Jonathan's side. "Did you tangle with renegade Comanches?"

Jonathan hated to disappoint the bright-eyed lad. "Sorry, but I've yet to see a single Comanche brave anywhere near here."

Robby hung over the side of the trough to get a better look at Jonathan's bruised hands. "Shucks, but you must have been fighting someone. If one of the hands got out of line with you, we'll fire him before sundown."

Robby was studying him with a delighted grin, and Jonathan couldn't help wondering why Lamar had two fine sons while his own darling boy had died. Forcing himself away from such troubling comparisons, he looked back toward the house and worried Robby might be the only Bendalin still speaking to him. Even that couldn't last much longer.

Robby followed Jonathan's distracted glance and again came to the wrong conclusion. "Jonathan? If you're really hurt, we'd better go and find Eliza Kate. She's got some salve that'll fix you up just fine in a day or two."

Jonathan pulled his aching hands out of the lukewarm water. It had been so long since he'd hit another man, he'd forgotten the agony he'd have to endure afterward. Still, finally being able to give Lamar what he deserved was well worth it. He curled his swollen fingers, but couldn't tighten them into a fist.

"I appreciate your concern, Robby, but it's not a good idea to bother your sister."

"Why not? Eliza Kate likes you." Robby lowered his voice to a conspiratorial whisper. "Don't let on that I told you, but I've seen her eyeing you when she thinks no one's looking."

Jonathan couldn't help smiling, but he was relieved Robby hadn't noticed how much time he'd also spent observing Eliza Kate. "That's real flattering, but she's not going to be eyeing me now, because I was fighting with your father."

Robby's pale brows compressed in furious disbelief. "But why? Aren't you two friends?"

Jonathan genuinely liked Robby and knew no good purpose would be served in tarnishing the boy's admiration for his father. He struggled to tell at least part of the truth, even if he dared not reveal all of it. "No, we're not. Lawrence is a close friend, but your father and I never have seen eye to eye. He said something today that I just couldn't abide, and I hit him. I don't recommend fighting. Usually it's just plain stupid, but today, well, I couldn't help myself."

Feeling thoroughly confused and sick at heart, Robby backed away. "I ought to look after my horse."

"Yes, you should, but before you do, your father wants your mother to believe he's gone into town, so at supper, please don't let on what really happened."

"You still plan on joining us for supper?" Robby asked incredulously.

"Yes, I do, and I'll do my best to make your mother think this was a particularly fine day. I could sure use your help."

Obviously torn by that request, Robby nodded, grabbed his pony's reins, and led him on into the barn. Jonathan hadn't really expected much in the way of help, but he was certain Robby would keep quiet about the fight for his mother's sake. Eliza Kate and Ricky would never upset their dear mother at supper either, which meant his worst problem might simply be maintaining a secure grip on his fork.

Jonathan shoved his hands back into the tepid water and wondered how Lawrence was getting along. He could not even imagine what Lawrence would say to Flossie Mae, or how she might respond, other than with more sweetly voiced lies.

"God, what a mess," he muttered under his breath, but damn it all, it wasn't his fault that Lamar was the worst of brothers. Still, to Jonathan's mind, it didn't matter that Lamar was responsible for the way Lawrence's romance would surely end; this was just another sorry example of how everyone close to him came to grief.

He hung his head and fought off the sorrow that threatened to suck him down into a darkness without end. He'd lived in that wretched abyss too long to risk a return, and yet there was a haunting appeal to a known misery compared to the tragedy he'd watched uncoil that day. He tried not to think about Eliza Kate, but it would have been far easier to cease breathing.

Jonathan's mood hadn't improved by the time he entered the parlor that evening. Only Delia offered a welcoming smile, while Robby stared out a window, and Ricky looked as though he hadn't waited for the cover of darkness to raid the liquor cabinet.

Then there was Eliza Kate who sat primly beside Delia and was as unwilling as her brothers to meet his gaze. She was dressed in the gray gown, which flattered her slender figure without revealing a pleasing glimpse of the soft swells hidden beneath the tucked bodice. She had been no happier with him the first time he'd seen her in it, and he wondered if that distressing memory had prompted her to wear it again that night.

"Both Lamar and Lawrence are in town," Delia explained apologetically. "So it will be a rather quiet evening. I do hope you won't mind."

"Not at all," Jonathan replied. "Frankly, I'd welcome a quiet evening for a change."

At that comment, Eliza Kate's head came up with a snap, and the look she shot Jonathan stung far more than his pride. He couldn't blame her for being angry, and part of him welcomed the hatred that would ease the pain of parting. But he'd never chosen the easy path in life, not even once.

Certain none of them would enjoy a bite of supper with him there to dampen the already somber mood, Jonathan promptly discounted the need to remain for Delia's sake. "I'm worried about Lawrence," he announced. "Perhaps I'd better ride into town and check on him."

"But why, dear?" Delia inquired, her innocent gaze wide with wonder.

While Jonathan gave the appropriate reply, he directed his response to Eliza Kate. "I fear he's fallen in love with the wrong woman."

Delia raised pale hands to lightly rouged cheeks. "Oh no! How can that be?"

Eliza Kate heard so much more than concern in Jonathan's deep voice, and recognizing a clear challenge to all she held dear, she issued a challenge of her own. "I assume you're referring to Mae Leroux, but if Lawrence loves her, how can she possibly be the wrong woman?"

The question was so naïvely endearing, Jonathan had to smile. But he also noticed Ricky's deepening glower, and that Robby had begun to clutch the windowsill with a white-knuckled grip. Clearly their mother had raised them to behave as gentlemen, but he doubted they could contain their disapproval through an entire meal.

He lowered his voice, hoping his response wouldn't come across as a lecture. "You enjoy sitting out in the garden reading romantic poetry, Eliza Kate, but life isn't always so pretty. I'm worried that Lawrence has walked, no make that been led," Jonathan stressed, "into a real ugly situation. Now tonight I could either sit here and pretend it didn't happen, or go into town and do whatever I can to make certain he gets home all right."

Equally convinced that was the proper course, Ricky pushed himself out of his chair and rose to his full height. "I'm going with you."

"Thanks, but I doubt it will take two of us," Jonathan said.

"I know Fort Worth a whole lot better than you do," Ricky countered, and with a quick glance toward his mother, he warned Jonathan not to argue.

From what Jonathan knew of Ricky's habits, he supposed the young man probably did know where Lawrence would go to nurse a broken heart. "All right then, let's be on our way," he agreed.

"And I'll have to stay here with the women," Robby complained.

"That's enough, Robby," Eliza Kate cautioned firmly. She gave her mother's hand a light pat, then rose to approach Jonathan. "Allow me to walk you to the door."

Jonathan knew she'd do exactly as she pleased, regardless of his response and merely nodded. "I hope you'll forgive me for leaving so abruptly, Mrs. Bendalin, but I'd be poor company for you while I'm preoccupied with Lawrence's welfare."

"Of course," Delia answered sweetly. "You must do whatever you think is best."

Eliza Kate not only walked Jonathan and Ricky to the front door, she went out onto the porch with them. Her expression then filled with a righteous rage, and she folded her arms across her chest. "Suppose you tell me exactly what's going on here, Mr. Blair."

Ricky raised both hands to plead. "Believe me, sis, you don't want to know."

Undaunted, Eliza fixed her gaze on Jonathan. "Oh, but I do. In fact, I insist upon hearing the whole story you dodged this afternoon."

Ricky shook his head in disgust and turned away to lean on the porch rail, but he glanced over his shoulder to sympathize with Jonathan. "I warned her, but as usual she refuses to listen. Go ahead and tell her whatever you like."

"I don't like any of it," Jonathan said darkly. He stared at Eliza Kate, wishing that she'd thought better of pushing him so hard, but her gaze didn't soften. If anything, her resolve appeared to grow stronger by the second, and he quickly tired of protecting Lamar. For a moment, he was at a loss as to where to begin but then chose the most obvious point.

"Have you ever heard of the Rosedale Hotel?" he asked.

Eliza tossed her head impatiently. "Of course. It's a whorehouse my father owns. What does it have to do with Lawrence and a pretty milliner?"

Jonathan couldn't believe his ears. "Lamar actually told you about the Rosedale?"

"No, of course not," Eliza assured him, "but I've heard rumors for years. One of our hands might not have noticed I was nearby when he bragged to a friend. Sometimes I've overheard conversations in town. You'd be surprised what men will reveal when they don't realize a woman is listening, which is most of the time, by the way, and completely beside the point."

Ricky's shoulders were shaking slightly from laughter, but Jonathan failed to see any humor in the whole ugly situation. "Just how much do you know about the Rosedale?" he asked him.

"As much as any man in Fort Worth," Ricky admitted as he turned to rest his elbows on the rail. "Which is all I care to say in front of my sister. Father wouldn't tell me anything this afternoon, but once I heard Flossie Mae's name, I understood enough to piece it together."

Eliza Kate rested her fists on her hips. "Are you telling me that Mae or Flossie, if that's her real name, has something to do with the Rosedale?"

That was so much easier to admit than that Flossie Mae Kemble was her father's mistress, but Jonathan still resorted to a reluctant shrug as he replied. "Yes, ma'am, she apparently does, and I happen to believe Lawrence deserves a lot better."

Eliza just stared at him. From what he'd said, there were only three parts to the equation: Lawrence, Mae Leroux, and the Rosedale. "But if Mae Leroux once worked at the Rosedale," she argued, "then surely my father must have known."

"You're a whole lot smarter than that, Eliza Kate," Ricky chided.

Eliza Kate glanced between the two men. Apparently extremely uncomfortable, Jonathan was nervously shifting his stance. Ricky, on the other hand, was grinning smugly as though for once he knew something she didn't. "Father knew," she surmised aloud.

She had such a marvelously expressive face, Jonathan could have given the precise instant she took her conclusion a step further. The horror filling her eyes sickened him, but he was the last person who could ease her pain. Instead, he took her arm and escorted her to the door.

"You need to keep your mother company tonight. I sure hope Lawrence won't do anything desperate, but I can't prevent it standing here. Come on, Rick. Let's find your uncle and bring him home."

Eliza watched them walk to the barn before she entered the house, but she felt numb, and the echoes of an ancient fear coursed through her. She thought her father was probably asleep, and knew he needed his rest to heal, but she longed to hike up her skirts, race up the stairs, and confront him.

Instead, she paused a moment to compose herself, and walked into the parlor wearing a confident smile. After all, it was a mask she'd worn for years, and she could maintain the pose for one more night.

As Jonathan and Ricky started down the road into town, Red Warrior and Harlequin were eager to race, but the men held their mounts to an even pace. An uneasy companion, Ricky cleared his throat but it failed to smooth the harshness from his voice. "I'm doing this for my uncle, but regardless of the cause, I'll not forgive what you did to my father."

Even with his hands still aching, Jonathan didn't feel the least bit vulnerable or threatened. "I don't care if you forgive me or not, but let me get this straight, you actually believe it was a good idea for your father to have one of his whores pose as a widowed milliner when it could only break Lawrence's heart?"

"It wasn't one of his whores," Ricky insisted. "It was Flossie Mae Kemble. She's a madam."

"I fail to see the difference."

"That's because you've never met Flossie Mae," Ricky replied. "She'd never hurt Uncle Lawrence."

"This argument is too stupid to continue," Jonathan responded, thinking Ricky's opinions were as twisted as Lamar's. They traveled through the darkness without exchanging another word until they reached the outskirts of Fort Worth, and even then they couldn't agree.

"We might as well begin with the Rosedale," Ricky offered.

"No. I want to meet the real Madame Leroux and find out what she knows about Lawrence."

"Probably nothing," Ricky replied. "It's a waste of time."

"Then go where you like," Jonathan ordered, and recalling the location of the shop from the times he'd walked through town, he rode to the milliner's without checking to see if Ricky was following.

Madame Leroux was tallying figures in her ledger when the knocking began at her door. She ignored it for a minute or two, but when the noise grew increasingly annoying, she left her private apartment to respond. She'd not expected the caller to be such a handsome devil, but the fierceness of his expression made her sorry she'd opened her door.

"If it is a gift you want, *monsieur*, I must insist you return Monday morning."

"I've no need of frilly hats," Jonathan informed her. "I'm looking for Lawrence Bendalin. Have you seen him today?"

With scant hope of avoiding the persistent man, Madame Leroux leaned against the door to bar his entrance to the shop. "He stopped by briefly earlier. A woman sent him a message, and I believe he went in search of her."

"Really?" Jonathan felt Ricky moving up too close behind him and took a step back to brush him out of his way. "Do you know her name?"

"I have no idea, *monsieur*. Mr. Bendalin and I are barely acquainted."

"You are Madame Leroux, are you not?"

"Yes, of course. This is my shop. Who else would I be at this hour?"

Jonathan just shook his head. "Nowadays, one never knows."

Ricky waited until the milliner had closed her door, then he gestured toward their horses. "I hope you'll listen to me now. Let's go on over to the Rosedale."

"I'll not set foot in the cursed place," Jonathan vowed. He yanked the reins from the hitching post and swung himself up on Red Warrior.

"Then I'll go," Ricky offered as he mounted Harlequin. "They all know me there."

"I'll just bet they do." Jonathan flexed his hands and

welcomed the resulting pain as a sharp reminder of how serious their mission truly was.

"You don't like any of us, do you?"

"Quit baiting me," Jonathan ordered. The street was crowded with men out looking for a good time on a Saturday night, but he knew Lawrence didn't enjoy walking enough to be out for a stroll. After a moment's thought, he realized Flossie Mae must have been the woman who'd sent Lawrence the message, so the Rosedale probably wasn't such a stupid place to visit after all.

"All right," he agreed. "I'll follow you to the Rosedale, but I'm still not going inside. Just see what you can find out and be quick about it."

Ricky flashed a wide grin, then shoved his hat back on his head. "Most men wouldn't pass up the chance to stop by the Rosedale. Are you just worried about Uncle Lawrence, or are you getting sweet on Eliza Kate?"

Jonathan drew a deep breath as he ran several possible responses through his mind. With Rick and Eliza Kate being close, Rick was sure to repeat whatever he said, and he didn't want Eliza to be any more furious with him than she already was. "Any man would adore your sister," he replied flippantly, "but she's safe at home, and we've no idea where Lawrence is."

Greatly relieved Jonathan hadn't shown even a tiny glimmer of interest in Eliza Kate, Ricky let the subject drop. "I'll bet you ten dollars my uncle's at the Rosedale getting drunk with some real charming company."

Lawrence had been too excited to meet Mae Leroux for Jonathan to believe such a preposterous suggestion. "You're forgetting I know you backed Red Warrior in the race and haven't got a cent left to wager. I doubt you'll hear anything but lies at the Rosedale. But on the off chance one of the girls does know something, we'll go there, but I'm not waiting outside more than five minutes before I start looking elsewhere."

"Bastard," Ricky muttered under his breath, but he led

the way and rather enjoyed having Jonathan Blair covering his back that Saturday night.

Eliza Kate was too distraught to taste more than her lightly
buttered potatoes at supper, but despite Robby's initial
complaint, he appeared to thoroughly enjoy being the
lone male at the table. He'd kept their mother so entertained with tales of his school chums that the meal had
passed quickly. Then he'd volunteered to escort Delia upstairs and read to her.

As the pair slowly climbed the stairs, Eliza Kate was
touched by how attentive each was to the other. She was
so pleased her mother possessed the energy to welcome
Robby's lively company. Certain they would enjoy the remainder of the evening without any help from her, she
fled the house for the peace of the garden.

The scent of night-blooming jasmine filled the air, lur-
ing her along the paths until she reached the bench beside the grape arbor. She sat down, folded her hands in
her lap, and drank in the tranquility of the night, but she
was restless even there.

Her father was so badly beaten he might hide in his
room for days. Her dear uncle had embraced love with
such joy, but surely that evening he'd discovered his
adored Mae was more at home in a bordello than a millinery shop. That her father could have instigated such a
tragic romance was too awful to even contemplate, and
yet she was tormented by the idea.

She curled up on the bench and hugged her knees. Her
home had been such an orderly place until Jonathan Blair
had arrived. Perhaps he had simply bewitched her, she
agonized, but still every choice he'd forced her to make
had been entirely her own. She could blame only herself
for falling in love with a soft-spoken man who had now
revealed a violent temper.

She rubbed the spot where the bruise had faded from
her hand, but other than the time he'd spoken of his late
wife, his touch had always been gentle, feather-light. He

treated her as though she were precious to him, and when she considered how deeply concerned he was for Lawrence, she couldn't help wishing he held her father in a similar high regard.

She clasped her arms and rocked slowly back and forth like a keening child. Tomorrow there would be no place to hide, but for the night, she took comfort from the shadowed garden and prayed somehow there had simply been a terrible mistake and that Mae Leroux really was the sweet woman Lawrence loved. Before long, she rested her head against the back of the bench and dozed off, but the sound of a lumbering wagon rattling into the yard startled her awake shortly after dawn.

Fearing the worst, she raced along the carefully tended paths, then burst through the gate and sprinted across the yard. Jonathan was at the back of the ramshackle wagon untying Red Warrior, Harlequin, and one of their dapple-grays, while Ricky was still atop the wagon's sloping seat, contending with a pair of dusty mules. Before she reached the wagon, Jonathan dropped his mount's reins and cut her off.

"You'd better stop right here," he warned and tightened his grasp on her waist.

Eliza pushed against his arms and struggled to break free. "Lawrence isn't dead, is he? Oh, please, tell me that isn't his body in the wagon."

She was still wearing the prim gray dress. Her hair was a mass of tangled curls, and Jonathan was shocked to realize she'd waited up all night for them. He'd thought she trusted him more than that.

"No, he isn't dead," he assured her, "but he'll probably wish he were when he comes to. We found him in a cantina on the road to Dallas, and it wasn't the kind of place that serves quality liquor."

Eliza still squirmed, hoping to get at least a glimpse of her uncle. "Is that the only problem? He's just drunk?"

Jonathan glanced toward Ricky, who'd finally gotten the

mules under control. "Well, I'm ashamed to admit he was in a fight."

"A fight?" Ricky shouted. "You should have been there, Eliza Kate. It was the wildest brawl I've ever seen." He wrapped the mules' reins around the brake, jumped down, raised his arms to snap his fingers, and danced around in a tight circle.

"Look," he exclaimed. "There's not a mark on either of us, but we broke most of the tables and chairs, and left a dozen men out cold on the floor. I'll never be able to go back there again, but I doubt I'd want to."

Amazed that Ricky was still so full of life after the night they'd had, Jonathan smiled slowly, but Eliza couldn't imagine how anyone could find brawling in a cantina amusing. "If you don't mind, I'd rather not hear the details. Just get Lawrence cleaned up and into his own bed before anyone sees him. He embarrasses so easily, and I don't want him to think the hands are laughing at him."

"No, ma'am, neither do I," Jonathan replied. "Why don't you go on back in the house, and we'll carry Lawrence up the back stairs."

Eliza Kate wanted to make certain her uncle truly was unharmed, but with both Jonathan and Ricky blocking the way, she gave up trying. "All right, but just tell me one thing. "Did you talk with Mae or Flossie, whatever her name is? What did she say?"

"That's two questions," Jonathan pointed out.

"Stop teasing me," Eliza cried, too tired and still too angry with him for hurting her father to enjoy silly games.

"She wouldn't see us," Ricky answered. "And from what I was told, she refused to see Lawrence when he came looking for her. Maybe she's ashamed of deceiving him, but it sure looks as though it's over between them."

As she backed away from Jonathan, tears flooded Eliza Kate's eyes. "This is all so unfair. I've not seen Lawrence so happy in years. Why couldn't his beautiful dreams have come true?"

Jonathan bit back a caustic reply before it crossed his

lips, but he understood how fleeting dreams could be and knew her heartbreak was as deep as his own. "Go on up to your room and get ready for the day," he suggested softly. "You can count on us to take real good care of Lawrence."

With little choice, Eliza Kate turned away, but she couldn't help wondering if Jonathan ever ached for someone to take good care of him. "Things can't get much worse," she murmured to herself, but then she remembered Fletcher Monroe couldn't stay in Galveston forever.

"Dear God, what am I going to tell him?" she wondered aloud, but unlike Flossie, she'd never willingly deceive a man who loved her. It was just that the truth was going to be awfully difficult to tell.

Chapter Fifteen

Sunday morning, Flossie Mae was awakened by the sound of distant church bells. Her eyes were still swollen slits, and when she refused to eat a bite of breakfast or even take a sip of water, Belle panicked and summoned Dr. Burnett.

Clay Burnett was a local boy who'd gone to medical school after the war. He'd come home to Fort Worth to build his practice and had quickly become popular with the townspeople. The girls at the Rosedale liked him because he provided effective treatment without sanctimoniously striving to save their souls. He was also Delia Bendalin's physician and the last man Flossie wished to consult.

Clay pulled up a chair and reached for Flossie's wrist. "I'm pleased to find you still have a pulse, Mrs. Kemble. If the sheriff hasn't gone after the man who attacked you, I'll be happy to give the brute a taste of his own medicine."

Flossie assumed that was a physician's idea of humor but she was too deeply depressed to laugh. "Thanks, but there's no need." Clay was an attractive man, but just a blur to her now, although she could easily visualize his concerned frown. "Please just go away and leave me alone."

"You know I can't do that. Now, I've got all morning to sit here and chat. Suppose you tell me what happened."

Flossie Mae wasn't even tempted to confide the truth. "I fell out of bed," she murmured instead.

Clay chuckled in spite of himself. "It looks as though you fell off the roof."

"Feels like it too," Flossie admitted, and she made no attempt to stem the tears that trickled down her cheeks and soaked her pillow. "Please just go away."

"I'd be a poor excuse for a physician if I abandoned you in your hour of need, Mrs. Kemble, but I'll be happy to allow you to rest after you've sipped this cup of tea."

"Promise?"

"You have my word on it," Clay promised, and he waited for her to raise herself up slightly before he brought the delicate porcelain cup to her lips. "The Rosedale employs a couple of big, muscular men to protect the girls from contentious callers. How did the bastard who beat you get past them?"

Flossie hadn't realized she was thirsty, but she savored the soothing tea before she replied. "No one slipped by. I just fell out of bed."

Clay kept offering the flavorful brew until she had drained the cup. He then set it aside, postponed his promise to leave, and picked up a piece of toast. He broke off a tiny bite and guided it to her lips. "You think Lamar will believe that preposterous tale?" he asked.

The tea had whet her appetite, and her initial insistence that he leave was forgotten. Flossie obediently ate the toast while she sought a coherent answer to his question. Finally a reasonable reply occurred to her. "He knows I'm often clumsy."

Clay brushed the last of the toast crumbs from his hands. "And that's what you expect me to believe as well?"

"Yes, sir, I do." Flossie closed her eyes and hoped he'd allow her to simply die in peace. She yawned and snuggled down under her covers.

"Rest a day or two," Clay encouraged. "I'll come back to check up on you."

"You needn't bother," Flossie argued softly.

"Mrs. Kemble—" Clay began, but believing she'd already fallen asleep, he picked up his leather bag and left the room.

Flossie Mae wasn't actually asleep. She was dreamily recalling the time she'd spent with Lawrence. She could remember his every expression and gesture, the pleasant warmth of his voice, and the slow sweetness of his touch. Losing him hurt so much worse than anything Lamar could ever do to her, and she doubted Dr. Burnett had a remedy for a broken heart.

She really didn't want a cure. She just wanted to die while her last memories would be of Lawrence and the hours he'd truly loved her.

Lawrence didn't awaken until late afternoon. Jonathan had thoughtfully drawn his bedroom curtains, and for an instant, the hazy light made him think he'd passed out in the cantina where he'd fully intended to goad a bandit into shooting him, or failing in that risky endeavor, had meant to drink himself to death. Swiftly recognizing more familiar surroundings, he was overcome with furious disappointment. He rolled over to sit up, but an excruciating bolt of pain tore through his head, and he collapsed against his pillow and clamped his eyes shut.

Maybe he had died, he hoped momentarily, but the warm comfort of his own bed made that possibility appear remote. He didn't remember coming home though and idly wondered how he had gotten there. From the little bit he did recall, the cantina had been full of cutthroats whose evil glances should have terrified him. But last night, he hadn't cared whether or not he lived or died. Perhaps that had made him far more dangerous than any of his larcenous companions.

Disgusted to still be alive, he lay awash in misery until someone began rudely pounding on his door. "Go away!" he shouted angrily.

Not wishing to disturb Lawrence if he were still asleep, Jonathan had rapped lightly, and he was startled by the fury of his friend's response. Nevertheless, he opened the door slightly and peered in. "I just wanted to make certain that you're still among the living."

Lawrence grabbed a glass sitting on his nightstand and hurled it toward the door. His aim was off by at least a yard, and it bounced off the wall and rolled across the floor. "Leave me be," he yelled, and not up to facing Jonathan or anyone else, he rolled back on his side and drew the quilt up over his head.

Believing he should offer some words of comfort, Jonathan hesitated, but nothing profound or even remotely appropriate came to mind. "I'm real sorry," he finally murmured and quietly closed the door.

Eliza had meant to look in on Lawrence herself, but having found Jonathan outside his door, she'd drawn back to wait at the end of the hall. For a long moment she watched her lover stand with his head bowed. Certain he must be as unhappy as she, she turned back toward the stairs. Unfortunately, Jonathan's senses were far too keen for her to go unnoticed. When he called her name, she froze as though she'd been caught at some terrible mischief.

Rather than putting on church clothes, Eliza Kate had changed into the white blouse and split skirt she wore most days. She still looked every bit as distracted as when Jonathan had last seen her at dawn. He wondered if she'd been able to get any rest that day. He hadn't even tried. For the moment, going down the stairs was too great an effort, so when he reached the landing, he leaned back against the wall and crossed his arms loosely over his chest.

"Do you want me to leave?" he asked pointedly.

Not expecting such a dire question, Eliza Kate caught her breath. She could barely stand the prospect of facing her family at dinner, and Jonathan expected her to make a reasoned decision on something so important to them both?

While her thoughts were a tortured jumble of forbidden hopes and desperate fears, her heart ached with the pain he'd caused her. There were a great many reasons to encourage him to go, but frantic for a compelling incentive to make him stay, she quickly grasped the most obvious.

"You can't leave," she blurted out in a frantic whisper. "You promised to race Fletcher again."

In spite of the darkness of his mood, Jonathan broke into a rich, rolling laugh that bubbled up clear from his soul. "My God, how can you even remember that stupid race?" he asked when he finally caught his breath.

"I damn near killed your father. Last night, one of the desperados crowding that cantina would surely have shot Lawrence if Ricky and I hadn't arrived to save him; but Ricky swears that timely rescue doesn't make up for the beating I gave your father. Robby's steering clear of me as though I were a rattler poised to strike. Your poor mother has absolutely no idea of the chaos swirling around her, and you think I ought to stay and race Fletcher?"

Maybe it was lack of sleep, or more tension than any man could sanely carry, but Jonathan began to laugh again, and although he held his sides, he just couldn't control himself.

Eliza feared he had lost his mind. She realized that in describing her family, he'd made no reference to her. "Don't I matter at all?" she asked. Her voice was so soft, she hardly expected him to hear.

But as always, Jonathan was intensely aware of her. He

brushed the tears of laughter from his eyes and straightened up. "Hell yes, you matter. That's why I offered to leave."

Another far more attractive option immediately occurred to Eliza Kate, but because it had obviously escaped him, she simply sneered. "If that's the very best you can do, you don't need my permission to take your leave."

Her finely shaped chin was raised at an all-too-familiar tilt, and exasperated with the willful beauty, Jonathan reached out to catch her elbow before she could escape him down the stairs. "No, I don't think I'm quite ready to bid you good-bye after all," he declared with a newfound resolve.

Too proud to throw herself into his arms in gratitude, Eliza Kate regarded him with a forbidding stare. "My father told Mother that on his way home last night, his horse stumbled in the dark. He claims he fell upon a jagged rock. She would never think to doubt his excuse, although he looks more as though he's been trampled in a stampede.

"I swear there are days when I feel as though I'm an actress in some lengthy farce; but I've no copy of the play and don't know my lines."

Clearly she was furious with him, and Jonathan couldn't blame her, but she was so very beautiful with her eyes flashing fiery sparks and her cheeks rosy with anger that it was all he could do to release her rather than yank her into a tight embrace. "The way I see it, this play's a tragedy rather than a farce, but I know exactly what you mean. That's also why I don't give a damn about racing Fletcher."

"Is there anything you do care about?" Eliza challenged, and when his eyes narrowed menacingly, she turned her back on him, this time fully intending to escape.

"Eliza Kate!" Jonathan breathed out. "You saw what I did to your father. What do you suppose Lawrence will do to him as soon as he's able to leave his bed?"

Caught in mid stride, Eliza could neither turn back to

confront Jonathan anew nor continue downstairs without giving his taunting question the serious consideration it deserved. Though it would be completely out of character, her tenderhearted uncle had been severely provoked, and she would not fault him if he went after her father in a blind rage.

In the next instant, the certain fury of Lawrence's anger blurred with her own, and overwhelmed by a scalding flood of memories, she sank down on the steps and rested her head in her hands. Her mother had always insisted upon ladylike behavior, and she'd never been allowed to vent her own anger with her father. Fortunately, she was no longer a child who idolized him despite his many faults.

Jonathan had meant to make her think, not rob her of her composure. Without a moment's hesitation, he sat down beside her and patted her back as he would a sobbing child. "Please don't cry," he urged persuasively. "I'll find a way to keep Lawrence from doing anything he'll regret."

Although startled by the sudden softening of his tone, Eliza Kate straightened to emphatically reject his sympathy, and there was not even a hint of tears in her eyes. "You've misunderstood. I've been furiously angry with my father myself. Ricky and Robby were too young to realize what was happening, but I'll never forget the day Father and Uncle Lawrence left to fight for the Confederacy.

"I love my mother dearly, but although she somehow survived the perils of childbirth three times, she's never been strong. Although I was only nine years old when my father left us, it was obvious to me that Mother would never be able to run the ranch on her own."

"So you took over," Jonathan observed quietly. With a slow smile he imagined her as a beautiful child shaking her fist at her father rather than blowing kisses as he rode away. He'd not realized until then that Lamar had abandoned his whole family as cruelly as he had Lawrence.

"Oh yes, I most certainly did," Eliza responded proudly.

"We had even more hands then than we do now because Father didn't want the ranch overrun by the Comanches while he was away. Anyway, I was so angry that he'd gone off on what he claimed would be a brief adventure, that I managed this place with the resolve worthy of a British queen.

"Mother would stand beside me and simply smile her sad, sweet smile. Then the *vaqueros* would be so completely enchanted they would rush to do her bidding without ever realizing that I was the one issuing the orders. By the time my father and uncle finally returned home, I'd forgotten what it meant to be a child. I suppose that must have happened to a great many children during the war."

Touched by the story of the courageous girl she had been, and the glorious woman she'd become, Jonathan drew her into his arms and rested his chin lightly against her golden curls. "That cursed war made us all old before our time," he murmured softly.

She'd never admitted to being angry with her father to anyone, but surprisingly relieved by the revelation, she was content to rest in Jonathan's embrace. Still, she couldn't help wondering why he'd offered to leave when surely he must have known how badly she would want him to stay.

Had he merely longed to hear her beg for more of his company? she worried. That made little sense to her, and yet he had asked the question in such an off-hand manner, as though her answer held little meaning for him.

Despite the warmth of his gentle embrace, she had never been more confused. But before she could make sense of anything that had happened in the last two days, she heard a hoarse cry and looked down to find Robby at the bottom of the stairs. He appeared to be shocked to find them together, but she saw his tears as he bolted for the door.

"Oh damn," she swore, and without a word to Jonathan, she sprang to her feet and ran after her brother.

Jonathan allowed the soft folds of her skirt to slip through his hands without grabbing hold, but as he leaned back against the stairs on his elbows, he shook his head. For just a moment, they'd been as close as they were in his bed; Robby had seen a lot more than he should have. It didn't actually surprise him that Eliza Kate had gone after the boy. Her family held so much of her heart, he doubted she'd ever have any love left over for him.

Striving to convince himself that was a good thing, he rose to go to his room and rest before before a dinner that was sure to be as polite as hell, and every bit as unpleasant as his worst nightmares.

As he crossed the landing, he caught a glimpse of Carmen carrying a tray into Lawrence's room. There was no time to warn her away. Expecting the worst, he paused, but when only silence ensued, he supposed Lawrence might be out of things to throw. If that were the case, he hoped Carmen had better luck with him than he had.

The first time he'd seen the dark-eyed young woman, he'd thought there had been a certain fondness to her gaze despite Lawrence's insistence that she was Delia's maid and nothing more. Well, perhaps now she would be precisely what Lawrence needed. At least he sure hoped so.

As he climbed the stairs to the third floor, he swore if he ever built another house, it would be a simple cabin with a single story where he'd never have to worry about being caught in a compromising position on the damn stairs.

"Mr. Lawrence?" Carmen nudged the door closed with her hip. "I've brought you some of the vegetable soup you like so much."

Hovering on the edge of sleep, Lawrence groaned. He was far too unhappy to be embarrassed about being seen in such a sorry state, but he assumed Jonathan must have sent her, and that really annoyed him.

"Tell Jonathan to mind his own business," he yelled. "Better yet, tell him to go straight to hell!"

Astonished by such uncharacteristic rudeness, Carmen

placed the tray on the dresser and approached the bed slowly. "I've not spoken with Mr. Blair," she advised coolly. "I was worried about you and came here on my own."

"That's even worse," Lawrence replied with a disgusted snort. "I don't need to be fed like an infant."

"I didn't plan on feeding you," Carmen insisted. "I just thought you might need some pleasant company."

It was the word *need* that caught Lawrence's attention, and he sat up despite the resulting agony in his head. His stomach lurched, but he swallowed hard to control the bile rising in his throat.

"And why would I be in such dire need of company, Carmen? Is the whole house talking about my being lonely?"

Carmen had never seen anything but the most gentlemanly behavior from the usually mild-mannered young man, and she took a cautious step away from the bed. "No, sir. I meant no disrespect."

She was shrinking away from him now as most women did, and the memory of Mae's smile suddenly flashed in his mind. Mae had always approached him as though he were still handsome and strong. God help him, he could almost feel her tender touch on his bare shoulder and the joy of her exuberant kisses.

"Did you hope I'd invite you into my bed?" Lawrence asked suddenly.

"Mr. Lawrence," Carmen said, gasping.

"You know I don't love you, so perhaps you'd prefer a straight business proposition. I'll pay you double what you earn looking after Delia, and I won't demand your attentions every night."

Carmen slammed the door on her way out, and relieved he would be spared her condescending company in the future, Lawrence flopped back down across his bed and prayed he'd not dream of Mae while he slept.

Eliza Kate chased Robby across the yard, into the barn, and right up the ladder into the loft. When he threw himself down near the open hay doors, she dropped to her knees and stretched out beside him on the coarse mound of hay. "Robby, I know you're upset, but please let me explain," she begged and struggled to catch her breath.

"I saw you kissing Blair," Robby complained, stubbornly refusing to look at her.

"No, you didn't," Eliza denied truthfully. "That may be what you think you saw, but Jonathan was just giving me a comforting hug because I was so unhappy."

Robby squirmed his hips to get more comfortable in the loose hay and rested his chin on clenched fists. "I hate Blair, and I'm going to tell Fletcher you were kissing him."

Shocked by the vehemence of his tone, Eliza sucked in a deep breath but the familiar fresh scent of the hay proved jarring. She'd done far more than merely kiss Jonathan, but she wasn't about to confide in her little brother. "You don't even like Fletcher," she argued instead. "Besides, I've changed my mind, and I'm not going to marry him."

His mood brightening, Robby sat up, but just as quickly, his expression filled with horror. "You're not going to marry Blair, are you? I know I never liked Fletcher much, but at least he never gave Father a beating."

Not feeling up to defending Jonathan any further, Eliza pushed herself into a sitting position and hugged her knees. "Things are a terrible mess, aren't they? But none of it is your fault. From what I can gather, Jonathan and Father have never liked each other."

"Yeah," Robby admitted grudgingly. "That's what Jonathan told me."

"Really?" At the moment, Eliza Kate didn't like her father much herself. She simply didn't understand how he could ever have imagined that Lawrence would be happy with some girl from the Rosedale. She hoped Robby didn't know anything about that disastrous affair.

"Something must have happened between them during the war," she suggested absently, "but I doubt either of them will ever tell us what it was."

Robby nodded thoughtfully. "Maybe Uncle Lawrence will if you ask him real nice."

"I don't think Lawrence knows," Eliza mused aloud, and in an instant she realized her uncle had never questioned why it had been Jonathan who'd carried him to safety after he'd been shot, rather than his own brother. She rubbed her arms against a sudden chill and glanced away.

Robby studied his sister's pensive frown a long moment, and then growing restless, jumped to his feet. "Well, I'll bet Father has a real good reason to hate Blair, and so do I. Why's he still hanging around where he isn't wanted? Hasn't he got the good sense to leave?"

"He's got plenty of sense, Robby, but he promised to race Fletcher a second time, and he means to keep his word." The excuse sounded even more ridiculous now than when she'd first offered it. She wasn't surprised when Robby just scoffed, scrambled back down the ladder, and ran away.

This time Eliza Kate didn't pursue him, but she also didn't hurry back to the house. Thinking they could use some fresh flowers for the dinner table, she took a detour through the garden, but forgot all about creating a bouquet when she found Carmen sobbing by the lily pond.

"What's wrong?" Eliza hastened to ask. "Has something happened to Mother?"

Carmen shook her head, but continued to weep as she provided a sputtering account of Lawrence's insulting offer. "What must he think of me?" she wailed. "I thought he was such a nice man, but now, I don't ever want to see him again."

Eliza sat beside Carmen and slid her arm around her shoulders. "Please don't carry on so," she soothed gently. "Lawrence has just had a dreadful shock, and obviously he isn't taking it well. I'm sure he'll offer a sincere apology in a day or so."

"I don't want to stay here that long," Carmen moaned, too humiliated to be satisfied with a mere apology.

"Please don't think of leaving us. Mother needs you,

Carmen. We all do. You mustn't think too badly of Lawrence. He's just not himself today." Eliza kept talking in a soothing tone until Carmen gulped a final sob and dried her eyes.

"Mother should be awake from her nap now, and she'll be waiting for you to help her dress for dinner. Will you go to her, please?" Eliza asked. "She is always so grateful for your kind attention."

"I love your mother, I really do," Carmen exclaimed. "But after today, I don't ever want to see Mr. Lawrence again. Please promise me I won't have to."

"You just leave him to me. I'll make certain he finds his manners," Eliza Kate promised firmly.

Carmen rose on shaky legs and took a hesitant step toward the house. "I used to love it here," she confided softly, and then rushed away.

Eliza Kate stayed behind to gather her thoughts, but she understood the gentle maid's dismay. When her dear uncle began making lewd suggestions to the help, they were in terrible straits indeed.

When she could delay no longer, she left the sweetly scented garden refuge for the house, where she fully intended to tell her uncle what she thought of him for terrorizing Carmen in such a shameful fashion. It wasn't until she reached his door that she acknowledged her own behavior was no longer above reproach.

Had it been that same afternoon that she'd bragged to Jonathan about how well she'd once run the ranch? What a ludicrous boast that seemed now that she was a grown woman and saw people as they truly were rather than as a young girl had longed for them to be.

"I used to love it here too," she murmured softly to herself, and then shoving aside her own sorrow, she knocked boldly on her uncle's door. When he responded with a muffled curse, she turned the crystal doorknob and walked in.

"I thought you had more courage," she challenged as she approached his bed. "You needn't tell me how much love hurts, because I know that pain well, but you're too fine a man to wallow in self-pity as you have today. If you can't pull yourself together in time for dinner, I'll understand, but if you ever speak another cross word to Carmen or any of our other help, I'll take a buggy whip to you."

Lawrence opened one eye and observed his niece standing with her hands on her hips and an expression as furious as her words. "Get out of here, Eliza Kate."

"I will not," Eliza swore emphatically. "Despite your current disheveled appearance and foul temper, I expect better of you. What possessed you to offer Carmen money to sleep with you? Don't you know she adores you?"

Lawrence had both eyes open, but he had to hold his head as he sat up. "I'm too sick to argue with you," he replied.

"Well, you ought to feel sick for saying such a stupid thing. Women do have feelings, and Carmen didn't deserve to be treated so badly."

"I just wanted her to go away," Lawrence moaned.

"Then you should have politely asked her to leave rather than insulting her so rudely. Now what do you intend to do about Mae Leroux?"

It hurt even to hear her name, and Lawrence shook his head and was instantly sorry. He ran his fingers through his hair, making it stick out like a porcupine's quills. The shadow of his beard made his thin features appear gaunt, and there was no mistaking the darkness of his mood.

"There is no Mae Leroux," he swore. "Or at least there isn't for me."

"How do you know?" Eliza asked. "Did you speak with her last night?"

Lawrence's head had begun to pound with a painful throb. "There is no Mae Leroux," he repeated in time with the pulsing ache.

Her thoughts taking a new direction, Eliza sat down on the foot of his bed. "You were thrilled with someone, Uncle Lawrence. That woman still exists. Perhaps you ought to hear her side of the story."

Lawrence dropped his hands and stared at her with cold fury. "There is no woman. There's only a clever whore who took me for a fool. Now get out of here before I find a horse whip to use on you."

He looked as though he meant it, too, and Eliza thought better of continuing the argument. Believing righteous anger was preferable to the silent misery in which she'd found him, she hid her smile as she went toward the door. She spotted a glass resting against the baseboard, scooped it up, and set it on the tray of tepid soup on his dresser.

"Oh, by the way," she remarked, "I thanked Jonathan and Ricky for bringing you home this morning, but you really ought to thank them again yourself when you feel up to it."

When he thought of the helpful pair, Lawrence had a vague recollection of a flying table. "Wait. Was there a fight?"

"From what Ricky says, it was a brawl. But obviously your side won. Shall I ask Jonathan to come and describe it for you?"

"Good Lord, no. I want to forget yesterday entirely."

"That's understandable, but I do hope you'll feel better tomorrow." Eliza pulled the door closed before Lawrence could comment, but she still thought it would be a good idea to have Jonathan look in on him later.

Chapter Sixteen

Eliza Kate was amazed when her father found the strength that evening to escort her mother into the parlor before dinner. The right side of his face was more badly bruised than the left, providing clear evidence that Jonathan must throw a harder punch with his left hand than his right.

She'd not known he was left-handed. It was such a small

thing but a stunning example of how little she truly knew
about him. She was also shocked by just how quickly her
thoughts had strayed to Jonathan when surely her father's
battered appearance should have evoked at least a small
flutter of sympathy.

She offered a faint smile in greeting, but she couldn't
actually feel anything but dismay. She simply could not
understand what could have prompted him to involve
Lawrence in a romance with a prostitute when the relationship could only have been doomed from the very beginning. How could he have treated his only brother in
such a cavalier fashion? she wondered, all the while knowing he'd not deign to justify his actions should she be bold
enough to inquire.

Not only was her father's face horribly bruised, but he
was also walking stiffly, as though he'd sprained his back
and was in pain. He was obviously putting on a brave show
for his wife and family, but the damage to his appearance
presented an all too vivid reminder of an afternoon Eliza
Kate would rather forget.

Ricky was only a step behind his parents. "Uncle
Lawrence doesn't feel up to dining with us, and Jonathan
volunteered to keep him company."

Delia's finely arched brows dipped in a slight frown.
"Poor Lawrence. Well, if he has to be ill, it's fortunate his
friend is here to keep him entertained."

"Isn't it though?" Lamar agreed with thinly veiled dis-
taste.

Ricky rolled his eyes, but only Eliza Kate caught the
gesture. That their mother had forgotten how worried
they'd all been about Lawrence the previous evening
could be seen as a blessing she supposed, but the mounting need to create a placid life for Delia's benefit was
becoming an increasingly heavy burden for Eliza Kate.

She turned toward Robby, who was sullenly stacking
checkers on the game table by the fireplace. He'd formed
a steady column with the black, but atop them, the red
were beginning to list precariously. Eliza wondered what

he was thinking and feared it was incredibly sad.

"Something sure smells good," Ricky commented enthusiastically, and with a broad gesture, he encouraged them all toward the dining room.

Eliza Kate slipped her arm around Robby's shoulders for a gentle hug as they moved toward their places at the table. She covered a yawn, but was so tired she could barely focus on her plate, and during the meal contributed little to the others' meandering attempts at conversation. Delia smiled often as she ate, while Lamar approached his meal with the deliberate care of a man who feared the painful consequence of too sudden a move.

Eliza continued to study her father. She could appreciate his efforts to provide them all with a comfortable home, but for the first time she was puzzled as to why he'd not found ranching a sufficient challenge. She'd seen his flaws so clearly as a child, but once he'd returned from the war, she'd allowed the devoted attention he showered on her mother to cloud her perceptions.

Then Jonathan had arrived, and since that splendid morning, she'd been observing her father's actions with a newfound curiosity. She wasn't pleased by what she'd seen either. She noticed Ricky frequently glancing their father's way and wondered if he weren't equally troubled.

Ricky was such a brash young man. She was grateful he'd not been old enough to serve the Confederacy, for surely he'd not have survived the war. She'd never had a drop of success taming his recklessness; but now that her once perfectly predictable life had veered off course, she was beginning to suspect she and Ricky were more alike than she'd ever dreamed.

As for Robby, the handsome boy mirrored her despair. He moved food around his plate without eating more than a few tiny bites until they were served a rich berry cobbler for dessert. Then he asked for seconds, and his mood brightening, he accepted Ricky's challenge of a game of checkers, while their parents promptly excused themselves and went upstairs for the night.

Unable to stay awake herself, Eliza Kate soon followed. Upon reaching her room, she glanced down the hall to where Lawrence's door was slightly ajar. She could smell the faint aroma of pipe tobacco. She'd not thought Lawrence would feel well enough yet to smoke, but hoped he and Jonathan were having a good talk. Dismissing them with another wide yawn, she entered her own room and prepared for bed.

Jonathan sat sprawled across an overstuffed chair near the window. He'd eaten every bite of his dinner, and then finished off what Lawrence didn't want of his. Now pleasantly full, he was feeling too good to be drawn into his friend's misery. He just let him rail on about how badly Flossie Mae had treated him, until he was so bored, he couldn't listen to another word of complaint.

"It's a terrible shame Mae wasn't what she seemed," he interrupted finally. "But there's something to be said for an experience that makes you appreciate being alive. They don't present themselves that often."

Stunned by Jonathan's observation, Lawrence set aside the pipe he seldom smoked and waved away a lingering sweetly scented haze. "You're not suggesting I thank her for what she did," he scoffed.

"It might strike you as farfetched, but it's not a bad idea. She made you believe not only in yourself, but in life, and that's a rare gift."

Unconvinced, Lawrence continued to seethe. "No. It was all a rotten, evil trick."

Jonathan couldn't comprehend how such an intelligent man could be so blind and weighed his words with extra care. "You're forgetting that Flossie Mae works for your brother. Who's trick do you think it really was?"

Lawrence responded with an angry snort. "You heard Lamar. He didn't mean anything by it. He just wanted me to have a chance to be with a woman again. He couldn't have known how far she'd take it."

Jonathan wished Lamar were capable of showing half that brotherly loyalty and compassion. "I sure hope you'll tell Lamar that the next time he wants to do you a favor, he ought to leave his whores out of it."

"After the beating you gave him? No, he'll not make that mistake again."

As Jonathan saw it, Lamar made mistakes more often than not, but he had been awake for too many hours to argue the point when Lawrence insisted upon defending him. Instead, he pushed himself out of the comfortable chair. "You might have slept most of the day, but I didn't. I'm going to turn in."

Lawrence waited until Jonathan reached the door. "About last night," he called. "Should you ever find me drunk in another filthy cantina, just leave me there."

Insulted that Lawrence was too bitter to appreciate the great favor he'd done him, Jonathan quietly closed the bedroom door without responding. Although it was still early, the house was quiet, and he went straight to Eliza Kate's room. When she didn't answer his soft knock, he opened her door and peered in.

Sound asleep, Eliza obediently moved over at Jonathan's first nudge and then relaxed into the soft cradle of his arms. She was warm and pliant, and the rhythm of her deep, even breathing didn't quicken at all. Jonathan lay still to enjoy the peace of the moment; but even as tired as he was, his mind refused to stop churning.

While Eliza Kate's tightly knit family was still close, he could sense their ties beginning to fray. Curled up beside her, he couldn't help believing that he was the one causing her comfortable life to unravel. As he saw it, so much of their life was a sham or a blatant refusal to face the truth, but what could he offer in its place? Plagued by that sorry dilemma, he rolled off the bed and left her, but he rested no more easily alone.

*   *   *

It wasn't until she awakened Monday morning that Eliza Kate noticed Jonathan's scent on her pillows, and she feared his tender kiss had flavored more than her dreams. She sat up with a start and fought the cold fury that threatened to make this day as awful as the last couple. With the whole household unsettled, she couldn't believe Jonathan thought he belonged in her bed.

She'd been so frightened that he would leave, but to enter her room uninvited was an outrageous imposition. Not knowing whether he had simply missed her, or merely wished to stir up additional trouble was doubly distressing. For her to go up to his room was one thing, she reasoned. For him to slip into hers as though she'd boldly enticed him, was quite another.

Quickly up and dressed in her riding clothes, she tramped down the stairs, grabbed her hat and scarf as she swept out the door and nearly ran on out to the barn. Jonathan was already there, leaning against the corral and looking mighty pleased with himself. She took immediate exception to his grin.

"How did you sleep last night?" she asked in a challenging whisper.

Jonathan chuckled and adjusted the angle of his hat. "Quite well, thank you, but somehow I thought you'd already know that."

Eliza moved closer than she usually dared when someone might be watching. "What was it you really wanted, to be with me, or to infuriate my father all over again?"

At that insulting question, all hint of amusement vanished from Jonathan's expression. He glanced away to get his temper in check, then looked down at Eliza and made a hushed observation. "If that's all you think of me, then I'm no better off than Lawrence."

Eliza Kate raised her hand to slap him clear into the next county, but he caught her wrist before she came close to his cheek. Just as she had surmised, he'd used his left hand. "Let me go," she mouthed angrily.

Jonathan just shook his head. "I'll admit to being in

your room last night, and I won't deny sharing your bed for a few minutes. I didn't believe I'd be overstepping my bounds, but obviously you think otherwise."

Eliza Kate had spent her whole life caring for others, and now the one time she'd worried about herself, she'd hurt the man who meant the whole world to her. Ashamed of herself, she ceased resisting his hold, and he slid his fingers down her arm in a gentle caress.

"I'm sorry, but things are just so awful here," she murmured, "and I don't want them to get any worse."

Jonathan could see she was sincerely troubled and nodded slightly to accept her apology. "I don't believe that's even possible."

He was teasing her again, but this time she managed a smile and took his hand. His knuckles were scraped, the fingers still slightly swollen, and yet his grasp felt not only familiar, but right. "I didn't realize you were left-handed."

"Does it matter?" he asked and gave her fingers a gentle squeeze.

"No. It's just that I know so little about you."

Puzzled she'd suddenly be anxious about such a small detail, Jonathan drew her close. "You know everything that matters," he assured her.

She knew he'd been born on the Trail of Tears, fought in a wretched war, and lost the wife and child he adored. What she didn't know was if she'd ever touch his heart. Unwilling to ask that question, she forced a smile. "Well, let's hope so. How did your conversation go with Lawrence last night?"

Her sudden change of subject startled Jonathan, but he made an honest effort to follow along. "It wasn't the most pleasant meal we've ever shared. He's mad at me for pulling him out of the cantina, but it scarcely compares to the furious anger he's heaped on Flossie Mae. He blames her for everything."

Eliza was surprised but not at all relieved. "And not my father?"

Jonathan sucked in a deep breath. "No, he actually believes Lamar just wanted him to have a good time."

Eliza caught the sarcasm that had crept into his voice. "But you don't believe that, do you?"

Jonathan quit trying to fool her. "Of course not, and I doubt you do either."

Embarrassed that she could only find one way to view her father's despicable actions, Eliza pulled her hand free of his and stepped away. "No, he was definitely up to something, and it couldn't have been simply a desire to show Lawrence a good time. Obviously he didn't expect to get caught, which means he and Flossie Mae must have had some sort of plan for ending the affair."

Giving her imagination free rein, Eliza pursed her lips thoughtfully. "What do you suppose Flossie Mae would tell us if we asked her?"

Jonathan barely caught his mouth before it dropped open. "You can't want to meet her."

"Why not? Lawrence described her in such glowing terms, but now it sounds as though he'd rather damn her to hell than admit she broke his heart. I can't help wondering how she feels about all this. Aren't you curious?"

Jonathan shoved his hands in his hip pockets. "Sure, but not nearly enough to seek her out at the Rosedale."

"Then just come along, and I'll do all the talking."

Jonathan began silently counting to ten. Eliza was doing what she'd always done: taking the lead to make things right. This time he doubted that it was even possible, but he had to admire her zeal.

She might have just noticed that he was left-handed, but God help him, he had known from the hour they'd met that she liked to have her own way. Yes, sir. She'd confided how well she'd once run the ranch, but that didn't mean he appreciated being ordered around like one of the hands.

Jonathan usually moved with an almost liquid strength, but Eliza saw him stubbornly plant himself where he stood and feared they'd not made a bit of progress toward reaching a meaningful accord. "You don't want to go, do you?" she asked.

"No, I don't, and I don't think you ought to go either."

Eliza wondered if his wife had been a sweet little thing who'd always done exactly what she was told. She couldn't be that woman even if she tried, and she certainly wasn't tempted to become a pale copy of his late wife.

"I wanted Lawrence to find someone to love. I encouraged his interest in Mae Leroux, and you did too," she reminded him. "Maybe you don't feel responsible for how unhappy he is now, but I can't just idly wait for him to get over it on his own when it took him years to find the courage to court a woman.

"I'm sorry you don't see things the same way, but you're not my father, and even if he forbade me to speak to Flossie Mae, I'd do it anyway." Frustrated, she gestured helplessly. "I just want the truth, Jonathan. Isn't that a worthy goal?"

Her last bit of defiance had weakened Jonathan's resolve, and a mention of the truth won him over completely. A slow smile tugged at the corner of his mouth. "Yes, it sure is, but the Rosedale sure seems like a peculiar place to conduct a search."

"My father will never tell us what happened. Lawrence was completely bamboozled. That leaves only Flossie Mae to relate the whole story, or have you another suggestion?"

Jonathan shrugged. "Not when you put it that way, but Flossie Mae can't possibly be the type of woman you'd want to meet."

Eliza Kate eyed him warily. "You're speaking from experience, I suppose?"

Too late Jonathan realized he'd painted himself into a real uncomfortable corner. "That's not the kind of question a woman usually asks a man," he cautioned. "Do you really want a truthful answer?"

Unwilling to back down, Eliza Kate straightened her shoulders. "From you, always."

Jonathan glanced toward Red Warrior. Saddled and

ready for the morning ride, the stallion appeared to be
following their every word with keen interest. As always,
Jonathan envied the horse his uncomplicated life.

"It isn't easy to admit I've been that lonely, but yes, I've
paid for a woman's favors; but I was never unfaithful to
my wife."

Eliza Kate believed him, but she still couldn't hide her
disappointment. "I understand," she assured him. "If I
hadn't met you, I probably would have married Fletcher
Monroe. That would have been a far worse mistake than
paying for agreeable company. Now we're wasting a good
morning standing here. Can't we continue our chat on
the way into town?"

"Sure, but do you see what the truth will get you?" he
asked pointedly.

Eliza Kate swung herself up into Patches's saddle.
"When have you ever settled for anything less?"

"Never," Jonathan swore, but he doubted the way he'd
kept quiet since he'd arrived at the Trinity Star Ranch
qualified as being truthful.

"Then quit stalling and let's go."

"Yes, ma'am," Jonathan reluctantly conceded. He'd had
their mounts saddled, but this was definitely not going to
be the romantic ride he'd been envisioning.

Lamar watched the scene out in the yard with growing
alarm. He'd warned Eliza Kate to stay away from Jonathan
Blair, but there she was cozying up to the man in plain
view of anyone who cared to look. He relaxed slightly as
she stepped away and hoped she was giving the bastard a
difficult time, which she certainly knew how to do. Then
she moved close again, and Lamar could barely stifle the
low growl rumbling deep in his throat.

His only daughter was engaged to Fletcher Monroe, but
there she was nearly dancing around Jonathan Blair with
flirtatious grace. It sickened him to see them together. He
hated Blair. How could she stand to be near him?

Blair had tried to kill him, might have succeeded if

Ricky and Lawrence hadn't belatedly gotten control of the situation. That he'd had to rely on his son and invalid brother to save him from such a sorry fate rankled him still. He wasn't a weak man, but Blair had fought like a demon.

Blair hated him, but hell, the feeling was mutual. Unfortunately, from the looks of things, Blair sure didn't hate Eliza Kate. Lamar curled his hands at his sides, wishing with all his might that he could strangle Jonathan Blair and nail his hide to the side of the barn. Once he told Fletcher how Eliza Kate had been carrying on with Blair, his partner would help him do it too.

Lamar's whole face ached when he tried to smile, but after they'd won big on the coming race, he was going to invite Fletcher to help him put Jonathan Blair in his place—permanently.

Monday morning, Flossie Mae awakened with an almost suffocating sense of dread. She expected Lamar to come into town, and she didn't want to see him again as long as she lived. Although it was still agony to move, she pushed herself up and off the bed, then flung out her arms to maintain her balance. She weaved and came dangerously close to collapsing on the rug, but after sitting down to rest a moment, did better on her second try. On her third, she took a couple of steps toward the wardrobe where only a few garments remained.

She stumbled, lurched into it, and leaned against the wide double doors to catch her breath. Then certain she could make it down the stairs with the help of a couple of the girls, she grew almost frantic to leave before Lamar arrived. Thanks to the years she'd spent at the Rosedale, she had plenty of savings in the bank. Lamar would find her quickly if she moved into one of the hotels, but Fort Worth had several modest boardinghouses he'd never think to check.

She felt sick to her stomach as she made her way to the vanity. She slumped down on the padded bench but didn't dare look in the mirror as she slowly brushed her hair. She owned a hat with a veil, and in her sweet widow's gown, she'd not draw a bit of notice on the street, providing she could actually make it to the street.

She did feel slightly better than yesterday, but dared not wait for the improvement to her health that tomorrow would no doubt bring. She had to get out of the Rosedale, and prayed she could simply disappear until she was strong enough to make plans to leave Fort Worth altogether. She was too dizzy to ponder possible destinations, but the fact that she'd have the money to start a small business, perhaps even become a milliner, provided all she needed in the way of courage that morning.

Jonathan kept a close watch on Eliza Kate as they rode into town. He knew her to be a sensible young woman, as well as a most passionate one, but clearly she was unable to dismiss his brief liaisons with other women as quickly as he'd hoped. He watched the chill of disappointment seep into her bones, and it startled him to feel her emotions so deeply.

He leaned down to grab Patches's bridle and pulled the mare to a halt beside Red Warrior. "Would you rather I'd just dodged your question or lied?" he challenged.

Rather than meet his steady gaze, Eliza Kate fussed with her gloves. "No, of course not. You've lived more than thirty years. I imagine you've gotten yourself into all sorts of trouble you'd rather not admit. The next time I ask an impertinent question, just tell me it's none of my business. Maybe we'll both be better off."

Jonathan feared he'd merely embarrassed her rather than eased her mind and nearly groaned in frustration. "Well, at least I've never owned a whorehouse. Come on, let's go."

Eliza Kate didn't appreciate that taunt a bit, but he'd made her think, and she wasn't at all pleased where her thoughts led. By the time they'd reached the Rosedale, she'd silently rehearsed her questions so as to focus her inquiries on Lawrence and carefully omit any reference to her father's habits.

After leaving their horses at the hitching post, she would have walked right through the front door, but Jonathan snagged her arm and led her around back. "The main entrance is for customers, although I doubt anyone's here this early. The back door should be a private entrance for the girls." He knocked loudly, and then stepped back and gestured for Eliza Kate to approach.

When a sleepy-eyed young woman with burgundy hair opened the door, Eliza wasted no time in introducing herself as Lamar's daughter. "Please tell Flossie Mae that Miss Bendalin's come to speak with her. I'll wait right here. Now go on, hurry."

Jonathan knew Eliza would not appreciate his pointing out that she had the makings of a fine madam herself, but he sure thought it. He scraped the toe of his boot in the dirt, and when the wait grew uncomfortably long, he took a couple of steps to kick an empty liquor bottle out of the way.

"I wonder what could be keeping her?" he asked.

"We are awfully early," Eliza noted. "Maybe she wasn't dressed."

"There's still time to leave," Jonathan offered hopefully.

Eliza Kate crossed her arms over her chest and glared. "Not likely."

In the next instant, the back door swung open and Belle peered out. She was dressed in a pink silk wrapper and hadn't yet combed last night's tangles from her hair. "I'm sorry, Miss Bendalin, I didn't really believe Agnes when she told me it was you."

Eliza sent Jonathan an incredulous glance. This woman was pretty, but she seemed much too young to have been Lawrence's widow. "Are you Flossie Mae?" she inquired.

The burgundy-haired young woman leaned into view. "Shucks, no. This is Belle, and I'm Agnes. Flossie Mae's gone."

"Gone where?" Eliza asked. "If she'll not be away long,

we'll go and have breakfast and come back."

Belle raised her hand to her hair in a futile attempt to smooth out the frazzled mess before sweeping Jonathan with a slow, admiring glance. "Flossie Mae's left the Rosedale for good," she explained in a seductive whisper. "She gave away all her fancy clothes last Friday, and today, she's already up and gone."

"You mean she's left town?" Eliza glanced toward Jonathan for help, but he shook his head.

"Sure looks that way," Agnes replied, slipping by Belle. "I wish we could help, but I don't think Flossie Mae wants to be found."

"Why not?" Eliza pressed. "Is she in some kind of trouble?"

Belle elbowed Agnes out of her way but her attention remained firmly focused on Jonathan as she smoothed her hands down her hips. "You could say that, but I'm still here."

Agnes put her hand on Belle's shoulder to tug her back inside the doorway. "What's the matter with you? Can't you see that he's Miss Bendalin's man? Try and act like a lady. I'm sorry, Miss Bendalin. Some of our girls have no manners at all."

"And you do?" Belle asked in dismay.

"Well, yes, I've got a hell of a lot more than you," Agnes countered.

Eliza Kate hadn't expected the situation to get so quickly out of hand. Flustered by their reference to Jonathan, she raised her voice to a near shout in hopes of preventing one of them from punching the other. "Ladies, please. Even if Flossie Mae isn't here, perhaps you could tell us a little about her. Do you know where she was from?"

"Georgia." Still exchanging murderous looks, the women replied in a harsh chorus.

"She was widowed during the war," Agnes interjected quickly. "Had to take care of herself as best she could."

She went suddenly still. "Well, that's her story to tell, not ours."

"Yes, of course," Eliza agreed, "but you must know something more. Why'd she give away all her fancy clothes? Wasn't that an unusual thing to do?"

"Mighty unusual," Belle announced, "but she was up to something over at the millinery shop." She regarded Agnes with a knowing smirk. "Of course, we were best friends, and I'll not reveal just what."

"You were never best friends!" Agnes cried.

"Ladies," Eliza again broke in. "Thank you. You've been very helpful." She supposed she should have come prepared to pay them, but she'd expected to meet Flossie Mae, not this silly pair. "I'm sorry to have bothered you so early." She began to back away, and Jonathan again took her arm.

Giving the handsome man one last try, Belle wiggled her fingers in a flirtatious wave, but Agnes grabbed her hand and yanked her back inside. The door slammed shut, and Jonathan burst into laughter.

"I'm sorry," he said. "I know you'd hoped to learn a lot more."

Nothing had gone as Eliza had hoped. Chagrined, she pulled her lower lip through her teeth. "On the contrary," she argued. "I discovered a great deal. For one thing, I hadn't realized prostitutes were so young."

"Not all of them are, but the young ones are the most popular."

As they reached their horses, Eliza shot him a sidelong glance. "You're pretty popular yourself."

"Well, thank God, I'm *your* man. That saved me from Belle's clutches," Jonathan replied, chuckling heartily.

Eliza had been badly embarrassed when Agnes had made that uncalled for reference, but she was absolutely mortified Jonathan would tease her about it. She took a moment to mount Patches and revealed more than she'd meant to with her wistful response. "You're your own man, Jonathan Blair. Anyone can see that."

Jonathan slid into Red Warrior's saddle with an easy stretch, then tipped his hat slightly. "Glad you noticed, ma'am. Now if we hurry, we might find a few strips of bacon left over from breakfast."

The exasperating morning had robbed Eliza Kate of her appetite. "We can always find you something to eat, but I just want to talk with my uncle."

"If he's in no better mood than yesterday, I doubt that would be wise."

Eliza Kate brushed her heels against Patches's sides to hurry the mare along. "We went looking for the truth, remember? Lawrence needs to know Flossie Mae really was a widow. That she gave away her fancy clothes indicates she planned to make a change in her life. That she's left the Rosedale proves it."

Eliza paused to look up at Jonathan. "Maybe she really loved Lawrence. It's important for him to know that."

Jonathan was truly amazed that she'd come up with such a fanciful interpretation of the few facts they'd gleaned. "You're missing the whole point," he scolded. "Maybe she just figured that Lawrence was rich, and that he'd buy her a nice house and a dozen new wardrobes. It doesn't change the fact of what she was, and that's what he'll never forgive."

They were well out of town before Eliza Kate thought that sad prediction through. "Lawrence thought Mae was so special, and I can't help believing she must be nothing at all like Belle and Agnes. But what you're really saying is that men insist upon virtue in their women while women are expected to overlook whatever dalliances men might have. That's very unfair."

Jonathan noticed the sparkle of tears in her eyes and feared he knew right where this conversation was headed. "That's only some men, Eliza Kate, not all of us."

Eliza Kate had hoped he'd say that he loved her, and that she'd never be the object of another man's scorn for having taken him as her lover. Instead he swept the horizon with an impatient glance as though there was nothing more to discuss. Coward that she was, she dared not beg him for the truth he'd sworn to tell.

Chapter Seventeen

After Eliza Kate and Jonathan parted company at the barn, she entered the house through the back door. She was discouraged the morning hadn't gone nearly as well as she'd hoped, but when she found her uncle in his shirt-sleeves straightening up the study, she promptly seized the opportunity to speak with him and fetched a feather duster.

She knocked lightly as she came through the door. "Good morning, Uncle Lawrence. It's high time we gave this room a thorough cleaning. You may know where everything belongs, but I can dust the books before you replace them on the shelves."

Lawrence slammed a thick dictionary down on the desk and barely glanced her way. "No, thanks. I'd rather handle this without your company."

Both his expression and tone were coldly forbidding, but Eliza hadn't expected him to be in the best of moods and simply ignored his cold rebuff and switched strategies. She stepped gingerly over the books littering the rug and lowered her voice to a compelling hush.

"Has it never occurred to you that I might appreciate yours?"

Lawrence paused to shift through an old ledger before responding. "I'm no fit company for anyone today."

"Well, regardless of the darkness of your mood, I'd value your advice."

Lawrence responded with a rude snort and tossed the ledger on the desk. "What weighty problem could you possibly have?"

That he could not even imagine her grappling with a

significant dilemma hurt Eliza so much that before she could catch it, the truth simply sprang from her lips. "I've fallen in love with a man my parents will never accept, and we've been carrying on in a scandalous fashion."

Caught completely off guard, Lawrence's angry frown dissolved into an incredulous grin, and then tickled by her stricken expression, he burst out laughing. "Oh, Eliza Kate, that's absolutely ridiculous, but I apologize for being so curt with you just now. Please stay and help me."

Aghast at what she'd revealed, Eliza fought to draw a breath, but her uncle continued to chuckle as though she'd made up an outlandish confession simply to shock him. That hurt her all the more, but she was deeply grateful that he'd not taken her seriously. She reached for the small stepladder that lay overturned in the corner, set it upright, and sat down. Now forcing herself into a picture of prim reflection, she twirled the duster in her hands.

"I really do need your advice about Fletcher," she confided, for he posed a problem she truly needed to share. "I've no longer any interest in marrying him. I tried, but failed, to tell him so before he left for Galveston. He'll be back any day, and then I'll have to confront the issue head-on."

Lawrence had to bite the inside of his mouth to keep from shouting for joy, but he was delighted she'd finally come to her senses. "I see," he mused thoughtfully. He leaned against the desk and folded his arms across his chest. "Have you told your father?"

"No. Things have been far too hectic the last few days for heart-to-heart chats. I know he'll be as furious as Fletcher though, and I'd rather avoid another awful scene here."

"That's understandable." Lawrence fought to maintain an expression of sympathetic concern but it was a real challenge while he felt so elated. "Fletcher will undoubtedly demand an explanation for your change of heart."

"Yes, I know he will, but no matter what I say, he'll argue that I'm wrong, or not thinking clearly, or making a dreadful mistake. But I don't love him, and nothing he could possibly say will change how I feel."

Lawrence understood her fears for he could easily imagine Fletcher browbeating her for hours. "But you must at least be fond of him, and he'll probably strive to convince you that you'll grow to love him in time."

Eliza Kate's shoulders slumped, and she ceased fiddling with the duster. She'd told Lawrence the truth, but because he'd not believed her, she certainly couldn't admit Jonathan had stolen her heart as well as her virtue. "You're undoubtedly right, but while Fletcher has many admirable qualities, he'll never be the man for me."

Convinced by the seriousness of her expression, Lawrence relaxed slightly. "To tell you the truth, I've always thought Fletcher was too full of himself, but because you seemed to like him, I kept silent. If you want, I could be there to provide moral support when you announce your decision to him and your father."

"Oh, would you, Uncle?" Eliza left the stepladder to give him a kiss on the cheek. She was greatly relieved he'd volunteered his help, but still hesitated to work Flossie Mae into the conversation.

"Now that that's settled, let's get busy," she encouraged, and she moved the stepladder aside to begin dusting the books that hadn't fallen from the shelves while Lawrence sorted those that had. With but an occasional comment on a forgotten novel, they worked in companionable silence for nearly an hour before Eliza sat down to rest.

"You've always been so good to me," she began, gathering her thoughts to tackle his problems. "I've never doubted that you have my best interests at heart, and I hope you trust me to care as much for you."

Also in need of a break, Lawrence slid into his chair behind the desk and wiped his forehead on his shirtsleeve. "Of course I do, although it's a mite difficult to believe you're old enough to entertain marriage proposals. It seems only yesterday that you and Ricky were playing tag around the barn."

It was an unexpectedly pleasant memory, and Eliza smiled. She loved both her brothers dearly. "I'd forgotten how much we loved that game when we were small. Did Father feel well enough to go into town today, or did Ricky take Robby to school this morning?"

"Ricky took him. Your father's not going anywhere for another day or two, but we probably ought to postpone our chat with him until he's feeling better."

"I'll be glad to postpone it as long as possible." They were again talking in their usual easy manner, and Eliza hoped the courage to offer him advice wouldn't desert her. "There's something I need to say about Mae Leroux."

"Good God," Lawrence said, gasping, and he raised his hand in an emphatic demand for silence.

"Just listen a minute," Eliza rushed on. "I know her name is really Flossie Mae. I've also learned she actually is a widow from Georgia. She gave away her fancy clothes last week, and now she's left the Rosedale Hotel. It's plain she means to change her life, and it could very well be because she met you. She may have fallen in love with you, and I know you cared for her. I believe you owe it to yourself to find her."

Lawrence leaned forward to prop his elbows on the desk and covered his eyes with his hands, but nothing could have stopped a fierce red haze from blurring his vision. He caught little of what Eliza Kate said after that, but he could no longer think of Mae and love in the same breath. When he straightened up, the gleam in his eyes was murderous.

"You are never to speak that slut's name in my presence again. What did you do, go down to the Rosedale and interview her friends?"

"If they could be called that," Eliza readily admitted. "Jonathan went with me, so it wasn't as ill-advised as you seem to believe."

"I thought Jonathan had more sense," Lawrence muttered under his breath. "Get out of here. Go entertain your mother until it's time to eat. I can finish what's left to do here on my own."

Eliza Kate rose and left as he'd asked, but only because she hoped he'd use the time alone to consider what she'd told him.

Fletcher Monroe returned to Fort Worth that afternoon. He made a brief stop at the office, then went straight to the Trinity Star Ranch rather than his own. When Carmen answered the door, he pushed right by her. "Where's Lamar? I expected to find him in town."

"He's not feeling his best today, sir, and I believe he's in his room resting."

"Then he'll appreciate good news," Fletcher exclaimed proudly, and after handing her his hat, he bounded up the stairs two at a time.

Carmen hung the hat on the hall tree, but was uncertain what to do next. Fletcher Monroe might be Lamar's business partner, but she doubted he was permitted free run of the Bendalin home. Fearful she should have stopped him, although she'd not known how, she hurried to the kitchen to warn the cook to expect a guest for dinner.

Fletcher whistled happily as he strode down the hall. Then realizing Delia might be napping, he fell silent and lightened his step. He'd been in Lamar's bedroom a time or two, and certain he had the right door, he knocked lightly and whispered, "It's Fletcher, and I've good news."

Lamar called to his partner, then carefully rolled off his bed. Obviously in pain, he straightened up slowly, but there was nothing he could do about his face. "I'm glad to hear there's good news somewhere," he said and tightened the belt on his robe.

As Fletcher entered, he was so shocked by Lamar's scrapes and bruises it took him a long moment to remember to close the door. "Good Lord, what happened to you?"

With no reason to lie for Fletcher's benefit, Lamar

blurted out the truth. "I was attacked by Jonathan Blair. This looks worse than it is, but there's no sense going into town and inviting a lot of stupid jokes at my expense."

"You've not canceled the race?" Fletcher asked much too quickly.

Lamar stared coldly at his partner's fearful expression. "I'm touched by your concern for my welfare. It warms my heart to know you hold me in such high regard."

Ignoring Lamar's sarcasm, Fletcher laced his hands behind his back and began to pace near the foot of the large four-poster bed. "Of course I'm distressed to see you've taken a beating, but we stand to win a great deal of money on Saturday's race, and that's sure to soothe your feelings. Please tell me it's still being held."

Lamar lacked the energy to remain standing for more than a few minutes and moved across the spacious room to the wing chair by the window. He lowered himself into it slowly, but still looked uncomfortable. "Quite frankly, I'd forgotten all about the blasted race, but Blair's still here, so apparently he intends to run. Now that's enough about him. Tell me what happened in Galveston."

Fletcher was relieved he'd finally be able to relate the story he'd polished all the way home, and he provided a lengthy and glowing account of how swiftly he'd handled the recalcitrant captain. "We'll have no more problems with him, nor with anyone else transporting our whiskey, I believe it's safe to say."

"Well, let's hope not," Lamar replied, but his distracted glance was focused on the view of the garden from his window rather than his proud partner's wide smirk. "I hate to admit this, but with you away, I fear Eliza Kate may have been spending far too much time with Jonathan Blair."

"My God! What could she possibly see in him?" Fletcher responded angrily.

Lamar sighed as though Fletcher were being deliberately obtuse. "I agree he's a totally unsuitable companion, but the bastard is remarkably handsome. Eliza's disobeyed my clear order to avoid him, but now that you're here, I trust you'll make her forget Blair was ever passably amusing."

The sunlight sucked from his triumphant afternoon, Fletcher headed for the door. "I'll put an end to their friendship this very minute."

"Wait," Lamar cautioned. "As you were so swift to point out, we'll win too much to risk having the race canceled. Leave Blair alone for the time being, and after the race, help me give him what he truly deserves."

Understanding completely, Fletcher rested his hand lightly on the crystal doorknob. "Have the Comanches staged any new raids near here?"

"No, I don't believe they have, but wouldn't it be unfortunate if Blair were to be set upon by a particularly vicious band of renegades?"

A sly smile brightened Fletcher's glance. "Yes, it would be a terrible shame for him to meet with such a dreadful end. If you'll excuse me, I'd like to pay a call on your daughter."

"Please do, and you might as well join us for dinner."

"Thank you. I shall look forward to it," Fletcher replied, and with the buoyancy returned to his step, he hurried away.

Eliza Kate was wading in the lily pond when Fletcher suddenly strode into view. She'd been lost in a blissfully tranquil moment, but then she'd not expected anyone to catch her in such a juvenile pursuit. She smiled as though she stepped into the pond every afternoon, and wished Lawrence were there to help her as he'd promised.

Unfortunately, her uncle had apparently headed for the liquor cabinet soon after she'd left the study, and by the midday meal, he'd been no better than a morose lump. Soon afterward, he'd mumbled his usual excuse about pain in his leg and gone upstairs to rest until dinner. She could not blame him for abandoning her, however, when he'd not known Fletcher would arrive that very day.

When Eliza smiled as though romping in the pond were an acceptable pastime, Fletcher halted several paces away and rested his hands on his hips. "Just what is it you think you're doing?" he inquired.

Eliza was holding her riding skirt above her knees to keep it dry, and with a graceful swish, moved a large leaf aside with her toe. "Nothing particularly mysterious, Fletcher. I'm just having fun."

Fletcher took another step closer, but remained at a cautious distance to avoid being splashed should she slip and fall. "You're a grown woman, my dear, and once we're wed, I'll expect you to behave in a far more circumspect fashion."

"Is that so?" Eliza moved around the pond with a slow, dancing rhythm. "I'm in my own garden, so there's no one to care how I behave."

"Well, I care!" Fletcher bellowed.

Eliza knew precisely what she was doing, but now that she had the chance, she couldn't resist goading him into an argument that might even inspire him to break their engagement. "You needn't shout at me, Fletcher. The afternoon is warm, and the lily pond is delightfully cool. Why don't you pull off your boots and socks, roll up your trousers, and join me?" she invited with a coquettish dip of her head.

"What's happened to you, Eliza Kate? You've always been such a sensible young woman. Now get out of that pond this instant."

Eliza ignored his command and instead continued her leisurely stroll through the water lilies. She knew she ought to simply tell him good-bye for good, but try as she might, the right words wouldn't come. When Fletcher suddenly reached out to grab her arm, she cried out, and barely managed to stay on her feet as she yanked herself free.

"Is that how you intend to treat your wife?" She shrank away into the far corner of the pond. "Will you expect me to obey your every whim as though I were one of your servants?"

Fletcher was so furiously angry with her, he was ready to step into the pond fully clothed and yank her out, but Jonathan Blair came whistling down the path before he could move. "Go away," he shouted at him. "This is a private conversation, and we don't wish to be disturbed."

"That true?" Jonathan asked as he continued on down the walkway. "I could have sworn I heard you calling my name, Eliza Kate."

Eliza recalled only a horrified scream, but couldn't help wondering if she hadn't meant for him to hear and come running. She was never certain where he was when they weren't together. He insisted upon keeping busy and helped out on the ranch whenever he could, so it was possible he'd been in the barn or out by Red Warrior's corral. Still, she didn't really think she'd made that much noise.

Unless, of course, he'd been listening. Cheered by that thought, she smiled. "Fletcher's trying to tell me what to do, but I'm enjoying wading in this lovely pond far too much to listen."

Jonathan walked right up to the edge of the pond, and slid his hands into his hip pockets. "Sure looks like fun to me. Why don't you just get in with her, Fletcher?"

Fletcher rolled his eyes to the heavens. "You're obviously not a good influence."

"I'm not?" Jonathan shook his head regretfully. "I had absolutely no idea. Why didn't you tell me I wasn't a good influence, Eliza Kate? I might have been able to mend my ways." He looked contrite for a second, then winked at her, sat down on the nearest bench, and yanked off his boots.

"Just what is it you think you're doing?" Fletcher asked, gasping.

"I've some time before dinner and thought I might enjoy wading too. Are you sure you won't join us?" Jonathan set his boots and socks aside, then stood and stepped into the pond.

"Say, this does feel good," he exclaimed.

"Well, I'll not hang around to watch you two cavort like children," Fletcher announced, and he started back up the path with an agitated stride.

"Hey, Monroe!" Jonathan called. "Did you know Eliza Kate loves to climb trees?"

Fletcher swung right around and came back. "Tell me he's not serious," he demanded.

Eliza laughed and nearly slipped, but Jonathan caught her elbow and kept her upright. "You were right, Fletcher. I've been such a serious person for so long, I'd forgotten how much fun it is to simply play. You ought to try climbing a tree now and again too. The view is marvelous, and I highly recommend it."

Fletcher's expression turned grim. "Please tell your mother that I asked after her, but I'll not be staying for dinner. Play all you wish, but after Saturday's race, I'll expect you to behave like the lady you were raised to be."

Eliza failed to respond before Fletcher turned his back on her a second time, but she could feel Jonathan observing her reaction and sure hoped he wasn't as disappointed in her as Fletcher obviously was. She took his hand and gave his fingers a fond squeeze.

"I didn't expect him to catch me here in the pond, and this just didn't seem like the best place to hold a serious conversation about marriage, or reveal that I no longer wish to be his wife."

Jonathan licked his lips, and then leaned down and kissed her. "You worry far too much, sugar. Let's just wade in the lilies and forget there ever was a Fletcher Monroe."

Eliza was so lost in his smile that truly Fletcher did cease to exist. There was only Jonathan Blair, and she loved everything about him. When after a few minutes he swung her up into his arms, and then sat down on the low wall surrounding the pond to cradle her in his lap, she squealed in delighted surprise.

"You're awfully bold, Mr. Blair."

He'd been out searching for Lawrence on Saturday night and shared her bed only briefly on Sunday. Now he was so anxious for the evening to arrive to make love to her again, he could barely contain his desire. He nuzzled her fragrant curls and whispered an enticing suggestion in her ear.

"Do you think all you need do is offer softly voiced invitations, and I'll come running to your room?" she asked.

"If you want more, please say so, and I'll gladly do it, because I'd sure hate to spend another night without you."

His deep kiss silenced whatever protest she might have made, but truly, none entered her thoughts until she recalled Fletcher's taunt about the race. She couldn't bear to think Jonathan had stayed only to race Fletcher, but he'd never given her any reason to believe otherwise. She ended the intoxicating kiss while she still could and leaned back slightly to study his satisfied smile, but she left her arms looped around his neck.

"You certainly don't seem worried about Saturday's race," she observed softly. "I was astonished when you didn't win handily the first time, but what will you do if you also lose the second race?"

Her expression was thoughtful, but what Jonathan noticed was how quickly his kisses lent her lips a seductively swollen pout. Nor could he mistake the glow of affection that made the blue of her eyes all the more bright. She was so comfortably posed on his lap, it seemed her usual perch. That they fit together so smoothly in bed and out was no surprise, but he could not help wondering at the true nature of her question.

"I'm not going to lose a second time," he finally assured her, but he thought it far more likely she'd hoped he'd describe his plans for the coming weeks.

His dark lashes made shadows on his cheeks, but what Eliza recognized in his beautiful light eyes was a stubborn determination not to think past Saturday no matter what the race might bring. It was only Monday, so they had four precious days left to share before the weekend. Still, she was glad she hadn't broken her engagement to Fletcher because if he'd suspected the truth and then canceled the race, they'd not even have that.

She rested her forehead against Jonathan's and took a deep breath to silence her fears. "We shouldn't be sitting here like this."

Jonathan couldn't argue, but he was so relieved by how quickly she had forgotten Fletcher that it was impossible for him to be concerned with propriety. He had not once paused to consider how she did it, but just being with her made him happy. God, how he needed that blessing to continue.

A flash of guilt and sorrow tightened his chest, but his smile remained smoothly confident. "I'd like to sit here with you until evening and watch the moon rise, but I know we're pressing our luck."

Reluctantly, he took a firm grip on her waist to set her on her feet, then stood, and stepped out of the pond to offer his hand. As she took it and moved by him, he murmured against her flowing curls, "Thank you."

Puzzled, Eliza Kate sat down to pull on her boots. "You're very welcome, of course, but for what?"

"For making me laugh. It's something I didn't expect." He sat down beside her and reached for his own boots. He'd polished them every day since he'd arrived, but they were still badly worn. With a low chuckle, he realized that was the least of his problems, but he vowed to buy a new pair—and soon.

"Oh, Jonathan, you have such a marvelous laugh, that I don't mind inspiring it, but I'm afraid Fletcher was right," Eliza admitted sadly. "I am too serious to crave more than a few minutes of unbridled fun; then I begin to fret."

Unfortunately, Jonathan knew it to be true. "I'm taking that as a challenge, ma'am, and I intend to give you far more than a few minutes of pleasure as soon as you can get away tonight."

His hand grazed hers as he leaned down to give her a quick kiss before they left to go their separate ways, and as always, Eliza felt a delicious thrill. She glanced over her shoulder to watch him walk away, his posture so very straight and proud. It made her heart ache to think how long her memories would have to last and how empty her life would be without him.

She took her time returning to the house, then nearly collided with Carmen as she came through the door. Both young women jumped back, but Eliza was the first to apologize. "I'm so sorry. I should have been paying closer attention to where I was going."

"No, the fault was all mine," Carmen insisted. "Your mother sent me to find you. There's nothing wrong. She just wants to speak with you."

"Thank you." Eliza rushed up the back stairs, all the while hoping her mother wouldn't notice that the hem of her skirt was still damp. Not that she was ashamed of wading in the pond, but such uncharacteristic foolishness would be difficult to explain to the woman who depended upon her for cool competence.

Delia was comfortably cuddled in a favorite quilt on the window seat, and as her daughter entered her room, she offered only a slight nod in greeting. "For some reason, I couldn't sleep this afternoon, so I've just been sitting here, enjoying my garden. There were so many interesting things happening, I scarcely know where to begin, but I do hope you realize it's a very good thing that my room overlooks the lily pond rather than your father's."

Delia usually took such long naps that Eliza hadn't even considered she might be observed. Robby made so much noise, she would have heard him coming before he actually ran by the pond, and Ricky had no interest in flowers. The one person she'd cared to see had been with her, but surely her mother had had ample opportunity to observe that.

Eliza had spent years shielding her mother from unpleasant truths, but Jonathan didn't fit that, or any other category. Searching for the proper words to explain rather than excuse their behavior, she approached the window seat slowly. "It was an incredibly lovely afternoon, so warm and clear."

"I doubt Fletcher would agree, and he'll be here long after the dashing Mr. Blair is gone," Delia replied. She traced her quilt's unique floral pattern with her fingertips. Inspired by her love of roses, the design was her own, and the ladies of the church sewing circle had helped to complete the thousands of intricate stitches. It was one of her most cherished possessions.

"I do hope you'll save this beautiful quilt," Delia murmured softly. "Like all my pretty things, I want you to have it."

"Mother, please." Eliza Kate sat down at the end of the window seat by Delia's feet. "It makes me so sad when you talk that way."

Delia continued to concentrate on the gentle curve of a winding stem and answered without looking up. "Fletcher adores you, and he'll not take you away where I could never see you or hold my precious grandbabies."

Her mother's anguish tore at Eliza Kate's heart, and she reached out to take her pale hands in a fond clasp. Her mother had always been delicate, but now each time they touched, there was less for Eliza Kate to hold. Soon, like the subtle fragrance of her perfume, she would fade completely.

"I'm not leaving you, Mother," she promised. "Please don't worry that I might. Jonathan won't ask me to accompany him when he leaves for California, and I won't beg him to stay. But after he's gone, I want no regrets. So please don't tell Father that you saw us together. It will only make it much too difficult for all of us."

Delia gazed longingly at her daughter. "Things are already difficult. We all know I'm dying, even if no one has the courage to speak the words. Who'll look after your father and the boys if you leave? Lawrence isn't up to the task. Am I asking too much of you, dearest? I am so sorry, but it seems neither of us really has a choice."

Unable to hold back her tears, Eliza drew her mother into a warm embrace and rocked her gently. She had not consciously chosen to love Jonathan, she just did. With the very same sense of certainty, she knew that he would not ask her to choose between him and her family. She had not known love could bring such incredible pain, and yet she would not have missed knowing him for anything.

Gathering her strength for her mother's sake, she kissed her cheek and sat back. "Let's dress with special care for dinner, as though it were a party. Fletcher apologized for not being able to join us, but I'll not miss him. I hope you won't either."

Delia's smile was shy and sweet. "As long as my family is together here, I don't need other guests."

"We'll always be here for you, Mother. Always," Eliza Kate promised sincerely, but she refused to consider how quickly her mother might leave them and what an awful void her absence would bring.

Chapter Eighteen

Flossie Mae lay curled on a narrow iron bed, tightly clutching a small satin pillow, but no matter how often she shifted position, her whole body ached as badly as her disheartened spirit. She was accustomed to the nearly continuous piano music and commotion of the Rosedale, and while she had deliberately sought out a quiet boardinghouse, she hadn't realized how eerie the stately calm would actually be.

With a concerted effort she focused on the only decorative touch in her small rented room, a lovely watercolor seascape in which some talented artist had captured the ocean's haunting vitality in subtle bands of blue and gray. The painting's delicate hues offered a welcome respite from her anguish. Blessed with a vivid imagination, perhaps a gift of her sadly circumscribed childhood, she could almost feel the chilly ocean breeze and catch its exotic scent. Swept along on her own salty tears, for a few precious moments she became part of the lonely stretch of beach and heard the waves' churning roar.

When her bruises faded, she might be tempted to go down to the gulf and locate another charming boarding-house where she could sit on the porch and pass her days observing the ships gliding along the horizon. Eventually, she might even book passage to some faraway port. She had seldom traveled, and then never for pleasure, yet even to contemplate a cruise now exhausted her.

Too tired and sad to appreciate the company of the other boarders or to offer them any cheer, she remained in her simply furnished room and ate the evening meal from a tray. She sipped the small bowl of potato soup and ate a bite of bread, but left the remainder of her supper untouched. She did drink all the tea in the sweet little china pot and hoped her landlady would not be insulted by her lack of appetite.

Slipping out of her black dress and into a nightgown was a dreaded chore, but with exaggerated care she forced herself to prepare for bed, where in dreams she could again be with Lawrence. Dreams were all she had left of him, and she dared not waste a minute of those.

That same evening, Jonathan finally took note of the individual silver salt cellars on the Bendalins's table. He liked his food plain and never bothered to add more seasoning than the cook had provided. He watched Lamar add a heavy sprinkling of salt and pepper without bothering to first taste his food.

That impulsive habit was yet another difference between them, but it was Lamar's satisfied smirk that annoyed Jonathan most. He refused to speculate on what

twisted thought Lamar might find amusing and preferred
to assume Fletcher Monroe must have brought good news
concerning their business ventures.

He then dismissed Lamar to wonder how Lawrence had
made it safely down the stairs when he appeared to be so
drunk he was having difficulty guiding his fork to his
mouth. Every few minutes, he'd sit up with a jerk, as
though shocked to discover he'd fallen into such a careless slump he was in danger of sliding right out of his
chair.

Jonathan fought not to glance Eliza Kate's way too often, but her laughter kept drawing his attention. Unfortunately, it was a brittle sound rather than the throaty
giggle he often coaxed from her. He winked at her, but
her answering smile wavered and tore at his heart.

He forced himself to look away and again focused on
his companions. Ricky was teasing Robby with his customary vigor, while Delia softly defended her younger son.
She had taken no more than a few tiny bites of her meal.
Her eyes were a bit too bright that night, and her fair skin
ghostly pale. Eliza Kate was observing her mother with an
anxious glance, and Jonathan doubted she had eaten
much either.

When he looked down, he was astonished to find only
a small puddle of gravy remained on his own dinner plate.
When a few minutes later, Eliza Kate encouraged him to
have more, he replied with a polite refusal. In a reflective
mood, he recalled the first strained meal he'd shared with
the Bendalins, and he was disgusted by how rapidly he'd
become accustomed to their gracious hospitality.

My God, he groaned inwardly, he'd been with them two
weeks, and he'd only meant to stop by for a brief chat
with Lawrence. Of course, he'd not expected Eliza Kate
to pose such a fascinating diversion, but was he so completely enchanted by her that the coming days would slide
into years without his ever making a conscious decision to
spend the rest of his life on the Trinity Star Ranch?

It was an appalling possibility, and still the prospect of

remaining with Eliza Kate teased his wounded soul. He
knew she deserved a far better man than he. Even on the
best of days, he skated on the raw edge of a despair so
deep it threatened to suck her right down with him. He
absolutely refused to risk that tragedy. Growing desperate
to put some distance between himself and the hauntingly
lovely young woman, he turned to Lawrence for the perfect excuse to escape the suddenly suffocating confines of
the dining room.

"Lawrence, we need to discuss Saturday's race," Jonathan announced abruptly. "Please excuse us." Before anyone could object, he had risen to help Lawrence from his
chair. Then with a firm hand, he guided the muddled
man out of the room and up the stairs.

Jonathan kept a tight grip on his friend's upper arm
until they reached Lawrence's room. He shouldered open
the door, then waited to release the inebriated man when
he was within easy reach of his bed. As expected,
Lawrence simply unfolded face-down across the thickly
padded quilt.

"Believe me," Jonathan vowed in deadly earnest, "I know
how badly it hurts to lose the woman you love, but—"

"I despise the slut," Lawrence swore, his words slurred
more by emotion than whiskey.

"Obviously," Jonathan argued with undisguised sarcasm.
"Why else would you try to drink yourself to death while
your family politely overlooks the attempt? I didn't save
your life to watch you throw it away. If you want Mae, then
sober up and go after her, but liquor won't wash her out
of your blood."

Lawrence raised his head slightly, and even bleary eyed,
caught the fierceness of Jonathan's expression. "You'd
know from experience?"

"Oh, hell yes, I know. Now stop wallowing in self-pity.
Mae touched your heart. Calling her vile names won't
erase what you and she shared. You ought to be man
enough to forgive her lies or simply choose to forget her."

Lawrence growled through clenched teeth. "I'll never forget her!" The painful admission caught him by surprise, and ashamed to be so weak, he dropped his head in defeat.

Jonathan leaned against a bedpost. "You were tough enough to survive being shot. Losing one pretty woman won't kill you."

"You self-righteous bastard," Lawrence hissed. "You're so damn sure what's good for me, but I don't see you out looking for another wife."

The insult caught Jonathan off guard, but thinking of Eliza Kate, he answered with surprising candor. "There's no need to search. Now go to sleep, and tomorrow avoid the temptation to drown your sorrows. I expect you to handle the money on Saturday, and it looks as though you'll need a few days to clear your head."

With a defeated sigh, Lawrence flopped over on his back and flung his arm over his eyes. "Saturday is a lifetime away."

Jonathan was all too aware of how soon he'd have to force himself to leave Eliza Kate, and to him, the remaining days consumed the space of a heartbeat. While he stood fighting a silent battle with his heart, Lawrence fell asleep where he lay, forcing Jonathan to ease off his friend's coat and boots. He then rolled the end of the quilt over him, and far too restless to remain in the house, left to prowl the garden.

He yanked off his tie and tucked it in his coat pocket, but even in the sweetly scented shadows he felt confined and soon shoved open the gate to head out across the open prairie. A solitary figure in the gathering dusk, he still felt Eliza Kate's presence, and with every stride his savage hunger for her brushed the shimmering edge of madness. Surely it was insanity to want her as badly as he did. Everyone he had ever loved had died far too young, and it was much easier to blame a curse than to believe it mere coincidence.

He refused to choose such a sorry fate for Eliza Kate

when she was so full of life she almost glowed. The very
last thing he wanted to do was leave her, even for her own
good; but he didn't trust fate to allow them a contented
life together. He could not speak of love either, for to
declare himself and then say good-bye would be far too
cruel. He did love her though and would forever.

It was after midnight when he finally returned to the
Bendalins's majestic home. By then, the only light shone
in his own bedroom window. He climbed the back stairs
with a weary step, but his fatigue vanished the instant he
pushed open his door and found Eliza Kate, demurely
dressed in her lace nightgown, sound asleep on his bed.

He'd just walked miles steadfastly refusing to curse her
with a deadly love, but when her eagerness to be with him
was so compelling, he could not refuse. Surely what he
was about to do was wrong, but none of his silent argu-
ments was strong enough to send him back out into the
night.

He drew in a ragged breath, then locked his door, and
leaned back against it to yank off his boots. He quietly set
them aside before stripping off his coat and shirt. He
draped the clothes over the armchair, then crossed to the
bed, and climbed over Eliza Kate to stretch out behind
her. He snuggled close, slid his fingers through her flowing hair, and brought a curl to his lips.

It was so easy to become lost in her and the joy she gave
with every caress. Although he had fought hard, he'd
failed to break the link between them; their bond simply
ran too deep. Drawing closer to Eliza's subtly perfumed
warmth, he tightened his embrace, and she arched her
back to press against his chest. He dipped his head to
place a light kiss on her shoulder and vowed to remember
very precious second of this, their last night together.

Eliza Kate yawned and stretched as she came awake.
Jonathan's arm was curled around her waist, and she
laced her fingers in his. Still sleepy, she spoke in a seductive sigh. "I've never cared much for the night. It was simply lost time before you came to us. Now I look forward

to the end of the day with a craving only you can satisfy."

Jonathan muffled a low moan in her fragrant curls, then propped his head on his elbow. "Thank you. I wish I had a gift for such poetic speeches."

Eliza Kate turned toward him with another languid stretch. "It was a sincere compliment, Mr. Blair. Have I simply embarrassed you?" She hoped not, when it was all she could do not to swear that she'd love him forever.

The fullness of her breasts brushed his chest, and Jonathan slid his hand between them to catch a tender nipple between his thumb and forefinger. He felt her shiver through her gown and increased the pressure. "No. You cause me such exquisite discomfort it does not even have a name."

The lamp gave his eyes a silvery gleam, but the sadness in their depths tugged on Eliza's heart. She wanted his thoughts focused on their future rather than his tragic past. "Despite your denial, you're very clever with words," she scolded softly.

Jonathan raised himself up to move over her. "Is that all you admire about me?" he asked before kissing her so deeply he left them both breathless.

When she'd first come to his room and found him gone, Eliza had been so frightened she'd quickly flung open the wardrobe to make certain he'd not left and taken everything he owned with him. His clothes were there, however, all clean and neatly pressed, but she'd not been reassured. He'd bolted from the dining room as though he'd been desperate to flee. She could not bear to think he'd wanted to escape her.

"Shall I prepare you a list?" she asked flippantly. He was still wearing his trousers, but she ran her hands over his hips to savor the feel of him through the cloth.

"You're all I need," Jonathan breathed out against the tempting softness of her lips. He traced their graceful bow with the tip of his tongue, and she wrapped her arms around his neck to lure him past all reason.

As he pulled away her gown to lave her breasts, she

responded with the sparkling laugh he'd missed at dinner. He'd not realized how much he enjoyed her laughter and the way it made emotion overflow his heart. As she unbuckled his belt, he recalled the morning he'd found her perched in the oak tree. He'd done all the laughing that day although it had been more than a year since he'd found anything passably amusing.

Now she'd boldly strip away his clothing, and he was uncertain who had taught whom to make love with such gleeful abandon. He adored her, but with every luscious kiss became more haunted by the specter of impending doom. If the fates already suspected how deeply she filled his heart, then he'd be no better able to protect her from harm than he had Mary Claire.

Striving to vanquish his ghosts, Eliza Kate welcomed Jonathan's desperate passion and thought that while he might describe the Cherokee as a civilized tribe, there was a wildness in him no amount of culture could ever tame. It was what she loved most about him. He was his own man, and she was his as she'd been born to be.

Even so, she was no more willing than he to think past that glorious moment. Thrilled by his strength, she wound herself around him and wished that like the most tenacious vine, she might remain coiled around him forever. She drank in his scent, absorbed his heat, and moved beneath him to draw him down into her own exotic dream where the ecstasy they created together danced and swelled to a near soul-shattering crescendo.

Left shaken by the fury of their entwined desire, and yet blissfully sated, she couldn't bear to waste another minute in sleep, so held Jonathan cradled in her arms while she prayed that his dreams would at last be of her. She reluctantly released him to return to her own bed before dawn, but she was far too excited to rest.

There had been a stunning tenderness to their lovemaking that night, and she hoped with all her heart the change in Jonathan had been sparked by love. What she craved were the words he'd yet to speak, and as she dressed for their morning ride, she imagined him rehearsing the devoted promises she longed to hear.

She also thought it possible that Jonathan might sleep until noon, but as she left the house, she found him waiting by the corral. He was leaning against the gate, his ankles crossed, and his arms folded over his chest. His hat was tipped low against the early-morning sun, and he was so still she thought he might be napping.

Then he flicked the angle of his hat to look up at her, and his expression was as coldly forbidding as the morning they'd met. Frightened, she halted in mid-stride. She'd not eaten, but still her stomach lurched then tightened into a painful knot. She swayed slightly, and unable to take another step, forced him to come to her.

"What's wrong?" she asked as soon as he was close enough to hear her anguished whisper. She'd longed to hear some sweet, romantic declaration, but clearly there was nothing even remotely like love on his mind today.

His heart breaking, Jonathan had no easy answer. Last night had convinced him he couldn't spend the next four nights creating an unforgettable farewell and then ride out of her life after the race Saturday. Nor could he share another meal with her family while his hopeless dreams threatened to rip him in two. His gear was already tied behind his saddle, and he was anxious to ride out before he lost his resolve as well as his heart.

"Let's go on out to the river," he stated calmly.

It was a command rather than an invitation, and Eliza Kate's terror increased tenfold. She shot a quick glance over her shoulder, but neither of her parents stood on the front porch monitoring their stilted conversation. "First you'll have to tell me what's wrong," she demanded hoarsely.

"Not a damn thing," Jonathan forced himself to lie. "It's too pretty a morning to waste here. Let's go on out to the river like we usually do."

His condescending tone struck her as false rather than soothing, and trusting her instincts, she feared this would be another in an awful string of difficult days. She'd shed too many tears last Saturday when he'd nearly beaten her father to death to break down in front of him now.

"If you've something to say to me, please do so right here," she demanded. "You needn't fear that I'll become so hysterical you'll have to toss me in the Trinity River to calm me down."

Jonathan damned his own lack of finesse where she was concerned and relaxed a knee to strike a more casual pose. He shoved his hands in his hip pockets. "That thought hadn't even occurred to me," he said convincingly, but he had feared she'd cry, and then he might have been the one to need a long swim to calm down.

Eliza Kate straightened her posture proudly. "Mr. Blair, something is obviously troubling you. Just spit it out, and save us the bother of a ride as tiresome as this conversation is fast becoming."

The sun was now well up in the sky, and Jonathan again ducked his head to avoid the glare. He worried the dirt with the scuffed toe of his boot, and anxious to deliver his wretched news, spoke at a brisk clip.

"You know I've never been comfortable in your home. I'll stay for the race since a lot of people are counting on me to show up, but I've decided to camp out by the river until Saturday. That's no complaint of your hospitality. I just need to get away and spend some time alone."

Already filled with a numbing dread, what Eliza heard loud and clear was his desperate desire to escape *her*. After all the glorious nights they'd shared, she couldn't understand how he could bring himself to leave her for even an hour. Clearly she didn't know him at all, and he could not even begin to understand her.

"Look at me," she ordered sharply.

Jonathan's head jerked up, and what he found facing him was the coolly confident Miss Bendalin who'd once offered no more than a quick drink at her river. It was easy to hate that haughty bitch, but he knew she wasn't the real Eliza Kate. Preferring bitter anger to tears, he nodded. "You already have my full attention."

"Good. If you ever told me, I've forgotten. What was your late wife's name?"

Baffled by such a seemingly irrelevant question, Jonathan took a moment to respond. "Mary Claire."

"Well, Mary Claire must have been a remarkable woman, and I intend to name my first daughter after her. Good luck on the race. I doubt I'll attend."

With that surprising announcement, Eliza Kate drew on a healthy dose of pride to recover her usual grace. She abruptly turned on her heel, and marched toward the house, leaving Jonathan to stare after her with an incredulous gape.

That she'd promised to name her daughter for Mary Claire flummoxed him completely. Then she'd brushed him off as though the time they'd spent together was no more than a shared cup of tea—and a cold one at that.

He slapped his hat against his thigh and swore a particularly obscene oath. To protect her, he'd had no choice other than to make a clean break, but he'd not expected her to toss him aside like a moldy potato peel. He cursed all the way across the yard to Red Warrior, then mounted and rode away with the speed that was sure to leave Fletcher Monroe's mighty black stallion snorting dust.

As soon as she entered her home, Eliza ducked into the parlor and collapsed in her father's chair. She pounded clenched fists on her knees but refused to give voice to the anguished tears bottled inside. She couldn't understand why Jonathan didn't want her, didn't ache for her, but she'd not fall victim to another bout of tears. Instead, she cursed the fate that had sent him into her life when he was so lost in the past he couldn't return her love.

Awash in sorrow, she didn't even look up when nearly an hour later Lawrence entered the room and made straight for the liquor cabinet. He'd already unlocked the door and reached for a crystal decanter before he realized he wasn't alone. He froze for an instant, then replaced the decanter, and closed and locked the cabinet with guilty haste.

"It's a beautiful day. Why aren't you out riding?" he asked.

Eliza Kate didn't recall ever seeing her uncle drink in the morning, but she knew why he was distraught and didn't question or judge the wisdom of his actions. Instead, she provided a highly censored version of her latest conversation with Jonathan.

Feeling blindsided, Lawrence sank down on the sofa and leaned forward to cradle his head in his hands. "Oh no. This is all my fault," he moaned. "He was only trying to help me last night, but I dredged up his wife. He was my best friend, and that was a rotten thing to do when it's plain he still misses her so badly."

For one horrible moment, Eliza wondered if it had been Lawrence's taunt that had prompted Jonathan to disappear for several hours last night. Had he been mourning his wife and then returned to make love to her? He had seemed so very loving, but had she merely served as a convenient substitute for the woman he'd lost? After all, he'd not come to her; she'd been lying in wait for him. Perhaps it was his conscience that had sent him away that morning, and if that were truly the case, then she was glad he was gone.

Thoroughly discouraged, she fought to focus on her uncle's lament, but she could barely speak over the tears knotting her throat. "I'm sure Jonathan will always be your best friend, but you can't blame him for wanting to get away from us. We'd overwhelm most people, and Lord knows, Father will be elated to find him gone."

Lawrence responded with a rude snort. "Yes, there's never been any love lost between those two."

Grasping at the faint hope of affecting a reconciliation, Eliza Kate leaned forward. "What actually happened between Father and Jonathan to create such enmity?" she asked.

Although still angry with himself as well as the world,

Lawrence sat up and shook his head. "It was a long time ago. Besides, since it involves your father, it's an inappropriate subject for discussion."

"So what? Most of our conversations of late could be described as inappropriate but that doesn't mean they weren't worthwhile. Please tell me what you know." Expecting that some dreadful argument was at the core of the problem, she held her breath; but Lawrence just rubbed his face as though he were as weary as she felt.

"I know the three of you met during the war when tempers were running high," she began. "But if it wasn't an argument that separated them, could Father have been jealous of your friendship with Jonathan? After all, you were his kid brother."

"I still am," Lawrence pointed out with a faint smile, but he remained lost in thought. "I've often wondered about one incident. But it's probably best not to pursue it after all these years."

"If it's lingered in your mind, then clearly it's worth pursuing," Eliza persisted, equally certain she was entitled to know what troubled him; if there were any way to help her father and Jonathan see eye to eye, she'd seize it.

Lawrence rose unsteadily. "Oh, Eliza Kate, they're just two stubborn, strong-willed men. Look at Jonathan and Fletcher as another example. Did they take to each other?"

Eliza laughed at the comparison. "No, they definitely did not. I see what you mean though. Sometimes people don't need a reason not to like each other."

Reminded of her last angry encounter with Fletcher, she let the matter of the animosity between her father and Jonathan drop, but she noted Lawrence's pensive frown. "Jonathan's just left our home, not the state of Texas. Why don't you ride out to see him? He'll not travel far before making camp. I don't believe he took any provisions with him, and he'd undoubtedly welcome a gift of food."

Lawrence gave her hand a squeeze as they entered the dining room to join the others for breakfast. "There are too many fish in the river for him to starve, but it's sweet of you to worry about him. I'll give him a day or two to get bored with his own company. Then he might be happier to see me."

"What a sensible idea, Uncle." Eliza's smile was sincere, but her thoughts were elsewhere. She'd just realized that after she'd advised him to follow his heart with Mae, she'd be a bigger fool than Jonathan to let him ride out of her life without making a single attempt to convince him to stay.

She would also wait a couple of days, because it would take her that long to devise a logical plea for something she feared only the heart could comprehend. She was also clinging to the hope the break would give Jonathan the opportunity to miss her and perhaps even to see the error of his ways.

She already missed him terribly. The dining room might hold the savory scent of fried bacon, but even the most delicious of breakfasts wouldn't fill the hollow beneath her heart.

Chapter Nineteen

Before Eliza Kate and Lawrence could be seated, Lamar came rushing down the stairs and burst into the dining room.

"Eliza Kate, your mother is feeling poorly this morning, and I'm sending for Dr. Burnett. Will you please go up and sit with her until he arrives? Carmen is with her now, but I'd prefer family."

"Of course." Eliza caught her uncle's eye and recognized her own panic mirrored in his frantic glance. Lawrence and her mother were very close, and before making her way to the door, Eliza paused to rest her hand lightly on his sleeve.

"You'll come up to say good morning when you can?" she asked.

Lawrence looked queasy, but he nodded. "Perhaps after Burnett's visit. We mustn't tire her."

Agreeing with his thoughtful suggestion, Eliza Kate hurried on up the stairs. Whenever her mother felt in the slightest bit ill, the whole household came to a hushed standstill, but it was always especially difficult for Eliza Kate. Unlike many of the others, she had never fooled herself into believing her mother would recover her strength. As a result, she regarded every setback as another ominous step toward death.

It was not a fear she would allow her mother to glimpse, however, and she smiled warmly as she entered her bedroom. "There's no need for you to stay, Carmen," she quickly assured the maid. "I'll ring if there's anything we require."

Clearly concerned for her mistress, Carmen frowned slightly, but then with practiced ease, she excused herself and left the room.

"Your father is an alarmist," Delia insisted before covering a wide yawn. "But since you're here, we might as well talk a while." She patted the place at her side, then snuggled down under her covers and smoothed fluttering fingertips along the scalloped border of her rose-patterned quilt.

Eliza Kate took the place she'd often occupied and caught her mother's hand. It was such a delicate hand, scarcely larger than a child's. "You needn't pretend with me. How are you really feeling?"

Delia shrugged slightly. "I'm not ill, simply too tired to leave this comfortable bed so early in the day. I'm sure to feel more energetic by this afternoon."

Eliza Kate recognized the wistful tone in her mother's voice and hoped she wasn't being overly optimistic. "It's another beautiful day. Perhaps you'll feel up to visiting the garden."

Delia covered another protracted yawn, then began to

smile. "The garden is especially lovely this spring. It would be perfect for an outdoor wedding."

"A wedding, Mother?" Taken aback, Eliza Kate promptly released her hand with a fond pat, nearly leaped to her feet, and crossed the spacious room to the window that overlooked the magnificent garden. She forced herself to focus on the colorful scene spread below rather than on the unlikely prospect of a charming wedding in which she'd be the bride.

"I know everyone assumes I'll marry Fletcher, but it's become increasingly obvious to me that we're not a good match. In fact, a marriage between us would be a dreadful mistake, and I should have told him so long before this."

"Oh, dear," Delia exclaimed, her interest keen. "Fletcher can't be expected to take such a shocking announcement well."

Eliza Kate sank down on the cushioned window seat. "No, he'll probably make an awful scene, but Uncle Lawrence has offered his support. His presence should serve to keep Fletcher's anger in check, but I'd rather have him hate me now than resent me every day for the rest of our lives."

"What a disheartening prediction. Why would he resent you, my darling?"

"I don't love him. In fact, I'm not even sure that I like him anymore."

Delia needed a long moment to consider her daughter's surprising change of heart. "Please don't forget that Fletcher is your father's partner, so you must take care not to be cruel, for your father's sake as well as Fletcher's."

"Don't worry, Mother. You've raised me to behave as a lady should." But all of her mother's diligent tutoring had been forgotten once she'd met Jonathan. Despite the resulting pain, she wasn't a bit sorry either.

Delia raised herself up slightly, but even in profile she could appreciate her daughter's pensive frown. "I'm beginning to fear I've raised you to be too much of a lady."

Intrigued, Eliza Kate turned to face her mother

squarely. "How can such a catastrophe even be possible?" she asked with a smile.

"I'm not teasing, my love. I meant for you always to temper your remarks with compassion, but perhaps what you've truly mastered is the art of censoring your emotions."

Her mother had not been nearly so astute of late, and although Eliza appreciated it as a good sign, she'd not admit to becoming so adept at hiding her feelings that not even her own mother could see through her act.

"You may be right, but Fletcher is unlikely to agree no matter how tactfully I dash his hopes for our marriage."

"You owe him the truth, of course, and I hope you'll not lie to yourself either," Delia added softly.

Eliza Kate felt as though Jonathan had drenched her in the truth that morning, and it might be years before her heartbreak began to subside. "I know the truth in my own heart. That's why I can't marry Fletcher Monroe."

Rather than meet her mother's inquisitive glance, she turned again to the serene view of the garden. "No matter how compassionate my words, Fletcher will be furious, and so will Father. We might as well prepare for the worst."

"I wish I weren't too sleepy to offer sage advice," Delia murmured before drawing a deep breath. "Their disappointment will be understandable, but it's your sorrow that troubles me now. If my mind isn't completed muddled, I seem to recall we've discussed Jonathan Blair on more than one occasion. Is he the real problem?"

Eliza wished she could swear her mother to secrecy and confide in her, but since that was impossible, she responded with a sad, sweet smile. "He doesn't love me."

Delia struggled to remain awake. "I find that difficult to believe."

"Yes, you would, but then you're my mother so you're prejudiced."

"Would you like for me to speak with him?"

Embarrassed by the offer, Eliza tensed. "What could you possibly say?"

Delia sank deeper into her pillows as she pondered her options. "I used to be so much better at this," she apologized. She glanced toward Eliza Kate and gestured with a lazy wave. "I would tell him to throw off the heavy burden of sorrow he's wrapped around himself as tightly as a winter coat. He's a fine man and deserves the happiness he'd find with you. He simply needs to recapture his belief in love."

A painful lump tightened Eliza's throat. "That's such a sweet thought, Mother. Jonathan and I have been happy together, but after all he's suffered, it's simply not enough."

"He's no fool, dearest. Perhaps all he needs is a little more time." Delia sighed softly and closed her eyes.

Before Eliza Kate could point out that time was a luxury they simply didn't have, her mother had fallen asleep. She was tired herself, but too anxious about her mother's declining health to doze off while she waited for Dr. Burnett. When he arrived a little after ten o'clock, she left the room to allow him the privacy to examine his patient.

She paced the hall like a caged lion until the physician finally pulled Delia's door closed. She rushed toward him, but one glance at his troubled expression sent her hopes plummeting. "She's not just overtired, is she?" she whispered fretfully.

Clay Burnett slipped his arm around her shoulders and guided her toward the stairs. "Let's go on down to the parlor, and I'll explain everything to you and your father at the same time."

His gentle touch was meant to be comforting, but Eliza Kate pulled away. "No, wait. It's best if I understand first, because Father will never accept bad news."

Clay sighed helplessly. "Can you blame him? He loves your mother so, but she's very weak, and there's nothing more I can do for her. I do want you to encourage her to eat, even if she only swallows a few bites at each meal.

She's not in any pain, but it won't do her any good to drown in her family's anguished tears."

Eliza understood his admonition completely. "You needn't worry. We're all accomplished at putting on a brave front for Mother. We'll not fail her now."

"No, of course, you won't. They taught us a phrase in medical school: Appreciate every minute you have with your loved ones. I'm sorry I've nothing more profound to recommend, but do enjoy your remaining time with your mother. She regards you and your brothers as her life's greatest blessing. I'll stop by to see her as often as I possibly can."

Eliza Kate dug her nails into her palms. She had already lost Jonathan, and now all too soon, she was going to lose her darling mother as well. Her family would never need her more, and yet she felt as dry as dust, with nothing more to give.

"Thank you, Dr. Burnett. I know Mother always enjoys seeing you. We all do."

"Thank you, but I wish I could offer more than my company. Now tell me what happened to your father. He looks as though he was on the losing end of a fistfight, and I simply can't imagine Lamar Bendalin brawling."

Eliza Kate fell in beside him as they made their way down the wide staircase. "No, indeed," she lied smoothly. "He simply suffered a fall from his horse."

When Eliza and Dr. Burnett entered the parlor, her father and Lawrence quickly came forward to meet them, but nothing the sympathetic young physician offered could erase the fear in the men's eyes.

Though Jonathan had never minded his own company, the day dragged on with little to do other than fish, which he'd never much enjoyed, and battle his own warring emotions. He welcomed the setting sun but soon found the darkness compounded his restlessness tenfold. He moved his bedroll repeatedly, but couldn't locate a smooth stretch of earth on the rise above the river. When he finally did fall asleep, he slept poorly and awakened with the dawn.

Unrefreshed, he washed in the chill river and struggled to understand why he felt so wretchedly unhappy when he was positive he'd done the right thing. He'd been certain that without him, Eliza Kate would have the chance to lead a full and happy life, but now he was torn by guilt as though he'd found her clinging to a crumbling cliff and simply turned his back and walked away.

He fought to dispel that troubling image by exercising Red Warrior and brushing the horse's coat until it nearly sparkled in the sunlight. Then he exchanged his boots for his moccasins and ran sprints along the riverbank while the powerful stallion grazed. Rather than ease the tension tearing him apart, however, running only served to focus his thoughts and intensify his overriding sense of regret.

Each time he thought of Eliza Kate, which was with every breath, he was reminded of her parting taunt. Clearly she intended to have a slew of beautiful daughters, but who would be their father? He absolutely could not abide the thought of her marrying Fletcher Monroe. But if not Fletcher, then whom did she intend to wed? he agonized.

It was late afternoon before he realized he'd forgotten to toss a line in the river. Red Warrior was chomping his way through the spring grass, but the tender greens weren't in the least bit appetizing to Jonathan. He cursed his own stupidity in not packing a hunk of cheese or a few biscuits before he'd left the Trinity Star, but as he finally got down to the business of catching his dinner, he was buffeted by a sudden burst of cold north wind. The sky swiftly filled with dark roiling clouds, and he was soon splattered with huge raindrops.

He had a tarp he quickly angled across the mesquite trees to provide Red Warrior with shelter from the storm, but he stood out in the rain until he was soaked clear through. The angry sky matched his mood, and he cheered a sudden bolt of lightning and shouted back at the thunder.

Inspired, he tore off his shirt and danced about, daring the lightning to strike him dead. When the bright fingers of electricity only tickled the far horizon, he spun and whirled, whooped and growled, then made great flying kicks, but despite his frantic efforts to attract the fury of the storm, he went unscathed.

Conceding defeat, he fell to his knees in the mud, and as his tears mingled with the pounding rain, he finally came to grips with how desperately he missed Eliza Kate. The storm-swollen Trinity River now flowed by him with a threatening roar, but his only fears were for the lovely young woman who filled his heart with a desperate yearning for the peace of her embrace.

He could feel her calling to him above the howling wind and knew he had to answer. Growing ever more intense, the fierce storm fought his every step, but he welcomed the challenge, gathered his soggy belongings, saddled Red Warrior, and headed for home.

Eliza Kate had seen the sky darken and with the first gust of chill northern wind had prayed Jonathan would find shelter from the coming storm. He was ever present in her thoughts, but her family's pressing needs prevented her from sacrificing her pride to ride out and make certain he was safe. Forced into bed by sheer exhaustion, she awoke the instant Jonathan cracked open her door.

Rain dripped off his hat and coat to puddle around his boots. In her dimly lit room, he appeared as a fluid apparition more suited to the ghost of a shipwreck than one defiantly haunting the Texas plains, but rather than cry out in alarm, she sprang from her bed to welcome him.

"Oh, Jonathan, look at you. You're soaked clear to the skin." She pulled him into her room, tossed his hat aside, and reached for the buttons on his coat.

Jonathan kicked the door closed behind him and caught her wrists in a near-bruising grip. She was dressed in her lacy white nightgown, and her trailing curls spilled over her shoulders in tantalizing disarray. Thrilled by how promptly she'd come to his aid, he clutched her tightly.

"Now wait just a minute, Miss Bendalin," he cautioned softly. "Before you strip me naked, there's something I need to ask."

Thinking this a bizarre time for a proposal, Eliza Kate still wanted to scream, Yes! Instead, she relaxed against him and licked her lips nervously. "What is it?"

"Mary Claire would have been real honored to have a namesake, but who's going to father all your pretty daughters?"

She was pressed so tightly against his chest that her nightgown was fast becoming as wet as his coat, but what she felt was his underlying strength rather than the rain's icy chill. The time they'd spent apart had been far too harrowing for her to mask her emotions, but late at night, discretion demanded a whisper rather than an enthusiastic shout.

"I had hoped it would be you," she admitted freely.

Elated, Jonathan shifted his hands to her waist, plucked her off her feet, and kissed her soundly so that she could not possibly mistake his intentions. "That's the answer I was hoping for, but you know I'm not your father's first choice," he reminded her.

"But we're talking about our lives, not his, and I love you too dearly to feel disloyal. Now let's get you out of those wet clothes. I don't want you to die of pneumonia just when you've come to your senses."

"My senses?" Jonathan chuckled. "Oh hell, let's not argue. I want to do the right thing, and I'll speak with your father first thing tomorrow morning."

For a few precious moments, he'd distracted her so completely, she'd forgotten how inopportune the time was. "No, you mustn't," she said as she eased Jonathan out of his wet coat. That he wasn't wearing a shirt struck her as odd, but she was too preoccupied with having him near to comment.

"Mother's not doing well, and Father's dropped everything to be with her. He's still not gone into town and claims his businesses will all have to take care of themselves."

Jonathan couldn't help wondering how things were going at the Rosedale, then was ashamed of himself. "I like your mother," he responded. "What does her doctor say?"

Eliza went to her washstand for towels and handed Jonathan one to dry his hair while she rubbed the other over his shoulders and back. "I don't even want to whisper the words, but she's dying."

Jonathan remembered his last dinner with the Bendalins, the stilted affair that had sent him spiraling right back down into his old torments. Delia had appeared touchingly frail that evening, and if her health had slipped since then, he doubted she had much longer to live.

"I picked a real poor time to leave you," he murmured apologetically. Delia hadn't been well when he'd arrived, so he doubted anyone would curse him if she died, but he had to fight hard not to shoulder the blame.

"Maybe I shouldn't have come back," he announced suddenly. "Misery haunts me wherever I go."

"Stop that this instant!" Eliza Kate scolded. "My mother has been blessed in so many ways, and meeting you is surely one of them. Now please, get out of those wet clothes, if for no other reason than that you're making a mess of my floor."

"Yes, Miss Bendalin. Maybe I ought to go on up to my room," he offered.

Eliza Kate already had her hands on his belt buckle. His skin was like ice, and his nipples frozen buds. "You'll do no such thing, and stop calling me Miss Bendalin. I want you in my bed where I can keep you warm."

"I hadn't even noticed I was cold," Jonathan said, laughing. She was fussing over him as a mother would, and he found her lavish attentions surprisingly endearing. He leaned down to kiss her and wound his fingers in her hair to hold her close. As always, the temptation to lose himself in her was strong.

When he finally caught himself and drew away, he breathed out a husky promise, "I do love you. Don't ever doubt that."

"Oh, Jonathan." Eliza Kate desperately wanted for them to be happy together. He was so very handsome in a dark suit, and she longed to wear a beautiful gown for the garden wedding her mother had imagined, but such a joyous celebration was impossible for them now. Nor could she push her panicked mind past her family's sorrow to consider how she and Jonathan would live or even where they might reside once they were wed.

"Everything's such an awful mess," she said, sighing sadly. "Please just come to bed and hold me until I believe it will be all right."

Jonathan welcomed her invitation, but he knew better than to leave his wet clothing scattered about her room. He quickly rolled everything up and laid it in the bowl on her washstand, then moved his boots away from her door. He caught her hand as they moved toward the bed, then had the presence of mind to go back and turn the key in the lock.

Once they'd reached the bed, Jonathan eased Eliza Kate out of her gown, slid under the covers, and pulled her into his arms. In that very instant, the house was rocked by a stunning bolt of lightning, and they clung to each other through the thunder's deafening roar. It was a disastrous omen in his view, but he had already fought to leave her and failed.

Her hands were on him, warming him as she'd promised, but he needed so much more than the comfort she craved. He needed all of her, her spirit, her beauty, her courage, which made her want him no matter how often he gave her a damn good reason to turn away.

"I will love you until the last drop of rain falls to earth," he murmured before her delicious kisses made it impossible to speak.

Eliza Kate slid her fingers through his hair. Thick and damp like ebony ribbons, it brushed over the fullness of her breasts as he spread a flurry of tender kisses down her body. Shivering with desire, she arched to press against him. He had been so cold, but was now infused with a passionate heat, and she was the one to cling to his warmth.

She savored each caress with a seductive moan and fought to make their loving last forever, but all too soon the night dissolved into morning. Then they had to part for a day that held not a glimmer of Jonathan's beautiful promises nor Eliza Kate's blissful dreams.

Chapter Twenty

Thursday morning, Lawrence met Jonathan on the second-floor landing and shook his head in disbelief. "I didn't expect to see you back here before Saturday's race."

He grasped the handrail to ease his way down the stairs and continued in an apologetic tone. "I meant to ride out and look for you, truly I did, but with Delia—" he mumbled a prayer under his breath and shrugged helplessly. "Then the storm hit yesterday, and I'd missed my chance."

"It's all right," Jonathan assured him. "As you can see, I survived just fine on my own."

"As you always do, but why are you dressed in my suit so early in the day? Please tell me you don't plan on going out again in this awful storm."

Jonathan chuckled as he reached the bottom of the stairs and stepped out into the foyer. "No, I've more sense than that; but all my clothes got wet in the downpour and are being laundered and dried, so I've simply nothing else to wear."

"Oh yes, of course, that makes sense." Lawrence led the

way into the dining room. The table was already set for breakfast, and tantalizing aromas were drifting in from the kitchen, but they were the first to arrive for the morning meal. Appearing desperately weary, Lawrence sank into his chair and leaned forward to rest his elbows on the table.

With great effort, he formed a smile. "Well, even if it was only to get out of the rain, I'm glad you're here. We're in sore need of a cool head now that Delia's situation has grown so terribly sad."

"I was real sorry to hear about her." Rather than take his usual place, Jonathan circled the long table to approach the window. The driving rain made a misty blur of Delia's lovely garden, but its beauty remained undimmed in his mind's eye.

"I mean to do whatever I can, or whatever Lamar will accept," Jonathan promised his companion, "but I'll need your help as well. I've decided to remain in Fort Worth, and I hope to win enough on Saturday's race to purchase land for a ranch, or at the very least, a sizable down payment."

"A ranch?" Stunned, Lawrence slumped back in his chair, but the seriousness of Jonathan's expression convinced him of his sincerity. "Why, that's wonderful news. I'd despaired of ever convincing you to remain here with us."

"Not *here*," Jonathan emphasized. "I want my own spread with more land than Red Warrior can gallop across in a day."

Lawrence's amazement continued to grow, for he'd never known Jonathan to make such ambitious plans. "What changed your mind about Texas?" he wondered aloud.

Jonathan wet his lips, tasted a delicious hint of Eliza Kate, and had to suppress a soft moan. He definitely wanted her, but he also longed to create lives worth living for them both. He needed to share his goals with her first, however, rather than confide his burgeoning dreams in Lawrence.

He shrugged off the question. "Let's just say I've finally found something more compelling than my nightmares."

Though still curious, Lawrence had learned through bitter experience the utter futility of prying into his friend's motives. It was frustrating, but a price he willingly paid to maintain their friendship. "Well, regardless of what might have prompted your return to ranching, it's terrific news. I suppose remaining here with us was out of the question after your falling out with Lamar."

Eliza Kate entered the dining room in time to hear that last remark. " 'Falling out,' is a gross understatement, Uncle."

"Yes, I'll concede that point," Lawrence quickly replied. "But Jonathan's decided to make his home here in Texas. Isn't that terrific news?"

Lawrence was watching her closely, obviously keenly interested in her reaction, but she dared not admit just how thrilled she truly was. Instead, she glanced over his head to meet Jonathan's gaze, and he winked at her. It was such a sly gesture, and yet so dear, she scarcely knew how to respond.

"Why, yes, that's marvelous news, and probably the only happy note we'll hear today. Please forgive me for not joining you gentlemen for breakfast, but I want to make certain Mother's tray is prepared as I directed. Then I'll eat with her and give Father some time to rest."

Eliza Kate swept through the door leading to the kitchen before Jonathan could volunteer his assistance, and he was left feeling as though he'd failed her in some important way. An all-too-familiar guilt washed through him, and he grabbed the opportunity before it was lost.

"Excuse me a second," he called to Lawrence, and he followed Eliza through the door into the spacious butler's pantry that connected the dining room with the kitchen. With breakfast preparations underway, the kitchen beckoned with a buttery warmth, but as soon as he entered, he was greeted with such shocked glances he doubted any of the Bendalin men ever visited that part of the house.

The cook stepped away from the heat of the stove and wiped her hands on her apron while Carmen and the two young serving girls merely gasped and gaped. Fortunately, Eliza Kate still had her wits about her and came back toward him.

"Is there something you need, Jonathan?" she asked sweetly.

Ignoring their startled audience, he dropped his voice to an enticing whisper. "Yes. I want to help you. Isn't there something I can do?"

Certain there must be a job that would suit his talents, Eliza Kate sifted through all that needed to be done, and her brothers quickly came to mind. "The rain's too heavy for Robby to go into town for school, and Ricky hasn't the patience to help him with his lessons. Could you make certain that he's keeping up with his studies?"

Jonathan didn't believe Robby was even speaking to him, but he'd not remind her of that sad fact. "Sure, and regardless of how low his store of patience might be, I'll do what I can to convince Ricky to keep an eye on his little brother."

"Thank you, that's very thoughtful."

There were faint shadows beneath her eyes, and Jonathan doubted she had slept any better than he had the last two nights. At least last night he'd been able to hold her, but neither of them had gotten much sleep. "Is there anything I could do for your mother?" he asked.

Touched by the concern in his voice and expression, Eliza Kate readily understood how desperately he wished to be of service. She also considered how this situation must be affecting him emotionally. "You've seen far too much death and dying," she answered in a hushed whisper. "I'll not ask for more than a prayer."

"You don't have to ask," Jonathan replied forcefully. "I'll go and pick some flowers for your mother's breakfast tray."

As he turned to go, Eliza Kate reached out to catch his hand. When he paused to bring it to his lips, she stepped close rather than pull away. "No, it's enough that you offered. I'll not send you out in the rain."

"I'll walk between the raindrops," Jonathan teased before releasing her, and with a ready grin for the kitchen's other occupants, he made a quick exit through the side door.

Eliza Kate then became the sole object of four flabbergasted stares. Had there been a giant tarantula perched on her shoulder, the servants could not have appeared more incredulous. She chose to ignore their apparently outraged sensibilities.

"He's an extremely charming man," she said instead. "He's probably very hungry as well. Now why don't we all get back to work? I want a poached egg, some warm buttered bread, and a fresh pot of chamomile tea for Mother."

Carmen had already placed a napkin and silverware on a lacquer-ware tray, but Eliza Kate had not had time to look for a vase before Jonathan returned with a handful of rosebuds. His hair was damp and raindrops glittered on his shoulders, but his smile was no less bright.

"Oh, those are lovely," Eliza exclaimed, and without thinking, she reached up to kiss him. It wasn't a chaste kiss to the cheek either, but a warm, spontaneous burst of affection she placed right on his smiling mouth.

Pleased that she'd cast aside her usual reserve, Jonathan responded with a mock bow. "You're very welcome, ma'am." He nodded toward the cluster of wide-eyed servants. "Ladies." Then he brushed the rain off his suit jacket and returned to the dining room.

"Let's hope the rain lets up today," he remarked as he joined Lawrence at the table. "Red Warrior won't complain about running in mud, but poor weather will make for a smaller crowd and keep the wagers down."

Jonathan had continued their conversation without

missing a beat, but Lawrence's thoughts had strayed. "Where were you just now?" he asked.

Jonathan didn't care for the suspicious gleam in his friend's eye, and cautiously chose to play innocent. "I went to get some flowers for Delia's breakfast tray. I told you I wanted to be helpful."

Lawrence regarded his old friend with a thoughtful stare. "You just wanted to make yourself useful?"

"Of course. Now where are Robby and Rick? Shouldn't they be here for breakfast, or should I go upstairs, wake them, and get them dressed? Your niece can't be expected to do everything with her mother so ill."

"No, of course not, but you needn't bother. The boys will come downstairs when they're hungry."

"All right then. Do you have any idea of what properties might be available near Fort Worth?" Jonathan wasn't sure he could convince Eliza Kate to leave the Trinity Star, but he thought the closer his home was to hers, the easier the task would be. "The land's awfully pretty around here."

"I've always thought so," Lawrence agreed, and completely distracted, he ceased to consider Jonathan's brief trip outside. "Give me a few hours to think about it. There might be some smaller ranches that you could acquire at a reasonable price and consolidate into one. Of course, it might be wise to wait and see how much you win. Then you'll have a better idea of what you can actually afford."

Confident that wouldn't be necessary, Jonathan struck a casual pose, and gazed up at the ceiling. "As long as the property is large and close, I'll find the money."

Lamar paused on the stairs. He didn't make a habit of eavesdropping in his own home, but he was too vitally interested in the conversation taking place in the dining room to enter and interrupt. As he listened, he didn't know which was worse, that Jonathan believed he'd win Saturday's race, or that he intended to use his winnings to buy land and become their neighbor.

Then with a sudden burst of generosity, he decided to allow Jonathan to make whatever grandiose plans he might like. After all, he'd not live long enough to bring any of his schemes to fruition.

Although Delia had slept through most of the last two days, Lamar had insisted she was much better that morning. Eliza Kate feared it was merely wishful thinking until she found her mother sitting up in bed looking both rested and pretty.

"Good morning, Mother. I don't have to ask how you are when it's so plain you're feeling better."

Delia leaned back slightly to allow Eliza Kate to place the breakfast tray across her lap. "Yes, I'm fine, thank you. Aren't these roses lovely?" she exclaimed.

She drank in their sweet perfume before reaching for her napkin. "I do wish you hadn't gone out in the rain to pick them though. Whatever will we do if you fall ill?"

Eliza Kate poured her mother a cup of tea, then set the teapot on the marble-topped bedside table. She pulled a rosewood chair up close to the bed and sat down. "Jonathan was kind enough to fetch the flowers, which won't endanger his health. He's a very strong young man."

Delia looked slightly puzzled as she began breaking tiny bits of buttered bread into the bowl containing her poached egg. She stirred the mixture, and savored a bite before meeting her daughter's gaze.

"I know I've heard the name, but I can't recall just who Jonathan is. Is he anyone important?"

Eliza Kate felt as though she'd been kicked in the stomach and had to swallow hard. Carmen had brushed and styled her mother's hair attractively. Her lacy nightgown was freshly laundered and pressed, but the invalid in the bed was merely a lovely shell of the vibrant woman she'd once been. Eliza felt a burst of now-familiar pain and was ashamed to miss her mother so terribly while she was still alive.

"Jonathan Blair is a good friend of Lawrence's from the war," she reminded her gently.

"Is he really? Please thank him for the flowers." For

several minutes, Delia continued eating her breakfast. "I can't imagine why I'm so hungry this morning. Do you suppose I could have some chicken soup at noon? I've always loved chicken soup."

"I'm sure we can arrange it," Eliza replied confidently, for it was a simple matter compared with having to deal with her mother's continued decline. She laced her hands in her lap and watched her mother eat with slow, dainty bites. She couldn't remember the last time her mother had shown any interest in food, but that she had forgotten someone as significant as Jonathan Blair was heartbreaking.

Eliza bit her lip until she tasted blood, and then she talked about the roses, which her mother could still appreciate. There were three yellow buds just opening, two of the most beautiful red, and a single white bloom, which made Eliza think not of a bride's bouquet, but of inevitable loss. For half an hour, they chatted easily, but of nothing that mattered, and when Lamar came to sit with his wife, Eliza barely made it out the door before she burst into tears.

She muffled her sobs with her hands, but when she reached her own room, she flung herself across the bed and cried herself to sleep. When she awoke two hours later, she remembered the chicken soup, and went racing downstairs, hoping against hope that the cook already had it simmering on the stove. When she found potato soup instead, she nearly wept again.

"Mother wants chicken soup," Eliza Kate insisted. "The rest of the family will surely eat all the potato, but please, we've just got to have some chicken soup for Mother."

The cook was a petite gray-haired woman who'd been with the Bendalins since before the Civil War. She admired Delia enormously and would have produced soup from stones had her mistress requested it. "Please don't fret, Miss Eliza. You had chicken and dumplings on the menu for dinner, so it will be no trouble to cook up some chicken soup for your mother. You need to get more rest, child. I can manage things here."

"Yes, of course, you can," Eliza concurred. "It's just the rain. I hate being cooped up inside."

The cook gestured toward the window. "There's a little sun peeking through the clouds. We might have a nice afternoon yet."

Drawn toward the light, Eliza Kate crossed the room. "The garden will be an awful mess," she murmured to herself, but she welcomed the prospect of pulling on a pair of gardening gloves and pruning back the damaged branches and vines. Desperate to leave the house, she watched anxiously as the sky slowly lightened, then ran for her hat and gloves.

Ricky and Robby had appeared for breakfast about the time Jonathan was ready to leave the table, but he had stayed and made the effort to engage the boys in conversation for Eliza's sake. He had had limited success until he had mentioned schoolwork, but then with a prod from Ricky, who'd shown more interest than Jonathan had been led to expect, Robby had reluctantly admitted to needing a little help with long division.

Although Jonathan thought Lawrence would make a far better math tutor, he nevertheless shrugged off his jacket and sent Robby upstairs for his arithmetic book and some paper and did his best to assign him some interesting problems. By the time the sun had finally broken through the clouds, Robby had gotten so quick with his numbers, Jonathan felt he'd earned some time to play.

Robby went whooping out the front door and dashed off toward the barn, but Jonathan intended to spend his time with Eliza Kate rather than his horse. When he found her raking leaves in the garden, he reached for the rake.

"Here, let me do that for you," he offered.

Eliza Kate's lips were set in a thin line, and rather than relax her fierce grip on the rake, she scraped it over the damp bricks with a savage swipe. "No, thank you. I want to clear the walkways myself."

Warned away by her tone, Jonathan took a cautious backward step. "I can understand how a little exercise would be welcome, but there's too much work for one pretty woman to do."

"I'm not usually alone," Eliza countered. "We have men who work as gardeners, but they've ridden out with the other hands to check on how the stock fared in the rain."

As Jonathan saw it, that still meant she was all alone. He looked around and noticed the bedraggled heap of flowers beside the shed. "Looks like the sweet peas could use a little attention. Maybe I'll string up a new trellis for them."

"The twine's in the shed," Eliza answered without glancing up.

"I'll see to it then." Jonathan thought Eliza probably needed a lot more than exercise, but because he'd never had any success drawing her out, he left her to tend to the sweet peas.

They lay in a fragrant tangle, but with a little gentle urging, he got the windblown plants upright and reattached to the side of the shed. He stepped back to admire his work, then noticed the lily pond was chock-full of dead leaves.

He remembered the day he and Eliza Kate had sent Fletcher Monroe off in a stuttering huff and grabbed a bucket from the shed. Rather than wade, he meant to drag the pail along the edge of the water to clear the leaves. It was an effective technique, but wasn't nearly as much fun as wading had been.

Eliza Kate spent more time watching Jonathan than raking, and by the time he'd scooped out most of the leaves from the pond, she'd calmed down enough to regret being so short with him. She leaned the rake against the shed and joined him at the pond. The benches were still damp, but she sat down on one anyway.

"My mother doesn't remember you," she revealed dejectedly. "She was quite lucid when we talked about you on Tuesday, although Dr. Burnett believed she was slipping away. Now, I don't know what to think. Maybe she'll be with us for weeks rather than days, but even when I'm with her, I miss the mother she used to be."

Eliza paused to wipe away a tear. "I'm so sorry. I shouldn't burden you with my sorrow when you have so much of your own."

More sorry than sad, Jonathan set the bucket on the low wall surrounding the pond and sat down. He removed Eliza's gloves with a quick tug, gave her fingers a comforting squeeze, and wished he knew equally soothing words.

Last night he'd danced with lightning in the hope he'd be struck dead, but something earth-shattering *had* happened to him. He was no longer the tormented man he'd been when they'd met, but the storm could take no credit for the alteration. It was Eliza Kate who'd filled his heart with hope and prompted a much-needed change for the better.

"There was a time when I shied away from everyone, even you," he recalled regretfully. "But that's over now. I know you want to be brave for your family, but please feel free to cry all you need to with me. I can take it."

"But you shouldn't have to," Eliza Kate mumbled through a choked sob.

"It's my choice," Jonathan emphasized. "Life being what it is, the sorrow often outweighs the joy. But as long as I'm alive, you'll not have to face your troubles alone."

His smile was as warm as his tender promise and after a deep breath, Eliza truly did feel better. "Thank you. I guess I'm just hanging on too tight when it's time to let go and simply accept whatever comes."

Jonathan nodded and placed a loving kiss in her palm. "I wish I could promise we'll always be happy, but you'd know that would be a lie."

"Only too well," Eliza murmured. She rested her head

against his shoulder and was grateful for that single moment of bliss.

By Saturday, the sky was a bright clear blue, and the ground near the Hanging Tree was thoroughly dry. Anticipation of another entertaining party at Fletcher Monroe's, as much as the desire to see an exciting race, had prompted an even larger crowd to head for the Trinity Star Ranch than had attended the first event. Coal Dust was again the clear favorite, but Lawrence gracefully accepted all bets while confidently backing Red Warrior with his own money as well as Jonathan's.

Delia had yet to summon the energy to leave her bed, but had continued to be in good spirits. When Dr. Burnett assured her family that she was in no immediate danger, Lamar insisted that Eliza Kate ride out to the race with him in the buggy.

Eliza saw through her father's ploy and was positive he was more interested in giving Fletcher another opportunity to impress her than in providing a respite from her mother's care. Confident Carmen would be attentive to her mother's needs, she had no qualms about leaving the house for a short while. As before, however, she hoped to see Jonathan win and looked forward to attending the race for his sake.

She dressed in a ruffled blue gown and wore an attractive straw hat with trailing blue ribbons rather than bother with a parasol. Her brothers rode behind their father's buggy, and while they still looked rather sheepish over the disadvantage they'd created for Red Warrior in the first race, she was certain they also expected the red stallion to be victorious.

They left their buggy at the edge of the crowd milling around the Hanging Tree, and Lamar went off in search of last-minute wagers. Ricky and Robby circled off to the east where they'd had a good view of the first race. Left on her own, Eliza began threading her way through the noisy crowd. It wasn't long, however, before Fletcher caught up with her.

With so much dependent upon her mother's health, Eliza had refused to allow Jonathan to discuss an engagement, let alone set a wedding date, but knowing someday soon they'd be husband and wife was enough to inspire her to be gracious. "Good morning, Fletcher. I must say that you look supremely confident," she observed.

"And you look so very beautiful, Eliza Kate," Fletcher replied effusively. "It's a good thing Coal Dust won't be nearly as distracted by your presence today as I'm sure to be."

"You're flattering me as always, Fletcher." He was apparently inclined to overlook how furious he'd been with her for daring to wade in her own pond. She'd not forgotten it though and was more grateful than ever that Jonathan had arrived before she'd married a man she thought less of with each new day.

She paused to adjust the angle of her hat before continuing in an off-hand manner, "I do hope Coal Dust will give Red Warrior some real competition. That's what everyone's come to see."

Though somewhat startled by her comment, Fletcher leaned close to whisper, "Most of these folks just want to win a few dollars and be invited to the party afterward. You'll come to the victory celebration, won't you?"

Jonathan hadn't made any plans to entertain the crowd, but she knew most of the people milling about were backing Coal Dust and so didn't deserve an invitation to her home anyway. "I wouldn't miss it," she assured him with a charming flutter of her long lashes. "Good luck."

"Thank you. I brought my buggy again and will escort you to my home after the race."

"How thoughtful," Eliza replied, although she had absolutely no intention of going anywhere with him ever again. As he began to describe just how handily he intended to beat Jonathan, she responded with a noncommittal nod, but he seemed not to notice her complete lack of enthusiasm for his company.

"Isn't it almost noon?" she interrupted to inquire.

"Why, yes, I believe it is." He dipped under the brim of her hat to plant a quick kiss on her cheek. "Don't leave without me," he ordered, and then with a careless shove, he parted the crowd and surged into it.

Quickly forgetting their conversation, Eliza hurried to follow Fletcher through a narrow opening between two families carrying small children. She struggled to get closer to the front to wish Jonathan good luck, but with everyone having the same intention, she was caught in the midst of the throng. Even standing on her tiptoes, she couldn't see more than a bright flash of Red Warrior's white mane.

Then Jonathan swung himself up on his stallion's back. His jet-black hair caught the sun's brilliant gleam, and Eliza could mistake him for no other. She watched him scan the crowd and felt a burst of pride knowing he was searching for her. She jumped and waved, but before he'd seen her, her father caught her arm and took her hand in a firm grasp.

"Don't encourage him, Eliza Kate," he said harshly. "By Monday he'll be gone, and I pray quickly forgotten. Now there's Fletcher on Coal Dust. I want to hear you cheering for him."

"I'd rather have stayed at home," Eliza answered, but a sudden shout from a bystander kept her defiant retort from being heard. *I should have spoken up long before this,* she worried. She had wanted to create a tranquil life for her mother, but the burden of her secret was proving too heavy to bear. She was going to have to confess her love for Jonathan—and soon.

As the crowd lurched forward, she was jostled and might have fallen and been trampled had her father not quickly slipped his arm around her waist to keep her upright and safe. In other times, such devoted parental attention would have been welcome, but now, she merely felt trapped in his arms and couldn't wait to break free.

Jonathan spotted Ricky and Robby, but couldn't locate Eliza Kate until he noticed Lamar's hat bobbing in the crowd. Then she was easily recognizable at her father's side, but she was looking away, rather than straining for a glimpse of the men riding in the race. That was disappointing, but if everything went as smoothly as he expected in the next few minutes, he'd win enough money to claim Eliza Kate as his wife.

Then rather than delay the wedding for Delia's sake, he intended to convince Eliza Kate to have a small ceremony that her mother could attend. He'd marry her in her mother's bedroom if he had to, but convincing Lamar to give her away willingly wouldn't be easy. He didn't relish the prospect of another bloody confrontation with him, but if that's what it took, then he was ready.

"Come on," he shouted to Fletcher. "If you delay any longer, your horse will die of old age before we run this race."

"It's still a minute to twelve!" Fletcher shouted back.

Jonathan maneuvered Red Warrior into place. "Then let's count to sixty. One, two, three . . ."

Fletcher swore, but joined in. They were running the same course as before, and while he counted, he reviewed his strategy. The red stallion was fast, but he was confident Coal Dust would beat him again. So confident in fact, that he'd encouraged Lamar to join him in wagering an enormous sum. It was an exhilarating risk, but all he'd thought about was how rich he and Lamar would be when Coal Dust won.

When Jonathan reached forty, he turned for a last glimpse of Eliza Kate and found Lamar had guided her toward the front row of spectators. He was glad she'd have a good view of the race, because he intended to give her plenty to see. He waved to her, then set his sights on the outcropping of rocks that marked the turn.

He bent low and whispered, "Let's show them how you can fly, Red."

In the next instant, the starter's pistol sounded, and this time Jonathan gave his stallion his head and made no move to check his speed. Halfway to the rocks, the magnificent red horse was streaking over the course at a blistering pace while with each stride Coal Dust fell farther behind. Jonathan held Red Warrior to a tight circle as they raced around the rocks, and when they headed back toward the Hanging Tree, still gathering speed, they were too far ahead to be caught.

Jonathan and Red Warrior flew by the finish line a full five lengths ahead of Fletcher and Coal Dust. Few cared how much money they'd lost on Coal Dust when they'd just seen the race of a lifetime, and the crowd cheered with loud whistles and rebel yells as though every one of them had backed Red Warrior.

Lamar, however, stood in stunned silence. Then the enormity of what had just happened struck him full force. "My God," he gasped.

Like those around her, Eliza Kate had been excitedly dancing a jig, but she turned to find her father so pale she feared he might faint. Her happiness shattered, she grabbed for his lapels and held on tightly to keep him on his feet.

"What's wrong? Are you ill?" she cried.

The crowd was still cheering wildly, but chilled clear through, Lamar heard only the wild beating of his own heart. "This can't be," he moaned.

"Father, what's wrong?" Terrified, Eliza strengthened her hold on him. He'd always been so strong, but now he scarcely appeared to be breathing.

Lamar knew he was ruined, but he'd be damned if he'd let Jonathan Blair get away with beating him like this. "Never," he breathed out in a hoarse cry, and he brought up his hands to break Eliza Kate's hold on him. He then took her hand in a bruising grip and yanking her along behind him, broke out of the crowd and ran toward the buggy.

Horrified, Eliza Kate was certain there must be something dreadfully wrong with her father. She stumbled and had to grab for the back of his coat, but he scarcely slowed his pace. Frantic, she turned to look for Jonathan, but he was lost in the widening swirls of the ecstatic crowd. Despite all his promises, she was in terrible trouble and alone.

Chapter Twenty-one

Jonathan let Red Warrior gallop fifty yards past the cheering crowd before he drew back on the reins to slow him. The powerful stallion came to a prancing halt, and Jonathan turned back to find Fletcher had ridden Coal Dust within a few yards of them. Elated by his easy win, Jonathan couldn't suppress a wide grin and waved.

Rather than respond with a curse, obscene gesture, or shouted demand for a rematch, Fletcher slumped forward and nearly fell from his saddle. He stumbled as his feet hit the ground, then collapsed in the dirt and sat sprawled with his head cradled in his hands.

Dismounting with a graceful leap, Jonathan dropped his reins and left Red Warrior to graze before approaching Fletcher. "It was only a race," he cajoled. "You needn't take losing that hard."

Fletcher glanced over his shoulder and was relieved to find no one had broken away from the lively crowd to run toward them. "You don't understand," he moaned. "I was so certain I'd win."

Jonathan stood back, shoved his hands in his hip pockets, and watched Fletcher bawl like a baby. He'd never liked the man, and this pathetic display disgusted him thoroughly. "Pull yourself together," he ordered harshly. "If this is the biggest disappointment you've ever had, then you're damn lucky. If you want another race, just say so."

Fletcher began to shake. He wrapped his arms around his chest and grabbed hold of his shirtsleeves to control the tremors. Tears continued to trickle down his flushed cheeks. "How'd I beat you the first time?" he whined.

Jonathan couldn't believe the man had forgotten the story Lawrence had circulated. "You must have heard Ricky was running a stud service. Not surprisingly, Red had an off day as a result; but it was still a close race," he reminded him.

Fletcher stared past Jonathan to Red Warrior and shook his head incredulously. "He ran like a demon today."

Jonathan let his satisfied grin slide into a taunting smirk. "That he did. Probably will the next time, too, but I'll still give you another race if you want it." He used the toe of his moccasin to carve a wide arc in the grass rather than issue a direct challenge, but it was all he could do not to gloat.

Fletcher had sincerely believed the race would give his wealth a considerable boost, but with the stunning loss, his carefully constructed world had caved in on him. Sick clear through, he began to rock back and forth.

"And suffer another humiliation?" he cried. "Good God, no."

Jonathan had seen too much real misery in his life to tolerate another moment of such self-pity. In a single confident stride, he reached his pitiful opponent and leaned down to grasp his arms. Then with an agile jerk, he stood Fletcher on his feet. When the distraught man swayed slightly, Jonathan was tempted to shake him.

"Those are your friends back there, not mine. Now show some courage so they'll not recognize you for the coward you are." He gave Fletcher a helpful shove to start him walking back toward the crowd.

Fletcher wiped his eyes on his shirtsleeve, then glared angrily at Jonathan, but he had to reach out for Coal Dust to steady himself. "I'll get you for this," he threatened darkly.

Jonathan laughed off the warning and gestured with

both hands. "Come on. You want to fight me? Let's do it right here while we've got a crowd eager to watch. I might even win a few hundred bucks more, if anyone would be crazy enough to back you in the bout, which I doubt."

Fletcher wasn't fool enough to fight such a tall, muscular man with his fists, but rather than face his friends, who must have also lost a great deal of money, he called upon his last bit of dignity to draw himself up into his saddle. Then after a hate-filled glance toward Jonathan, he rode across the open prairie toward the ranch he was terrified he would lose.

Lamar whipped the horses in a wild dash for home, and Eliza Kate had to hang on to the side of the buggy for fear of being bounced right out on the ground. Should that catastrophe occur, she doubted her father would even notice. He'd not answered her frantic questions, and with his face contorted into a horrifying mask, she could only assume he must be wracked with excruciating pain. Powerless to help when she didn't even understand what the problem truly was, she prayed simply to reach home safely.

Lamar slowed the team as the buggy clattered across the yard, but he drove right on into the barn before jumping out. "I can't face your mother," he called over his shoulder. "Don't tell her what happened until I decide what to do."

Eliza Kate scrambled out of the buggy. Her hat was clinging by the bow she'd tied under her chin and bounced against her shoulder blades as she ran after him. "Wait! What is it I'm not supposed to tell Mother?" she called.

Her father disappeared into the house without answering. Shaken by his bizarre behavior, Eliza Kate turned back to the barn to make certain someone would unhitch the team and cool the horses down, but there was no one in sight. With no idea what she should or should not confide in her mother, she assumed all the hands had gone to the race and was grateful for a compelling chore. She had always understood the predictable problems horses presented, but men were far more complex creatures and often posed such baffling dilemmas she had no idea where to begin.

When she finally entered the house, it was cool and strangely quiet. She found the door to the study closed and turned the knob gently, but the bolt had been thrown. Apparently her father didn't wish to be disturbed until he'd solved his nameless problem, but she wished he'd trusted her enough to confide in her. She also wished Jonathan and Lawrence would hurry home, and then maybe they could make some sense of her father's puzzling actions.

She'd thought the race would be fun, and it certainly had been exciting, but she'd expected to celebrate with Jonathan, rather than being forced to return home. Something was dreadfully wrong, she just knew it, and her father was relying on her to keep her mother from finding out. Just as her mother had always depended upon her to keep the household's petty problems from troubling her father.

Caught in the middle, she wanted to scream and stamp her feet in frustration, but in such a strained family, she couldn't give vent to her temper. Instead with great effort, she swallowed her anger and went to her own room to remove her hat and freshen up before looking in on her mother.

She'd not eaten much in the last few days. She'd told her family she wished to eat with her mother, and let her mother think she'd eaten with the family. Now her hands shook as she splashed cool water on her face and patted herself dry. Her cheeks remained flushed, and she hoped her mother would blame the sun. She sprinkled a few drops of perfume on her fingertips and combed her hands through her long curls. Too anxious to do more, she left her hair falling free.

As she entered her mother's room, Carmen closed her

book and left her bedside vigil. "How is she?" Eliza Kate whispered.

"She's resting peacefully," Carmen replied. "Are you going to wake her to have something to eat?"

Eliza Kate shook her head emphatically and held the door open for Carmen to leave. She didn't take the chair at the bedside, however, but slowly wandered the room. It was filled with her mother's prized possessions, cluttered really, and yet kept immaculately dusted. The air was scented with the lavender sachet that perfumed her mother's lingerie, and though Eliza had a compassionate purpose in being there, she felt as though she were intruding.

Restless, she wondered what was taking Jonathan so awfully long to join her. Not that she'd dashed home to be with him after the first race. No indeed, she'd gone to Fletcher's party and suffered through several miserable hours before she'd finally sought out the fascinating man who'd captured her heart. The tardiness of her arrival hadn't been lost on him either.

He wasn't the type to stay away out of spite though. She hoped he was still accepting congratulations, but she was badly disappointed not to be enjoying the excitement with him. She could easily imagine all the pretty young women who'd been so eager to meet him at Fletcher's party crowding around him now. They'd wear adoring smiles and be aflutter with flirtatious compliments. He'd be flattered as any man would, but would he consider her unexplained absence reason enough to flirt in return? she worried.

She rubbed her temples to derail that jealous train of thought, but her mind held no peace, and she was immediately overwhelmed with her family's sorrow. Before seeking solace at her favorite place on the window seat, she circled the wide bed to satisfy herself that her mother really was resting comfortably. Her fears allayed for the moment, she slipped off her shoes and curled up on the window seat.

She'd had months to adjust to the tragic change in her dear mother, but now her father's behavior had suddenly spiraled out of control. No, that wasn't entirely true, she began to fret. A downward shift in his mood had coincided with Jonathan's arrival. Perhaps that was why the result of today's race had upset him so badly. He'd mentioned something about Jonathan being gone by Monday. But then he'd not known his own daughter had inspired Jonathan to choose Texas over California for his home.

She leaned back against the wall and looped her arms around her knees. With her father locked in the study, she could not confess to him how deep her feelings for Jonathan ran, but she was sick of pretending otherwise. But where was Jonathan? And how had she come to believe in him so completely when she'd always relied solely on herself? she wondered. Was that why she felt so unsettled? Had she grabbed so eagerly for the comfort he offered that she felt bereft without it?

Her mother sighed softly in her sleep, and Eliza turned toward her. For as long as she could remember, she'd admired her mother as the perfect Southern belle. She was gracious and warm, a loving mother who'd not once had a thought in conflict with her husband's. She accepted his decision in all matters, and had been lost without him during the war.

Eliza had shouldered the burden of the family then: what would she do if her father no longer played his part? What if he was unwilling, or God forbid, unable to lead? She'd felt responsible for her family's welfare and happiness for so long, but she'd not had to bear the economic burden as well.

There was Uncle Lawrence, of course. Dear, sad Lawrence who'd fallen in love with the wrong woman— or so he believed. He kept the books for her father's various business enterprises, so he ought to be able to manage them equally well, but could he summon the strength to actually do it?

Her thoughts in a painful muddle, she looked out over

the garden and wished she'd thought to pick a fresh bouquet for the room before she'd come upstairs. She'd do it later, but for now, she rested her head against a window pane and wondered if Jonathan were missing her as badly as she missed him.

Jonathan rode up to Lawrence, but stayed well clear of the flurry of pretty girls surrounding him. He noticed a flash of red hair amid the beribboned hats and marveled at the veritable rainbow of ruffled parasols before a twittering giggle pierced the air. Then with the grace of a *corps de ballet*, the whole feminine contingent turned as one. Their welcoming smiles were bright, but just a touch predatory, and because the only woman he cared to see wasn't among them, he cautiously remained astride Red Warrior.

"How'd we do?" he shouted to Lawrence.

A flash of worry crossed Lawrence's face, but he tipped his hat. "You'll be real happy," he promised.

Jonathan wasn't even tempted to discuss their winnings in more detail in front of dozens of people he didn't know. "Where's your brother and Eliza Kate?" he asked instead.

"Lamar was probably worried about being away from Delia," Lawrence guessed, then hoping to amuse his pretty companions, he added, "Or maybe he and Eliza Kate went to console Fletcher."

"He certainly needs it," Jonathan said, laughing and taking care not to trample any lovely ladies, he turned Red Warrior away from the crowd. When a careful sweep of the gathering convinced him Eliza Kate was gone, he headed for home.

Deeply disappointed, Bess Perry voiced a small startled cry and turned to Lawrence with a petulant complaint. "You promised to introduce us."

The beautiful sisters, Deborah and Rachel Webster, frowned in dismay. "Yes, you did, Mr. Bendalin, but you just let your friend ride away without making the slightest attempt to invite him to stay," Rachel complained.

Carol Ann Ferguson was too irate to giggle, but her voice rose sharply. "I'm real peeved with you, Mr. Bendalin. How is Mr. Blair going to make friends if you don't introduce him to your most cherished acquaintances?"

Though he would never describe them in that way, Lawrence raised his hands in mock surrender. "I do apologize, ladies, but Jonathan just isn't much for socializing. After such an important race, it's obvious he was more concerned about assuring Red Warrior's comfort than seeing to yours."

Not entirely convinced they hadn't just been unfavorably compared to a horse, the young women gathered around Lawrence broke away in gossiping pairs. Not one remained to chat with him. He wasn't surprised, but he felt doubly awkward to be left standing alone while people were clustered all around him still excitedly exchanging their views on the spectacular race.

He overheard a half-dozen accounts, but in each one, praise for Red Warrior's speed overshadowed any disappointment in Coal Dust's poor showing. A few men had actually won some money, and by ecstatically bragging about their keen eye for horseflesh, they were making those who'd lost feel all the worse.

Rather than bundles of cash, Lawrence had a pocketful of markers from gentlemen who'd cover their losses as soon as the banks opened Monday morning. He wasn't worried about any of them welshing on their bets because they all regarded a gentleman's word as his bond. With the utmost tact and decorum, money would simply be withdrawn from their accounts and deposited in the one Lawrence would insist Jonathan open. He would be depositing a generous amount in his own account, even though he had no real use for his own winnings.

His leg had begun to ache, and thinking it time to return home, he headed toward his horse. He had just skirted a boisterous group of hands from the Trinity Star when he caught sight of a petite, fair-haired woman standing not twenty feet away. His heart skipped a beat and his fervent hope that it might be Mae left him breathless.

Then the woman hugged a friend good-bye and turned toward him, and he recognized her as someone he'd met at church. She was with her husband, who held their small son in his arms, and as the handsome family walked away toward their buggy, Lawrence was overwhelmed by a crushing sense of loss.

He had sworn that he felt nothing but contempt for Mae, but when a mere glimpse of a woman who resembled her had been every bit as exhilarating as Red Warrior's easy victory, he had ample proof of his own lie. He wasn't over her at all, and with a heavy heart, he feared he might never be.

Jonathan knocked lightly at Delia's door, and Eliza Kate hurried to let him in. "What happened?" he whispered. "I looked for you after the race, but you'd disappeared."

Eliza brought a warning finger to her lips, then took his hand and led him over to the window seat where they could sit together comfortably. "Father insisted we leave," she confided softly, but when she saw that Jonathan was still elated about his victory, she thought better of adding the disturbing description of her father's peculiar mood.

"It was such a thrilling race," she complimented him eagerly. "At least I was there to see you win, and you did it as easily as you should have the first time."

Jonathan wanted that race forgotten and promptly changed the subject. "Looks like Lawrence and I won quite a bit of money. I was real excited about buying land for a ranch. Then about halfway here I realized I'd have to find a place with a house already standing so we'll have somewhere to live while we build ourselves a home."

His eyes were aglow with a teasing light, and he looked years younger than when they'd met. He'd been such a solemn soul then, and she hoped with all her heart he'd always be as content as he was that very minute. As for her own outlook, she was enormously worried and sent an apprehensive glance toward her mother.

Jonathan followed her gaze and spoke softly to reassure her. "I know you need to be here for your mother. But please don't forget just how badly I want us to be together."

He folded his hands over hers. "You're trembling." He slid his thumb across her pulse and noticed the dark bruise encircling her left hand. "My God, who did this to you?" he asked anxiously.

Eliza scarcely knew where to begin. "You know I bruise easily," she hedged. "Father just took my hand to escort me to the buggy."

Jonathan wrapped his fingers around the telltale marks. "Looks more like he grabbed hold. What did he do, yank you along behind him as he ran?"

That was precisely what he'd done, but she was loath to admit it when Jonathan and her father got along so poorly. Her eyes stung with the threat of tears, and she fought to blink them away. Rather than dwell on her own torment, she longed to hear more of his wonderful plans.

"Please," she offered apologetically, "it doesn't concern you."

"The hell it doesn't," Jonathan argued. "I'll not allow anyone to manhandle you."

"Hush! Keep your voice down," Eliza begged. "We mustn't wake Mother."

"I'm already awake," Delia called in a dreamy whisper. "Are you Jonathan? Come close and give me a better look at you."

Although they were forced to leave the issue unsettled, Jonathan's narrowed glance warned Eliza Kate he was only calling a temporary truce. His expression relaxed into a concerned smile as he stood and approached the bed.

"I'm real sorry to have disturbed your rest, Mrs. Bendalin. How are you feeling today?"

Delia stretched languidly before replying. "I'm still rather tired I'm afraid. I do remember you now. It was just your name I'd forgotten. Are you sweet on my Eliza Kate?"

In Jonathan's mind, that was far too innocent a term for the passionate devotion he felt for her spirited daughter, and his smile took on a decidedly guilty slant. Eliza Kate had followed him to the bedside, and he winked at her before responding. "Yes, ma'am, I sure am."

"Why don't you look happy about it, my darling?"

Eliza slid her hand into Jonathan's, and as he squeezed her fingers gently, she found a tremulous smile. "I am happy, Mother. It's all just a little overwhelming."

"Well, then, why don't you have Carmen bring me a nice bowl of chicken soup, and then you and Jonathan should go for a stroll in the garden. The beauty of the flowers always brings me peace of mind."

"Thank you for that wonderful suggestion, Mrs. Bendalin," Jonathan was quick to reply. Then with a far more delicate touch than Lamar had shown, he guided Eliza Kate from the room.

It was an easy matter for Eliza Kate to send a bowl of soup up to her mother, but as she stepped out onto the garden walk, she couldn't bear to look up at Jonathan. He'd not asked her to choose between her father and him, but the demand had been clear in his strident tone.

All the damage from the storm had been swept away, and stalling for time, she lingered at the roses. "Tell me more about the ranch you hope to own. Have you chosen a name yet?"

This was not where Jonathan had wished to continue their conversation, but he understood her reticence to admit what had happened and played along. In the next instant, he had a splendid name. "I thought I'd call it the Texas Belle, for you."

Surprised, and yet incredibly flattered, Eliza traced the delicate stem of a red rose and wondered at his motives. "That's an extravagant gesture," she murmured. "Or perhaps, you're merely teasing me."

"About our ranch?" Jonathan scoffed. "I wouldn't do that. I intend to create a fine ranch that will make you proud."

Her defenses dissolved, Eliza turned toward him, and the sweetness of his smile touched her as deeply as his loving promise. He took a first tentative step toward her, and she went to him eagerly. She slid her arms around his narrow hips and rested her head on his chest where his steady heartbeat made a reassuring rhythm.

"I'd be proud if we owned no more than ten acres and lived in a shack," she vowed convincingly.

Jonathan chuckled way back in his throat and combed his fingers through her cascading curls. "It's difficult to believe you'd be satisfied with so little after growing up here."

Now delighted to look up at him, Eliza Kate tipped her head. "That's just it. I have grown up, and you're what's important to me, not what you might own."

Jonathan wanted to believe that was true, but it was enough to hear her say it. "And you're what's important to me, my love, and anyone who bruises your beautiful skin will have to answer to me."

He'd turned their conversation full circle. Eliza Kate hadn't meant to hand him such an easy advantage. Disgusted with herself rather than him, she dropped her arms and backed away. "My father has enough trouble without another bitter confrontation with you. If you care so much about me, then you'll grant this request: forgive him and let the matter drop."

Jonathan widened his stance and rested his hands on his hips. "I'll not forgive him for hurting you. Not now, not ever."

Uncomfortable under his determined gaze, Eliza had a sinking premonition that this horrid impasse would not be their last. If that were truly the case, then she'd need a garden at least as large as her mother's if she were ever going to find peace with Jonathan Blair.

"I'm not your wife yet," she reminded him, and her

scowl was every bit as darkly threatening as his.

Jonathan responded with a knowing nod. "You're wrong about that too," he cautioned. "You've been my wife since the night we first made love. It's an ancient custom and not one solely reserved for savages; but rather than accept my word, perhaps you'd care to hear your father's opinion."

Suddenly feeling faint, Eliza barely made it to the closest bench, where she nearly fell rather than sitting with her usual grace. When Jonathan knelt beside her, his concerned expression appeared real, but she was so badly frightened, she couldn't be certain what she saw.

"Is that all this has ever been?" she whispered accusingly. "Just some fiendish plot to get even with my father for something that happened during that cursed war?"

She was as pale as a ghost, but before Jonathan could defend himself against her awful charge, Lawrence entered the garden and hurried toward them. "Oh, damn it all," Jonathan swore, and he stood to shield a badly shaken Eliza Kate from her uncle's view.

"You'll not believe what's happened," Lawrence began as soon as he'd reached them. "Lamar and Fletcher didn't just place large bets on Coal Dust, they borrowed against everything they owned to do so. They had bets with several different men so I had no idea what they'd done until Lamar blurted out the truth just now. He expects me to find a way to save the ranch, which will take every penny I won and probably cost him the liquor business, and the new buildings downtown as well. God, what an awful mess."

Lawrence moved past Jonathan to slump down on the bench beside Eliza Kate. "I'm so sorry. If only I'd known they'd taken such a stupid risk, I'd have found a way to call off the race." He leaned forward and rested his head in his hands. "I'm afraid I'm going to be sick."

Eliza Kate laid her hand on his back and patted soothingly. "It can't possibly be as bad as that, Uncle. Father's never been an intemperate man." But the financial catastrophe Lawrence described made her father's horrified reaction to Red Warrior's win easily understandable. She glanced up at Jonathan, who was watching her with a coldly detached stare she recognized all too well.

"You'd be thrilled if my father were ruined, wouldn't you?" she challenged.

"Of course, not," Jonathan denied, "but now it's plain why Fletcher was such a sore loser. Maybe he'd be willing to sell me his ranch at a good price."

Grasping for hope, Lawrence peeked through his fingers. "Wait a minute. Before you go off spending your winnings, let's talk with Lamar."

Jonathan sent Eliza Kate a questioning glance, but she couldn't be certain it didn't hold more of a dare. "Maybe you'd like to buy the Rosedale Hotel," she suggested caustically.

"Not when I've got my heart set on owning a ranch," Jonathan replied, "but perhaps your father and I can strike a bargain on another of his valuable assets."

"Do you think so?" Lawrence pushed himself off the bench and reached out to take Jonathan's arm. "If you can see your way clear to help us out, we'd sure appreciate it. Wouldn't we, Eliza Kate?"

Eliza Kate didn't know how to respond to that absurd question when she strongly suspected she must be the unnamed asset Jonathan craved. She wanted to scream that her father would never sell her off like prized livestock; but at the same time, the ugly bruise on her hand made her wonder if she'd have time to pack her clothes.

Chapter Twenty-two

Eliza Kate's tears blurred the enchanting beauty of the garden, but she was not even tempted to sit and weep while Jonathan and her father struck some hateful bargain that would surely ruin all their lives. If either of them thought they could use her as a pawn in their long-running feud, then they simply had another think coming. She rose from the bench, and although weaving slightly, made her way down the path and followed the men through the back door.

Lawrence had already entered the study, but Jonathan stood at the doorway, his outstretched arm casually propped against the jamb. He looked surprised by her arrival, but she ducked under his elbow before he could stop her and approached her father, who sat slumped behind the desk.

"With Mother so ill, no one's been thinking clearly," she began resolutely. "Offer her failing health as an excuse, and surely the men you owe will allow you the necessary time to pay off your bets."

A flicker of hope lit Lamar's gaze. "Would that work, Lawrence?"

Lawrence pulled up a chair for Eliza Kate, but when she refused it, he moved it closer to the desk and sat down to face his brother. "We could ask your good friends for time, but some of the bets you placed with Fletcher were with men who'd like nothing better than to seize everything you own. They won't look kindly on a request for time. I'll give you all I won to pay them off, but it's not going to be enough. We'll have to sell what property we can Monday morning before anyone can realize what's happened and take advantage of the fact you're in desperate straits."

"Fletcher ought to be here," Lamar said, moaning. "We're partners, and I'll only receive half the profits on anything the two of us sell."

Eliza Kate could feel Jonathan watching her and fought the impulse to glance his way, but the compulsion swiftly proved undeniably strong. She'd expected him to be wearing a satisfied smirk over the quandary her father had stupidly created for himself, but instead, his brow was furrowed by a slight frown. Confused by his apparent sympathy, she struggled to stay focused on the more pressing issue. There would be plenty of money after the cattle drive, but it wouldn't begin for several weeks, and they needed cash now.

"You've given Mother some exquisite jewelry over the years," she reminded her father. "It must be worth thousands."

"I'll not sell my darling's jewelry," Lamar bellowed. "My God, what have I done?" Utterly defeated, he crossed his arms on the desk, rested his head, and choked back a sob.

Eliza Kate was accustomed to handling problems in a straightforward manner, but she'd never encountered such a threatening situation and simply didn't know what else to suggest. She sent her uncle an imploring glance, but equally troubled, he shrugged helplessly and hung his head.

"We have until Monday," Jonathan offered quietly. "That's plenty of time to devise a plan."

"We?" Lamar peered up at Jonathan, his eyes bloodshot and brimming with tears.

Jonathan ignored the question of his participation and continued calmly. "You own the Rosedale Hotel outright, don't you?"

Lamar cast a fearful glance toward Eliza Kate, but he was sufficiently encouraged to sit up. "Yes, I do."

"That enterprise brings in so much money, you ought to be able to arrange a trade to cover a substantial portion of what you owe. Your whiskey business has to be another gold mine. Take in a couple more partners in exchange for what you owe. I'll throw in most of the cash I won for your promise to supply me with enough cattle to start my own herd as soon as I've bought land for a ranch."

Eliza Kate couldn't believe he'd be willing to give away what he'd won when owning a ranch meant so much to him, to them both. It was their whole future, or so she'd thought. "But how will you buy land if you give Father your winnings?" she asked fretfully.

Jonathan shrugged as though it were a small favor. "I

own the fastest horse in Texas. I'll just keep racing him, and I can guarantee there will be plenty more men as arrogant as Fletcher Monroe who'll line up for the chance to beat me. The odds won't ever be as good as they were today, so it might take a while, but I'll get the money together to purchase land before too long."

Lamar sat up and regarded Jonathan with a suspicious stare. "It's not like you to be so damn generous where I'm concerned. You've got to want more than prize cattle."

Jonathan nodded to concede the point, but his wicked smile was meant for Eliza Kate. "That I do. I want your consent to marry your lovely daughter, and because I know how much she'd like to have her mother attend the ceremony, I want to hold the wedding this very afternoon."

Lamar's mouth fell agape, but Lawrence responded with a hoarse shout. Then he glanced up at Eliza Kate and was amazed to discover she didn't appear nearly as shocked by Jonathan's bold request as he and his brother. "I'd absolutely no idea," he stammered. "Lamar, what do you think?"

Lamar felt as though his very blood had caught fire. He'd already loosened his collar, but it didn't help him breathe any easier. That he'd bet so much more than he could sanely afford to lose would severely damage his reputation as an astute businessman with everyone who mattered in Fort Worth. He had to give Jonathan credit for coming up with a way to save his holdings by taking in partners, but he still needed his enemy's winnings as well as Lawrence's. He felt sick clear through.

His only ray of hope was how swiftly Jonathan's bride would be widowed, and he had to bite the inside of his mouth to contain his joy. "You actually want this rogue for a husband, Eliza Kate? The whole town is sure to call your children half-breeds. Can you live with that disgrace?"

Though she thought the question rude in the extreme, this wasn't the ghastly scene she had envisioned. Now that

Jonathan had offered his help coupled with a gentlemanly request for her hand, rather than a high-handed demand, she was ashamed to have ever doubted his motives. He must have been deeply insulted, but he was smiling as though he'd already forgotten, and her answer came easily.

"No one will dare insult our children," she answered confidently. "I like the idea of marrying Jonathan today too. Mother's been talking about a garden wedding. Perhaps you could carry her downstairs."

"Easily," Lamar agreed grudgingly. "She weighs no more than a feather pillow. But first, I want your pledge in writing, Jonathan. I'll not give you Eliza Kate today and have you laugh in my face on Monday."

"He'd never do that," Eliza swore.

Impressed by how readily she'd defended him, Jonathan finally stepped into the study to take her hand in a tender clasp. "I appreciate your confidence in me, sweetheart, but I don't mind putting our agreement in writing. After all, I sure don't want to be greeted with a snide snicker when I ask for the cattle your father's promised."

"I'll not cheat you," Lamar vowed darkly. "Write it up, Lawrence. You're far better at wording contracts than I."

Lawrence compared Jonathan and Eliza Katè's fond smiles with his brother's furious scowl and just shook his head sadly. "I don't believe any of this, but if we're hosting a wedding today, we need to send someone into town for Reverend Adams."

"I'll send Ricky," Eliza Kate offered. "Are he and Robby home yet?"

Jonathan leaned down to kiss her parted lips lightly and overlooked Lamar's rude snort. "I'll get the preacher. Now you just go on upstairs and tell your mother about the wedding. The two of you will want to dress in your finest, won't you?"

Flustered, Eliza tucked a stray curl behind her ear. "Yes, of course, we will. Forgive me, I'm not thinking very clearly, I'm afraid."

"Well, it's not every day that a woman gets married, so you're forgiven," Jonathan teased, and he laughed when she blew him a kiss on her way out the door.

Once she had left them, however, all trace of humor left his expression. He turned to the Bendalin brothers. "Now let's get that contract drawn up. It's my wedding day, and I've no time to waste arguing with either of you."

"Right. I'll have it ready in no time," Lawrence replied, but he could scarcely believe the somber friend who'd sworn he'd never remarry was about to take his beautiful niece for a wife.

Eliza Kate had eaten so little in the last week that Delia's wedding gown was a perfect fit. She quickly remedied the fact the cream-colored dress was a good three inches too short by adding an ivory satin petticoat as an underskirt to create a graceful ruffle. With pale stockings and ivory slippers, she turned in front of her mother's standing mirror and thought she looked just fine until she noticed she'd forgotten to style her hair.

She swore softly under her breath and with a quick flip of her hairbrush and an artful twist of lacy ribbon, she had her curls tied atop her head. She raised her skirt as she neared her mother's bed.

"How do I look?" she asked.

"Exquisitely beautiful, as always," Delia assured her. "You must wear my pearls."

Delia's intricately carved jewelry box sat on the vanity and Eliza Kate quickly opened it and found the pearls. She slipped them around her neck, fastened the diamond clasp, and donned the matching drop earrings. She admired the pearls's warm glow in the vanity mirror and understood why her father couldn't bear to sell her mother's cherished gifts.

"There." Eliza smoothed the drape of her skirt. "I do believe we're finally ready."

Carmen had helped Delia to dress in a peach silk gown that blended so perfectly with her pale coloring, she seemed almost aglow. "Isn't this the moment when I'm supposed to impart some motherly wisdom?"

Eliza could readily imagine how awkward that conversation might be between an innocent young bride and a doting mother who'd deliberately kept her daughter ignorant of the joys of the marriage bed, but her mother had confided all she truly needed to know years ago.

"We've already had that conversation, Mother, and though I am Jonathan's second wife, I know he loves me, and I have never loved another man."

"You are happy then?" Delia inquired softly.

Eliza Kate was near tears so often of late, but on that afternoon, she wanted simply to enjoy the happiness she'd found with Jonathan. "Yes, deliriously so. Now let me call Father to help you downstairs before Jonathan comes to his senses and leaves me standing in the garden with only a handful of roses rather than a fine husband."

Delia's laugh was a delicate musical trill. "How silly you are. He'll not abandon you, not today, not ever."

Eliza Kate certainly hoped not and gave her mother's cheek a fleeting kiss before leaving to summon her father.

Lawrence leaned close to Jonathan to whisper, "Are you really sure you want to go through with this?"

Jonathan ran a finger around the inside of his collar as he considered how best to answer such a ridiculous question. They were gathered in the grassy picnic area near the grape arbor. He'd expected only the immediate family to attend the wedding, but someone had invited all the servants and what looked like every *vaquero* within three miles of the house. He'd never cared for crowds, and this was the second one he'd had to endure in a single day.

He drew in a deep breath and rocked back on the heels of the brand-new boots he'd barely had time to buy. "I'd not have proposed in the first place if I had any doubts about marrying Eliza Kate, and I sure wouldn't have asked you to be my best man either."

Lawrence had the sinking feeling he had caught only a

small fraction of what was happening around him and understood even less. "You mean you and Eliza Kate had discussed marriage before today?"

"Is that so difficult to believe?" Jonathan wiggled his toes. For a new pair of boots, these were surprisingly comfortable, but he was sorry there hadn't been time for him to buy a suit. Lawrence's fit well enough, but it just didn't seem right to be getting married in another man's clothes.

Before Lawrence could provide a response that didn't insult his best friend, Lamar carried Delia to a nearby bench. He sat with her perched upon his right knee, but despite her graceful pose, it was apparent she'd not be able to sit up without his discreet assistance. That pained Lawrence deeply, and he struggled not to ruin Eliza Kate's wedding with tears for Delia.

With her mother dependent upon her father's assistance to attend the ceremony, and her uncle serving as best man, Eliza Kate had considered herself fortunate to have two handsome brothers to escort her down the brick path to where the minister, Jonathan, and Lawrence were waiting. She'd attended several lovely traditional weddings over the years, but the garden setting was so very beautiful, she didn't mind not having an organist to provide the appropriate music or a crush of friends in fine clothes.

She'd not bothered with a veil, when upon this of all days she wanted to see clearly. As she and her brothers reached Reverend Adams, Ricky gallantly placed her hand on Jonathan's arm, then he and Robby remained close rather than join their parents on the bench. She heard appreciative murmurs from those gathered to witness her marriage, but it was Jonathan's hushed greeting that meant the world to her.

As Reverend Adams cleared his throat and began the ceremony, Jonathan glanced down at Eliza Kate's bouquet of white roses tied with ivory satin streamers. The fragile blossoms were as beautiful as his bride, but he could not help recalling an earlier wedding in which he'd stood beside another young woman who'd regarded him with an equally adoring gaze.

He had promised to love Mary Claire until they were parted by death and he had, but he'd not realized until Eliza Kate had taken her place at his side just how difficult it would be to repeat those same sacred vows a second time. That he meant every word gave him the confidence to speak the loving promises clearly, but he vowed in his heart, this would be the last time.

While in town, he'd bought a gold wedding band along with the locket he'd admired, yet even as he slipped the ring on Eliza Kate's finger, he could feel the old heartache tugging at his soul. He gave it a fierce mental shove, but it wasn't until the close of the ceremony, when Eliza Kate stood on her tiptoes to return his kiss that he truly felt free of the past. It was only a brief display of affection, all that decorum allowed, but he responded by wrapping his arms around her waist and lifting her clear off the ground.

Eliza Kate squealed with delight and held on tightly, but when Jonathan placed her gently on her feet, she was sufficiently composed to take his hand and lead him the short distance to her parents. She bent down to kiss them both, and then turned to toss her bouquet to Carmen.

"You'll be the next bride!" she called with a sparkling laugh.

Carmen blushed a deep red, and then after burying her face in the flowers to hide her dismay, she fled to the house to assist with the dinner preparations, intent upon making the important meal as perfect as could be. The other servants swiftly followed, which left the *vaqueros* to file by and offer their awkward congratulations to the newlyweds.

Dinner began at sunset, but Delia sipped only a few mouthfuls of soup before begging everyone's forgiveness and returning to her bed. Lamar remained upstairs with her, and Eliza Kate was left to celebrate her marriage with her new husband, uncle, and brothers. She was exhausted, but so happy she felt no need to converse while they dined, and Jonathan had never indulged in idle chatter.

Lawrence was ashamed he'd been so lost in his own misery that he'd not known how close Eliza Kate and Jonathan had become, while Ricky and Robby hadn't really recovered from their initial astonishment at the match. None of them seemed to know what to say, which created a series of increasingly uncomfortable silences.

"Are you taking Eliza Kate on a honeymoon?" Robby suddenly blurted.

Now without the means to provide more than a trip into town, Jonathan appeared rather perplexed. "I'd sure like to, Robby, but it will have to wait awhile. Neither of us wants to be away as long as your mother isn't well."

Robby twirled his fork in his mashed potatoes. "But she's not going to get any better, is she?"

"Now, Robby," Lawrence begged, "we mustn't lose hope."

The last few weeks had not been easy for Robby. He couldn't help fearing death would soon rob him of a mother, and that day Eliza Kate had deserted him for Jonathan Blair. He was frightened of being left alone in the world and more than a little angry.

"I know the truth, and I wish you'd all stop treating me like a baby," he cried, and with a forceful shove, he left the table and bolted from the room.

"I'll go after him," Ricky volunteered almost too quickly, and after pausing to grab another forkful of roast beef, he ran after his kid brother.

"Oh, dear," Lawrence sighed. "I'm so sorry, Eliza Kate. I know this isn't the wedding night you'd hoped to have. Well, not your wedding night, of course, but—"

Jonathan burst out laughing as his friend's embarrassment grew as deep as his blush. "It's all right, Lawrence. We know what you mean. I didn't really expect Ricky and Robby to be all that happy about my marrying their sister. It will take them a while to adjust."

Eliza Kate hurriedly blotted her lips. "Look, I told them in no uncertain terms that they're to treat you well. That wasn't even about you. It was about Mother."

"If you say so," Jonathan agreed amicably. "I'm sorry I can't take you to Paris or somewhere equally grand."

"I don't need Paris," Eliza Kate declared. "I'll be happy right here with you."

Lawrence felt so out of place he nearly churned in his seat. "You two ought to be alone. I'm not really hungry anyway."

"Stay put," Jonathan ordered. "Now this might strike you as a mite strange rather than romantic, but I'd like to take Eliza Kate out of here tonight and camp out on the prairie. We'll come back Monday morning, and I'll go into Fort Worth with you to do what we can to keep Lamar solvent."

"Camp out?" Lawrence couldn't believe his ears. "You want to take your bride out on the prairie like some—"

"Wild Indian?" Jonathan supplied.

"Well, no, I didn't mean Indian," Lawrence argued, but clearly that was precisely where he'd been headed, and he struggled to dig himself out of another mortifying hole. "It just doesn't seem like the best way to begin a marriage."

Jonathan slanted Eliza Kate a questioning glance, but she shook her head. They both knew this wouldn't be their first time together, but there was no reason to confide that fact to her shy uncle. "If I'm unhappy, I'm sure Jonathan will bring me home, won't you, dear?"

"Your home is with me now," Jonathan reminded her, "but yes, I'll bring you back here before Monday if you wish."

"You see, Uncle? Jonathan will be a wonderful husband, regardless of where we sleep."

Regarding that reference as far too intimate, Lawrence slid his hand over his eyes and suddenly remembered his conversation with Eliza Kate while straightening up the study. He was then appalled by how quickly he'd dismissed the shocking confession he now feared was true. That meant Jonathan had played him for a fool, and the realization cut him deeply.

"When you told me you'd been carrying on with someone your folks wouldn't accept, you were talking about Jonathan, weren't you?"

Her uncle's challenging question had been delivered in a surprisingly hostile tone, and Eliza Kate was grateful Jonathan was seated beside her so she could reach for his hand. "I was upset when I said it, but yes, I was referring to him."

Lawrence glared at his old friend. "And I begged you to stay here," he muttered regretfully and slowly got to his feet. "Clearly trusting you around Eliza Kate was the worst mistake I've ever made. You know I'm not strong enough to fight you, but I'd sure like to. It's a relief I won't have to look at either of you until Monday. Good night."

Wounded by her beloved uncle's bitter condemnation, Eliza Kate let him leave the room without responding, but she felt as though her whole family had abandoned her when she had every right to their love and best wishes. Although Jonathan tightened his hold on her hand, she had to use her free hand to blot her tears on her napkin.

"I'm so sorry," she murmured. "This should have been such a happy time."

"No, I'm the one who's sorry," Jonathan countered. "Now let's get out of here before the cook comes in to give me a piece of her mind."

Eliza Kate thought that possibility highly unlikely, but she was every bit as eager to get away as he. Eventually they'd have to come back though, and the painful problems they were leaving behind would all be waiting.

Jonathan and Eliza Kate changed into their riding clothes and rode out to the river where they'd met. As soon as they'd unsaddled their horses, they were in each other's arms. Eliza Kate clung to her new husband, her kisses as ardent as her love, but he soon grew breathless and broke away.

"I've a present for you," he said. He dug in his pocket for a flat paper package. "It's not nearly as beautiful as your mother's pearls, but it's something I've been wanting to give you."

"A gift?" Eliza Kate hadn't expected one. "There was no time for me to buy you a present."

The moon was bright enough for Jonathan to appreciate her dismay, and he slid his hand around her neck to pull her close for a quick kiss. He slid his thumb along her jaw in a light caress. "You've already given me more than you'll ever know. Now open it."

Eliza's hands shook slightly as she accepted the small package. She stepped back to peel away the paper. "Oh, Jonathan, what a beautiful locket. I love it." She dropped it into his hand and turned her back toward him. Her hair was still piled on her head and out of his way. "Help me put it on, please."

Jonathan fumbled with the delicate clasp. "I should have given it to you while there was still enough light to make this easy, but the barn just didn't seem like a romantic spot. There, I've got it."

Eliza Kate ran her fingers over the shiny gold heart. "I love it and you. We'll have to have photographs taken so I can carry your portrait with me always."

"Now there's a thought." Jonathan drew her back against his chest. There was so much he longed to promise her, but putting his dreams into words was still difficult with the persistent fear that merely speaking them aloud would turn them to dust. For a long moment, he just held her tightly and let the splendor of the starry night surround them.

Eliza Kate relaxed against him, and gathering courage from his warmth, rushed to say something she felt must be said. "The first time we were together, it was your tears that woke me. You were hurt I'd left you, but—"

Jonathan turned her slowly in his arms and silenced

what he considered an unnecessary apology with a tender kiss. "It doesn't matter now," he assured her.

Eliza braced her hands on his chest. "Oh, but it does, because I knew you were crying for your wife and son. I know you'll never love me as much as you did Mary Claire, but—"

"If you don't hush, I'm going to have a hard time stifling the impulse to strangle you," Jonathan cautioned, and he kissed her with all the emotion overflowing his heart until he felt her go weak against him. Then he pulled her down into the grass and cradled her across his lap.

"How many times have I asked you what you were thinking?" he complained. "A dozen or more? Have you been worried all this time that you might be the woman in my arms while another owned my heart?"

Eliza considered it an encouraging sign that he was annoyed with her silence, but she'd lacked the courage to voice her fears. Now that she was his wife, she'd simply have to live with them. "It's the truth, isn't it?"

Jonathan smothered a curse in her curls, but nearly crushed her in his arms. "No, it's not the truth. Any nightmares I have are about the war. Men bled to death in my arms, and that's not something I'll ever forget, but those ghastly dreams don't come as often anymore. If my tears woke you, those nightmares were the cause; Mary Claire is another problem altogether. You needn't compete with her."

Jonathan struggled for a way to show her how badly she'd misjudged his affection and finally found one. "Let's look at it this way: which of your brothers do you love the most?"

"Oh, Jonathan, what an awful question. I love them both."

Jonathan didn't respond; he just waited for her to consider her answer more fully. He pulled the lacy ribbon from her hair and let the curls slide over her shoulders in gentle disarray. He loved her golden hair, but then she possessed so many delightful attributes, and he loved each one.

Eliza Kate understood precisely what he was doing, but remained unconvinced. "That's really not the same. Parents don't love their children in the same way they love each other, and I don't love my family the way I love you."

Jonathan glanced up at the stars for inspiration. "I knew the first time I saw you riding toward me that you'd be trouble, but did I ride the other way? Oh no, I followed you home instead. Now look where that's gotten me. I'm married to a woman who doesn't believe I love her."

Eliza Kate laced her fingers in his. "I know you love me."

"Then what, exactly, is your complaint, sweetheart?"

Eliza was ashamed to have been so clumsy he'd missed her point. "I'm not complaining," she denied in an anguished whisper. "I'm just saying I understand you'll always love Mary Claire more."

Jonathan had to remind himself that this was their wedding night, and no matter how long it took, he was going to be patient because he sure as hell didn't want to begin their marriage with a terrible argument and most especially not one over as ridiculous a misunderstanding as this. She'd once told him words merely got in their way. Taking her advice, he leaned down to tickle her ear with the tip of his tongue.

Eliza Kate couldn't suppress a throaty giggle, but when she covered her ear with her hand, he began to suck on her fingertips. She slid her hand up the side of his face into his hair to escape that torment, but he responded by shifting his weight toward her and rolled them both onto the grass in a tangled sprawl.

Eliza Kate had expected a grudging nod, or perhaps a mumbled apology that she'd never be first in his heart, but Jonathan kissed her until she couldn't think at all, and when he began to unbutton her blouse, she reached for his belt buckle. Before she could loosen his belt, however, he captured her hand.

"No," he warned. "Don't touch me until you believe I love you."

"I do believe," Eliza assured him.

"No, you don't," Jonathan murmured against the smooth swell above her lace-trimmed camisole. "You don't believe a word I say." He caught her other hand and raised her arms above her head where he could hold her wrists with his left hand while his right traced teasing circles over her breasts and lower.

He loved exploring every inch of her. Her floral fragrance was intoxicating, and she tasted so incredibly good. He soon discovered just how impossible it was to undress her while holding her wrists. He had to concentrate on her mouth then, but kissing her moist lips and delving into her honeyed sweetness fueled his passions as well as hers. Reluctantly, he released her captive wrists, but rather than escape him, she responded by slipping her hands beneath his shirt to caress his chest, and the silent battle to win her confidence was lost.

Then in a frantic rush, they cast their clothes aside and showed little care while they spread out their blankets. Desperately eager to please her, Jonathan gathered Eliza Kate into his arms and called upon his last bit of restraint to enter her with gentle, teasing thrusts. He then withdrew to trace her sensitive cleft with the blunt tip of his manhood. He repeated his tender torture until she locked her ankles over his thighs and drew him down into her heated core where pleasure awaited with a trembling fury. On a final deep plunge, he felt her convulse around him and with a triumphant cry, truly became her husband.

They lay entwined for what seemed like hours before Jonathan could finally draw the breath to speak. Eliza's eyelashes fluttered against his arm so he knew she was awake. "I hold nothing back when I'm with you," he whispered softly, "no thoughts, no unspoken regrets, no love for another woman. It's all for you. I'm sorry I didn't tell you that the first time we made love. I never meant to cause you a moment's doubt."

Eliza Kate believed him and smiled as she propped her head on her elbow. She wished the dawn would never arrive, but intended to make the most of the night while it lasted. "Thank you for saying it now. The first time I saw you kneeling beside the river, I thought you looked dangerous."

Jonathan laughed way back in his throat, and the sound echoed against the river's steady roar. "And now you know that I am."

With a graceful ease, Eliza Kate rose to straddle him. "Yes, my darling, and now I know all manner of dangerous things too. Shall I show you a few?"

"My God, woman—" He'd almost said she'd be the death of him, but he'd caught himself before it was too late. He reached up to roll the pale pink tips of her breasts between his fingers and prayed this time he and his bride would grow old together.

Chapter Twenty-three

Monday morning came all too swiftly for Eliza Kate. She'd found an exquisite ecstasy awakening in Jonathan's arms and reveled in the fact she had every right to be there. Despite a cushion of blankets, the ground had been a poor substitute for the feather mattress her pampered existence had led her to expect, but she'd shaken off the resulting aches and stiffness rather than voice a single complaint. She simply wanted to be with Jonathan, and for two nights and a day she'd found paradise with him out there on the prairie.

Now her eyes lit with rapt fascination as she watched him shave. He'd propped a small metal mirror in a convenient crook of a mesquite tree, then used a misshapen bar of soap and water from the river to create lather. With each deft stroke, his razor caught the sun with a brilliant gleam but it scarcely rivaled the sheen of his ebony hair.

He was clad only in black pants and boots, and the intricate interplay of muscles shifting across his broad back created a handsome sight indeed. He had a lean, powerful build, and yet held her with a tenderness that made her reluctant ever to leave his arms. She knew her family needed her at home, but what she truly needed was more of the silver-eyed devil who'd won her heart.

Sadness swept through her as she came up behind him. She rested her palms on his narrow waist, then slid her fingertips into his front pockets to caress the hollow of his hips. "I don't want to go home," she breathed out in a dreamy sigh.

"Neither do I," Jonathan quickly agreed, "but I promised to pull your father out of the fire, and I'll not go back on my word."

"I'd not have wed a man who would," Eliza advised pointedly, but also resigned to the depressing fact they had little choice about how they spent the day, she dropped her hands to smooth out her riding skirt. "It doesn't follow that I'm looking forward to leaving here though."

Jonathan stepped away to scoop up a handful of water to rinse his face and then dipped his razor in the river to shake off the last of the soap and whiskers before slipping all his shaving gear into his saddlebags. He was used to traveling light and sleeping under the stars, but while he'd been eager to take Eliza Kate away, he couldn't really believe she wasn't equally eager to return to the comforts of home.

"I'll take that as a compliment to my attentive company rather than the fine accommodations I've provided here," he teased.

"Take it anyway you like, Mr. Blair," Eliza nearly purred.

That she'd now flirt with him so boldly made Jonathan laugh appreciatively, but he was not so distracted he forgot the task at hand. He shook out a clean shirt and pulled it on. It was a pearl gray that very nearly matched his eyes, and he buttoned it up before shoving the tail into his pants and fastening his belt. The holster containing his Navy Colt was rolled up in his saddlebags, but he saw no reason to strap it on for the ride home.

Thinking they were ready to leave, he scanned their campsite a last time to make certain they'd erased all trace of their presence. Satisfied they had, he picked up his saddlebags. "Are you ready?" he asked.

They had already saddled their horses and with no real reason to delay other than desire, Eliza Kate took a very small step toward her mare. "Yes. That's a handsome shirt. Other than when you dress for dinner, I've not seen you wear anything but black."

"I'm glad you like it, ma'am. I didn't have much time to supplement my wardrobe before our wedding, but you can count on me to do better from now on."

Eliza Kate was the one to laugh then, and all at once she realized how often they had laughed of late. In the last few days, Jonathan had revealed the charming, jovial side of his nature that had made her uncle's stories about him so wonderfully entertaining. She wanted that man with her always and kissed him soundly before mounting Patches.

Jonathan favored his bride with frequent smiles as they headed for home, but his true mood was far from relaxed. He considered helping to pay off Lamar's debts a regrettable obligation, but was hoping that while in town, he could line up another race or two. Red Warrior was strong, but he didn't want to race his prize stallion so often the citizens of Fort Worth grew bored with the sport. He'd have to select his opponents with care to create a worthy challenge, which meant he'd need Lawrence's advice. Unfortunately, that was where their troubles with horse races had begun.

Eliza Kate was equally preoccupied, and by the time her stately home came into view, she was so melancholy she was nearly in tears. Her mother would never be well, and in his inept response to his gambling debts, her father had shown himself to be more coward than confident businessman. She wondered how much of his comfortable life was built on pretense, and her thoughts rapidly led to the most logical conclusion.

"I think I know why it was you, rather than my father, who rescued Uncle Lawrence when he was shot," she announced abruptly.

Jonathan drew Red Warrior to a halt and reached down to catch Patches's reins. In the two nights and a day they'd been married, they'd not spent all their time making love. They'd also held long, intimate conversations to settle lingering misunderstandings and create dreams he'd not have dared hope would come true without her. When the past held so little significance for him anymore, he had no wish to jeopardize their newfound harmony to expose ancient wrongs.

"Let's not pursue that line of thinking, sweetheart," he cautioned "No good can possibly come from it."

Unwilling to back down when she felt she was on the verge of an important truth, Eliza Kate squared her shoulders. "My father abandoned us to go play at war. I've already told you what I think of him for that. Despite his success, it's doubtful he's changed much over the years. When he realized how much money he'd lost on Saturday, he ran and hid like a frightened child.

"I'll bet that's exactly what he did when his kid brother fell. He has to know you saw him abandon Lawrence. That's why he hates you."

She shook her head sadly. "That first morning when he walked into the dining room and found you there, he paled as though he were ill. I'll bet he was sick with fear. You may be too honorable a man to tell Lawrence about his brother's cowardice, but you can't disillusion me. I already know my father's deeply flawed."

Jonathan couldn't provide an argument there. "You're very wise," he said without really answering her question, "but I'd rather not have your father accuse me of working to turn you against him. After what happened with Flossie

Mae, Lawrence sure doesn't need another hefty dose of the truth either. Your father and I will never be friends, but I don't have to admire him to be civil, and for your sake, I mean to do whatever I can to keep the peace between us."

"For my sake?" Eliza Kate probed skeptically.

"Oh, hell yes," Jonathan exclaimed. "There's something about how beautiful you look perched in an oak tree that would melt the hardest heart."

Satisfied he'd confirmed her suspicions, Eliza Kate thought better of requesting details about the day Lawrence had been wounded; instead, she nodded toward the house. "As long as I melted yours, I'm happy. Let's hope the day passes quickly so that we can make love again."

"Now you're melting more than my heart," Jonathan replied with a deep chuckle. He doffed his hat and waved it to create a cooling breeze, then tapped his heels against Red Warrior's sides to send him on up to the barn. Eliza Kate and Patches quickly followed.

Lawrence had been watching for the newlyweds' return and hurried out onto the porch to greet them. They were holding hands and laughing as they came toward him, and though their easy exchange of affection embarrassed him, he still hated to put an end to their fun.

"You better hurry on up to your mother, Eliza Kate. It looks as though attending your wedding was simply too much for her. Dr. Burnett was here yesterday, and he's promised to come again this morning."

Eliza Kate had bathed in the river, and Jonathan had brushed her hair, but she didn't feel nearly well enough groomed to visit her mother. "Give me a few minutes to change my clothes, and I'll spend the whole day with her." She leaned up to give Jonathan a quick kiss, but Lawrence tapped her arm.

"I wouldn't waste any time changing clothes," he advised and quickly looked away.

Eliza Kate accepted his warning with a numbing sense of dread, and after a fearful parting glance for Jonathan, she entered the house and raced up the stairs. That she'd not wanted to come home created a guilty weight on her heart, for now she feared she ought not to have risked spending even an hour away.

Lawrence waited until he was certain Eliza Kate was out of earshot to speak. Even then, he adopted a cautious whisper. "Delia slept most of the time you were gone, and even with Eliza Kate home, she might not awaken. Lamar asked me to stay here and look after things until the doctor arrives, but you ought to go on into town. I'll give you the markers from the men who owe us money. They should be waiting at the bank. Open an account and deposit your winnings.

"Lamar went to see Fletcher yesterday, and I guess Fletcher was drunk and in an awful state. Lamar told him we'd thought of a way to get them out of debt with as little pain as possible. Apparently Fletcher wasn't convinced, and Lamar's gone over there again this morning to escort him into town.

"Ricky took Robby to school, and then he's going on over to the freight warehouse to begin an inventory. The kid surprised me. He knows his father's in trouble, and he wants to help out wherever he can. Maybe all he's needed is a real job to do."

"Possibly," Jonathan murmured, but he thoughtfully didn't add that Ricky would probably make a hurried stop at the Rosedale Hotel on his way through Fort Worth.

"I'll start for town as soon as Dr. Burnett arrives," Lawrence continued, "but I want Lamar and Fletcher to take care of their major debts on their own before we contribute our winnings."

Jonathan was relieved he'd not have to insist upon that prudent sequence himself. "That's fine with me. Maybe it will give us time to decide who we'd like to race against next."

Lawrence fumbled in his vest pocket for the list he'd

made. "I've already jotted down the best prospects. You want some breakfast before you go?"

"No, thank you. I'll get something to eat in town. But I would like to borrow a horse. I've been riding Red Warrior, but with so many men wagering against him and losing, it's probably not a good idea to parade him through town, or leave him tied at a hitching post."

"I'd not even considered the risk," Lawrence replied, clearly embarrassed by the oversight. "You're right, of course. Either of the grays are good mounts. Take your pick. Come on, I'll walk you to the barn."

Jonathan wasn't pleased about having to go to the bank alone, but because he intended to buy property for a ranch, he knew he ought to get used to handling his financial affairs on his own. He tried to concentrate on that thought rather than how damn generous he was being with Lamar, who wouldn't deserve a nickel if he hadn't fathered Eliza Kate.

"Do you know much about Delia's people?" he asked.

Lawrence was taken aback for a moment, but then thought he understood Jonathan's question. "Yes, I sure do. She's a Devereaux from Louisiana. It's a fine family, but all that's left of her branch are a few distant cousins who reside in New Orleans. Apparently they've exchanged a few letters over the years, but they aren't close. There's no one to summon to bid her good-bye."

"I'm sorry to hear that," Jonathan replied, but someday soon, he wanted to hear all about Delia's family to better appreciate his remarkable Eliza Kate.

As they entered the barn, he grabbed his saddle and slung it over his shoulder and led the way down the line of stalls where the Bendalins kept their riding horses. The barn was well-tended and smelled of fresh straw and hay. With Ricky, Robby, and their father gone, several of the wide, roomy stalls were empty.

"Delia has Lamar and her children," Lawrence mused absently. "That's all she's ever needed."

Loving Eliza Kate as he did, Jonathan could easily understand how Delia's life was complete, but he felt an odd chill and couldn't wait to leave the shadowed barn for the sunlight where the tragic specter of his mother-in-law's imminent death wouldn't hover so oppressively.

Jonathan had never enjoyed the ride into Fort Worth, but that morning he felt a prickly itch of foreboding. He knew giving away the major portion of his winnings was the right thing to do when he could scarcely enjoy his good fortune if his new bride's family was impoverished. Still, he sensed something bad coming and could no longer shrug it off as a widower's lingering despair.

He eyed the outcropping of rocks ahead with a deeply suspicious glance. He'd always regarded it as the perfect cover for an ambush, but what fool would rob him on the way to the bank? he rationalized. Then he remembered the markers tucked into his hip pocket. If those disappeared, a lot of men might not bother paying off their wagers, especially if the man who'd been carrying them were dead.

During the war, he'd developed a finely honed sense of danger, and because he'd been uneasy even before he'd left the ranch, he'd worn his Navy Colt. He ran his hand over the silky smooth handle. Samuel Colt had made revolvers for the Northern Army, but that didn't mean the fine weapon hadn't found its way into Confederate hands. Jonathan had gotten his from a Union officer who'd been taken captive in the first months of the war, and it had served him well ever since.

Ever since his initial trip into town with Lawrence, he'd been apprehensive along that particular stretch of road, but he'd passed by safely every time. He wondered if his imagination might not be playing tricks on him. Either that, or the old caution that had kept him alive during the war had surfaced, and he wasn't inclined to question why.

Far too smart to wander into an ambush, he studied the surrounding terrain, but it was so rough and uneven he'd not risk a borrowed horse galloping across it to avoid the outcropping. With the road providing soft footing, however, he had no misgivings about clucking his tongue and tapping his heels against the gray gelding's sides to urge him into a gallop.

Finding the horse surprisingly eager to run, he crouched low on his back and was nearly clear of the tumbled boulders when the shots he dreaded actually rang out. He dipped lower still, then angled his mount toward the closest patch of scrub brush, which offered his only hope of cover. He drew his weapon as he rolled off the gray, but no other shots were fired. He kept low and tossed his hat aside to present a smaller target while the handsome gelding ran on in a wide arc without him, then circled back and in an easy canter headed for home.

Not about to chase the horse, nor to waste ammunition firing on an unseen enemy, Jonathan waited, every muscle tensed. When the wait grew uncomfortably long, he shielded himself behind the brush and crept closer. He hoped for a glimpse of the man who wished him dead, and it took him a moment to realize a dark stain marring the sun-bleached stones might be blood.

He waited another couple of minutes, then broke out into the open in a wild zigzagging dash toward the rocks. His new boots raked the gravel and sent up billowing puffs of dust as he reached their base, but he was greeted with an eerie silence. He pressed against the rocks to catch his breath, but he didn't need another round of gunfire to feel the continued threat of danger.

With his revolver still tightly clutched in his left hand, he started a slow climb over the boulders, but he hadn't gotten but six feet off the ground when he saw a body wedged between a jagged split in the rocks. The man lay directly below the gory stain, and he wasn't moving.

Jonathan had seen more than one such instance of idiocy during the war and readily guessed what must have happened. The man and his partner or partners had probably taken up positions on either side of the road.

Because he'd not ridden Red Warrior, nor worn a black shirt, they must not have recognized him until he'd raced between them. Caught by surprise, apparently they'd both fired, and one must have shot the other.

He'd really hoped he'd seen his last dead man. Shaken, he had to push himself to keep on climbing until he could peer over the top of the rocks and across the road. The boulders were more widely scattered on the other side, and from this vantage point, he caught sight of a couple of pinto ponies. He dropped back and clung to the rock. If their mounts were still there, that meant the other man either wouldn't, or couldn't, leave his partner.

Jonathan sucked in a deep breath and weighed his options. Not liking any that came to mind, he eased his way back down to where he could reach the fallen man. The poor soul was lying face down, but his head was cocked at a peculiar angle. Jonathan looked up at the blood-smeared rocks and then at the man's bloody sleeve.

It appeared the luckless fellow had taken a bullet in the arm, lost his footing, and broken his neck in the fall. "That's a real stupid way to die," he muttered, and wondering if by any chance he'd know the bushwhacker, he leaned down to turn the oddly loose head toward the sky.

"Oh, dear God," Jonathan breathed, for it was Fletcher Monroe in cast-off clothing.

He knew who'd been riding with Fletcher that morning, and had he taken the time to eat breakfast, he would have lost it as a roiling nausea swept through him. He was positive Lawrence would never have been a party to this murderous scheme, but clearly Lamar had taken pains to send his sons into town, and make certain his brother remained at home so Jonathan would be out on the road alone.

"How considerate of him." Jonathan spat in disgust and narrowly missed splattering Fletcher's body. Apparently Lamar had thought of everything, except the possibility his quarry might not be clothed in black and astride Red Warrior. But that was only a minor mistake: plotting to kill his new son-in-law was the monumental blunder.

A high-pitched screech pulled Jonathan's gaze toward the sky where a lone vulture had already begun to circle. He was tempted to leave Fletcher where he lay, but if Lamar were truly desperate enough to shoot him on the road, he'd not have taken off on foot. That meant he had to be lurking nearby, and disposing of Fletcher's body would just have to wait until he found Lamar.

He shoved his Colt into his holster, and then sprinted back to the scrub brush. Positive Lamar wasn't above shooting him in the back, he cautiously crept along the ground wherever the brush grew sparse and crossed the road well below the rocks. Then keeping away from the trail, he approached the tethered ponies with the stealth that had often served him well as a scout.

The pintos were only slightly larger than Eliza Kate's Patches. Unshod, they had obviously been ridden to leave hoofprints others would assume had been left by a Comanche band. It was just another piece of evidence that this was no last-minute attack. Sick clear through, Jonathan drew his revolver for his own protection.

"Fletcher's dead, Lamar," he yelled. "You might as well come out with your hands up."

There were a dozen places for a man to hide, and Jonathan swept them all with a wary eye. The vulture continued its fierce cawing, and a second bird joined in, but there was no response from Lamar Bendalin. He was still there though—Jonathan could feel him.

"Let's settle this between ourselves, Lamar. There's no reason to draw the sheriff into it while Delia's so ill," he shouted.

He waited, his other senses alert as he listened attentively for some clue to Lamar's whereabouts. He glanced back toward the ponies, but they were standing so still they appeared to have dozed off.

"I know you weren't pleased to have me join your family, but I won't shoot you. Come on out, and we'll concoct a believable story and go on home," he coaxed.

Just when he was about to give up and risk a hazardous

search through the rocks, a handful of gravel went sailing into the air. It was off to the right, in an area he'd skirted on the way to the ponies. Leery, he moved for cover before again circling to approach from the opposite direction.

He'd assumed Lamar was just scared out of his wits and hiding, but when he found his father-in-law, he was clutching a bloody shoulder wound. His revolver had been tossed aside, but clearly he wasn't strong enough to use it even if it had been within easy reach.

"Don't leave me to the buzzards," Lamar begged hoarsely.

Jonathan leaned down to retrieve Lamar's pistol and tossed it well out of reach before holstering his own weapon. He then squatted beside him. The tumbled boulders were closely spaced, providing little room between them. The scent of blood brought back the worst of his war memories, but he'd seen men survive similar wounds and thought Lamar might just be mean enough to live to tell some preposterous lie about this catastrophe.

"Leave a wounded man?" Jonathan chided. "Surely you jest. I ran through cannon fire to save Lawrence, and while I'd surely love to leave you to the scorpions, I won't. Can you still sit on a horse?"

Jonathan's face swam before Lamar in a menacing blur. "I doubt it," he said moaning.

"Well, unfortunately, the ill-trained beast I was riding ran off, and neither of your little Indian ponies will carry two men. I'll have to boost you onto one and walk beside you to keep you from sliding off in the dirt."

Lamar coughed, and bloody bubbles dribbled through his lips. "You'd help me get home?"

"You're family, Pa," Jonathan reminded him sarcastically, but it now looked to him as though Lamar had taken a bullet in the lungs. That wasn't good at all. "We'll just hope Dr. Burnett overtakes us before we've gone too far."

Jonathan stood and bent to help Lamar rise, but it was a struggle for both men. Faint from loss of blood, Lamar could barely stand, and walking over the rocky ground was impossible for him. Jonathan wrapped his arms around Lamar and hung on to his belt to half-carry, half-drag him out to the ponies.

Too weak to attempt mounting one, Lamar slid from Jonathan's grasp and collapsed on the stony ground. "It's no use," he cried. "I can't ride."

"All right, give me a minute to rig a travois, and we'll drag you home behind these fine little ponies."

Lamar lay back and with a fear-glazed gaze watched the buzzards swoop lower with each lazy circle. Jonathan opened his mouth to exhort him to show more courage, but then remembered Lamar had none to begin with. He had already unsaddled the horses and cut a hunk of saddle blanket to stem the blood seeping through Lamar's clenched fingers when he heard the rattle of an approaching buggy.

"Sounds like we're in luck," he said, and he quickly made his way out to the road. He'd met Dr. Burnett on one of his visits with Delia, and recognizing him easily, waved him to a halt.

Clay Burnett also recognized Jonathan, but his blood-stained shirt frightened him badly. "My God, man, what's happened?"

There was no easy way to answer that question and stalling for time, Jonathan wiped the sweat from his eyes on his sleeve and made a mental note to fetch his hat. "There's been an ambush. Fletcher Monroe's dead over yonder, and Lamar's badly wounded. Come help me get him home."

Clay looped the reins around the brake handle and jumped down from his buggy. "Who'd want to ambush Fletcher and Lamar?" he called, but Jonathan didn't stop to answer.

Eliza Kate was pacing her mother's room when Lawrence rapped lightly at the door. One look at his frantic expression was enough to lure her out into the hallway, but

rather than explain what was wrong, he grabbed her hand
and rushed her to the stairs. When she reached the landing, she looked down to find Jonathan standing in the
foyer. Certain the blood he was bathed in was his own,
she brushed by her uncle and nearly flew down the stairs.

Jonathan caught her at the bottom and held her at
arm's length. "Your father's been shot," he confided in a
hushed voice. "Dr. Burnett helped me to bring him home,
but it doesn't look good."

"Shot? But who would do such an awful thing?" Eliza
studied her husband's coldly aloof expression and feared
the worst. "Oh no, this doesn't have anything to do with
you, does it?" Then before he could answer, she rushed
on, "Where is he?"

Lawrence had reached the foyer by then and grasped
Eliza Kate's elbow. "We've laid him in the dining room,
where the doctor can tend him more easily."

Frightened and confused, Eliza stared up at Jonathan.
"You must tell me everything later," she insisted, and hurried into the dining room.

Shaken, Lawrence leaned back against the newel post.
"What can you possibly tell her?" he asked.

Uncertain where to begin, Jonathan shrugged dejectedly. "The truth, I suppose. You'd better go on in with
your brother."

Lawrence nodded, but he was so disappointed in Lamar, it took him a moment to find the strength to follow
Eliza Kate. Lamar was stretched out on the dining table
while Dr. Burnett worked on his shoulder, but Lawrence
feared his brother was past saving. He was not even certain
he wanted Lamar to live if he'd have to face a charge of
attempted murder. That terrible thought compounded
his fear with a painful burst of guilt.

"What can I do?" he inquired softly.

Clay glanced over his shoulder. "The bleeding's nearly
stopped, but you could still pray."

In their haste to take care of Lamar, they'd scattered
the chairs lining the table, and as Lawrence moved one

toward the wall, he caught a glimpse of Jonathan at the doorway. His friend had made no move to change out of his blood-splattered shirt, and Lawrence feared the shooting might have deepened his layer of invisible scars.

Overwhelmed by guilt, Lawrence sank into his chair and mumbled a prayer. He'd known how little Lamar and Jonathan liked each other when he'd begged his dear friend to extend his visit. He'd not cared about Lamar's feelings then, but only his own deep concern that Eliza Kate not wed Fletcher Monroe. Now Fletcher's body was growing cold in the barn, and it looked as though Lamar might not survive the day.

Convinced the tragedy was entirely his fault, he leaned forward and rested his head in his hands. He'd lost track of the time before he heard Lamar call his name in an anguished whisper. "Yes?" he responded eagerly, and he shoved away from his chair with a clumsy stretch and approached the table.

Clay had cut away Lamar's shirt and swathed his shoulder in bandages, but the injured man's skin was nearly as pale as the white cotton crisscrossing his shoulder and chest. He was propped up at an angle, but his breathing had grown shallow. He gestured with his good arm for Lawrence to come close.

"I was afraid," he whispered.

Lawrence circled the table to grip his hand. "Please don't talk," he urged. "You need every bit of your strength to recover."

Lamar closed his eyes for so long he appeared to have fallen asleep, but then he looked straight at Lawrence. "When you were shot, I was too frightened to save you. It's been my shame all these years. Can you forgive me?"

That Lamar had abandoned him was a possibility Lawrence had steadfastly refused to consider, but now confronted with the damning truth, he could only nod. "Yes, of course, I forgive you. I'm here, I'm well. What does it matter now?"

"It has always mattered," Lamar admitted with a small

strangled cry. He saw Eliza Kate hovering near but couldn't bear to look at her. "I want to be with Delia. Will you take me upstairs?"

Lawrence glanced toward the physician, who immediately shook his head regretfully. "Why don't we bring Delia to you, Lamar? Clay's worked awfully hard on your shoulder, and we mustn't risk reopening your wound."

"Delia," Lamar murmured plaintively.

"I'll bring her," Jonathan leaned into the room to volunteer. In less than a minute, he reappeared with the frail woman wrapped in her rose quilt. Two pillows dangled from his hand, and Eliza Kate quickly grabbed them.

She tucked one under her father's head and placed the other beside it. "There. I think Mother will rest comfortably here."

Jonathan circled the table to ease Delia down beside Lamar where he could wrap his good arm around her. "I tried to wake her, but failed," he apologized.

"I'm sure it doesn't matter," Eliza Kate told him. She'd not seen the cook and Carmen slip into the room, but they were weeping softly in the corner. She sent them a brave smile and then squeezed her husband's hand. It was as cold as ice.

Lamar wound his fingers in his wife's silvery hair. "I have always loved you," he whispered. "You are my life."

To everyone's surprise, Delia snuggled against him and sighed sweetly. "I love you, too, Lamar. You have been the very best of husbands."

A hushed silence filled the room until Eliza Kate remembered her brothers. "Someone should send for the boys," she murmured.

"We did," Jonathan leaned down to whisper, "but they'll arrive too late."

In the next moment, Eliza Kate felt a gentle flutter against her cheek. The caress was as light as an angel's kiss and graced with the sweet scent of her mother's perfume. She had sincerely believed the last months had prepared her for this inevitable loss, but the wrenching heartbreak caught her full force.

Clay Burnett leaned over the table, and then sighed sadly. "I'm so sorry. But we've lost them both."

Eliza Kate turned to reach for Jonathan, but he had vanished, and the cry that came from her very soul was for him.

Chapter Twenty-four

Eliza Kate found Jonathan seated on the back steps with his head cradled in his hands. His shoulders were shaking with great wracking sobs as though it had been his own dear parents who'd just died in each other's arms. He was such a strong man, she couldn't understand why his sorrow should be so deep.

She had come seeking his comfort, but clearly he was in greater need of hers. She knelt in front of him and rested her hands lightly on his knees. "Lawrence told me what happened, my darling, and none of this was your fault."

Appalled that she'd found him in such a sorry state, Jonathan quickly dried his eyes on his sleeve and raked his hands through his hair. He then laced his fingers in hers and held on tight.

"You're wrong. Had I not stopped here to visit, today's tragedy wouldn't have happened. My greatest fear has been that the demons stalking me would harm you, but I took you anyway."

The despair in his gaze rocked Eliza Kate, but she refused to accept his awful doubts as fact. "I don't believe the world is populated with demons who wreak havoc on kind-hearted people who'd never harm others. I'm also certain that you've taken nothing from me. Everything I've given, myself, my love, it's been a gift, not a theft.

You've never held me hostage. I am yours solely because I wish to be."

The sweetness of her words washed over him like a cooling rain, but his chest felt so tight he could hardly breathe. He gave it a conscious effort, then wondered if he might not be better off surrendering to the pain and suffocating right there on the steps.

"You don't understand," he complained darkly. "Your father's never liked me, but I doubt he'd have tried to kill me had he not lost so much on Saturday's race." Jonathan paused to consider how much he wished to confide, but he swiftly decided any deception would be pointless now.

"I lost the first race on purpose, Eliza Kate. Lawrence thought I'd done it to embarrass Fletcher when I beat him handily in the rematch, but he was wrong. I held Red back and pulled him wide because I couldn't think of any other way to stay with you."

Eliza's eyes widened in amazement. "You deliberately lost that race because of me?" she inquired incredulously. "I'd no idea, simply none." Her most vivid memory of that Saturday was not of the race, but of the thrilling night they'd spent together.

She needed a long moment to absorb his astonishing confession. "Well, that was certainly a reckless strategy, but it worked extremely well, didn't it?"

Jonathan brought her hands to his lips and kissed her fingertips. "Better than I could have dreamed, but don't you see, if I'd run the first race honestly, no one would have won or lost much money. There wouldn't have been such large wagers placed on the second race, and your father and Fletcher would never have become so desperate for revenge they'd have staged an ambush meant to leave me lying dead in the road."

Eliza frowned slightly as she recalled a curious comment of her father's. "Last Saturday, my father scolded me for cheering for you. He swore you'd be gone on Monday but Fletcher would still be here. I thought perhaps he'd not heard that you planned to remain in Texas, but now I wonder if he might not have plotted your death even before the race was run."

Chilled clear to the marrow by that ghastly prospect, she moved to sit beside her husband and hugged his arm. "I knew he was weak, but God help us, could he really have been evil?"

Jonathan wiped the last of the moisture from his eyes with his fingertips. What he'd observed was such a thoughtful plan it had even included unshod ponies. It was possible Lamar could have drawn it together between Saturday afternoon and Monday morning, but Jonathan couldn't help suspecting the plot had been brewing for a whole lot longer.

He had never needed his wife's affectionate understanding more, but guilt-ridden, he slipped free of her grasp and stood to confront her squarely. "It really doesn't matter if Lamar had been plotting to kill me since the day Robert E. Lee surrendered. What matters is that we've not been wed a week, and already your parents are dead. I can't take the risk anything worse will happen to you. I won't," he emphasized stubbornly.

Eliza Kate rose to defend herself as well as their marriage. "My father was a charming man, but we both know he didn't have much in the way of character. That he died trying to kill you is an outrage I'll never forgive, for it shows just how little he thought of me as well as you. He was probably always jealous of you for being the better man, but he couldn't have plotted to rob me of the husband I hold so dear if he truly loved me.

"I absolutely refuse to allow you to blame yourself for his death when he brought it on himself with his own malicious hatred. As for my mother, she was in poor health when you arrived. That she died before learning what a scoundrel my father truly was is a blessing, and surely it was God's will that she died when she did.

"I'll understand if you wish to leave Texas, but you'll not go alone. I'm coming with you, and I don't care if we don't have anything more than we had over the weekend.

We'll have each other, and that's such a precious gift, it's more than enough for me."

Though deeply flattered, Jonathan was afraid she'd blindly chosen to ignore the terrible risk loving him brought. He'd never regarded himself as eloquent and wished he were able to wage a more forceful argument. Heartsick to be doing such a poor job of convincing her, he looked out over the enchanting garden.

"We ought to bury your mother with her roses," he suggested absently.

"Yes, it's the perfect spot for them both. The part of my father that loved my mother was really the very best of him. It's a shame there was so much more that wasn't nearly as honorable."

Jonathan shifted his weight anxiously but couldn't get comfortable regardless of his pose. "I appreciate your devotion to me, really I do, but it's not just bad luck that haunts me. It's absolute doom."

Again discounting his fears as absurd, Eliza Kate came toward him. When he tried to back away, she grabbed hold of his bloodstained shirt and began to unbutton it. "You know I'm stubborn, and I'll admit to being proud, but Red Warrior must have thrown you one too many times if you actually believe I'll allow you to walk out on me regardless of how noble you may consider your reason."

"Red's never thrown me," Jonathan argued.

"I'm glad to hear it. Now you need to get rid of this shirt before Ricky and Robby arrive."

Jonathan caught her hands but was careful to keep his hold feather light. "Shirts are easy to change. It's my fate that's so relentlessly black."

Eliza Kate stood on her tiptoes to kiss him. Her expression was still tinged with sadness, but lit with hope. "Maybe it was, but you found me, didn't you?"

Meeting Eliza Kate Bendalin had indeed been the best piece of luck Jonathan had ever had, but he was so thoroughly depressed, the thought brought only a slight smile.

"Yes, but it's cost you your parents, and I can't really believe you'd leave your home to head out for nowhere with me. What would Lawrence and your brothers do without you?"

He appeared to be resigned to losing her, and yet Eliza Kate sensed a spark of hope fighting to burst through his fears. "Before you came, I was needed here, it's true, but I was also on a path leading me straight to Fletcher Monroe. I was far too busy caring for others to sense the emptiness in my own life and ask what it was I truly wanted. I didn't even know what delicious possibilities existed before you appeared.

"Not knowing you would have been the real tragedy, my love, and whatever heartbreak I feel today, it won't dim my passion for you. You warned me life has more sorrow than joy, but you also promised never to leave me. I'm going to hold you to that vow, but I'll add one of my own: I will never abandon you either."

Tears flooded over her lashes as she slipped her arms around his waist and pressed close to hug him tight. "No matter how long our time together might be, I have no fear of death. I don't believe love ever dies, my darling. It lives in the fragrance of the flowers and the warmth of the sun, and like the beauty of the earth, I will be with you always."

Jonathan smothered a grateful sigh in her curls and wrapped her in a near-crushing embrace. Surely he'd wed the most loving creature ever born, and together they'd erase the darkness of his past. There was so much to do, brothers to comfort, and funerals to plan, but for now his heart swelled with love and the hope for a thousand bright tomorrows.

The funeral had drawn one of the largest crowds of mourners Lawrence had ever seen, and he sincerely appreciated all the loving condolences sent his way, but he just wasn't ready to return to the ranch, where he knew callers would stream by all afternoon. After the rest of the family had left for home, he wandered to the rear of the church and slid into the last pew.

It had been a harrowing week, and he had been so busy wrapping up Lamar's affairs that he'd had little time to contemplate how greatly his own life would change. Ricky had been of great help, looking after Robby with a brotherly concern that had amazed them all. The boys had helped him to build their parents' coffins and dig their graves in the rose garden. All the while the brothers had shown a resilience and maturity he'd had to struggle to match.

Eliza Kate and Jonathan had planned today's memorial service, as well as the one held earlier in the week for Fletcher Monroe. Jonathan had insisted upon describing Lamar and his partner's deaths as the result of a regrettable hunting accident. While Lawrence had argued that was an outlandish interpretation of the facts, he'd at last given in. For his nephews' sakes, because he'd not wanted his brother's last treachery exposed.

He was through hiding from the truth, however. He'd long suspected that Lamar had not behaved honorably when he'd been shot, but he'd taken the easy path and avoided the issue rather than confront him over it. But it seemed with that choice he'd been hiding not only from the ugliness of the war, but from life itself.

Now with Lamar gone, he'd become the head of the Bendalin clan, but he didn't feel much like a patriarch. He just felt incredibly sad and alone. He looked up at the high-beamed ceiling that gave the hymns he'd loved from childhood such a resonant sound. He'd forgotten how much he'd once loved attending church, and thought maybe it was time he made the effort to get himself into town on Sunday for service.

He sat back to appreciate the colorful profusion of flowers banking the altar. They'd come from gardens all over town. Lamar and Delia had had a great many friends, and now it was time he cultivated some of his own. Thinking he ought to be getting on home to help Eliza Kate and

Jonathan with their guests, he'd just grabbed the back of the adjacent pew when a veiled woman dressed in black entered by the side door.

She moved toward the front of the church and paused to inhale the fragrance of the white roses in a wicker basket by the pulpit before taking a place in the front pew. Her head bowed, she appeared to be lost in prayer but a foul stream of curses flooded Lawrence's mind. He couldn't believe Mae would dare show herself in church, but as he rose to tell her so to her face, he wondered if perhaps he'd again mistaken another woman for the lying madam.

He slumped back down in his seat in an effort to think things through before he made a complete fool of himself with some petite woman who was probably one of Delia's dearest friends rather than a popular prostitute. That he could still imagine Mae in a place she was highly unlikely to visit embarrassed him. He had been so in love with the woman he'd believed her to be, and for the first time, he wished he'd been the one to die rather than Lamar. No one would have missed him, and Lamar had a fine family who loved him.

Feeling thoroughly dejected, he stared down at his hands until he heard the soft rustle of satin. When he glanced up, the tardy mourner was at his side, and as she raised her veil, he saw it was Mae after all. That she was even more beautiful than he had recalled took his breath away, but then he noticed the faint green shadow of a fading bruise marring her right eye and cheek, and his expression filled with horror.

Mae had expected as much and reached out to touch his shoulder and keep him in his seat. "Wait. I'd hoped to see you before I left town, but certainly not on such a sad occasion. Please accept my condolences for the loss of your brother and his wife."

She looked and sounded like the fine lady she had pretended to be, and Lawrence wasn't sure how to reply. Then a sufficiently rude retort sprang from his lips. "You look as though you've been beaten. Were you finally caught in one of your outrageous lies?"

Flossie Mae knew she deserved whatever abuse he cared to heap on her, and she reacted with admirable restraint rather than anger. "After being with you, I refused to sleep with Lamar. He very nearly killed me for defying him, but it was worth it."

There wasn't the slightest trace of duplicity in her expression, but then, there never had been. Torn between a desperate desire to believe her, and the sinking fear he was again being played for a fool, Lawrence fought for control of his warring emotions. After a long, awkward pause, he scooted over.

"Sit down," he ordered. "And for once, just tell me the truth. If it's even possible," he taunted.

Flossie Mae took the place at his side, but sat forward to rest her elbow along the back of the next pew. She had played this scene out in her mind a thousand times, but no matter how artfully she had worded her part, he'd always turned his back on her and walked away.

"Other than to pretend to be Mae Leroux, I never lied to you. My name is Mae, Flossie Mae, but I'm going by Mae now. It was my own lonely childhood I described, my own dear husband who died in the battle of Shiloh. It was what I didn't tell you about the years following the war that truly mattered though. I was ashamed to admit I'd trusted a man who swiftly abandoned me with no way to survive except to rely on what I could earn with a shapely body."

Sickened, Lawrence was positive he didn't want to hear any more. "I don't care—"

"No, please listen," she rushed on. "I realize it's too late for us, but there's one thing you must understand. I meant it when I said I loved you. Foolishly I'd dreamed of marrying you and leading a respectable life. Lamar wouldn't have allowed it, of course. But meeting you did prompt me to give away my garish wardrobe, and I would definitely have left the Rosedale no matter what had happened between us.

"You made me feel alive for the first time since the war, and I sincerely wanted to be the woman I was with you. I actually was that woman once, and I allowed my dreams for a life with you to overrule my reason. That was very selfish of me, and you're too fine a gentleman to have suffered the shame I caused you."

Even after all she'd been through, Mae had too much pride to beg, but she did extend her small, gloved hand. "I wish you the best life has to offer, Lawrence. I will always love you and be sorry I disappointed you so badly."

Lawrence saw the tremor in her hand and certain she was about to withdraw it, he grabbed hold. "I don't know what to believe," he said, sighing sadly. As always, Mae's words had touched his heart, or what was left of the shriveled organ. "Perhaps I've been an even greater fool than I thought."

"Oh no," Mae argued. "You mustn't think ill of yourself. You're simply too honest to suspect the awful trick Lamar and I played on you."

Lawrence sought the precise term, but he was so excited to be with her again, and at the same time appalled by the thrill, that he could barely think at all. "Yes, it was unkind."

"It was much worse than unkind," Mae said regretfully. "It was cruel. Horrid."

She withdrew her hand from his and used her handkerchief to dry the tears threatening to blur her vision and spoil these few remaining minutes with him. He looked so pale and thin. She longed to reach out to stroke his silvery hair, but certain he'd slap her hand away, she worried the lacy edge of her handkerchief instead.

"Please forgive me for interrupting your prayers. I'd not have embarrassed your family by attending the funeral, but I did want to come by the church for a few minutes at least."

Fearing she was about to bolt, Lawrence again reached

for her hand and covered it with both of his. "Where are you staying?" he asked.

Hope surged through her, and she pressed his fingers lightly as she scanned his expression for a glimmer of sympathy for her plight. Unfortunately, he merely looked annoyed, and she lowered her expectations accordingly. "I have a room at Mary McBride's boardinghouse. It's a respectable place, or at least it was until I arrived."

Lawrence had an excellent grasp of figures, but nothing about Mae and him fit into neat columns or added up to predictable sums. He had missed her so much that he longed to trust his heart where she was concerned, but he'd been too badly hurt to believe his judgment was sound. He didn't want to part this way though and pursed his lips thoughtfully.

"Will you take me there?" he asked politely.

Confused, Mae broke free of his grasp and rolled her damp handkerchief into a tiny wad. "If you like, but why would you wish to go?"

Lawrence shrugged in frustration. "I would just like to talk, and there will be too many people out at the ranch this afternoon for me to take you home now."

Mae's first thought was that he intended to make her apologize to his whole family, or at least what was left of it, for the awful trick she'd played on him. "Oh please," she murmured. "Don't ask to me to go out to the ranch."

Her golden-brown eyes appeared huge and shone with a tear-brightened fear Lawrence didn't understand, but he felt such a powerful tug on his emotions he had to glance away. She had a magical appeal, but perhaps he was merely bewitched.

"You mentioned leaving town. Where is it you wish to live?" he asked.

That she had ever imagined being welcomed into the Bendalin home struck her as lunacy now. Her future was so bleak. It really didn't matter where she might reside, but she did have one prerequisite. "I want to go so far away no one will know me," she replied in a fervent prayer.

"Won't that be awfully lonely?" Lawrence inquired.

"Loneliness is all I know," Mae replied sadly.

What Lawrence felt then was a wave of sorrow lapping at his very soul. He thought back to the Saturday night he'd found her at the Rosedale, and this time, he was furiously angry with himself rather than her.

"I should never have let you send me away," he blurted, and his voice rolled against the high ceiling with a booming echo. "When your friend brought me that ridiculous message about being dead, I should have searched the whole damn hotel until I found you."

Flossie raised her hand to trace the last faint evidence of the awful beating. "I meant what I said about Lamar. Another few blows, and he would surely have killed me. I couldn't face you when I could neither see nor walk. I felt dead in every way that mattered. Besides, once you'd discovered that I lived at the Rosedale, there wasn't any hope for us. The whole town knows what I am—or was," she amended abruptly. "People would have laughed at you, and I couldn't have borne that."

"What people?"

"You know what people." Mae nearly moaned. "The whole blasted town."

"And what is that to us?" Lawrence asked.

"Please. I've already admitted my dreams were a selfish delusion, but I never meant to hurt you."

Lawrence drew in a deep breath and was surprised the mingled fragrances of the flowers had drifted so far from the altar. It was the exotic perfume of hope, and as it dissolved his doubts, he seized it eagerly. "You haven't heard my dreams yet but after meeting you, I began to long for more than simply being the favorite uncle in my brother's family.

"Lamar's left me with a mountain of debt, for which I'm partly to blame, but I do believe Jonathan Blair and I are well on our way to covering all his losses. I'll always miss my brother, but it's high time I admitted his flaws and lived my own life. It's taken me a long while to realize I deserve to be happy, and nothing would make me happier than to be with you."

That he would forgive her deceit was more than Mae had any right to expect, but that he would say something so dear overwhelmed her and instantly reduced her to tears. She covered her face with her hands and sobbed for the beautiful dream she dared not believe would ever come true.

Lawrence raised his arms to hold her, but he was uncertain just how. Then recognizing he was again being confined by needless fears, he drew her into a fond embrace and hung on as though he'd never let her go. "My dearest," he hushed, "you mustn't carry on so. You'll make yourself ill."

Mae leaned back slightly and hiccupped between sobs. "I would love to be with you, too, but I can't, Lawrence. You deserve a woman who's led an exemplary life, someone who's above reproach, not some—"

"Damn it all, Mae. I know what I want, so stop arguing with me. Let's just go and pack up your things, and I'll take you home right now. If it creates a scandal this town never forgets, I won't care a bit. All I need is your promise that you'll marry me just as soon as it can be arranged."

Mae swept his expression with a frantic gaze. He looked so heartbreakingly sincere, but surely he was simply too good to appreciate what a truly awful scandal marrying her would create. She could already feel it overtaking them, and as swiftly as the spring rain flooded the arroyos, it would drown them both.

"I love you dearly," she assured him, "but please, we mustn't rush into anything."

"I've waited my whole life for you," Lawrence declared confidently. "Take as long as you wish to get used to the idea, but you are going to marry me. Is that understood?"

Mae was amazed by the severity of his tone. "Why, Lawrence, I had no idea you could be so determined."

Lawrence was ashamed to admit he just hadn't cared enough about anything to set a determined course until now. "I hope it's a pleasant surprise. Now let's go and get your things," he urged.

Flossie rose on unsteady legs. "It isn't far, but you ought to drive your buggy around to the back. The gossips all sit on the front porch and chatter endlessly about whomever walks by."

"I know the type," he assured her, but he was sorely tempted to park his buggy out front and introduce himself to the whole lot. Not wanting to embarrass her, however, he took her suggestion, and they entered the white frame house through the rear door. He followed her down the narrow hall to a room barely large enough to hold a bed and dresser. Drawn to the charming seascape opposite the bed, he studied it as Mae began to collect her belongings.

"This is quite lovely," he murmured appreciatively.

"Isn't it though? It's all that's kept me sane."

"Then let's take it with us." Lawrence reached up to remove the painting from the wall.

Mae hadn't considered buying it from her landlady, but was delighted that he had suggested it. She knew the Bendalin house was large and supposed she could find a nice place to hang it. Suddenly recalling she wasn't the only person involved, she caught herself before she began redecorating the whole house in her mind. She slumped down on the bed.

"I forgot all about Ricky," she said, breathing out in an anguished sigh.

Still clutching the painting, Lawrence leaned back against her door. "I know he frequents the Rosedale," he said, but despite his vow to start facing disagreeable truths, he couldn't bring himself to ask the most obvious question. Still, the sad possibility that she'd slept with his nephew darkened his gaze.

Unable to face him, Mae looked away. "*Frequents* is a good word. Ricky couldn't have been more than fourteen when he began sneaking into the hotel. The girls all knew who he was and just kissed his cheek and shooed him right on out. He kept coming back though, and one night, maybe a year or so later, a little red-haired girl named Sylvia invited him to spend the night. Lamar just laughed when he heard about it, and Ricky's been a frequent visitor ever since."

Mae glanced up at Lawrence through tear-spiked lashes. "I've always liked Ricky, but I was your brother's mistress. I never slept with anyone else, let alone his son."

"I didn't ask," Lawrence insisted.

"No, but you sure wanted to, and every time we meet one of your friends, you'll wonder; and it will eat away at you until your only feeling for me is contempt."

"Never!" Lawrence nearly shouted. "And you needn't worry about Ricky either. He'll not treat you with any disrespect, or he'll have to deal with me."

Mae ran her hand over the bed's faded quilt. It had come with the room, and she'd often traced the tiny stitches and wondered if they'd been sewn with love or dread. "I know you mean it now, but people have a tendency to overlook what they don't wish to see, until the sight is too hideous to ignore."

She had begun to try Lawrence's patience, but he studied the sad slope of her shoulders and was again pained by the lingering evidence of Lamar's brutal beating. "You're afraid to believe we have a chance at happiness," he stated sympathetically. "Don't you think I'm worried too? I can't run. I can barely walk without tripping over my own feet. What if you soon find my limp annoying?"

"Oh Lawrence, it's barely noticeable."

"No, it's pronounced, and you might soon come to regard it, and me, as pathetic."

"Never!" Flossie cried and knotted her fists tightly in her lap for emphasis.

A slow smile flirted across Lawrence's lips. "If I'm to accept that promise from you, then you'll have to accept mine that I'll never become disappointed in you. Is it a bargain?"

"It's scarcely a fair exchange."

"Well, I say it is," Lawrence argued.

Flossie shook her head in wonder. "I'd absolutely no idea you were such a stubborn man."

"There's a great deal you don't know about me," he cautioned, "but as long as you remember how dearly I love you, it will be enough."

Again on the verge of tears, Mae jumped at the sharp knock at the door. "Yes?" she called fretfully.

"It's Mrs. McBride. Is there a man in your room, Mrs. Kemble? You know I don't allow social visits in my tenant's rooms."

Mae's cheeks flushed with embarrassment, but Lawrence just moved aside and swung open the door. He introduced himself to the stout little woman in the hall, and then held out the seascape. "Mrs. Kemble is leaving, and I've come to help her pack. While I'm here, I'd like to purchase this charming watercolor, if I may. Are you acquainted with the artist?"

Mary McBride's startled glance careened between Lawrence, Mae, and the painting. "No, I can't say I am. A salesman, who came up short on his rent, left it here several years ago. Say, you're Lamar Bendalin's younger brother, aren't you?"

"Yes, ma'am, I surely am." He reached into his pocket and withdrew a five-dollar gold piece. "I believe this should be sufficient." Then he added several more coins. "Here's something for you as well."

He then turned to Mae. "Do we need to settle your bill, sweetheart?"

Flossie took in her landlady's astonished gasp and rose to finish gathering the few toilet articles and items of clothing she'd kept in the dresser. "No, darling, I paid for the month in advance."

"Fine. Is there anything else, Mrs. McBride?" Lawrence inquired.

"Well, no, I suppose not." She regarded the gleaming coins in her pudgy palm, appeared pleased, and dropped them into her pocket. "I'll just go and let our cook know there will be one less for supper."

"Thank you," Lawrence responded, and the instant she turned away, he closed the door. He then set the painting aside and turned the key in the lock. "I trust we'll not be disturbed again while you're packing."

Mae had already shoved everything into her carpetbag. She searched the room with a distracted glance, but she'd brought nothing, and now that they owned the painting, she'd leave nothing behind. "This is all I have," she revealed with a slight shrug. "A single dress, a few changes of lingerie, a nightgown, nothing else worth mentioning."

Lawrence nodded thoughtfully. "Then packing didn't take nearly as long as I'd anticipated, and it's still a little early to head out to the ranch."

Mae saw his glance stray toward the bed, but she wasn't insulted. "I've really missed you," she whispered before laying her bag aside.

As she crossed the narrow distance between them, Lawrence admired her graceful sway. "Tell me something," he began.

Mae appeared perplexed. "You already know all my shameful secrets. There's nothing else to tell."

Lawrence slid his arms around her waist to draw her near. "I just wondered if you like to dance."

"Is that all?" Mae licked her lips nervously. "Actually, I've never cared much for dancing, but if you enjoy it, I'll certainly try."

Relief washed through Lawrence, and he broke into a ready grin. "No, you needn't bother. I can't dance anymore."

Mae reached up on her tiptoes to kiss him. "Well, I'll certainly not miss it when you're so good at what you can do."

The flattering line had left her lips with practiced ease, but Lawrence didn't care if she'd repeated it earlier to other men. They were together again, and so in love, everything was new.

By the time the last guest had left for home, Eliza Kate was exhausted. When she heard the heavy front door swing open again, she actually moaned, but Jonathan, who was watching the doorway, broke into a wide smile. Curious as to whom he would greet so enthusiastically, Eliza turned to take his hand. When she saw her uncle and a petite woman in black, she knew precisely who it must be. Her brothers were seated behind her, but when they noticed a woman had entered, they rose and came forward.

Eliza had never met a madam, but she'd expected Flossie Mae to be a far more flamboyant creature than this dear person clinging to her uncle's arm. Because she'd witnessed her uncle's anguish, and his present unmistakable joy, she felt as though she knew her. Lawrence introduced her simply as Mrs. Kemble, but the name struck Eliza as far too formal.

"Please call me Eliza Kate," she offered graciously, "and I do hope you'll allow me to call you Mae."

"Yes, thank you. I have come to prefer it," Mae agreed. She was delighted by Jonathan's welcoming smile, but Lamar's sons were more reserved. "Good evening," she greeted them both.

Ricky hesitated a moment then stepped forward to brush Mae's check with a light kiss. "It's nice to meet you, Mrs. Kemble. I sure hope you'll feel at home here."

Robby stared up at his brother, then following his lead, remembered his manners. "Evening, ma'am."

That Ricky had chosen to forget how close she had been to his father was almost too much for Mae. She clung to Lawrence's arm all the more frantically and murmured a polite response to Robby's greeting.

"Why don't we go into the dining room and have some tea?" Eliza suggested. "Our friends brought us so many delicious cakes and pies, and I've not have a chance to sample any of them."

Mae doubted she could swallow a bite, but Lawrence escorted her to the long table where she'd once dreamed she'd take Delia's place. Now seated beside a man she truly loved, she gave silent thanks that her earlier fantasies hadn't come true.

Lawrence waited until everyone had been served his or her choice of desserts and had had a chance to swallow a few sips of tea. Then he cleared his throat. "You've always been like a brother to me, Jonathan. I know you want your own ranch, but I'd much rather you stayed on here at the Trinity Star as my partner."

"Our partner," Ricky and Robby added in a chorus, then chuckled at themselves.

"Yes, of course," Lawrence agreed. "That's precisely what I meant. You wanted a ranch in Texas, and the Trinity Star is among the best."

Jonathan noted his wife's delighted smile, but he couldn't agree. "That's very generous of you all," he replied, including the boys. "But I've been thinking that since Fletcher apparently didn't have any relatives who'll claim his spread, by the time his estate is sorted out, I might have won enough money racing Red Warrior to buy it."

Although he'd mentioned buying out Fletcher earlier, Eliza hadn't realized he was serious. "We do share one common boundary," she advised. "So it might be a very wise move to purchase Fletcher's ranch, but it will be expensive, won't it, Uncle?"

"It won't be cheap, but if we can't have you and Jonathan here, then Fletcher's place is a damn good alternative," Lawrence replied. "I sure wish money weren't in such short supply now."

Mae had managed only a few sips of tea, but she was listening attentively. "I have quite a bit set aside," she offered softly. "And now that I'm not leaving Fort Worth, I'll have no need of it. If it will help the family, then I want you to have it, Lawrence."

Lawrence opened his mouth to refuse, then realized

the money must have come from her share of the Rosedale's profits and that meant it was hers to do with as she chose. "Thank you, Mae. I want you to feel part of the family, but you don't have to buy your way in."

"Consider it a gift," Mae insisted.

Eliza Kate caught Jonathan's eye, and he nodded. Love was the greatest gift of all.

"So when's the wedding?" Robby asked.

Mae blushed and shook her head. "A wedding wouldn't be proper while the family's in mourning, Robby, but soon."

"Very soon," Lawrence vowed.

"The garden is such a lovely place for a wedding," Eliza recalled with a wistful smile. "Let's begin making our plans tomorrow, Mae."

As he so often did, Jonathan marveled at the grace of his wife's gestures, and the loving spirit flowing through her every word. He couldn't wait to paint a sign for the Texas Belle and hang it over the entrance to his own ranch; but as he glanced at the smiling faces gathered around the table, he knew that along with the wife he adored, these dear people were his family, and that meant he was already home.